What people are saying about …

ḣEALER

"In *Healer*, Linda Windsor combines a knack for thorough research and the skill to draw from it judiciously in telling an engaging story. She weaves together a rich and detailed tapestry of sixth-century life in Scotland. Her notes about Arthurian characters, the Grail Palace, and the bibliography are well worth reading. Linda has done her homework and written a fine story."

Randy Alcorn, author of *Safely Home* and *Deception*

"As a longtime, unabashed fan of Linda Windsor's novels, I have been waiting and hoping for a new medieval book from her for several years. Not only did *Healer* not disappoint, it exceeded my expectations. A beautiful, heart-pounding love story set firmly against a backdrop of clan fighting and supernatural warfare kept me glued to this book. The next book in this series cannot come soon enough!"

Tracey Bateman, author of *Thirsty*

"One of the best historical novels I've read in years. Windsor painted a picture that allowed me to journey through sixth-century Scotland—to laugh, to cry, to shout victory, and to praise God for watching over His own. Exquisitely written. Never-to-be-forgotten characters woven with a plot that touches the world we live in today."

DiAnn Mills, author of *A Woman Called Sage* and *Sworn to Protect*

"With the first book in her Brides of Alba trilogy, Linda Windsor beautifully melds Arthurian legend with early Christianity in an unforgettable story of forgiveness and reconciliation that captivated me at the first page and became my constant companion until the last. I impatiently await the next two books."

Tamara Leigh, author of *Leaving Carolina* and *Nowhere, Carolina*

"Windsor weaves together a rich tapestry of intrigue, love, and faith set in Arthurian Scotland. With her beautiful prose she transports you into Brenna and Ronan's world, a place where hope and light overcome despair and darkness. Prepare to be swept away by *Healer*."

Kathleen Fuller, best-selling author of the Hearts of Middlefield series

"Linda Windsor's *Healer* takes us back to a little-known time. Rich in historical atmosphere, memorable characters, deep emotion, and the triumph of faith—what more could a reader want?"

Lyn Cote, author of *Her Abundant Joy*

"This is a beautiful story, full of mystery, romance, and—most of all—redemption. Linda Windsor has written a breathtaking saga combining history and faith with imagination to create a page-turning tale that lingers long after the final paragraph. I can hardly wait for the next book!"

Janelle C. Schneider, author and spiritual director

hEALER

OTHER BOOKS
BY LINDA WINDSOR

HISTORICAL FICTION

Fires of Gleannmara Trilogy
Maire

Riona

Deirdre

The Brides of Alba Trilogy
Healer

Thief (Summer 2011)

Rebel (Summer 2012)

CONTEMPORARY ROMANCE

Piper Cove Chronicles
Wedding Bell Blues

For Pete's Sake

Moonstruck Series
Paper Moon

Fiesta Moon

Blue Moon

Along Came Jones

It Had To Be You

Not Exactly Eden

Hi Honey I'm Home

THE BRIDES OF ALBA

hEALER

LINDA WINDSOR

David C Cook®

transforming lives together

HEALER
Published by David C. Cook
4050 Lee Vance View
Colorado Springs, CO 80918 U.S.A.

David C. Cook Distribution Canada
55 Woodslee Avenue, Paris, Ontario, Canada N3L 3E5

David C. Cook U.K., Kingsway Communications
Eastbourne, East Sussex BN23 6NT, England

David C. Cook and the graphic circle C logo
are registered trademarks of Cook Communications Ministries.

This story is a work of fiction. All characters and events are the product of the author's
imagination. Any resemblance to any person, living or dead, is coincidental.

Scripture quotations are taken from the King James Version of the Bible. (Public
Domain.) The author has added italics to Scripture quotations for emphasis.

LCCN 2010921502
ISBN 978-1-4347-6478-2
eISBN 978-0-7814-0449-5

© 2010 Linda Windsor
Published in association with the literary agency of Alive Communications,
Inc., 7680 Goddard St., Suite 200, Colorado Springs, CO.

The Team: Ingrid Beck, Ramona Tucker, Amy Kiechlin,
Sarah Schultz, Caitlyn York, Karen Athen
Cover design: DogEared Design, Kirk DouPonce

Sixth-century map on p. 18–19 © 2010 Linda Windsor and David C. Cook

Printed in the United States of America
First Edition 2010

1 2 3 4 5 6 7 8 9 10

031210

To my mom and children,
for their support and sacrifices to allow me
time to research and write this novel.

My son Jeff's by-the-Good-Book faith helped keep me grounded,
while my daughter, Kelly, challenged me to find ways to fish for men
who would not heed Scripture from the other side of the boat.

To David C. Cook,
for giving me the wings to fly with this project.

And finally, to my Heavenly Father,
the Great Creator who would not let me be until
I wrote of the things He placed on my heart.
Thank You, Jesus, for Your love and grace.

Dear Reader,

Many of you are aware of my passion for historical research. When a friend forwarded me a magazine article about what happened to the Davidic line after the nation of Israel scattered (1 and 2 Kings), I became intrigued by the possibilities. So I started a three-year journey of earnest research that birthed this new series.

With the Brides of Alba series, I am once again stepping into the Dark Ages and surely controversial histories and traditions. It is set in the late sixth-century Scotland of Arthur, prince of Dalraida—the only historically documented Arthur. Most scholarly sources point to Arthur, Merlin, and even Guinevere/Gwenhyfar as titles, so it's easy to see why the Age of Arthur lasted over one hundred years. There was more than one Arthur. The Dark Ages become even darker when you consider that there was no standard for dating and even the records that exist are written in at least four different languages. Neither names, dates, place names, nor translations are completely reliable. So I quote eighth-century historian Nenius: "I have made a heap of all I could find."

The Prince Arthur of *Healer,* like his historical forefathers, had claim to the royal bloodline of David and that of the apostolic priestly line from the first-century family and friends of Jesus according to multiple sources. A few are listed in the Bibliography (see page 366). Because my hero and heroine are of similar heritage, they are greatly affected by the rules and traditions of these sacred lines. Just how they were affected, came from the Arthurian scholars' works highlighted in the booklist, Chadwick in particular. From these books come an Arthur and a Scotland/Britain that is unique to history, tradition, lore, and the Christian faith. (See *Arthurian Characters* on page 358 and *The Grail Palace* on page 363 for more.)

If figuring out who was who wasn't hard enough, I also tackled the task of showing our fledgling early church and faith struggle in this time before science evolved from what was known as *nature magic*—and from where nature magic was often supplemented or replaced by miracle or dark magic. It is the last two that involve the supernatural—divine miracle or demonic magic. *Nature magic* (protoscience) was the knowledge and use of the properties of God's wonderful creation, a knowledge practiced by my Christian heroine and accompanied by God. But sometimes it was used for evil and accompanied by dark magic. I can tell you that the research of some elements needed for the story left me unsettled and clinging to God's shirttail and Scripture for discernment.

I found myself reading and rereading the verses below as I worked on this novel and endeavored to show the difference between Christians and nonbelievers, as well as between the Christian Celtic or druidic priests, the Roman priests, and the nonbelieving druids. (Bear in mind that *druid* in that time was a word for all professionals—doctors, judges, poets, teachers, and protoscientists as well as priests. *Druid* meant "teacher, rabbi, magi, or master," not the dark, hooded stereotype assumed by many today.)

With regard to nature magic as well as the power of the Holy Spirit in the believer, I gravitated in my work to these verses:

> *While we look not at the things which are seen, but at the things which are not seen: for the things which are seen are temporal; but the things which are not seen are eternal.—2 Corinthians 4:18*

> *And he said, Unto you it is given to know the mysteries of the kingdom of God: but to others in parables; that seeing they might not see, and hearing they might not understand.—Luke 8:10*

> *Beloved, believe not every spirit, but try the spirits whether they are of God: because many false prophets are gone out into the world. Hereby know ye the Spirit of God: Every spirit that confesseth that Jesus Christ is come in the flesh is of God: And every spirit that confesseth not that Jesus Christ is come in the flesh is not of God: and this is that spirit of antichrist, whereof ye have heard that it should come; and even now already is it in the world.—1 John 4:1–3*

> *I am the vine, ye are the branches: He that abideth in me, and I in him, the same bringeth forth much fruit: for without me ye can do nothing.—John 15:5*

Many of you know how my daughter was stalked and assaulted in college, how she blamed and turned against God and became involved in Wicca, or white witchcraft. It was through research for another Dark Age series, the Fires of Gleannmara, that I learned by God's grace to witness to her effectively when she would not hear anything from the Word. I have included even more on this kind of research in *Healer*, Book One of the Brides of Alba series.

To reach my daughter, I had to *fish* from the other side of the boat. This was revealed to me once when I read the story of how the disciples had fished all night with no success. Then Jesus told them to try the other side of the vessel. They did and netted a boatload. My child would not listen to Scripture, but she was all ears for the history and oral traditions of the era that became the origins of many of today's New Age beliefs.

These historical and oral traditions underscored or clarified what Scripture revealed, separating the wheat from the chaff. They distinguish between works done for the glory of God, praising Him for creation and its properties (or use of nature magic, or protoscience), and those done for self-edification and/or to harm others. They reveal how most druids knew who Christ was—the Son and Messiah ordained by the Creator—because their forefathers had recorded the astrological phenomena of His birth star and the darkness after His death (see www. BethlehemStar.com to see how NASA technology and accepted history are used to affirm this). And they define the line between the light use of nature magic, often aided by the Holy Spirit, and the dark use of the same knowledge, aided by demons.

The results of my *fishing* were not as instant as that of the disciples. It took a journey of eight years before my daughter was ready to jump into the boat. But the net had been cast and repeatedly *mended* each time I found something new to share, something that built on common ground and carried her one step closer to Christ. Both mother and daughter emerged stronger from that storm—stronger in faith, friendship, and love. I share this story because maybe someone out there needs to know how to approach a beloved nonbeliever who will not hear Scripture or traditional witness ... but must be reached from the other side of the boat.

This is my passion. To reach out and enable others to reach out effectively to those who are swimming on the other side of the boat from the written Word with a net that will bring them to Christ, the Living Word.

With all my heart,

Linda Windsor

CHARACTER LIST

O'BYRNE Clan of Glenarden
(colors are red, black, and silver/gray)

Aeda—Tarlach's late royal Pictish wife; mother to Ronan, Caden, and Alyn

Ailill—bard

Alyn—Tarlach and Aeda's third son

Bron—a penniless cripple taken in by Brenna; from the Highlands with widowed mother

Caden—Tarlach and Aeda's second son

Cú—Tarlach's wolfhound

Dara—Glenarden's midwife

Egan O'Toole—Glenarden's champion

Gillis—master of the hounds

Kella O'Toole—Egan's daughter; foster sister to Ronan, Caden, and Alyn

Rhianon—Caden's wife from Gwenydd of North Wales; daughter of Idwal and Enda

Ronan—Tarlach and Aeda's eldest son and heir

Rory—Ronan's alias

Tarlach—clan chief/king, also known as the Glenarden; of royal Irish descent (Davidic bloodline)

Vychan—steward

GOWRYS Clan—Subclan of O'Byrnes
(colors are red and green)

Brenna—daughter of Llas and Joanna; heiress to Gowrys

Daniel—Donal's son and Gowrys princeling; hostage to the O'Byrnes

Donal—Brenna's cousin and current Gowrys clan chief

Ealga—Brenna's nurse and mentor; Joanna's cousin

Faol—Brenna's silver-white wolf

Joanna—Llas's slain queen and mother of Brenna, descended from British apostolic bloodline of Arimathea

Llas—father of Brenna; slain chieftain/king

Kingdom of GWYNEDD
(colors are pale blue and black)

Enda—Rhianon's mother

Heming—hunter and soldier of fortune

Idwal—Rhianon's father

Keena—Rhianon's maidservant since birth

PRIESTS

Brother Martin—the priest who tutored Brenna

Brother Michael—young priest who accompanies his senior Brother Martin

Dupric, bishop of Llandalf—wants to start a monastery on land where Brother Martin lives (a historical bishop who *may* also be Merlin Emrys)

ARTHURIAN CHARACTERS
(see page 358)

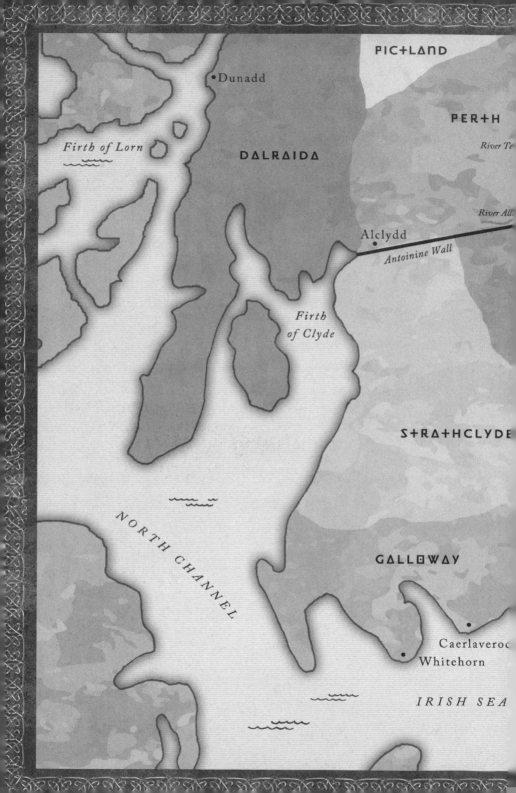

LATE 6TH
CENTURY
ALBA

Scone
Forteviot
River Tay

FIFE

Glenarden
Strighlagh

X Battle of
CAMLAN

Firth of Forth

Berwick

Din Edyn
Traprain
Law

King's Knot
River Carron
Falkirk

NORTH SEA

LOTHIAN
River Tweed

Fort Camlan

Lindisfarne

MANAU
Gododdin

Din Guardi

BERNICIA

GWENDOLEU

Hadrian's Wall

Carmelide

*Solway
Firth*

RHEGED

ELMET

pROLOGUE

Manau Gododdin, Alba
Sixth century AD

A deadly danger lurked in the sleepy hollow.

The night mist hung low above the crannog, cloaking the steep cliff that protected the fortress's back as well as the still, reflectionless water surrounding its other three sides. But that was not all it obscured. Warriors, some clad in the rich red, black, and silver of the O'Byrne clan, crept like a pack of wolves from leather and tarred curraghs onto the shore of the Gowrys rath.

The tall, bearded leader, hardened more by bitterness than war, lifted his head with a sudden uneasy awareness. Could she see him? Searching the murky darkness for the small village nestled about the keep, he envisioned the beautiful enchantress who'd captured his dreams night and day. 'Twould take more than the Gowrys fire-hardened stone tower to save her this night. With a sinister tilt of his lips, Tarlach O'Byrne raised his head and howled at the moon that refused to show its face. His words railed above the hushed scrape of the light, wicker-framed crafts his men drew onto the beach.

"Sister of Avalon or bride of Sheol, I promised you I'd have you. Tonight is the night, Joanna of Gowrys!"

Tarlach O'Byrne's roar tore through the thin veil of slumber that Queen Joanna had induced with a concoction of soothing herbs to thwart her sleeplessness of late. Her ears rang as he beat the flat of his battle-axe against the painted Red Hand on his breastplate. The image was as clear as if he stood at her bedside, yet none shared the room save her husband, sleeping beside her.

The queen grew cold all over, for in her mind's eye she could see Tarlach, leading his bloodthirsty minions into the inner rath, beyond the stockade and earthenwork fortifications where unsuspecting guards, long accustomed to the natural protection of the lake and cliff, fell victim to the enemy's silent but deadly weapons. Like creeping death, the O'Byrnes stole through the quiet cottages nestled in the enclosed grounds and made straight for the stone keep—for her beloved ... for herself ... for their child.

It was not the first time the scene had played out in her dream, yet now Joanna was awake.

Tonight is the night, Joanna of Gowrys.

Joanna clenched her hands in a tight fold against her breast, whispering, "Father, take these horrors away. Leave me sleep in peace yet one more night."

She inhaled deeply and slowly released her breath though it were her will, her troubled spirit. Instead of the blessed peace that usually came, filling her mind with a sweet, reassuring psalm, Tarlach's words boomed again and again, like the approach of war drums.

Joanna's blood congealed in her veins. This time it was real. Tarlach *was* here! She shook her husband with urgency. "He's here, Llas. Heaven help us, he's here!"

"Who, Beloved?" Still in the sway of sleep, Llas of Gowrys rolled over and reached instinctively for the axe he kept at the head of the box bed.

"Tarlach." The answer came dry from Joanna's throat.

The mention of Tarlach, once a friend and now a foe, cleared Llas's daze in an instant. He pulled Joanna to him long enough to remove the hated name from her lips with a fierce kiss. "God forgive me for not heeding your words, Beloved, for I cannot expect you to." The pain and guilt in his voice when he released her was as sharp as the sword he seized. Before Joanna could reply, a bloodcurdling scream erupted from the lower chamber of the round tower, affirming that the chieftain of Glenarden was in the keep. Shouting and the clash of metal vibrated in the air. Women and children screamed.

God have mercy!

With all her heart, Joanna called after Llas as he unbolted the door to join his men below. "I do forgive you, Llas. Now and always."

He mustn't go to the Other Side with this burden of guilt. She knew Llas understood her gift of second sight no more than he could the savage pangs of childbirth, though the gift had never foretold wrong, even when the outcome was disastrous and men dear to them were lost.

But none were as dear as the man who now paused at the door. Llas's eyes said it all. This was his last farewell. "Get the bairn, and lock yourself in here." The vibrant blue of his eyes turned to steel as resolve closed the floodgate of his emotion.

Joanna rushed to obey, her hand clutching the wooden bolt as she cried, "God protect you, love of my life."

But Llas didn't look back. He was already committed to the death struggle below. Wearing no more than his courage and determination, the chieftain of Gowrys disappeared into the dark, descending corridor, where flickering shadows cast by torches from the hall below danced on the walls like demons inviting him to the fires of Sheol.

Her worst nightmare all too real at last, Joanna slammed the door and slid the bolt in place. In the adjoining room, her infant daughter stirred in the soft bedclothes woven by Joanna's loving hand. Beyond the cradle, the babe's nurse, already awakened by the tumult, hurriedly pulled on her overdress.

"So it's come," the woman said, voice muffled by the volume of her garment.

"Aye, Ealga."

Ealga, her cousin and sister of Avalon, knew of Joanna's nightmarish vision. The first time, it came unbidden to Joanna on her wedding night, ripping away the sweet languor induced by nuptial passion. Trembling in her husband's arms, the new queen could not be comforted by Llas's vow that his foster brother would never turn against him, much less wage an ignoble attack in the dark of the night. The Glenarden king was a man of honor. Had they not fought side by side since coming of age together? Nothing could break such a bond.

Nothing but the twisting fingers of a jealous heart. Joanna had chosen Llas over Tarlach, even though the Joseph of the church had promised her to the latter. Joanna had ignored the high priest's reminder of the duty to which she'd been born and bred to follow the lead of her heart. And now Tarlach was here, just as her dreams had foretold.

Joanna cradled her baby to her chest, but it was no balm to the anguish chafing within her. Llas would never accept what she had long known—that she'd have to send their daughter away in the dark of night to escape the betrayal of his foster brother. That all left behind, save the Gowrys who lived in the fells above the lake, would die.

Father in Heaven, must it be so soon? Tears rolled down her face, soaking into the blankets as she nuzzled the dark curls of baby Brenna's head. The baby whimpered, sensing Joanna's distress.

"'Tis best we be on our way, Cousin, before the mite grows restless and gives us away." Using coals from the hearth, Ealga lit a small finger lamp on the bedside table. "We cannot let Brenna fall into *his* hands."

His. Ealga's intonation belied the need to say Tarlach's name. She'd had no use for their neighbor since coming from Avalon to Gowrys the moment the women of the Arimathean order learned that the young queen was with child. A few years Joanna's senior, Ealga had pledged herself to the mother and the baby she helped deliver.

"There is an evil in that one. You know it, Joanna," the nurse had said, time and again, about Tarlach O'Byrne.

Aye, Joanna knew it. But, like Llas, she hadn't wanted to believe it. Tarlach and Llas had been such good friends, comrades-in-arms fighting with Aedan MacGabran, sometimes against the northern Pictish tribes, other times against the Irish, and always against the Saxons. Then Tarlach was wounded in a skirmish, and Joanna was sent with an elder healer from the Holy Isle to nurse him back to health. It was the first time she'd met the Glenarden, offspring of an ancient royal lineage. As a descendant of an equally old priestly line, Joanna was to marry him when she came of age. Tarlach had fallen in love with her, but it was his foster brother, Llas, who had stolen Joanna's heart.

"Brenna is the hope of Gowrys—indeed, of Glenarden, too."

Ealga's soft words tempted Joanna back to the present, but the regret clawing at her would not let go. If only Bishop Dupric, who'd been sympathetic to Joanna's plight, could have pierced Tarlach's jealous rage with reason.

Joanna could still hear the holy man's assurance. "His anger will mellow in time, my child."

But it hadn't. Not even Aeda, a royal bride of Gododdin, who'd borne Tarlach sons eligible to rule both Pict and Scot, had diminished the Glenarden's wounded pride. The likes of love and hate knew no span of time or reason. Else, how could Joanna have chosen Llas, a lesser chief than Tarlach? How could she love her husband as fiercely today as when she'd pledged her love and life to him?

Heavenly Father! Joanna's knees nearly buckled from the weight of it all. *This is more than I can bear. I have seen my husband off to his death, and now I must send my child away to an unknown fate. Where are You?*

"Joanna." Ealga reached for the babe, her eyes brimming.

Mother's instinct caused Joanna to draw her child closer, resulting in a startled wail of protest. She'd trust Brenna to none other than Ealga. Her cousin would see Brenna taught, as Joanna had been, in the arts of healing passed down through the ages. Joanna handed the child over, along with half her heart. The remainder still beat raggedly within Joanna's chest for her husband.

"Go … quickly. I will delay Tarlach as long as I can bear it."

Death was the fate of anyone left in the madman's path. Yet Ealga made no attempt to change Joanna's decision to remain behind. This plan had been made between them after Brenna's birth. They had known Tarlach would come. That he'd never stop seeking Joanna. For her to accompany Ealga and the infant was to endanger their chance of escape and survival.

"God speed you to safety, Beloved." Joanna couldn't resist one last brush of the baby's head with her lips, one last sniff of sweet innocence. The scent reinforced Joanna's faltering courage to do what had to be done. She would carry it with her to her impending death, a reminder of what her sacrifice was for.

"I'll get the hatch to the souterrain."

Joanna hurried into the master bedchamber and tugged the heavy bed away from the wall to reveal a trapdoor leading to an underground cell. From there, Ealga would make her escape through a tunnel cavern that opened in the forest adjacent to the rocky wall at the keep's back. Four generations of her husband's kin had known of this escape from the lakeside crag. This night it protected not only their child, but future generations, for God had been kind enough to give Joanna a glimpse of what lay ahead for the woman her child would become. Hope would not die tonight, even though Joanna would.

As Ealga paused at the head of the stone steps, Joanna gave in to one last embrace of farewell. With the same fervor as the parting kiss her husband had given her, she conveyed to the nurse and child in her arms a lifetime of love, purged from the heart, the very soul of her being. It was good-bye for this time and place but not for eternity.

"God surround you with His angels." Joanna handed Ealga the finger lamp the nurse had lit earlier. The glow cast a halo upon the crown of the infant's head. Ever so tender, Joanna tucked the blanket over her baby daughter's dark curls. "Tell Brenna when she's old enough that her mother and father loved her very much."

"Greater love hath no man than this—"

Ealga broke off, unable to finish, but Joanna nodded, completing the rest in her mind: *That a man lay down his life for his friends.* Aye, this had to be a great love for it to hurt so much.

"I will see you again, Cousin," Ealga said. "Till then, this life of mine belongs to the bairn." The nurse turned abruptly to make her way down the steep steps, the infant clutched against her with one hand, the lamp in the other.

"Until we meet again." Joanna watched what remained of her tortured heart leave.

Father, I give them to You. You are my hope and stay. Give me courage to finish my task. Keep them in the palm of Your hand.

When the nurse and infant were swallowed by the darkness, Joanna slid the bed back over the hidden door. In moments they would be safe in the time-carved bowels of the hills and in the Rock of her faith.

Footsteps thundered closer, accompanied by the clash of metal and stone, on the stairs leading to the upper chambers. Death cries mingled with bloodthirsty growls of triumph. Joanna whispered a broken prayer for her husband's soul, for no man would set foot on the stairs while Llas still breathed. She ended with a plea for her own forgiveness as she took a jeweled dagger from its sheath and sat upon Llas's side of the bed, still warm from the heat of his body.

Cutting the silk ribbon confining the long braid of her hair, she shook her tresses loose. The regal cloak unfurled about her shoulders as she placed the ribbon on his pillow, remembering his joy in losing his fingers in her dark tresses. It was almost over … all but the final words she had for Tarlach O'Byrne.

Joanna neither blinked nor flinched as the keeper of the bolt gave way, splintering the solid oak frame. With a calm she never dreamed possible, she rose and turned to face her destiny. The terror outside the chamber burst in with Tarlach O'Byrne at its head.

"Your husband is dead, woman."

Though Joanna cringed inwardly as he raised the severed head of her beloved Llas, she struggled to show no sign of her shock at the sightless eyes that had once burned bright with life and love or the drip of blood that had short moments before pumped through her husband's veins. The dream had prepared her. Still, she was grateful for the bed between them bracing the slight buckle of her knees.

Tearing her gaze away, Joanna met that of Llas's murderer, and her horror-curdled blood became as glacial as her demeanor. "So I shall soon join him, sir."

There was no hint in this monster of the smitten warrior who'd once pledged his love to her. Tarlach's nostrils flared like those of a Pictish bull, and his chest heaved beneath the bloodstained crest of pledging hands on his breastplate. Truly the demon of envy had eaten away at his heart and soul like an insidious cancer.

"So you shall …" He licked blood spatter from his lips and smiled as though he savored the taste. "After—"

"After I've had a word with you, Tarlach O'Byrne."

"I'll have more than a word with you, ye coldhearted wench." With a snarl of contempt, Tarlach tossed aside his bloody trophy. "Bring in the lad, men."

Joanna swayed. The blade she hid within the folds of her gown pricked at flesh just below the cage of bone protecting her heart as Tarlach's son, the young heir of Glenarden, stumbled into the room ahead of the man's henchmen. Joanna had been at Ronan's birth, sent for in desperation when complications set in. She recalled stroking the baby boy's thick tuft of dark auburn hair, watching the color come to his cheeks with the life the good Lord breathed into him. Today his wild hair was black compared to his shock-blanched pallor. A nasty gash lay open across his peach-smooth face, bleeding scarlet beneath a wide, terrified gaze. Had the man no conscience, that he would expose a child to such carnage?

"God's mercy, Tarlach. Your son can be no more than six, and already he bears the scars of your bitterness and greed." Joanna resisted the natural urge to run to the lad and gather him into her arms. There was naught she could do for the child but pray that God would heal him of his demon father's scars.

So it will be, a familiar voice, a conviction beyond understanding, assured her.

"The lad must learn how to deal with the witchery of your likes," Tarlach shot back.

"The same *witchery* that saved him?" When would people like Tarlach ever learn? *"The secret things belong unto the LORD our God,"* Joanna quoted, *"but those things which are revealed belong unto us and to our children for ever, that we may do all the words of this law.* To do good for our fellow man in the manner of Christ," she explained.

She'd wonder to her last breath how anyone could call the knowledge of nature's healing properties *witchcraft*. Witchcraft was but its destructive fruit, the use of knowledge for harm or self-glorification, rather than giving the Creator credit for creation's properties.

"Ye did no good to me, Joanna lass. You—"

Suddenly the room flooded with a light from the nursery. A soldier carrying a smoking, blazing torch stopped just inside the adjoining door. "There's no sign of the bairn, milord," he said. "We've searched all the rooms."

Tarlach fixed a glare on Joanna.

When had his left eye begun to stray? the healer within her wondered.

"Where is the whelp?" he bellowed.

"In God's hands."

Brenna was safe. Llas was with his Maker. Joanna was but a few words from joining him. Tarlach started toward her, his axe raised in threat.

Now, she thought, *and God forgive me.* Joanna felt the sting of the dagger as it broke the yielding flesh just beneath her rib cage. There was naught left to do but fall upon it.

Tarlach swore as the torchlight glanced off the metal of the knife. "What manner of trickery is this? You seek to lure me close, then sting me with that?"

"The only sting you will know will be that of the vision God has given me. The Gowrys seed shall divide your mighty house and bring a peace beyond the ken of your wicked soul."

Joanna fell upon the bed, the blade thrusting into a heart already dead with grief. It was then that she saw him. Llas, whole and magnificent, had waited for her, reached for her. Joanna clasped his hand and turned in the brilliance that surrounded them. It bore them up and away from pain, loss, and hatred forever.

"No!" Tarlach leapt forward, realizing what Joanna had done. She would not rob him of this last pleasure. He'd not let her go. But to his horror, instead of leaving his hand at the throw, the axe took on the weight of a great stone, bearing his arm down to his side.

What witchery was this?

Joanna lay upon the bed, silent as death, yet the bite of her words assaulted his left arm with a thousand pinpricks, rendering battle-hardened muscles useless. The axe dropped harmless to the floor with a thud. Nay, she'd not do this to him. By sheer will, Tarlach dragged his unaccountably heavy legs to where the woman lay and turned her upon her back with his good arm.

Below her breastbone, scarlet spread on the pure white of her embroidered chemise in a circle from the jeweled hilt of the buried blade. Pain surged through his body from the same spot, as though she'd impaled him instead of herself. The invisible blade ripped through his right side and up into his brain. God's mercy, it felt as though his blood would burst from his temple, all but blinding him in its fierce rush.

How could Joanna lie so calm and lovely in the midst of this ugliness? How dare her lips tilt in mockery of him? Why, he'd hack her beautiful face into oblivion.

The Glenarden meant to reach for the dagger in his belt, but his rage turned on him as he had his onetime friend Llas. It took Tarlach unaware, slashing the air from his shuddering chest, denying him the use of every muscle. It was her … the beautiful, serene witch lying on the bed beside him. She'd cast one last spell.

"Father!"

Tarlach tried to answer his son, to call for his men, but all that emerged from his throat was a gagging, gurgling sound. Spittle seeped down his chin. His tongue rendered as useless as his arm, he drifted away from the clamor surrounding him. All that remained before oblivion claimed him was the memory of the last words from lips he'd once worshipped.

The Gowrys seed shall divide your mighty house and bring a peace beyond the ken of your wicked soul.

CHAPTER ONE

Glenarden, Manau Gododdin, Britain
Twenty years later

Although cold enough to frost one's breath, the day was as fair as the general mood of the gathering at the keep of Glenarden. The only clouds were those breaking away, fat with snow from the shrouded mountains—and the ever-present one upon the face of the bent old man who stood on the rampart of the gate tower. No longer able to ride much distance, Tarlach O'Byrne watched the procession form beyond.

Clansmen and kin, farmers and craftsmen—all turned out for the annual hunt, but they were more excited over the festivities that awaited their return. In the yard about the keep, gleemen in outlandish costumes practiced entertaining antics, delighting the children and teasing the kitchen servant or warrior who happened to pass too near. Great pits had been fired. On the spits over them were enough succulent shanks of venison, boar, and beef to feed the multitude of O'Byrnes and the guests from tribes in the kingdom under the old king's protection.

Below the ramparts, Ronan O'Byrne adjusted the woolen folds of his brat over his shoulders. Woven with the silver, black, and scarlet threads of the clan, it would keep the prince warm on this brisk day. A fine dappled gray snorted in eagerness as Ronan took his reins in hand and started toward the gate. Beyond, the people he would govern upon his father's death waited.

The youngest of the O'Byrne brothers rode through them, unable to contain his excitement any longer. "By father's aching bones, Ronan, what matters of great import keep you now?"

Were the pest any other but his youngest brother, Ronan might have scowled, deepening the scar that marked the indent of his cheek—the physical reminder of this travesty that began years ago. Alyn was the pride and joy of Glenarden, and Ronan was no exception to those who admired and loved the precocious youth.

"Only a raid on the mill by our *neighbors*," Ronan answered his youngest sibling.

His somber gaze belayed the lightness in his voice. The thieves had made off with Glenarden's reserve grain stores and the miller's quern. Ronan had already sent a replacement hand mill to the mistress. But now that the harvest was over and the excess had been sold, replacing the reserves would be harder. It galled Ronan to buy back his own produce at a higher price than he'd received from merchants in Carmelide. This was the hard lot he faced—this farce, or hunting down the scoundrels and taking back what was rightfully his.

Every year on the anniversary of the Gowrys slaughter, Tarlach insisted that the O'Byrne clan search the hills high and low for Llas and Joanna's heir. But instead of going off on a madman's goose chase after his imagined enemy—a mountain nymph who was rumored to shape-shift into a wolf at will—the O'Byrnes manpower was best spent ransacking and burning one of the Gowrys mountain settlements in retribution, for they were undoubtedly the culprits. It was the only reasoning the Gowrys thieves understood—burn their ramshackle hovels and take some of their meager stock in payment.

Even so, taking such actions only stalled their mischief for a little while. Then it was the same thing all over again. As it was, Ronan had sent trackers out to mark their escape route, lest the wrong camp be destroyed.

"Can I ride after them on the morrow with you?" Alyn's deep blue eyes, inherited from their Pictish mother, were alight with the idea of fighting and possible bloodshed—only because he'd never tasted it firsthand. "After the Witch's End?"

Disgust pulling at his mouth, Ronan mounted the broad and sturdy steed he'd acquired at last spring's fair. *Witch's End.* That's what Tarlach O'Byrne had dubbed the celebration of the massacre that had made him an invalid and driven him to the brink of insanity. In the old chief's demented thought, he'd brought justice to those who had betrayed him and stopped an enchantress forever. Sometimes, as on this particular day, it pushed him beyond reason, for it was a reminder that there was one thing left undone. The heiress of Gowrys still lived to threaten Glenarden … at least in his mind.

"The mill raid is no different from any other raid and will be handled as such," Ronan answered.

"So I can go?"

"Nay, return to your studies at the university." The hunt for a nonexistent witch was one thing, but Gowrys were skilled fighters.

"'Twould suit a Gowrys naught better than to send a son of Tarlach earthways with an arrow through your sixteen-year-old heart."

"So you and Caden will go after the brigands."

Alyn's dejection rivaled that of Tarlach's, except the youth's would be gone with the next change of the wind. The older O'Byrne's would not leave until his last breath faded in the air.

Ronan opened his mouth to assuage the lad when a downpour of water, icy as a northern fjord, struck him, soaking him through. "Herth's fire!" Startled, his gray gelding danced sideways, knocking into the door of the open gate. "Ho, Ballach," Ronan soothed the beast. "Easy laddie."

"Take that, you bandy-legged fodere!" a shrill voice sounded from above.

"Crom's breath, Kella, look what you've done," Alyn blustered, struggling to control his own spooked steed. "Called my brother a bandy-legged deceiver and soaked him through."

Wiping his hair away from his brow, Ronan spotted the cherub-faced perpetrator of the mischief peering over the battlement, eyes spitting fire. Lacking the ripeness of womanhood, Kella's overall appearance was unremarkable, but she surely lived up to her name with that indomitable warrior spirit, bundled in the innocence of youth. It was an innocence Ronan had never known. The daughter of Glenarden's champion, Kella O'Toole was like a breath of fresh air. For that Ronan could forgive her more impetuous moments.

"And for what, Milady Kella, do I deserve the title of a *bandy-legged fool*, much less this chilling shower?"

Kella gaped in dismay, speechless, as she took in Ronan's drenched state. But not for long. "Faith, 'twasn't meant for you, sir, but for Alyn! 'Tis the likes of him that finds the company of a scullery maid more delicious than mine."

Ronan cast an amused glance at his youngest brother, who had now turned as scarlet as the banners fluttering overhead.

"Ho, lad, what foolrede have ye been about?" Caden O'Byrne shouted from the midst of the mounted assembly in wait beyond the gate. Fair as the sun with a fiery temperament to match, the second of Tarlach's sons gave the indignant maid on the rampart a devilish wink.

"'Tis no one's business but my own," Alyn protested. "And certainly not that of a demented *child.*"

"Child, is it?"

Ronan swerved his horse out of range as Kella slung the empty bucket at Alyn. Her aim was hindered by the other girls close at her elbows, and the missile struck the ground an arm's length away from its intended target.

"I'll have you know I'm a full thirteen years."

"Then appeal to me a few years hence when, and if, your God-given sense returns," the youngest O'Byrne replied.

Ronan moved to the cover of the gatehouse and removed his drenched brat. Fortunately, the cloak had caught and shed the main of the attack. Already one of the servants approached with the plain blue one he wore about his business on the estate. Irritating as the mishap was, his lips quirked with humor as his aide helped him don the dry brat. It wasn't as princely as the O'Byrne colors, but it was more suited to Ronan's personal taste.

It was no secret that Egan O'Toole's daughter was smitten with Alyn. With brown hair spun with threads of gold and snapping eyes almost the same incredible shade, she would indeed blossom into a beauty someday. Meanwhile, the champion of Glenarden would do well to pray for maturity to temper Kella's bellicose manner, so that his daughter might win, rather than frighten, suitors.

Then there was Alyn, who hadn't sense enough to see a prize in the making. Ronan shook his head. His brother was too involved in living the existence of the carefree youth Ronan had been robbed of the night of the Gowrys bloodfest.

"So, are you now high and dry, Brother?" Caden O'Byrne called to Ronan with impatience.

Ronan's eyes narrowed. Always coveting what wasn't his, Caden would like nothing better than to lead the hunt without Ronan. Would God that Ronan could hand over Glenarden and all its responsibilities. But Caden was too rash, a man driven more by passion than thought.

"Have a heart, Beloved," a golden-haired beauty called down to him from the flock of twittering ladies on the rampart. Caden's new bride spared Ronan a glance. "Ronan's had much travail this morning already with the news of the Gowrys raid."

"Had he as fair and gentle a wife as I, I daresay his humor would be much improved." Ever the king of hearts, Caden signaled his horse to bow in Lady Rhianon's direction and blew his wife a kiss.

"No doubt it would, Brother," Ronan replied.

There was little merit in pointing out that the ambitious Lady Rhianon had first set her sights on him. No loss to Ronan, she seemed to make his more frivolous brother a happy man. The couple enjoyed the same revelry in dance and entertainment, not to mention the bower. Too often, its four walls failed to contain the merriment of their love play. Neither seemed to care that they were the talk of the keep. If anything, they gloried in the gossip and fed it all the more.

Battling down an annoying twinge of envy, Ronan made certain his cloak was fast, then swung up into the saddle again. Alyn's problems were easier to consider, not to mention more amusing. "Is your wench disarmed, Alyn?" Ronan shouted in jest as he left the cover of the gate once again.

Beyond Lady Kella's tempestuous reach for the moment, Alyn gave him a grudging nod.

Ronan brought his horse alongside his siblings, facing the gatehouse of the outer walls, where Tarlach O'Byrne would address the gathering. Like Alyn's, Caden's countenance was one of eagerness and excitement. How Ronan envied them both for their childhood. He longed to get away from the bitterness that festered within the walls of Glenarden. His had been an apprenticeship to a haunted madness.

Tarlach straightened as much as his gnarled and creaking joints would allow. "Remember the prophecy, *shons* of mine," he charged them. He raised his withered left arm as high as it would go. It had never regained its former power since the night he'd tried to attack Lady Joanna of Gowrys. Nor had his speech recovered. He slurred his words from time to time, more so in fatigue.

"The Gowrys *sheed* shall divide your mighty house ... shall divide your mighty *housh* and bring a peace beyond *itch* ken."

Ronan knew the words by heart. They were as indelibly etched in his memory as the bloody travesty he'd witnessed through a six-year-old's eyes. The quote was close, but whether Tarlach's failing mind or his guilt was accountable for leaving out *"peace beyond the ken of your wicked soul,"* only God knew. If He cared ... or even existed.

"Search every hill, every glen, every tree and shrub. Find the she-wolf and bring back her skin to hang as a trophy in the hall, and her heart to be devoured by the dogs. Take no nun-day repast. The future of Glenarden depends on the Gowrys whelp's death."

At the rousing cry of "O'Byrne!" rising from his fellow huntsmen and kin, Ronan turned the dapple gray with the group and cantered to the front, his rightful place as prince and heir. He didn't believe the girl child had survived these last twenty years, much less that she'd turned into a she-wolf because of her mother's sins. Nor did he wallow in hatred like his father.

A shudder ran through him, colder than the water that had drenched him earlier. Ronan looked to the west again, where thick clouds drifted away from the uplands. May he never become so obsessed with a female that his body and soul should waste away from within due to the gnawing of bitterness and fear. Superstitious fear.

On both sides of the winding, rutted road ahead lay rolling fields. Winter's breath was turning the last vestiges of harvest color to browns and grays. Low, round huts of wattle and daub, limed white and domed with honey-dark thatching, were scattered here and there. Gray smoke circled toward the sky from their peaks. Fat milk cows and chickens made themselves at home, searching for food. Beyond lay the river, teeming with fish enough for all.

Glenarden's prosperity was enough to satisfy Ronan. Nothing less would do for his clan. The tuath was already his in every manner save the last breath of Tarlach O'Byrne … though Ronan was in no hurry for that. Despite his troublesome tempers, Tarlach had been as good a father as he knew how, breaking the fosterage custom to rear his firstborn son under his own eye. A hard teacher he'd been, yet fair—equal with praise as with criticism.

"You are the arm I lost, lad," Tarlach told him again and again, especially when the drink had its way with him. "The hope and strength of Glenarden."

Ronan humored the old man as much as followed his orders. At midday, instead of stopping as usual for the nun repast, he paused for neither rest nor food for his men. They ate on the move—the fresh bread and cheese in the sacks provided by the keep's kitchen. The higher into the hills they went, the sharper the wind whipped through the narrow pass leading to the upper lakelands. Ronan was thankful that the former stronghold of the Gowrys wasn't much farther.

"Faith, 'tis colder than witches' milk," Caden swore from the ranks behind Ronan.

"Witches' milk?" the naive Alyn protested. "What would you know of such things?"

"A good deal more than a pup not yet dry behind the ears. 'Tis a fine drink on a hot summer day."

"Or for the fever," Egan O'Toole chimed in.

His poorly disguised snicker raised suspicion in the youth. "They play me false, don't they, Ronan?"

"Aye, ask our elder brother, lad," Caden remarked in a dry voice. "He has no sense of humor."

Somber, Ronan turned in his saddle. "I have one, Brother, but my duties do not afford me much use of it. As for your question, lad," he said to their younger brother, who rode next to Caden, "there's no such thing as witches, so there can be no witches' milk."

"What about the Lady Joanna?" Alyn asked. "She was a witch."

"Think, lad," Ronan replied. "If she'd truly possessed magic, would she or her kin have died? It was love and jealousy that addled Father."

"But love *is* magic, little brother," Caden put in. "Make no mistake."

"'Tis also loud enough to set tongues wagging all over the keep," Alyn piped up. He grinned at the round of raucous laughter that rippled around them at Caden's expense.

But Caden showed no shame. "That's the rejoicing, lad." He turned to the others. "Methinks our Lady Kella has little to fret over as yet." With a loud laugh, he clapped their red-faced little brother on the back.

Rather than allow the banter to prick or lift an already sore humor, Ronan focused on the first few flakes of snow already whirling in and about the pass ahead of them and the nightmare that already had begun. Twenty years before, this very pass had been just as cold and inhospitable. With possible flurries blowing up, Ronan had no inclination to prolong the outing.

The crannog, or stockaded peninsula, was now little more than a pile of rubble rising out of the lake water's edge. Cradled by overgrown fields and thick forest on three quarters of its periphery, the lake itself was as gray as the winter sky. On the fourth was the jut of land upon which Llas of Gowrys had restored an ancient broch, bracing it against the rise of the steep crag at its back. With no regard for what had been, yellow spots of gorse had taken root here and there in the tumble of blackened stone.

Ronan could still smell the blaze, hear the shrieks of the dying. Ignoring the curdling in the pit of his stomach, a remnant of the fear and horror a six-year-old dared not show, Ronan dispersed the group. "Egan, you and Alyn take your men and search north of the lake. Caden, take the others and search the south. When I sound the horn, everyone should make haste back here. The sooner we return to warm hearths and full noggins of ale, the better."

"I want to go with you," Alyn declared, sidling his brown pony next to Ronan's gray.

"I intend to stay here in the cover of yon ledge and build a fire," Ronan informed him, "but you are welcome to join me."

"I think not."

Alyn's expression of disdain almost made Ronan laugh.

"What if a raiding party of Gowrys happens upon you?" Caden spoke up. A rare concern knit his bushy golden brows.

"Then I shall invite them to the fire for a draught of witch's milk."

Caden laughed out loud. His square-jawed face, bristling with the golden shadow of his great mane of hair, was handsome by even a man's standard. "I misjudged you, Brother. I stand corrected on the account of humor but would still hold that you act too old for your twenty-six years."

"The Gowrys aren't given to visiting the place where they were so soundly trounced … and I'm no more than a horn's blow from help, should my sword not suffice," Ronan pointed out.

He had no taste for this nonsense. What he craved most at the moment was the peace that followed after the others rode off, whooping and beating their shields lest the spirits of the slain accost them.

The hush of the falling snow and the still testimony of the ruins were at least a welcome change from the ribald and oft querulous babble of the hall. Time alone, without demand, was to be savored, even in this ungodly cold and desolate place. All he had to do was keep the memories at bay.

A movement from just above a hawthorn thicket near the base of the cliff caught Ronan's eye, raising the hackles on the back of his neck. With feigned nonchalance he brushed away the snow accumulating on his leather-clad thigh and scanned the gray slope of rock as it donned the thickening winter white veil. Nothing.

At least he thought he'd seen something. A flash of white, with a tail—mayhaps a large dog. Beneath him, the gelding shivered. With a whinny, he sidestepped, tossing his black mane as if to confirm that he sensed danger as well. *A wolf?*

Drawing his sword in one hand, Ronan brought the horse under control with a steadying tone. "Easy, Ballach, easy."

The speckled horse quieted, his muscles as tense as Ronan's clenched jaw. The scene before him was still, like that of a tapestry. At his gentle nudge the horse started around shore toward the high stone cliff. Dog, wolf, or man, Ronan was certain the steel of his blade was all the protection he'd need.

CHAPTER TWO

From a lofty ledge in the steep slope of the rock cliff, Brenna of Gowrys watched the lone man on the horse pick a cautious route around the lake. The O'Byrnes had ridden off, but this one made his way straight for the thicket where Faol had disappeared. Whatever had possessed the wolf to venture that close to a human? She'd raised him from a pup to be like her, a hermit for the sake of survival.

And, like her, Faol was curious. Hadn't she come out this very day just to see the enemy that hunted her, ignoring her late nurse's warnings? Yet this one didn't wear the colors of the O'Byrnes, who'd abandoned him at the pass to hunt her down like wolves after a sheep. She didn't recognize the horse, either. It wasn't the short, sure-footed native breed, but larger and sleeker, built as though to race the wind rather than maneuver in the rocky uplands. This one had surely been brought across the sea from exotic places Brenna had but heard of.

Perhaps the man was a foreigner, too, a guest of the O'Byrnes. Stranger or nay, the sword he wielded as though it were a featherweight identified him as a danger—and, like the rest of them, a fool to be out in this weather.

Brenna flexed cold-stiffened fingers within the confines of her wrap. *Now who's the swineherd swearing the pig stinks?*

A quirk of a smile on her lips, Brenna drew her fur-lined cloak more closely about her. Like the rest of her clothing, it was made of remnants of coarse woolen cloth, except that she'd lined it with a patchwork of such fur as her bow and sling provided. A season's worth of hunting and skinning paid well in food and warmth. According to Ealga, rest her soul, the good Lord put everything on the earth a body might need.

Melancholy weighed the corners of Brenna's mouth. It had been two winters the dear woman who'd raised her had been gone, but Ealga had left a legacy of love and wisdom. A sister of Avalon's Isle, Ealga had taken a seven-year-old Brenna to the sea-swept marshland that had been granted to Joseph of Arimathea in the first century. The wattle-and-mud church he built in Glaston, beyond the claws of the Roman eagle that once occupied and then abandoned Albion's shores to the Saxon wolves, was now a holy community. It included a hospital, where Brenna had learned the arts and knowledge of healing handed down from those who'd personally known and learned from Christ, the Great Physician.

As an apprentice, Brenna had gathered and preserved herbs while applying herself to the religious and academic studies fit for the late Queen Joanna of Gowrys' daughter. When Brenna had reached the age of sixteen, Ealga brought her back to the Gododdin hills so that Joanna's prophecy for peace might be fulfilled before the Gowrys and O'Byrnes killed each other off. Although by what means Brenna was to bring down the house of the O'Byrnes, her guardian had not explained—if she even knew. God knew, Ealga assured her. He would not have given Joanna such a vision if He had no plan.

Surely being hunted like an animal by one clan and considered a messiah-like herald to war by the other wasn't part of the Creator's—

A flash of white amidst the trees below drew Brenna's attention from the stranger with a start. *Faol!* The silver-white wolf had circled and was stalking the man again. She bit her lip, subduing the urge to whistle for the animal to come to her. That would certainly draw the stranger's attention.

Though his horse nervously pranced along the bank, the man thankfully appeared oblivious to her pet's proximity. Aye, the animal would know what the man would not. Thanks be to God, the horse could not speak. The increasing wind wrapped the man's cloak about an able and muscular build, piquing her curiosity all the more. Had he a face as fine?

Not that she'd ever know. Brenna shook the morose reminder aside. Spawned by the loss of her one human companion, such notions smote her at the least expected times, always at war with her faith that God's grace was sufficient, even in loneliness.

The sudden hiss and thud of a flying arrow finding its mark cut short her unbidden longing. The stranger stiffened, arching backward. The sword fell from his hand. Impaired by his wind tossed cloak, he grabbed in futility at the missile lodged in his back with the other.

Brenna's sharp gaze fixed on the bright red and green fletching of the arrow. *God's mercy, he's been ambushed!*

A figure, garbed in the brown and gray of his surroundings, emerged from the thick forest at the edge of the bog. No clan colors did he boast. Yet the Gowrys' red and green fletching was on the arrows.

As she puzzled, the assailant drew back another deadly shaft and, with a banshee-like howl that caused his prey to turn toward him, let it fly at the staggered stranger. This time, the impact drove the victim backward, sending him off the horse's flank. The stranger struck the ground, breaking off the arrow in his back as he rolled over and to his feet with his sword in his good hand.

The assailant dashed back into the cover of the wood and after what seemed but a breath later emerged mounted on a brown horse, unremarkable compared to the fine dappled one that trotted off in the distance. With another bone-scraping howl, he charged the wounded man. The stranger, no novice to be sure, stood his ground before the pounding hooves of the oncoming steed, sword raised.

The ring of metal striking metal cracked sharp as thunder in a summer sky. The momentum carried the deadly predator past his target. He turned his horse, its nostrils blowing clouds in the cold air. His weakened prey staggered in a turn for the next onslaught, making no effort to run from the villain who charged at him again.

She had to do something. Brenna unslung her bow, but the distance was too great to ensure a hit. If she missed, she'd expose herself to the same danger. Caution and the urge to help the helpless warred within. She was a healer, not a slayer.

Beyond, the murderous intruder rode straight at the stranger. Even if he chose, the stranger could not reach the protection of the trees in time to escape the hooves of the snorting horse. Despite his effort to sidestep, the charging animal struck him a mighty blow, hurling him toward some ice-encrusted brush near the woods' edge.

The stranger dragged himself into the thin cover and reached for a stalwart sapling to pull himself to his feet. Below Brenna's perch on the rocky crag, the horseman brought his mount to an abrupt, rearing halt and dismounted. Drawing a short sword from his hip, he advanced for the kill.

Brenna leapt to her feet, throwing caution to the wind. But the shout on the tip of her tongue stalled as yet another banshee wail filled the winter hush of the landlocked basin—*animal, not human.*

From out of nowhere, a bolt of snarling, silver-white fur slammed into the assailant, knocking him over like a chess piece. The weapon in his hand flew, harmless, toward the now still man in the brush.

"Faol!" Surprise robbed Brenna's voice of its strength.

Faol took a stand over the blade, wedging himself between its owner and the fallen stranger. Teeth bared, his warning growl drifted to where Brenna watched in open-mouthed wonder. Faol had chosen to even the fight. Never had she known such pride and fear at the same time. The wolf was fiercely protective of Brenna, but of no other living soul—until now.

Would Faol let the burly assailant retreat? If the wolf did and the man fetched the bow Brenna could clearly see slung on the horse, would her wolf have sense enough to run? She searched the landscape beyond the standoff of man and beast. Where were the stranger's companions? How could this be happening?

Exactly as she anticipated, the intruder backed toward his steed for the weapon slung there. Her limbs thawed, clearing her mind for the action. She had no choice. Brenna drew an arrow from the quiver strapped across her back.

Nocking the arrow, she raised the weapon and pulled back the string. Second thought reared its head. She'd never shot a human.

But then, like as not, she'd not hit the man.

Below, the would-be murderer continued to curse the snarling wolf standing between him and his victim's body. Ever so surely, he reached for his quiver of arrows.

Brenna hesitated no more. *Father, send it straight and true, according to Thy will.*

She let the missile fly along with her breath. It shot up in a graceful arch and, much to her astonishment, ran through the leather protection of the assailant's hand, pinning it and the glove to the saddle. Given the distance, she'd aimed at his body, but this sufficed.

Startled, the man broke off the arrow to free his hand, all the while looking about in wild disbelief. Brenna ducked deep into the crevice. She'd done what she had to do, but a rise of queasiness now battled her alarm. Faith, would she have to tend the very wound she'd inflicted, or would he find and kill her first?

After an unendurable wait she peered out of her hiding place once more to find her answer.

Neither. For once, the superstition surrounding her and the ruins worked to her favor. Abandoning his victim and precious sword to the growling wolf, her target wrestled to mount his steed. The startled horse danced away, dragging him with one foot hung in the stirrup while he desperately grasped the saddle with his uninjured hand. His head swiveling to keep an eye on the growling wolf and seek the source of his attack, the would-be assassin hopped in three full circles, one of them through the shallows of the lake, before he managed to gain his seat.

There his courage caught up long enough for him to pause and snatch up the reins of the dapple gray, which had wandered a short distance down the shoreline. Disgust thinned Brenna's lips. The churl was not only a cowardly murderer, but a horse thief as well.

He could not be one of her clan, she hoped as much as prayed. Scratching a livelihood from the hills to which they'd been exiled had left the Gowrys so poor that the days of pageantry and marking their arrows with their colors were part of the past. Was it possible another enemy of the Glenarden used the same fletching?

Much as she was tempted to scurry down the rocky incline straight to the wounded man's aid, the years of caution instilled by Ealga prevailed. Running both horses as though every Gowrys' ghost were on his heels, the assailant grew smaller and smaller until he disappeared in the pass. Of course, he might return once he came to his senses. Worse yet, what if his victim's companions returned and found her in the open with no place to run?

But the stranger was clearly hurt, or perhaps, still as he lay, already dead. And Faol, which should mean *fool* rather than *wolf* ... well, Brenna wasn't certain what the wolf was up to. She'd never seen him behave in such a peculiar manner.

Am I healer or fugitive? Brenna listened intently to the hush of the surrounding hills, broken only by the occasional bluster of the wind. The weather was worsening. A fit man, or woman for that matter, wouldn't last long in this, much less one wounded and undoubtedly bleeding.

Inasmuch as ye have done it unto one of the least of these ... ye have done it unto Me. The sisters who taught her God's Word turned away no one in need. And neither would she—despite the poor company he kept.

The snow fell upon her descent as though hurled from Ben Ledi. Rare as they came, such snow-fat storms from the Mountain of Light that guarded the entrance to the Highlands made the steep slope all the more treacherous and closed off the passes, sometimes for weeks. Keen as she was to the signs of weather, Brenna hadn't expected this. But then nature did not always reveal its secrets.

Scree near the bottom of the slope sent Brenna sliding with the loose, ice-glazed stones into a dense thicket of scrub conifer and juniper. As she struggled to her feet, all speculation about nature's whimsy was banished by a rumbling in her ear. The howling wind had either picked up, or an accompanying drum of horses approached.

Pulling back into the cover of the wild brush, Brenna crouched in the narrow of a deer path, waiting until the horses and riders materialized. *O'Byrnes!* But would they see their fallen colleague? And—a terrible thought—would they see Faol?

Her heart beating twice its normal rate, Brenna eased a frozen branch of evergreen aside to look for her pet. Instead of shrinking deeper into the forest cover, Faol lay stretched out next to the man, his thick white coat blending with the snow-blanketed landscape.

Now 'twas certain the wolf was mad—his skin alone was worth a goodly sum. What was so exceedingly special about this man?

There were six riders at first. A fair-haired one sported the red, silver, and black colors of the O'Byrnes on the brat. Instead of riding around to where the stranger had fallen, they waited, fully mounted, and laughed amongst one another in a camaraderie Brenna might have envied under other circumstances. Faith, but she missed someone to speak to. Aside from a wolf and the too few visits from the hermit priest in the glen, there was no one.

Many were the nights Ealga had heralded her with tales of how her mother and father had met. How Llas of Gowrys and Tarlach of Glenarden had been best of comrades then. Until Llas met Brenna's mother, Joanna, who was since childhood betrothed by the church to Tarlach.

"To preserve the Grail lines, child," Ealga explained when Brenna wrestled with the unfairness of her mother being promised to someone she'd never met. "The O'Byrnes carry the Davidic blood passed on in Erin after the fall of the Holy City. And your dear mother, Joanna, carried the Briton royal *and* the apostolic blood of St. Joseph, come to these shores after the resurrection of our Lord."

"But Father wasn't royal or priestly?"

Brenna could still see Ealga's ever-patient, ever-loving smile. "His lineage was just as precious, but he wasn't among the chosen."

The chosen. Those gifted few who excelled in war and in their studies in universities like Glaston or Llanwit. Once versed in the arts and sciences of the ancients and the Word of God, these students were then groomed, according to his or her gifts, for the mission of the church.

"Tarlach was trained as a scholar, warrior, and king," Eagla told Brenna. "His quest? To keep the kingdom of Glenarden a Christian one. He was to wed Joanna, a Grail priestess of the most devout and scholarly of Briton and apostolic lineages."

Missionaries in their own way, Ealga had explained, these women sometimes married into a pagan court to seal an alliance and produce a Christian heir.

"What the swords of the Christian kings could not conquer, love did."

Brenna loved that part of her nurse's tales.

"But the sacred bloodlines have always been fostered and protected on all our isles by the church fathers. Arthur's is such a marriage. His mother, Ygraine's, and Aedan's. His aunt Morganna and Orkney's Cennalath as well."

But of most import to Brenna was that Joanna had renounced her honored calling to marry for love ... and paid a horrible price.

A boisterous "Ho!" from the far side of the abandoned lake rath pulled Brenna from past to present. More hunters approached ... including a dog handler and two great wolfhounds.

Brenna blanched. Dare she hope the blizzard would mask Faol's scent? If not—

The handler released the hounds, but instead of heading in Faol's direction, the dogs began to run in circles among the riders, barking wildly. The chaos caused the horses to rear and bolt so that the crazed canines were soon leashed again and led away toward the pass.

Brenna clasped her hands to her chest. *Father God be thanked!*

Meanwhile, the men below gestured and looked about, uncertain as to what to do about their missing comrade. With the tracks of the earlier conflict blotted out by the sudden increase of ground cover, there was little to make them look closely at the forest's edge, where Faol and the injured man lay still as death. Brenna could see them only because she knew where to look. She hoped, at least for Faol's sake, the wolf and man would not be seen. But for the man to survive ...

'Twas God's decision to make. Even as Brenna accepted the truth, her heart lacked the conviction that she knew she should feel. Since the day Brenna had found Faol, abandoned and half-starved, she was the only mother the orphaned wolf pup had known, just as Ealga had been hers. To lose her constant companion to the hunters ...

The men divided and circled the shore of the lake. Twice they rode past the spot where Faol and the still man lay in the cover of wild brush and snow, and twice the searchers missed seeing them. At long last they regrouped and left, led by the fair-haired man through the pass leading down to the lowland from the basin. Ealga had branded her parents' murderer as a golden-haired monster, so this strapping fellow was surely his son.

And there Faol lay next to his charge like a self-appointed guardian angel, escaped by a thousand heartbeats from her worst nightmare. *Father God be thanked.*

Brenna's knees ached as she straightened from her crouched position. Wriggling her toes in her deerskin boots, she warily studied the pass where the O'Byrnes had retreated. Even if they went straightaway to their fine keep, 'twould take the balance of the night by a leaping fire and considerable drink to thaw from this blizzard.

A howl sharper than the wind broke the hush surrounding her. *Faol.* Standing a few feet away from the fallen man, the wolf looked in her direction as if to say it was safe to come out and see what he'd done. The proud wag of his tail slung snow in all directions. Mother of mercy, he'd brought home prizes from his hunts before and left them at the entrance of the cave, but this surpassed them all.

CHAPTER THREE

Despite the icy weather pelting the mountainside, Brenna was sweat soaked by the time she and Faol dragged the unconscious man into the shelter of her home—a cave, but no ordinary one.

A crook in the entrance chamber, combined with the hide hung over the opening that separated the inner cave from the outer, cut the icy fingers of the wind off at the knuckle. The hot spring in the bowel of the mountain, a natural heat that drove them to the outer cave in summer, warmed the inner chamber.

"Thank you, Father God," she said, grateful that the stranger still breathed after being dragged on his cloak up a rocky mountainside. The glorious warmth embraced them, even though she'd banked the fire early that morning.

After covering the stranger with such blankets and skins as she had and propping his fine sword against the wall, Brenna stirred the coals on the hearth and added wood. Soon the fire's shadows danced on the walls and ceiling of the stone enclosure. As her aching fingers began to thaw, she watched the smoke swirl upward through a blackened fissure in the ceiling. Brenna could only guess where it exited.

Her stomach growled, reminding her that she'd not eaten since that morning. Tempting as it was to stuff down one of the cold bannocks she'd baked on the hearth the night before, Brenna turned her attentions to her patient. The oat flatbread would have to wait. A long night awaited her, but undoubtedly it would be even longer for him.

If he'd not bled too much already.

The frontal shaft, fired dead on at close range, had gone clean through his shoulder. But the one fired deceitfully at his back had broken off. Upon cutting away his velvet tunic and the embroidered linen shirt beneath, both as princely as the gold ring on his right hand, Brenna removed the absorbent fungus she'd stripped from a nearby ash and applied to the wounds before she had moved him. Now his muscled flesh, mottled with dried, blackened blood, began to ooze fresh blood. The cold must have slowed the bleed, for the bruising appeared little worse than when she'd covered the wounds at the beginning of their journey.

But now she knew the wounds needed to bleed freely to rid the body of contamination. And the broken shaft and arrowhead had to be removed, by whatever means necessary.

She began to assemble what she'd need for the surgery. Ealga's tools, now Brenna's own. Hot, healing water from the spring. Poultices of wood sorrel and bugle. Strips of cloth rent from her late nurse's clothing.

What if he's an O'Byrne?

The thought stopped Brenna in her tracks.

Fine time to be thinking such a thing. Not that she had a choice. Enemy or nay, she couldn't let him freeze to death, now, could she?

She was a healer. He didn't wear the O'Byrne colors. And he was God's child as much as she.

Father, he and I are in Your capable hands. If he is my enemy, let me conquer him with Your love.

Only in faith could Brenna bat down the doubts that curled like serpents about her resolve as she returned to her patient's side, ready to work. Fear was a lack of faith, Ealga said. And Brenna had faith. She was weaned on it by her nurse and Brother Martin, the hermit priest in the glen. Never mind that she'd led the life of a fugitive. Never mind that this man might be sworn to take her life. This was her duty. God would protect her for serving Him so. He would not fail her.

As though sensing her troubled thoughts, Faol left his favorite place by the hearth and came to her. After studying both her and the patient's still face, the wolf began to lick the unconscious man's cheek.

Brenna pushed the animal away affectionately. "Off with you now! You've done your part. Best leave his care to me."

Instead of going back to his rug by the hearth, Faol dropped next to her patient—diligent, if not wholly obedient.

"Silly pup," she fussed. "Now I have to clean my hands again."

But she was Faol's mama, and he was her guardian and dear companion. Love welled in Brenna to the brim. *And thank You, Father God, for my faithful, furry friend. I can't imagine life without him. Keep him safe and bless him with long life.*

Yet even as she prayed, she well knew that the wolf was hers for a time only. Like Ealga. She took a deep breath to break the vise closing on her heart.

Faol cocked his head at her.

"'Tis good for now, laddie," she whispered. Beyond that, Brenna could not bear to think, lest her fear of being alone again become unbearable. "Father God willing, we've a man's life to save."

Chilled to the bone, Caden of Glenarden led the dismal group of riders back to the fortress in the waning light of nightfall. He almost wished he were as frozen dead as his elder brother surely was by now, rather than tell Tarlach the dreaded news. At the lake, Caden first thought Ronan had tired of the waiting and, with the increasingly bad turn of weather, started back to Glenarden. Perhaps the howling wind had muffled his signal. But then the group came upon his brother's riderless horse wandering in the pass, the horn still tied to the saddle.

Evidently Ronan had tried to make it back to the keep, but something had gone wrong. They'd searched along the pass for any sign of Ronan or his possible assailant until the weather and darkening skies made it impossible to continue. Not even the dogs had a clue, not so much as a scent, although they'd behaved oddly about the lake, circling the riders and barking incessantly. The master of the hounds was at a loss to explain or control their behavior until they were well away from Gowrys' ruins. Only then did Gillis mutter something under his breath about spirits of the dead spooking his furred charges.

Shouts from the towers bracketing the main gate heralded their slow approach. The welcoming shouts smacked of relief, for the hunting party should have been back by midafternoon for the feast. Perhaps Caden should have sent Alyn back with O'Toole to let his father know what had happened.

Cursed hindsight. Caden excelled with it. But daylight fairly raced to fade, and the snow thickened in the pass until it was nigh impossible to see. Were Caden as superstitious as Gillis, he'd think death's angel curtained it off.

The aged oak gates of Glenarden swung open, preempting further speculation. Tarlach himself shuffled out into the weather, flanked by some of the clan elders. Caden couldn't see his father's face, but he knew his bent figure, broad as a bear and just as dangerous in a temper. And if he were not already in one, the clan chief would be upon finding out his precious heir was missing, probably dead. And his wrath would fall on Caden, who never measured up to Ronan.

Caden steeled himself, his fingers tightening on the reins of the riderless dappled stallion walking next to his own steed. God forgive him, he loved Ronan as a brother. Yet there was a part of Caden, a poison green part, that hated him and would not mourn the loss. Ronan had no fault in Tarlach's failing eyes. He'd fought like a warrior at age six. He was the unanimous choice of the lesser chieftains as Tarlach's heir. He was a wise administrator, cautious … everything Caden was not. Nay, Caden would not miss him overmuch. Perhaps now was the chance to show Tarlach his second son had merit too.

Eventually. For now, the present must be faced. For the first time, Caden noticed that even the wind had ceased its wail, as if in anticipation of a greater storm approaching. "Where is my son?" Tarlach's roar pierced the silence.

It took great effort not to remind the old man that two sons *were* present. "Ronan is missing, my lord father," he said instead. "We searched till the light failed us, all to no avail."

Tarlach staggered back as though struck broadside with a sword. A wounded growl erupted from his throat. An attendant rushed to the old lord's side, only to be shoved away. Tarlach tore the cloak away from his face, exposing his wild age-shot mane to the elements, and narrowed his eyes beneath the bush of his brow.

"I'll hear you inside." No offer, no invitation. An order.

"We looked ... " Alyn's young voice broke. "We looked everywhere, Father."

In the torchlight Tarlach's hardened features relaxed upon seeing his youngest son. "Aye, laddie, I'm sure you did. But come inside before you take a chill. My heart could not take the loss of another son."

"*If* Ronan is lost, milord," Caden said. It was a thin hope. One that might raise Tarlach's esteem of him, if he found Ronan. At least there would be a body to mourn. "I give you my word," he called to Tarlach as the old man turned to reenter the outer yard. "I will not rest until I find him."

Without acknowledgment, Tarlach continued his bent, shuffling walk through the round, thatched huts of those who lived within the protection of Glenarden's thick stockade walls and headed toward the raised stone keep in the center of the compound.

As if Caden did not exist in this world or in the old man's own bitter one. It wasn't new to Caden, but it hurt, twisting like a knife in his chest. Tearing open old scars and barely healed wounds. Again.

By the time the men had seen to their horses and had their grim audience with Tarlach, a feast fit for kings awaited them. But the air was far from the festive scenes portrayed on the tapestries hung along the wall. The pall of Ronan's disappearance blanketed the very air and choked any semblance of laughter. The eyes of man and woman alike blinked away mists of grief as the story circulated the room in hushed tones.

"Gowrys!" Tarlach spat the name of his enemy and slung his empty bronze cup across the table where his sons and honored guests sat. The remainder of the population gathered on benches about the fire pit. The cup rolled off the table and onto the floor, where Tarlach's hounds set upon investigating the untempting handout. A maid hastily retrieved it, wiping its rim with her apron, her eyes creeping to Ronan's seat beside the chieftain.

It was conspicuously empty. No one dared occupy it. Certainly not Caden. Not yet. He contented himself to be next to Rhianon, the bride he'd taken that spring. Never had Caden felt this way about a woman, and he had known more than his share.

Beyond Rhianon's golden crown of braided hair, interwoven with wine velvet ribbon to match her gown, Tarlach came into focus. He stared unsteadily at Caden, his head weaving from the drink in which he'd drowned himself. "*You* lost him, lad. *You* find him. You owe me that."

"On my honor, Father, I will find our brother and exact justice." Caden meant every word. He would prove himself invaluable to Tarlach. Indispensable. Now was his chance to show his father and his bride he was every bit his brother's equal.

Tarlach rose on wobbly legs and lifted his freshly filled cup. "Tomorrow, at dawn's light, we will search again for my firstborn. I will not mourn without a body. I will not!" He slammed the fist of his good arm on the table and leaned forward. "And if our search fails, then we will ride to the high hills at Leafbud and raze every Gowrys hovel until his fate is known to us."

"What if the wolf-witch has him?"

All heads turned toward the youngest O'Byrne. Alyn had been unusually quiet until now ... no doubt wracked with guilt for abandoning the search. In other men, Caden found such idealism disgusting. But in his youngest brother, it was pure charm.

The youth pressed on. "What if it wasn't the Gowrys, but she who spirited him off his horse?"

For a moment the room was as frozen as the hunting scene embroidered by Caden's late mother that hung on the wall. Glances, not words, were exchanged—some with fear and superstition, others with skepticism and mild amusement.

Tarlach thawed first, sinking into his chair as though the wind had been snatched from his lungs. Despite his rantings over the she-wolf, it was obvious that this had not crossed his fevered mind. In his mind, *he* was the hunter. The witch, if she existed, was the hunted. With a trembling hand the old man made the sign of the cross over his chest. His gesture was repeated here and there around the room.

Caden watched, fascinated to see the bear almost shrivel within the folds of his brat. Tarlach's lips moved, yet nothing came out of them. Nothing coherent.

"Father?" Alyn hastened to the old man's side. "I'm sorry I mentioned her. Of course she couldn't possibly overcome Ronan. He's a fine warrior."

"Oh she could, laddie. She could, she could, she .... " A whimper escaped Tarlach. "May God forgive me if it was I who put my son in her path." He switched his attention to Caden. "Were there wolf tracks?"

"Nay, Father. No tracks of any kind. Our own were covered almost as we made them."

"Aye, the storm," Tarlach recalled. "The storm none of us saw coming."

"As though hurled by vengeance," someone observed.

Tarlach began to rock back and forth, drawing his cloak closer over his round shoulders from the unseen storm pelting his conscience. "Magic. Her kind could do such things in olden days."

Caden started at the crackling voice of Rhianon's maidservant.

"Be sure, they still do, milord."

Keena, she was called—old, wizened, and filled with enough superstition for them all.

"By all your gods, woman, must you ever lurk about?" he demanded.

Keena bowed her head till all Caden could see was a wild tangle of salt-shot black hair. "I ever serve milady." Her humble words sorely lacked backbone. "Where she is, there I be."

Caden counted his blessings that it was not *always* the case.

"Regardless, old woman, none control the weather save nature itself." Caden had yet to see a druid who could control the weather, the tales of old be dashed. Predict it, yes. He'd seen pious priests plying God with prayer for favorable weather and studying the heavens for His signs. The same signs that had spoken to the farmer and fisherman since time began. No magic. Just astute observation.

Like as not, Caden knew Tarlach wrestled more with guilt and shame than fear. Guilt for betraying a foster brother over a woman and shame for attacking in the night like a coward and slaying the chieftain when he was still dazed with sleep. The only magic involved was that of love turned bad. It was Joanna's rejection of him that had changed the proud Christian warrior Tarlach had once been, one who had fought shoulder to shoulder with his foster brother in battle after battle to unite the Briton kingdoms against the Saxon and Pict.

As Caden glanced from his father to Rhianon, a glimmer of understanding flashed in Caden's mind, slaying his disdain. Truly if Rhianon turned against him, if she were taken from him, Caden would lose his mind. His fists clenched against the thought. The burning rage that flashed within him told Caden there was no telling the atrocities he might commit to avenge her loss.

With a loud moan, Tarlach grabbed his head, rocking. "Even now she stabs at my mind. Oh heartless vixen, be gone. Be gone!"

"Sshh, Father." Alyn gently coaxed Tarlach out of his chair and motioned for the steward to help him. "Caden?" the boy called over his shoulder in a plaintive tone.

Caden understood his brother's panic. Tarlach was given to violent headaches from time to time. The physician warned that a brain attack might finish the work of the one Tarlach experienced the night of the Witch's End.

Rhianon gathered her velvet skirts about her and rose. "Come, Keena," she said to her nurse. "Let us prepare a headache powder for his lordship … something with a calmative as well."

Caden caught her arm. "Nay, milady, let your nurse see to it. Your place is at my side. Vychan," he said, addressing Glenarden's steward. Tall and lean with snow creeping into his light brown hair and beard, the man had been in Tarlach's service for nigh on ten years, succeeding his father before him. "Go with Alyn to help my father to his quarters."

No stranger to Tarlach's fits, Vychan nodded grimly. "Aye, milord. I'll see to the Glenarden's needs *and* his head pain," he added with an unveiled look of distrust at Keena's retreating figure. There was no doubt the steward thought the crone a witch. However, any woman stranger to a comb or brush was suspect in Vychan's fastidious world.

Caden shoved his end of the bench he shared with his wife away from the table and stood to command attention away from the rush of aid to Tarlach. "Milords and ladies, many of you have seen the O'Byrne like this before. This day he's suffered a fierce blow, and the wine has done little to ease his pain. But it would pain him even more should one man or woman retire prematurely from the O'Byrne hospitality. For Tarlach's sake, let us eat and drink well, for we have a long day tomorrow. We will find my brother, alive or dead, and bring him home. We will give my father the peace he deserves!"

A chorus of "Huzzah" rose from every corner of the hall as Alyn guided Tarlach, still clutching his head, into an anteroom that had been converted into a bedchamber to save the aging lord from climbing the steps to the master bedchamber on the second floor. Ronan had taken that over at Tarlach's insistence.

"Ailill," Caden called to the clan bard, whose music had ceased upon Tarlach's outburst. "Play us a song of better times, for if ever there was a night our spirit needed bolstering, 'tis this."

As the music started, Caden slipped into the tooled leather seat vacated by his father. Batting away a dart of guilt, he helped himself to a choice piece of roast venison. He felt better already.

CHAPTER FOUR

Fever set in Brenna's patient the next day. After applying fresh drawing poultices, Brenna sought to bring the heat down by wrapping her patient in a cool linen sheet drenched in spring water steeped with yarrow and daisy and cooled by snow. At times his teeth chattered like the lid on a boiling pot as the man drifted somewhere between This World and the Other Side. Not even the honey-sweetened tea of willow bark and dried ginger that she coaxed into her patient hour after hour to restore the fluids flushed out by the fever made any difference.

His head in her lap, Brenna tried to coax the last bit through his lips when he flung out his arm, knocking the wooden cup from her hand and sending it rolling across the stone floor of the cave. Startled by both the suddenness of the action and the patient's strength, she inadvertently shrieked. Before Brenna knew it, Faol had the man's arm in his teeth. Warning rumbled in the wolf's throat.

"Gently, Faol," she sang in a voice that had soothed both man and wolf since she'd brought the stranger home. The wolf's dark gaze shifted from the now still man to Brenna. Ever so slowly the raised hairs on the animal's neck relaxed, as did his grip on the stranger's arm. "He knows not what he does, *cariad*. Now go to your rug."

As though he understood her every word, the white wolf obediently returned to his station, where a beet broth slowly warmed.

Brenna felt the damp linen sheet covering her patient's body. Still as hot as the skin beneath.

"Time for another bathing," she observed to no one in particular.

Brenna gathered a basin of water from the hot spring and added herbal oils to boost his strength and snow gathered from the mouth of the cave to cool the water once more. The bath would not only minister to the man but stay the stench of the infection-poisoned sweat his body threw off in its fierce battle for life … although there had been a distinct, pleasant scent in the velvet tunic she'd cut away from him. She couldn't quite make out the nature of it. An imported soap, perhaps. Very masculine. Very princely.

Who are you, my prince? And who would want you dead?

Yesterday it had been all she could manage to cleanse the flesh around the wound in order to treat it. Today more was needed. If God instructed His people to cleanse a dead man, surely the living needed cleansing even more for their battle against raging disease.

When she finished towel drying the man's thick mass of dark auburn hair, she sat back on her knees, her brow furrowing. The very idea of progressing beyond his wounds heated her face and staggered her pulse. The older women of Avalon sent the younger away when tending male patients. By the time Brenna reached the stage in training where she was allowed to stay, Ealga had spirited her back to the land of lakes set like jewels by God's hand into the mountainsides.

Father God, I would bring him clean unto You for healing. Banish this base curiosity worming into my thoughts like rot to an apple and use my lowly efforts to Your glory.

In spite of her order that Faol stay by the fire, the wolf inched closer and closer as she wrung out her cloth.

Bless him. "We can do this, Faol. His face first."

It was of exquisite proportion. His forehead was high to suggest intelligence, his cheekbones proud. The square of his jaw, like the Romanesque length of his nose, was angular and manly—like a statue she'd seen as a child traveling from the Avalon marshland back to her home in the mountains.

Once she'd finished his upper torso, trying not to admire it overmuch with eye or curious fingers, she studied the laces of his trousers and braided leather leggings, tied snugly about sturdy limbs. There had to be a way to remove the clothing and maintain decency.

"Remove only what is necessary."

Exactly, Brenna agreed as she remembered the long ago advice from her teachers. But given nature taking course over the long night, everything was necessary. Even as she painstakingly removed the clothing under the cover of a blanket, whispers of her fellow novices at Avalon regarding the bestial nature of that which prominently separated male from female plagued her. Word was that it had a consciousness of its own, even when the patient himself was unconscious.

How she wished for Ealga! But that was not possible. *Brenna* was now the healer. Trained, but untried in so many ways.

'Twill be no more than skinning the rabbit, she told herself. A few well-executed snips with her scissors on the outer seams, snatch out the *skin*—the man's clothing—and leave him his decency beneath the covers.

Though Brenna did her best, in her blindness and attempt to save the clothes that she might stitch them together again, she nicked him here and there with the sharpened tips of the blades. At length she tugged the last piece of clothing out from under the blanket—his braccae, inseam still intact—and breathed a sigh of relief. Then she crossed herself, praying for a steady hand for the washing to follow.

She did so by feel beneath the blanket—soaking, wiping, cooling—until she at last covered his bare feet and tucked them in snugly. Now wiser than she wished to be regarding the source of those nighttime whispers and giggles, she gathered up the clothing scattered on the floor, relying on work to bury her newfound knowledge deep into the recesses of her mind.

"Sure, I'll have a good deal of mending to do before our prince will have need of these," she said to her furry companion.

Across the enclosure Faol barked and backed away from the hearth with a low rumble.

"So it boils!" Brenna stuffed the clothing into a basket. "Thank you, Faol." Upon crossing to the hearth, she lifted the lid and checked the nutritious beetroot stew she was preparing. "We need to thin it down for our guest and add hawthorn, I think, for when he gains his senses. He'll need all the help we can afford for his pain."

Brenna ladled a portion of the brew into one of the two wooden bowls she possessed and put the linen bag of herbs she'd prepared into it. This done, she scooped a hot stone from the hearth and dropped it in to keep the mixture warm until the steeping was done.

"There we go."

When the broth had steeped sufficiently to give to the patient, Brenna knelt beside him once more. Pillows raised his head enough that she could slip the nourishment through the man's lips a scant spoonful at a time. Her patient strangled but once, wincing fiercely at the pain the convulsive coughing caused him. Brenna set aside the cup and held him, as if to protect him from the agony tearing at his wounds, until he finally quieted.

As he fell back against her lap and pillows, he briefly opened his eyes. Unfocused, his gaze darted, panic-stricken, about his surroundings. The hearth fire, the dried herbs strung on a line overhead, the old cupboard that housed the preparations Brenna had been putting together for the spring fair.

And then his gaze found hers and widened. "What the ... who ...?"

Brenna knew this raw fear surfacing in his fevered eyes. It was the same as that of the wild animals she brought home to nurse. A foreign place ... in the hands of a stranger ...

She smiled. "There now, you're safe within my care, sir, though gravely wounded. You mustn't stir overmuch—"

His lashes fluttered and surrendered to the persistent unconsciousness. The fever heightened the already ruddy hue of a man accustomed to the out-of-doors. Though she'd noticed, when dragging him onto the pallet the night before, that neither his hands nor gold ring were indicative of a life of skin-callusing labor. Nay, this one's calluses were those of a wealthy warrior, made by weapons and the reins of his horse.

Perhaps he was a noble kinsman of the O'Byrnes. That would account for the expensive clothes and fine steed he'd ridden. She ran her finger along his cheek, noticing for the first time a thin scar slashed across it. It was from long ago and well healed, perhaps since childhood.

"Who are you, fair stranger? Friend, foe, or innocent?"

The question haunted Brenna through the next week as her patient battled for his life against the burning possession of fever. It attacked his lungs, making him struggle for every breath. Yet when he coughed up the yellow drowning, the effort tore at his wounds. Brenna sang to him or soothed him with the psalms and Scripture she'd committed to memory while at Avalon. The voice had as much healing quality as the hands, her nurse had said.

When delirious nightmares punished him, she held him, talked him through his imagined travails, praying all the while that these dream demons were imagined. Yet the way he cringed in her arms and cursed vehemently at blood and gore, at murdering women and children, and at madmen and witches made them seem real. Too real ... and familiar.

Her only consolation came in his equal denouncement of the O'Byrnes and Gowrys. "'Twas foolrede! Neither side deserved to win. Tarlach claimed the victory, but he lost as much as the Gowrys."

"How could Tarlach lose more than his life?" Brenna ventured during one of the deliriums. Her blood ran cold with dread. Had the man in her arms been there? Had he seen her parents' massacre? Surely he'd been no more than a child at the time. "Was it his soul?"

The stranger looked at her as if she were an apparition and not what he saw in his tortured dementia. "His mind, lassie," he railed at her, his voice dry and cracking. "He lost his mind ... his honor. He had no right!"

"No right to what, sir?"

Ealga never dwelled much on the night of Brenna's parents' death, except to say that it was a bloody massacre, done in the dark and shame of night.

"The children, lassie. There was no need to kill children."

Aye, everyone had been murdered. All except for her and Ealga. The nurse had bundled Brenna off to the safety of the hills. Joanna of Gowrys had foreseen the event and made certain her daughter would be spared.

"God save the innocents! Would that I'd joined them, for they are surely better off than the likes of me now."

"What did you see? Did you see Lady Joanna … the witch?" If the stranger believed her mother was a witch, then he was Brenna's enemy to be sure.

He shook his head, clasping Brenna to him with his good arm. "Only if beauty and kindness be witchery. The dagger that killed her killed me as well. I am dead, but trapped in a living body, not much better off than Tarlach himself. I am too old to live and too young to die. 'Tis a damnable curse, worse than the one she put upon us."

Brenna's heart shuddered to a stop. "You're an O'Byrne." It was a statement, not a question. Her patient could be no other.

"Nay, never! I only go through the motions."

Relief washed over her, leaving confusion in its wake. If he was not an O'Byrne, who was he? Did she want to know? Could she ever close an eye again without fearing for her life?

"What motions, sir?"

"Life, milady. Better you should let me die."

The sheer force of his words shook her to the core. His was a torment that reached into the very recesses of his mind, far worse than what she'd battled thus far. His utter hopelessness explained why his improvement had been so slow. How tragic to possess cherished youth and wish it away for death! His despair seeped into her, overwhelming her.

Despite her closed eyes, she saw a young boy with burnished auburn hair, blood seeping down his cheek. But it was the horror in his eyes that riveted her, made her hold the man in her arms even tighter. No child should see what he had seen.

A sob wrenched free of her patient's throat, only to be caught and muffled against her as she cradled his head. "Hush, *a stór*," she cooed, bestowing without second thought the endearment that Eagla lavished upon her when the affairs of childhood—a skinned knee, a pet that died, or one that had to be let go—grew too great for Brenna to bear. Another and yet another sob shook the body of the man, but they poured from the heart of that boy. That poor, frightened child.

And as Brenna held him now, understanding dawned. That boy had never smiled again. Never laughed or loved. The blackness that had enshrouded his heart that night of terror wouldn't allow it. Brenna couldn't see the blackness, but somehow she knew it. This was what needed healing. His body was strong, but as long as this darkness imprisoned the spirit of the child he'd been, the man could not survive.

CHAPTER FIVE

Brenna surfaced from sleep on the wide pallet next to her patient. He was murmuring again … not that she could make out his words. A glance at the hearth told her that Faol had gone out, but as to whether it was night or day, she wasn't certain. She'd lost all sense of time and routine since bringing the stranger to her cave. Thankfully she'd been diligent in preparing for the long dark of winter and was well supplied with food, fuel for the fire, and medicinal herbs.

But the stranger wasn't healing. Not as he should. His wounds ran deeper than the flesh, challenging her expertise, while his cries and murmurings aroused compassion. If only she could relieve his nightmares, give him a reason to want to live.

And so she doted on him—singing, praying, reciting the Scriptures she'd been memorizing since she was old enough to speak. The Psalms were her favorites. In them she hoped he would hear the despair of God's beloved turn to praise again and again. The words would remind him and her of the joy of God's love, felt even in the darkest of times.

As she repeated verse after verse, she watched closely for the bat of an eyelash, a movement of his arm or lips—any sign of response.

But fever toyed with her, giving her hope one moment as it broke and returning to dash it the next. Her initial discomfort at ministering to the muscled planes of his body and that most male of his anatomy subsided with necessity.

As a precaution she introduced a concoction of barrenwort and like herbs as an essential part of the stranger's broth for their dulling effect on a man's baser nature. Granted, he was weak and harmless. For now. But until he was well enough to leave and as long as she shared the same pallet, she would continue that precaution.

During her chores Brenna found herself talking to the man as she did to Faol. She expected no answer but enjoyed the companionship she'd missed since Ealga's passing. As though he might be interested, she explained about the herbs and broths she made for him, all save the barrenwort, and spoke to him encouragingly about the healing of his wounds.

"You must recover, Adam." The name seemed to suit him, given he was her first male patient and all but naked except for a cloth wrap about his middle. "The Father has a destiny for you," she'd insisted, quoting Jeremiah. *"For I know the thoughts that I think toward you, saith the LORD, thoughts of peace, and not of evil, to give you an expected end."*

And what was that destiny? Brenna propped herself up on one elbow to study his sleeping face. Of course he'd leave. No one would voluntarily isolate himself as her circumstance demanded. Perhaps he'd ride off to fight with Arthur.

"Will you join our young Dux Bellorum and hold back the northern Picts from taking our beloved Manau? Or fight the Saxons to the south and east of us?"

Though this Arthur was the first to bear the title *and* the given name, his enemies were more than the nameless Romano-British commander general who held off the initial Saxon onslaughts further south when her parents were but babes. For safety's sake, it had been forbidden by law back then to address great personages by their given names—a deed punishable by death. But the previous Arthurs were also of the royal Davidic and priestly Arimathean bloodlines preserved by the church.

What if Adam were of like parentage? Brenna fingered the gold ring on his finger, looking for a symbol and finding naught but exquisite knotwork engraved upon it.

"Is your name recorded with those of the former Pendragons on the Sacred Isle, privy only to the church?" Brenna reached out and stroked his bristled jaw, giving rein to her imagination. "Have you blood royal roots here—a Pictish grandmother and a Scottish grandfather—like Arthur?"

While Arthur was the hope of Manau, the people called his father, Aedan, *uther*, terrible, for abandoning them to the enmity of the Northern Picts and Saxons in order to succeed his father, Gabran, to the grander Dalraida throne in the West. Even worse, Aedan married a Romano-British queen instead of a royal from the Gododdin lineage. It was at the blessing of the church, but poorly received in Manau, nonetheless. "Faith, *you* could already be married in that mire of matches … or worse, married in alliance to the O'Byrnes." Brenna's brow furrowed as she eyed the precious ring on his hand. "Regardless, you'll be going. Of that I'm sure."

A dread rooted in her chest, paining her already at the idea of being left alone once more. Granted, her companion hadn't replied

to the conversations she'd carried on with him, but he'd been there
and taken the edge off her loneliness.

Mathair Ealga said this was her worst fault: her reluctance to let
an animal go once she'd nurtured it to renewed health. Of all her
rescues, only Faol had come back. The white wolf went off at times
to hunt and, no doubt, mate, but he always returned.

"He'll take care of ye, child, until he brings ye one to take his place."

Brenna pondered her nurse's strange prediction as she rose to
build the fire for tea. Stirring the banked coals, she thought back to
the day Faol had singled out the stranger to protect, even at the risk
of the wolf's life. Suddenly she caught her breath, glancing sharply at
the sleeping figure lying on the nearby pallet.

Faith, had Ealga meant Faol would bring her a *man* instead of
another pup?

Nay! She dismissed the idea, focusing on adding kindling to the
glowing red coals. What wishful thinking that was. The kind that
could only lead to disappointment.

Perhaps a soak in the hot spring would wash away such nonsense from her addled brain. That's exactly what she needed. And
she would see to it as soon as Faol returned from his wandering to
keep an eye on the patient. The wolf would raise an alarm if Adam
should gain consciousness or move about so as to hurt himself. In the
meantime, the man needed to be fed.

Ronan O'Bryne swam through a fog-like world of imaginings as
thick as a bog mist. Some were horrifying, and others made him wish

he could remain there forever. He'd seen angels and demons, felt unbearable heat and brittle cold. Voices damned him to the depths of Hades on the one side and pulled him back on the other with heavenly song. There'd been pain; then he flew above it. Whatever came at him, he surrendered to it. He was tired of fighting. Ronan craved peace, yet it was the one thing that would not come.

His eyelids felt laden with lead rather than flesh as he forced them open. Above him a stone ceiling swirled slowly, blurring bunches of herbs and baskets strung on a rope across part of it. Their earthy scent mingled with the must of damp stone. It was not unpleasant. Just strange. Was he in a cave or a tomb? The dancing shadows of the herbs drew his attention across the ceiling and down to where a fire blazed in a cutout of rock to one side of the enclosure. The wall above it was blackened with soot from the rising smoke. A small pot hung from an iron trammel over the fire bed, but it was the large beast lying next to the blaze that arrested his breath.

The white wolf! So it *had* been real. Somewhere in his memory he recalled a giant of a wolf lying beside him. But as to the circumstances, he was at a loss.

As if sensing Ronan's consciousness, the animal raised its head and looked at him with shining eyes alight from the fire's glow. Unable to hold it longer, Ronan allowed his breath to escape slowly and closed his eyes again. He tried to make sense of what he'd seen, or thought he'd seen. So if the wolf was real, was the dark-haired angel with the heavenly voice also?

God's mercy, she'd drawn him to her from alternating bouts of utter blackness and relentless fires, battling for him with prayers and words of Scripture. There'd been something about her so familiar and inviting that he'd wanted to reach for her, touch her, cling to the promise of words he'd rejected in the past.

A white wolf. A raven-haired beauty. Hadn't Joanna of Gowrys been such a woman? Fragments of his memory circled in his brain until they finally connected. Joanna's image was indelibly etched in Ronan's mind. He searched through the fog until his angel materialized. The same dark hair and ivory skin. Such compassion when she looked at him.

A shiver razed his spine. Could the rumors of the Gowrys changeling be true? Was he in her lair?

Ronan cracked open one eye enough to see that the white wolf had lowered its head again. He didn't believe in such superstitious nonsense. Nonetheless, images began to drift into his consciousness like floating leaves in a fall breeze. One moment she sang to him like a sweet siren bent on drawing him from the pits of Hades. The next, there was the wolf licking his face, as though tasting a prospective meal.

Whatever the nature of his caregiver, he was in no position to do anything about it. Sorting delirium from reality would have to wait.

Just as Ronan began to drift away into oblivion, he sensed, rather than saw, the animal stir. With great effort he peeked in time to see the angel from his fevered recollections enter the cell. Her dark hair was wet and spread like a tangled shroud over her shoulders and the coarse, shapeless shift she wore.

"So it's not boiled, has it?" she said to the wolf as she rubbed both its ears with her hands. The affection reduced the huge animal to a tail-wagging pup that rolled over and exposed its belly for further attention. "And how is our patient?"

Ronan closed his eyes as she turned to look at him. Relief spread through him. He had not lost his mind. The woman and wolf were not one and the same.

"He didn't take much broth this morning. Once my hair is dry, I'll try to get him to eat again."

But she *was* real, Ronan realized with a pang of alarm. He cracked his gaze at her again. She was the very image of the woman he'd seen drive a dagger into her breast and curse his father forever. She could be none other than the long-lost daughter of Gowrys.

Humming to herself, the young woman sat down on a stool by the hearth and began to work a comb through her wet tresses, oblivious to his scrutiny. The motion twisted the loose shift about feminine curves that left no doubt that she was of age—and ripe enough to take a man's breath away had his aching chest not been so stingy with it. That Ronan well recognized her voice as his angel's conflicted with what he knew to be true. He was at the mercy of his sworn enemy.

A defensive rush shot through him. He tried lifting his head, but for all his effort, it might have been the cornerstone of Glenarden's hall. Truly God, if there was one, had a wicked sense of humor....

Ronan must have drifted off, for when he next was aware, the scent of food taunted his eyelids open. At a crude table near the hearth, the woman grimaced over a bowl in which she crushed something with a stone pestle. Her hair, now confined in a long black braid, swung as she worked.

"I'm hoping I can get some of this boiled venison into you, Adam. That is, if I can crush it fine enough," she said.

Ronan moved his eyes only, glancing about the stone cell. But the wolf was not there. So who was Adam?

"You must get stronger, or you'll never heal." She stopped and perused a shelf lined with jars and vials. "The drawing herbs and fever brews have done well by you, but it's time we strengthen the blood and muscles, lest they wane away." Her voice faded to a murmur as she read off the names of the medicines capped with linen and wax. "And we can't have that fine body waste away, now, can we?" she said, peeling back the cloth cap of one jar and measuring a bit of its content. She sprinkled it into the bowl and began grinding again.

What did she know of his body? Ronan moved a hand beneath the coverlets and found his answer. He was stripped naked as a newborn. Worse, he was too weary to care.

"I think you'll like this, Adam," she said, moving to the hearth, where she dipped out a steaming liquid into the bowl of crushed meat and herbs. "'Tis more palatable than the fever brews."

Ronan closed his eyes as she turned to look at him. Had he told her his name was Adam, or did she call him so for obvious reasons? Had he told her anything? Heaven help him, he couldn't remember.

Her slipper-clad feet were ever so light on the rug-covered stone floor as she approached. The fire at her back silhouetted long slender legs, shapely as they moved within—

"Oh!"

Ronan started with her exclamation of surprise.

"You're awake! Praise Father God, my prayers are answered."

Too late to feign sleep, Ronan held his tongue as she dropped to her knees and, brushing back the hair from his forehead, planted a kiss there. The firelight danced in the bluest eyes he'd ever seen, but a frown creased her brow.

"You still have some fever, but this is a wondrous improvement."

Ah, it wasn't affection. Not that he expected any. Ronan licked his dry, cracked lips. Try as he might, he had trouble mustering his voice.

"At last, you can tell me your name," she prompted.

His name. She didn't know it.

"Adam?" he ventured hoarsely.

Her laugh sounded as pure as the silver bell of a priest. "Nay, sir, that's the name I gave you, what with your being the first man I'd e'er seen in mother nature's all … and I'd wager Adam was no finer specimen." A second later her eyes widened, crimson splashing over her face. "Not that I noticed all that much. I only ministered as I was trained, of course."

Sassy, yet modest. An appealing contradiction.

"I … appreciate your candor, milady. And your ministrations." Were he not in such a wretched state, he might seize upon her embarrassment and ripen her cheeks even more.

"I pray your forgiveness, sir. I tend to say what I think." She twisted her loose shift in her fingers. "I fear my social skills are sorely lacking."

"I find them refreshing."

A smile quivered on her lips, as though she were loath to accept him at his word.

"Perhaps you can tell me how I came to be in your care and where—" He gestured at his surroundings. A terrible burning pain streaked through his right shoulder from both the back and the front, clashing and threatening to explode from within. Ronan ground his teeth to keep from crying out. "By my father's breath," he hissed, "what happened to me?"

The fog was gone completely now, banished by the blinding white agony.

"Lie still. You've angered your wounds with that sudden movement."

His caregiver's heart-shaped face mirrored concern and her lips—

He focused on them like a lifeline.

"You were ambushed by a bowman. I took one arrow from your back and the other went clean through your shoulder."

Ambush? Who—

Ronan blinked, fighting the lightheadedness that felt as though it would lift him off the pallet. The sweet scent of lavender accompanied the sharp breaths he inhaled as the woman leaned over him, cradling his head to her shoulder.

"There now, *cariad*."

Dearest. She called him *dearest*. Now he *really* wanted to remember.

"Be still, and it will pass. Breathe deeply and exhale just as hard. Come now. With me."

Ronan could feel her cheek against his ear, smooth and warm. Her fingers twined in his hair as she coached him to inhale and exhale fully. He couldn't discern if it was the distraction of the breathing or the sweetness of her presence that calmed the throbbing, but subside it did. It was intoxicating. *She* was intoxicating. She almost made him forget, drew him to another plane more comfortable and peaceful. A safe place. Perhaps she *was* a witch.

"Brenna will take care of you, but you must be still until the wound closes."

Nay, an enchantress called Brenna.

Ambushed. The word snagged his scattered attention once more. Ronan wanted to know more about that as well, but not now. For the moment, he was … at peace.

Chapter Six

The news of Ronan's death traveled quickly. A month to the day later, Gwenhyfar and her court were coming to pay respects to her late cousin Aeda's family. Glenarden was often a convenient stop along the queen's wintry journey from Camelot at Carmelide on the Solway to Arthur's eastern court at Strighlagh. But this time no effort was being spared, especially by Caden's wife.

Every tapestry in Glenarden's hall had been beaten and rehung. Extra pits were fired and freshly hunted game and river fish roasted over them. In the kitchen, the cooks had worked all night baking fresh breads and painting the flatbreads with food dyes. While Glenarden was wealthy by most standards, few royals had sufficient metal or wooden plates to serve more than the lord, his lady, and perhaps a special guest or two. The floral designs on the flatbreads were above and beyond, an effort surely to be noticed by their royal visitors.

Indeed, Rhianon's efforts were everywhere, assailing the senses. Despite fresh spring blossoms being weeks yet away, dried heather and fragrant herbs mixed with new rushes on the floors refreshed the winter stale of the keep.

Caden was prouder of the weapons and war trophies that hung along the sidewalls and from the rafters, marking the military prowess of the O'Byrne clan. And now that the Gowrys had paid for their trespass against his brother, more trophies would adorn the outer stockade. When the royal party approached, there would be no doubt in anyone's mind that Glenarden was a proper warlord's hall.

Would that Arthur himself were coming, Caden mused, stepping outside. Beyond the cluster of round huts topped with cones of thatch rose the stone and timber walls that protected the inner keep. Banners freshly made or repaired by the women during the long dark season flapped red, black, and silver in the brisk March wind. Along the timber ramparts his men hung the Gowrys' shields on the walls of the gatehouses as he'd instructed.

Sorely outnumbered, the Gowrys men had abandoned the fight and fled into the forest to hide with their families. A smile twitched on Caden's mouth at the thought of his enemies watching with their frightened women and children as the warriors of Glenarden razed their camp, burned the meager shelters constructed around it, and herded off such cattle as were to be found nearby.

'Twas penance long overdue. It had taken two weeks for the pass to clear enough for Caden to lead a search party for his late brother's remains. Likely due to wolves, there'd been nothing left to find except a common rusted sword and the broken shafts of two arrows, their red and green fletching and paint faded by their melting cover. But not so faint that the evidence didn't point straight to Ronan's murderers.

Caden made his way around the stone base of the keep to the rear of the compound, where the smithy's shed, the granaries, and stables lay. All was now his—including Ronan's fine dappled gelding. Here and there children darted about, laughing, challenging each other. Dogs barked and chased after them, scattering chickens about the muddy yard in a squawking frenzy. Above the din came the occasional shrill reprimand from an irate mother.

Meeting gazes with his servants, Caden returned the nods with one of his own, accepting his due as lord. That's what he was, except by ceremony. Tarlach had withdrawn to his quarters since Ronan had gone missing. Rarely did the old man come to the hall, even for meals. On the one hand, Caden preferred the freedom at his disposal. But there was a part of him that wanted his father to acknowledge him as the able and rightful heir to Glenarden. It gnawed at Caden like a dog on a tasty bone that such an admission would never happen. Tarlach blamed him for Ronan's loss.

"You should have never left your brother alone." The spiteful words haunted Caden like a demon spirit.

He mentally shook them off and sought out Ballach, as had been his custom every day since Ronan disappeared. Caden personally tended the steed in order to win his trust.

"Ho, there, Ballach," he said, dipping his hand deeply into the grain barrel before approaching the horse, so named for his speckled gray coat. Ballach shivered in spite of Caden's gentle murmur and warily nuzzled his outstretched hand.

"There's more where that came fr—"

Shouts sounded from the gate towers. The horse jerked away.

"Easy, laddie," Caden cajoled. "It sounds like our royal cousin and her court have come to pay their respects to your late master … and to honor your new."

Master of Glenarden by birth to his noble Pictish mother as well as by his Dalraidan father, Caden was in no hurry to meet the approaching royal retinue. Wasn't he as good as the Dux Bellorum, who'd been landless royalty until Aedan left to rule Dalraida and Arthur acquired Gwenhyfar's lands by marriage? Granted, Glenarden was just a part of Arthur's Gododdin, but its wealth was enough for Caden, especially since he and Rhianon were both second born. Such as they were left to make do in life without the sanction of God and, in Caden's case, without even the aid of the man who sired him. He'd been trained as a warrior alone, not a warrior king as Ronan had. Simply put, Caden had been expendable … until now.

Caden struck a lordly gait toward the main entrance where a herald clad in Camelot's blue with gold embroidery awaited his permission for the royal party to make its entrance. Arthur had adopted the blue of the Virgin as the color of his court since his trip to the Holy Land. Some said he'd had the image of her painted on his battleshield, although the banner of the Red Dragon still led his troops into battle.

"Prince of Glenarden, I salute you in the name of High Queen of the Celtic Kingdoms, Her Majesty Gwenhyfar," a herald announced upon entering the open gates.

The High Queen of the Celtic Kingdoms by marriage to Arthur, Dux Bellorum, waited for him.

Caden's chest swelled at the thought. "Glenarden welcomes Her Majesty and Court," he said magnanimously. He opened his arms to encompass all he owned … and ruled.

The flicker of torches around the perimeter of the great hall gave the embroidered figures and beasts on the tapesty by the Glenarden's table a life of their own. Even Tarlach came out of his self-enforced seclusion, dressed in the red, black, and gray plaid. For an instant, Caden thought the old man was returning to himself, for, though a crippled picture of former gallantry, Tarlach insisted that the queen take his leather chair at the center of the oak plank table.

But Queen Gwenhyfar would not hear of it. She graciously took one of the cushioned bench seats between Tarlach and Caden, endearing all who watched to her. With luminous green eyes, ever so slightly slanted, she studied the old lord.

Or was it the fine charcoal lining that gave them their exotic tilt? Caden wondered. Tales of the old ones suggested the Picts had come from the East in the long, long ago. Regardless, the woman's reputation for beauty could not be exaggerated. She grew lovelier each time he saw her. Merlin Emrys, the uncle of Arthur's father, Aedan, had done well by Arthur in choosing this Gwenhyfar. In a small way, it had redeemed Aedan, Arthur's father, for abandoning Manau to rule Dalraida.

"Do you think she is pleased?" Rhianon whispered. The opposite in coloring from the queen, his wife was a sun maid, golden and resplendent in her best wine-hued gown … and with a fire to match beneath the coverlets.

"How can she not be, my love? You and Vychan have outdone yourselves."

Rhianon and Vychan, Glenarden's steward, had put aside their silent battle for control of the keep and worked with flawless cohesion. Throughout the sumptuous feast, they continued to communicate with meaningful gazes or nods. The servants performed their assigned tasks like warriors drilled in hospitality.

And now that the meal was finished, etiquette allowed for the business of the kingdom to be discussed rather than family matters and idle talk. The business of *his* kingdom.

"Your father tires," the queen observed quietly. Although she spoke the same language, Gwenhyfar possessed the same Pictish accent as Caden's late mother. It put many of her British-born subjects off, even though she was fluent in the language of the Scot and Cymri peoples.

Caden gave Tarlach an embarrassed glance. The old man had nodded off in the midst of his meal, his head tilted ever to the left. "He sleeps more and more since Ronan's death ... as though he's eager to join my lost brother."

"So this recent raid upon the Gowrys was under your leadership alone?"

At last. Caden nodded, eager for his due recognition. "The shields hung on our outer walls were taken or left behind by the Gowrys men."

"Arthur does not question Glenarden's warrior might," the queen demured. "You and your men have proven yourselves many times over. Part of the reason for this visit, beyond the loss of your brother, is to seek Glenarden warriors for his next campaign."

"I'd like to lead them, your lordship willing," Egan O'Toole offered. The champion cast an anxious look at Caden.

"Aye." Caden turned back to his royal guest. "It goes without saying that Arthur will have what he asks of Glenarden." But wariness crept along Caden's spine.

Over the meal, the queen—as his late mother's concerned younger cousin—had lamented Ronan's loss and listened to Tarlach's ceaseless praise of his lost son. Now the commiserating gentlewoman had vanished. In her place was the warrior queen, who led her troops into battle.

"Do I detect displeasure in Your Majesty?" Caden asked. "For I can assure you, we do not make war without good cause."

Gwenhyfar's gaze was as hard as the green gem from the East adorning one of her rings. "My lord Arthur simply wishes that such conflicts be brought to us for just resolution. While our kings and chieftains war among themselves, killing each other off, the Saxons and the Miathi wait with bated breath, poised to attack when we've weakened or distracted each other."

Rhianon bristled at Caden's side. "My lord had absolute proof that our enemy took Ronan's life!"

"Then *I* would see it." The demand came not from the queen, but from one of her retinue seated around the central fire on benches. A bent, hooded man in an earthy brown cloak rose from a seat far away from the table of honor to a height nearly a full head taller than most. For all Caden knew, he was no more than a lowly manservant. Unnoticeable—until now.

Gwenhyfar laughed. "Merlin Emrys, you are ever a surprise to us. Did Arthur not think me capable of speaking on his behalf?"

Merlin Emrys here in Glenarden? Caden's astonishment echoed throughout the hall, even among the queen's retinue.

"Do come forward, friend," Gwenhyfar encouraged.

The merlin took his time in his approach, leaning heavily on a staff, the top of which had been carved out to house a crystal set in a silver cross. Light from the nearest torch struck the crystal stone embedded in the cross and cast beams in a hundred directions, drawing gasps of wonder from many of the onlookers. Caden hadn't seen it until now, but then Merlin Emrys hadn't intended to be seen beforehand. He was known as a master of disguise. Some claimed he actually shifted shape. Such was the difference between the minds of the educated noble class and the common folk, many of whom still held to their pagan gods and superstitions.

Rhianon was no exception. Though educated according to her rank, his bride still kept her favorite goddesses under her pillow, clinging to both the old ways and the new as many were wont to do. Caden himself held to nothing greater than himself and his ability with a sword.

Merlin tossed back his hood, revealing white hair flowing from the shaved ear-to-ear line of the druidic tonsure so typical of the Celtic Church. Head bowed slightly to the queen, he spoke in a surprisingly strong voice. "Milady, you were taught by one of my most illustrious colleagues on the Holy Isle. You are most capable of representing Arthur's position."

Caden wondered if the sage was as old as he looked. Though he was still tall by most standards, his shoulders were the rounded ones of a scholar from time spent over faded manuscripts, charts, and his curious experiments with the elements of nature. Yet he had clear, piercing blue eyes enfolded beneath a high weathered brow. They shifted from Gwenhyfar to Caden.

"I would like to see the arrows you found, milord."

"How could you possibly know about them?" Rhianon demanded, astonished.

Caden placed a restraining hand on his lady's thigh beneath the cover of the table. "Clearly someone from Glenarden carried the news to Arthur's court, milady."

The shock over being put before the judgment of the royal court in his own hall began to thaw in Caden's veins and was replaced with a growing simmer of indignation. Here, *he* was lord—not Arthur, nor his queen, and certainly not the seer some considered a prophet after the Old Testament order.

"Though I am vexed," Caden continued, "as to why such a trivial matter in the scheme of Arthur's concerns should merit a spy among us, who have long been among his staunchest supporters."

"I have my ways of discerning things," Merlin told him, nonplussed. "Though I remind you that the loss of any life is no trivial matter, milord."

And through it all, Tarlach slept! If this were not sign enough of the old man's incompetence, nothing would sway those still lamenting the loss of Ronan.

"Your *ways* of discernment, are they the same ways you of the church seek to forbid others?" It was no question Rhianon hurled at the man, but an accusation.

"Milady ..." Iron rang in Merlin's voice. "Neither I nor my brethren seek such restriction. The pursuit of knowledge in truth is an admirable quest. Our Creator is so great that at our best effort, we shall never know all there is to know of His creation."

Rather than Merlin's supposed supernatural abililty to see things, Caden thought it likely that a priest had brought the matter between Glenarden and Gowrys to the attention of Merlin Emrys. Caden searched the smoke-filled hall to see if the priestly recluse from the glen dared to show himself.

"That is not what I've heard from my family in Gwynedd," Rhianon persisted. "Riderch's was a most cruel attack, kin against kin, *simply because Myrddin and Gwendoleu clung to the old ways.*"

A collective breath held, for Christian and pagan alike awaited Merlin's reply.

"Milady, perhaps it is *your* sources that should be questioned and not mine," Merlin chided gently. "Yes, Riderch's attack on Gwendoleu's kingdom was unjust, but it was his greed to rule over more land *masked* as a religious intolerance. It only appeared the battle was over a nest of larks … of Riderch's Roman Church leanings against the bards of old druidic practice like King Gwendoleu's Merlin Sylvester."

That the Roman Church frowned upon the secular arts and knowledge pursued and taught along with the Word by its sister church in Albion was no secret. But thus far, the religious tolerance and practices of the bishops of Britain remained untouched by Rome's influence, for its ways were as old, if not older, than its Roman counterpart. Many of the Hebrew festivals and customs of the first century missionaries were held in both the western and eastern Camelot.

Merlin schooled his voice to that of a patient teacher with a child. "I think we *all* know that Arthur has the support of both Christian and non-Christian kings in his battles against the northern Picts and Saxons. But do you *also* know that the king who controls Carmelide in Gwynedd controls not only a rich commercial center but access to the whole belly of Albion? Greed, not church conflict, is why the clash at Arderydd happened. Christ Himself would have spat upon Riderch of Alcut's true motivation."

"But—" Rhianon bit off her objection as Caden tightened his fingers on her leg to silence her. Instead, she puffed at his side like an angry hen fit to burst.

Merlin raised his strong, clear voice for the benefit of the entire audience. "We must not throw Christ out with Riderch's filthy holy water, my children. Remember, the Dux Bellorum, and his father, the former Duke of War, are *both* descended from five centuries of our island's Pendragons. As such, they razed Riderch's dun at Alcut and established neutral rule in the late Gwendoleu's kingdom to protect these freedoms of faith and pursuit of knowledge for both Christian and pagan alike. The banner of the Pendragon has flown over Carmelide ever since."

And greed never would have crossed Arthur's mind, Caden thought wryly to himself. Landless before his marriage, Arthur now had dominion over Strighlagh, Manau Goddodin, and Carmelide, one of Albion's choicest commercial centers. Instead of calling Arthur "The Bear of Britain," Caden would call him "The Fox of Albion."

"My husband tries hard not to dictate his faith to the kings and princes pledged to him," Gwenhyfar spoke up. "For Christ Himself was no dictator. Though He showed us the only way to the Father, He gave us all the freedom to choose to follow that way. His is a rule of love."

"Not Arthur's," someone quipped from among those gathered near the back of the hall. Nervous laughter rippled in its wake.

"Who dares address the Queen of the Celtic Nations thus?" Caden exploded … though his mind was in the same moat as the offender's.

Gwenhyfar waved her hand in dismissal. "I take no offense. We need a touch of humor to lighten so dark and heavy a subject. And how could I argue when it is true?"

"Well said, milady," Merlin agreed.

"Our Duke of War, our Pendragon, must be a strong leader," the queen told the assembly. "But I know it gives Arthur no pleasure to make war upon his own kindred … to walk among the dead and dying who might have stood shoulder to shoulder with him to stop the Saxon storm that will snuff out all that is dear to the sons of Albion like a candle in the wind."

"According to the law of God, Riderch, the king of Alcut, might be forgiven," Merlin said, raising his staff to command undivided attention. "But to ensure the unity of this island, he still had to receive earthly justice. And that"—the master of oratory swept his staff in a circle around him—"is why this feuding among the clans and tribes must stop and stop *now*." He slammed the wooden staff onto the floor.

Caden bit his tongue, but his thoughts ran rampant. He had been part of Arthur's troops when the attack on Gwendoleu had taken place and saw no difference between it and the justice Caden recently delivered to the Gowrys. Merlin Emrys spoke out of both sides of his mouth, with one standard for his Arthur and yet another for Glenarden.

It was all right to exact revenge, evidently, if one forgave the enemy before annihilating him. So the O'Byrnes erred only in the spiritual realm, for they would never forgive the Gowrys for Ronan's death. Where was this freedom of choice to forgive or not to forgive, which Merlin claimed so boldly to defend?

"Now if I may," Emrys said, not bothering to face Caden with his request, "I would like to see the arrows you've determined to be irrefutable evidence."

Caden burned to fling his question at the prophet. Instead he turned to his steward. "Vychan, send the captain of the guard for the shield next to the gatehouse. The arrows are lashed to it … against the blood of its owner," Caden added in defiance. "It was a fit end for the cur."

Merlin whirled, his robes wrapping about his lean form, and nailed Caden with an ice-hard gaze. "The clan Gowrys is calling for a hostage and tribute from Glenarden, *milord,* both for an unrighteous attack. An attack in which a Gowrys prince was slain."

Caden clenched his fists on the edge of the table. "By my father's breath, they'll have none of it! We were within our rights."

"Perhaps if you'd gone through Camelot's justice, milord, instead of taking it into your own hands, it would not have come to this," Gwenhyfar counseled him, as calm as Caden was outraged. "But as it is, there is no witness to your brother's death."

"Or that Ronan is even dead," Merlin added, watching Caden closely.

Surely Emrys did not suspect him of—

The fury pounding in Caden's veins stumbled. Had the prophet seen something? Something Caden and his men had missed?

"Well, Ronan certainly didn't ride off with the fairies, now, did he?" Rhianon exclaimed. "Oh!" Like a child who'd said more than she should, she belatedly covered her mouth and braced against Caden for her share of the merlin's cold reprimand.

But not even the powerful Merlin Emrys was immune to such beauty and charm. "That at least, milady, we can agree upon."

A welcome titter of laughter swept through the room.

"Merlin, do join us at the table," Gwenhyfar spoke up, graciously salvaging the hospitality that had fallen by the wayside in the course of the prophet's appearance.

Caden would never forgive himself if Glenarden's name was besmirched for inattention to the law of hospitality. He bolted to his feet. "Forgive us, Queen Gwenhyfar ... Merlin."

Caden's gaze came to rest upon his father. To remove someone from the table was an affront, and it was filled to capacity with the favorites of both the queen and Glenarden. But Caden had to find a place for Merlin to join them. "P-perhaps we should help Father to bed before further discussion."

"Nay," Merlin objected. "Leave Tarlach be. I am content to remain with my companions there." He motioned to the place he'd abandoned further down the ranks of the hall guests. Although now that his identity was revealed, some were squirming uncomfortably at the thought of sitting next to a man of such power.

At the mention of his name, Tarlach stirred with a start. "Wh-what?" The old chieftain blinked at the prophet standing boldly in front of him. Instantly recognition disbursed the initial confusion in his eyes. He thumped the table with his good fist. "By all that's holy, Merlin Emrys!"

Genuine pleasure lit Merlin's face. "Tarlach, old friend. It has been a few years."

Tarlach cut his gaze to Caden. "Well, get up, laddie. Where are your manners? Give Merlin your seat."

The blood rush scorching Caden's face grew hotter still. Tarlach's seat was Caden's right as the real lord of Glenarden, but to suggest Caden leave the table altogether—

"Well go on, laddie. Are you deaf?"

The injustice rendered Caden speechless and still.

He felt Rhianon's gentle hand on his arm. "Take *my* seat, dearest." His wife rose and brushed her skirts free of imaginary bread crumbs, suddenly self-conscious as the focus of both the queen's and Merlin's gazes. "In truth, my head pains me with this change in the weather," she said. "So, if it please Her Majesty and Merlin, I—"

"By all means, Lady Rhianon." Gwenhyfar gave Rhianon a grateful look for her resourceful alternative to the dilemma. Or perhaps the queen was as relieved as Caden to have Rhianon's impulsive tongue removed from the tension that had seized the room.

The only challenge remaining for Caden now was to hold counsel over his own tongue … and hope Tarlach might not embarrass them all.

CHAPTER SEVEN

Past and present, reality and dream ... the ability to separate them plagued Ronan each time he struggled to open his eyes. Nonetheless, this time his senses alerted him to being manhandled. The gritty glue of sleep holding his eyelids fast finally gave way. There, above him, was the raven-haired nymph of his dreams, gently lifting his head into her lap. Her lochan blue eyes grew larger upon meeting his gaze.

"At last, you're awake!" She hugged his head in her delight, then planted a chaste kiss on his forehead. "And free of the fever, I might add."

She was very real. Warm and utterly captivating. Yet ... dangerous. Vague recollections of consciousness drifted to the forefront of his thoughts until they took form. Now he remembered. She was the long-lost seed of Gowrys, the daughter Tarlach feared would destroy Glenarden. Her name eluded him. Had he heard it?

Ronan tried to speak but found his tongue uncooperative. Anticipating his need, she tipped his head forward and eased a cup to his lips. Water.

"I fear I do not know your name," he managed at last. "Or how I came to be here."

"I am Brenna, and I'll tell you the rest when you tell me your name."

"Brenna of ...?" he prompted. Though she'd be a fool to admit her true identity.

"Of these hallowed hills," she answered simply. "Though some call me the wolf-woman. Have you heard such stories, sir?"

Her candor shocked Ronan. "Heard, but not believed."

She offered him more water. "And now it's your turn to tell me your name."

Another memory bobbed to the surface. "Adam?"

She blushed. "Nay, that is the name I gave you." She rustled the sheet covering him. "For reasons I need not explain."

Now he remembered. *Saucy, this one.*

"I'd have your real name, now that you've come to your senses."

"R-Rory." Better to use a name that began the same as his own. He only hoped he could remember it. Her charms had a way of scrambling his senses.

"Rory."

He liked the way she savored his name.

"It suits you, for you've a reddish cast to your hair and your clothing suggests kingly fortune. Are you from this province, Rory?"

Ronan chose his words carefully, for this Brenna was no fool. "A traveler through it many times, but born to the road, as my father before me."

"A soldier for hire or seeking tourney? You were well outfitted, at least with steed, clothing, and weapon," she explained hastily. "I'd say you were successful enough."

"Not hardly, or I'd not be here, feeling as though I'd been drained of all but my last breath." Ronan winced as he shifted his weight onto his good shoulder.

The pain swept even more of the cobwebs from his memory. Ambush, she'd said.

Now he remembered … at least parts of it. The impact of the arrow in his back. Another from the fore.

"Would that I'd worn my mail shirt, save I was out for a day's frolic, not combat." In his mind's eyes, he saw a faceless man on horseback, intent on running him down.

"So you remember now?"

"Bits here and there." He stared at the ceiling of the cave. "Though what was real and what was not, I'm sorely put to tell."

"Why then did you ride with O'Byrnes on such a *celebration?*"

The way Brenna said the word told Ronan he walked a delicate line between life and death, for he was in no condition to defend himself, even if his adversary was a woman.

"I was on my way to join Arthur in Strighlagh and accepted the hospitality of Glenarden." Ronan feigned astonishment. "Don't tell me that *you* are the wolf-woman the O'Byrnes sought?"

She drew back. "Now, do I look like a wolf, Sir Rory of the Road, or does he?" She pointed at the hearth where a monstrous-sized white wolf lay, watching Ronan with eyes like burning coals. "Though people do confuse us," she added with a not-so-grievous sigh. "And they have no delirium to blame for the mistake."

So she admitted to being the wolf-woman? Ronan couldn't take his eyes off her. She had the precociousness of a wood nymph and a voice sweet enough to shame an angel's.

"I meant no insult to you by my implication, milady, but to the fools who seek you." Though, Heaven help him, the woman and the wolf had seemed one and the same to his mind, giving him second thought. That is, when he could think at all. Ronan wondered just what he had told her in his delirium. "I pray I said nothing more in the fever that you found troubling."

From the shadow that fell over her face, Ronan had his answer.

"You've led a troubled life since childhood, Rory of the Road," she said. "Your childhood nightmares still haunt you."

Shame ran Ronan through. She knew him. But at the touch of her fingers on his cheek, turning his face to hers, he was amazed to see not anger or accusation, but tenderness and compassion swimming in her eyes.

"I saw what you saw as I held you," she told him. "At least in part. Whoever made you, no more than a child, take part in the Gowrys massacre was cruel and heartless."

She had *seen* what he saw? An involuntary shiver tripped along Ronan's spine. Still, she didn't seem to know who he was. Only that he'd been present at Tarlach's cowardly massacre. He fought to think above the emotions tangling his mind.

"My mother died when I was young. I had no choice but to follow my father on the road."

"So it was *he* who fought with the Glenarden." A single tear escaped her wet gaze. "Know this, Rory. The bloodshed was not your fault. I felt your horror at it all. I know you wanted to run away from it. I know you are still running from it."

Night upon night, but how—

"You must give those nightmares to God, or you will not heal.

At least, not here." She placed the palm of her hand over his heart. "God is waiting to forgive you, waiting for you to ask."

But could *she?*

She nodded, making him aware that he'd voiced his question. "Of course I forgive you. You did not want to be there. I even forgive the man who led the attack, for surely Tarlach O'Byrne was not the same man who'd been my father's best friend. Ealga—my nurse— said Tarlach was driven to madness by demons of lust and greed."

Demons still tormented Tarlach's crippled body. Demons of guilt.

"I pray for my enemy daily as Christ encouraged His followers to do. I pray for peace between the clans, that I might live a normal life outside this cave. And I have prayed over you even more, that God"—her voice broke—"that God would take away your childhood terror and shame."

That these tears could be for him strained Ronan's credulity beyond its limit. Say what she would with Tarlach beyond her reach, if she knew he was Tarlach's son ....

"No matter what Scripture says of forgiveness, milady, this forgiveness of yours of the men who murdered your kin and still force you to hide like a hunted animal ... it ... it isn't natural."

She sniffed, then wiped her eyes with her skirt. "Nay, Rory, it is not. Only by God's grace is it possible." She rocked back on her knees and sang, *"Look upward for manna, not backward for salt, or you'll become bitter, and all your own fault."* A melancholy sigh overtook her. "Ealga taught me that rhyme to live by. *'Don't be a Lot's wife,'* she'd say whenever I lamented leaving Glaston for this isolation."

"If what you say is true, then you are closer to God than I, Brenna of the Hallowed Hills." *And far more forgiving of Him.*

"Well," she said, fluffing up the pillow beneath his head, "then we shall have to work on that." She pushed herself up to her feet, mischief dancing where tears had been moments earlier. "You might start by asking forgiveness for the curses you've hurled at all manner of man and beast during your fever."

Ronan followed the graceful sway of Brenna's hips as she fetched a bowl from the table near the hearth. That was it? Her only concern was for *his* pain? For his soul? This was harder to accept than a woman who shape-changed into a wolf.

"I hope I never cursed you, lassie."

"Not once." Brenna picked up a round of flat bread from the table and tore off a piece, which she tossed to the wolf. It caught it with a snap of sharp teeth and swallowed it in one hungry gulp. "Although you've sworn heartily at Faol, the very one who saved ye."

She broke up more of the loaf into the bowl and filled it with hot broth from a pot over the fire.

Faol. Ronan translated the old tongue, not exactly surprised. "Wolf? So Faol is your *other* form?"

"Aye, to be sure he is, and I in two forms at once. Have you *ever* seen such magic?" Brenna snickered outright, making Ronan feel the bigger fool.

"Herth's fire, woman, the fever may have addled my brain, but I seem to recall awakening to the lapping tongue of a cold and wet-nosed hairy creature resembling a wolf."

She laughed, goading him all the more. "Well, it wasn't me."

As if floating down to the rug by the pallet, Brenna sank to her knees and put a cup of steaming broth next to her on the floor. Reaching behind him, she struggled dutifully to raise his head, so that he'd not choke.

Annoyed at the pleasure his confusion had given her, Ronan tried to raise it on his own but found it too heavy. Alarmed at his weakness, he tried moving his fingers and toes. To his relief, they worked, but the effort forced perspiration out all over his body.

"You mustn't strain yourself, Rory, nor become hysterical."

"I'm not hysterical!" Ronan ground out in frustration as she gathered his face to her shoulder in order to build up his pillows. She smelled like the fresh blossoms of a summer garden, yet he knew it to be the dead of winter. At least, he thought he did.

"How—" His beard-roughened cheek touched the flesh of a milk white shoulder, innocently bared during her ministration by her oversized shift. "How long have I been here?"

"Weeks," she grunted in an effort to ease him down without dropping him. "Even I've been hard pressed to keep full track of time. The fever has taken you on both sides of the veil between the here and after. At times I feared you'd not make your way back. I've left your side very little."

She took up the bowl. "Now open your mouth. Mayhaps I shan't have to bathe you after each feeding, now that you're awake enough to eat and regain your strength. You've been a dribbler."

Feeling foolish *and* helpless as a dribbling babe soured Ronan's humor all the more. "My apolog—" His sarcastic reply was arrested as she blew on the contents of the spoon to cool it for him, her lips pursed in such a manner as to do the opposite to his blood. His wounds put him at death's door, yet her simplest gesture injected him with an awareness he'd not known since the callow days of his manhood.

"I've added bread to your meal, now that you're awake, but we'll start with it soaked in broth."

Holding a cloth under his chin, she leaned forward and slipped the spoon between his lips. It was tasty enough in a plain way, not highly seasoned with spices from the Orient like the fare from Glenarden's kitchen.

"'Tis sweetened with honey to cover the taste of the herbs I've used to keep the gangrene at bay and fortify the blood," she informed him, following his wary glance at the dried herbs overhead.

Ronan grunted in response. Her mother had been reputed to be a healer with an uncanny knowledge of nature magic—the healing powers of herbs and plants the hills afforded. Joanna of Gowrys learned nature's secrets from the abbey at Glaston where they'd been taught since the first Christians arrived after the death of Christ. With those same secrets, she'd healed Tarlach's wounds and, according to Aeda, saved his mother and Ronan during a difficult childbirth.

"You said you'd tell me how I came to be here, if I told you my name," he reminded her. "There are pieces missing that I do not recall."

The tale was as incredible as she. Hidden among the rocks above the crannog, Brenna had witnessed the cowardly attack from the unknown assailant. As she spoke, Ronan's buried memories came to the fore with clarity. The white wolf she said she'd raised from a pup streaked once more across Ronan's pain-blurred vision of his would-be murderer approaching, sword raised for a blow that did not come.

"Faol took a strange liking to you, for reasons I cannot fathom. He has watched you as much as I, between his jaunts beyond the cave."

"Friendly fellow, eh?" Ronan couldn't help the edge in his voice, for he allowed not even his favorite hounds to lick him on the face.

"The fact is, he isn't usually. At least not to strangers." Brenna paused in thought, spoon in the bowl. "And I did have to push him away to keep him from licking your wounds."

Aha! His memory had not played him false. "Are you certain he wasn't after the blood?"

Brenna bristled at his skepticism. "He saved your life, sir. He drove the horse thief away and then laid beside you in the blizzard to keep you warm with his body until I could reach you."

His horse! Ronan closed his eyes a moment in frustration. So that's what the man was after. At first, Ronan thought his assailant might be a Gowrys, but his clothing was indistinct and of better quality than the highland clan could afford.

"At risk of his own life, I might add, for when the O'Byrnes regathered at the lake, they'd have surely tried to kill him, had they come upon you in the thicket. But look as they might, the snow made you impossible to see."

So the clan had looked for him. Ronan took a spoonful of the broth-soaked bread. And his attacker was naught but a common thief. Had he been of the rival clan, he'd surely not have attempted his final blow without hurling the name Gowrys in Ronan's face.

As sure as his shoulder ached, Ronan would hunt the thief down when he was recovered. A horse like Ballach was easily traced.

"So how'd you manage to get me here?" he asked when the bowl was nearly emptied. He hadn't realized that he was even hungry.

"Barely, and there's the truth. I had to drag you upon your cloak."

"Such slender and graceful limbs must be stronger than I'd have wagered."

"Strong enough, no more," she replied without pretension. She rose, taking the empty bowl with her. It was a smooth, flowing motion, utterly effortless. "This is the first entire bowl you've taken." She rewarded him with a smile that infected his own lips, as though her pleasure was his as well. "You'll be moving about on your own strength soon, if you continue to take nourishment like this."

Ronan wondered if that were really possible. He'd done nothing but open his mouth and swallow, yet his body was clammy with the effort. He tried to watch Brenna as she made quick work of cleaning up the table where she'd evidently eaten earlier, before he awoke. But moments after she poured some steaming water into a basin, Ronan drifted off into sleep.

Later, when he opened his eyes again, the fire was renewed with extra logs for the night, and the primitive lamp on the table had been blown out. A stirring next to him drew Ronan's attention to where Brenna approached his pallet. On meeting his gaze, she hesitated for an awkward moment before lying on it. Heavy as his eyelids were, Ronan could not close them now, not with this living, breathing woman curling up beside him, her back to him beneath the covers. The rough linen of her shift was all that separated his naked flesh from her own. That, and the small distance between them.

So she *had* slept with him, innocently of course. That had not been a dream. And she had held his head to her shoulder, all the while singing away his fiendish dreams, without any thought but to

soothe his troubled mind. It was her heartbeat that had calmed his—
not that of an imaginary angel, but of a real one. Except that then
he'd been in a netherworld, where reality and imagination blended
without distinction and sleep dominated all.

Now he was very much alert, very much aware that the most
gentle, enigmatic woman he'd ever met shared his bed. Even now the
warmth of her body beckoned him closer. Ronan turned abruptly,
his back to temptation. Herth's fire, he'd not sleep this night.

"Good night, Rory. Sleep well." Her weary sigh stroked his
senses. Absurdly, he wondered how his real name would sound on
such inviting lips. For the first time in his life, Ronan glimpsed an
inkling of the mad obsession his father suffered. The recognition
struck panic in his chest.

Was he bewitched? Reason reared to counter the notion, but
oddly enough, both it and his alarm were smothered by the slumber
he vowed would never come.

Ronan awoke with a start, slapping instinctively at the furred creature
licking his face. As punishment for his hasty movement, his wounds
screamed foul until he saw the pain flashing like lightning across his
eyelids. Swearing himself into complete wakefulness, he tried to ease
the burning throb with his good arm but froze instantly at the sight
of snarling canine teeth bared at him.

From behind him, the maid Brenna's sharp admonishment
backed the animal away. "Faol, shame on you!" With a rustle of covers, she crawled off the end of the pallet, shift askew, and rose to her

feet. "What fickleness is this, that ye'd save the man one day and eat him the next?"

She grabbed the fierce-eyed creature by the ears and shook its head roughly. "Shame on you, pup!" Then her voice lightened to that of a mother's teasing her child. "Been off on a gallivant, have you?" she asked, picking pine needles from his fur.

As if to apologize, the wolf reared up on its hind legs and placed its paws on the girl's shoulders. Ronan wrinkled his nose as it licked her about the face and neck, tail wagging happily. Had Brenna ever been kissed? By a man, that is.

"Dancin' will not earn you forgiveness, you ragged ball o'fur!" Brenna laughed, buckling to her knees under the large animal's weight. "'Tis a thrashing you deserve for growling at poor Rory so."

Not very likely, he observed as maid and wolf rolled on the rug before the hearth with giggles and growls. Until Brenna found Faol's weakness and started rubbing his belly. With a pitiful wail of surrender, the canine fell over on his back, one hind leg jerking in ticklish ecstasy.

"Look at this harmless little pup, Rory."

"If any creature's to put a tongue to my face, better a woman, not a blasted wolf!" Ronan snorted in indignation.

Chuckling, Brenna climbed to her feet and tossed more wood on the fire. "Ye provoked him, didn't ye?"

"What was I to do, waking nose-to-nose with a wild wolf?" Ronan declared. "Aye, I struck him away and, s'help me, am suffering the worse for it without your reproach."

Instead of showing offense, the girl studied him with curiosity. "You are a peculiar sort, Rory of the Road."

"And you're not, Brenna of the Hallowed Hills, who lives in a cave with a …" Ronan's voice trailed off as Faol lifted his head from the rug to stare at him. "Wolf."

"He senses your hostility even now."

Ronan lay back against his pillow and dislodged his good arm. It was as numb from his having slept upon it as his other was anguished. What else was to befall him? He flexed his fingers, glad to see they responded.

"Are you always so ill-tempered, Rory?"

"Only since I was ambushed by a murderous horse thief and awakened near dead in a cave tended by a madwoman and her pet wolf."

Instantly Ronan regretted his outburst, not because the wolf had risen and placed itself between him and the girl, but because of Brenna's stricken expression.

Her eyes narrowed. "'Tis my *madness* that's kept you alive, sir! Few men survive so many days of fever."

"I meant no discourtesy, Lady Brenna."

Her wounded look faded. "Well … at least I'm a mad *lady* now." She rolled the word off her tongue. "*Lady* Brenna. It has a pleasant ring to it."

Frustration riddled Ronan's voice. "My limbs outweigh my strength, I fear, and it's *that* which settles poorly with me, not you … or the wolf."

With every ounce of will Ronan possessed, he reached his hand out, palm upward toward the animal. Not only did he not trust it, but the effort was supreme in its toll upon his body. Unable to keep the limb suspended, he let it lay on the rug by the pallet until the

wolf warily moved closer and sniffed at his fingers. "Apologies to you
as well, Faol."

"It appears they are accepted, sir … by us both," Brenna added,
when the animal began to tentatively lick at his hand.

The last Ronan remembered, Faol settled down an arm's length
from the pallet and placed his furry chin on Ronan's outstretched
palm. Had the wolf decided to devour him, starting there at his
fingers, Ronan still could not have resisted the fatigue claiming him.

Chapter Eight

Under the impatient gaze of Faol, Brenna stripped the skin from a rabbit she'd trapped. The fur, along with others she'd dried during the Long Dark, would help replenish her supplies at the May Fair two months hence.

"Don't worry. The scraps are yours," she told her companion. And the fresh meat and barley would be a welcome change to Rory's diet. By the way he'd begun to screw up his face at the herbal broths that had brought him through the worst of his infirmity, one might think she was trying to poison him, rather than save him.

With a glance toward the pallet where he slept, Brenna set about cutting up the beastie and combined it with water and barley in a pot. For seasoning, she added salt and crushed rosemary, which she took from one of the bags that she'd sewn together over the winter's course. There was a pile of bags, each one fat with ground or powdered herbs that had dried overhead in the heat from the hearth. By May, she should have sufficient enough to take to the May Fair, where, dressed as a laddie, she'd exchange them to replenish her stores.

Mayhaps she'd buy a bolt of cloth at the fair to make herself a new dress, which she needed far more than a cloak. The woolen gunna she now wore over her shift was worn through at the sleeves, the elbows, and the hem, in spite of her many attempts to mend them. What clothing she had was cut down from Mathair Ealga's wardrobe. And when no longer fit for wear, she made the rags into bags for her herbs.

There was but one exception—a dress so dear she'd never once worn it. In anticipation of Tarlach's attack, her mother had packed the dress in a small chest along with some ribbons and a silver comb and had left the keepsakes for her baby daughter in the stone passage of their escape route. Sometimes Brenna shook out her mother's wedding dress, aired it, and carefully replaced it in the chest to await her own wedding day.

Not that she could foresee such an occasion.

Your will, Lord.

If only giving her loneliness to God would take it away. Instead it crept back again and again. She wiped her hands on a towel, sinking into thought. Thought that bade her turn and consider her patient.

To her surprise, Rory was no longer asleep but sitting upright on the pallet watching her intently. Although surely he had no clue what fancy had crossed her mind....

"Good morning, Brenna." He stifled a yawn with the back of his hand. "How long have you been afoot?"

Rory had improved by the day since the fever left. He ate without her aid and saw to nature's call on his own, though the effort wasted his energy quickly. But as he improved, an uneasy awareness of him as a man, rather than a patient, had begun to develop. Perhaps it was the way he watched her. Sometimes that russet-shaded gaze upon her reeled her senses as though she'd been caressed. And robbed her of wit.

"Um ... "

It really wasn't that difficult a question.

"Since before daybreak," she finally managed. Feeling more the fool, she pointed to the pot over the fire. "I trapped a rabbit for supper."

Thanks be for the herb that still protected her from a man's baser nature, for the way he warmed her with his eyes and smiles had her brain spinning widdershins. Yet even with her mind circling counter to the sun, she never forgot to slip the herb into his porridge or tea.

"*Finally*, fresh meat."

Sarcasm, after all her work?

"I have not only the finest healer in the land, but a huntress as well," he added hastily. Within the reddish brown thicket of his beard, a smile appeared.

Brenna's irritation deflated under its spell. "I should change your bandages and give you a bath, lest you become overripe to the nose," she thought aloud.

Instead of answering, Rory tossed back the covers, revealing the linen wrap he'd taken to wearing knotted about his waist for modesty's sake. It confounded Brenna that the sight of him, the thought of ministering to him, made her blush even more than the first time she'd tended him. True, he'd taken over his more intimate hygiene, but when she rubbed in the liniments designed to keep his muscles from withering with disuse, the ridges of sinew beneath her fingers filled her mind with all manner of dangerous fancy.

"You finish your breakfast while I get the water."

"No, not this time."

Brenna froze, the bucket dangling in her hand. "What?"

With a determined expression, her patient took a deep breath and walked to the table. "I think I am capable of walking to that healing spring you've told me about," he said upon reaching it. "You've done more than enough already, milady. I owe you much."

Milady. It sounded like a caress, the way he said it. Filled with gratitude and perhaps something more. It was a brave and charming front he presented, but as he sank onto the crude bench, his knees nearly buckled.

Brenna rushed to ease his descent. "Just because you can rise and walk to the table doesn't mean you can make the trek down to the pool," she chided him. "When you're stronger, I'll help you there, but for now, we'll make do with hand bathing and the oil rubs."

"I think I can walk."

"Down there, perhaps. But you'd be weak as a newborn kitten on the climb back."

Rory muttered something beneath his breath, his gallantry expired with his strength. "I have my pride, woman," he groused, slamming his fist on the table as if that would make her change her mind. "I'm weary of being coddled like a *naked* babe."

Naked. His intonation told Brenna she wasn't the only one growing more ill at ease ... though it was silly on both their parts. She was a healer. "Such modesty is a bit belated, don't you think, sir?" Before he could reply, Brenna put a finger to his lips, sheer mischief infecting her voice. "I promise I'll touch nothing I've not touched before."

"By my ancestors' bones, you're the saucy one."

"Aye, and you're the cantankerous one," she shot back, swinging the bucket as she dashed out of the room.

But her smile faded as his parting words caught up with her. "Enjoy riding the high horse while you may, milady, for your privilege grows shorter lived by the day."

Praise be for the barrenwort.

Rory had returned to the pallet by the time Brenna returned with the warm spring water. If his warning hadn't knocked the sass out of her, carrying the loaded bucket up the sloping tunnel had. Perhaps he'd learned that he was not as strong as he thought himself to be.

"I thought you'd be out for a brisk walk to still the blood by now," she quipped, pouring some of the water into a smaller basin.

Rory grunted in response, eyes remaining closed.

Alarm shot through her. "You didn't hurt yourself, did you?" She rushed to his side. "Did you fall?"

"No, I'm tired. Too tired to listen to all this clucking."

Heaven save her from such a childlike temperament. "Fine then." Brenna spun about to fetch her supplies. "You'll get your bath in silence, but a bath you *will* have."

"Then do it and be done. Not that I could stop you, if I were of a mind, with this confounded shoulder."

Ah, so that was it. His pride was sore. Well, what about hers? She'd spent countless hours, nay days, nursing him, and this was her reward?

"Move over," she said, on returning to his bedside. "You're not only acting like a petulant child, you're taking up the whole bed."

With another grunt, he complied, giving her room to kneel on the pallet rather than the hard stone floor. As she dropped to her knees, he turned his face away, straining the cords of his neck. Brenna hesitated, taking in the rise and fall of her patient's chest beneath the sheet pulled to his chin. The way his beard clung to the clenched box of his jaw. She guessed at the disapproving line surely formed by his lips.

"I'll be as fast—" She remembered her promise of silence.

Rory tensed as she tugged away the sheet to expose the dressing on his chest. It was still moist from the poultices, but no blood had congealed on it. A very good sign. Upon removing the bandages, she saw his flesh had begun to knit with little sign of the inflammation that had driven up his fever just days before. She had truly wondered if he'd survive, but God had answered her prayers. The worst had finally passed.

She probed ever so gently for any ooze of hidden infection. Nothing! Her spirit soared. She was at last her mother's daughter. God had used her for healing as He had Joanna. Just as Ealga said, it was what Brenna was created to do.

If only she could do more of it. Be safe enough to move to the village near the river glen and help others like this, instead of sending her medicines through Brother Martin while hiding in the wild.

But that was impossible. Just as her mother's gift flowed through her veins, Joanna's curse imprisoned her. *Lord, why give me such a gift, if I must keep it hidden?*

Beyond the sudden blur of despair in her eyes, Rory's shoulder came into focus. Brenna let go her longing for the future to grasp the present. The task now was to rebuild the strength he so sorely grieved.

With Your help, Father God.

Gently, Brenna sponged the healing mineral water over the wound, then dabbed it dry. She repeated the same process, cleansing Rory's arms and chest to his waist. When she stopped to pour the liniment on her palm to rub into the muscles surrounding it, Rory glanced down to see the damage that had dragged him to the pits of hell and back, but his expression was veiled. In truth, the wound looked small, considering the great toll it had taken on him.

As Brenna massaged in the herbal oils, his tension grew palpable.

"Relax, Rory. You must let me work the oil into your muscles."

"I *am* relaxed."

"I could crack an egg on your chest."

"If it would restore my strength, then have at it, *woman*."

She mimicked him. "Just turn your back to me, *man* ... and pray your other wounds are healing as nicely."

The exit wound from the frontal arrow was. The other, where the arrow had wedged in his shoulder blade, was not. At least it wasn't as well knit as the others. But after careful examination, Brenna was satisfied there was no infection. That she'd had to cut a larger opening to retrieve the arrow from Rory's back likely accounted for its slower healing. Brenna washed it, oiled carefully around it and its connecting sinew, and applied fresh poultices. Those she secured with strips of cloth.

"And now for the rest of you," she announced, easing him on his back again.

"I'll see to myself, thank you."

This irritability was becoming infectious. "What is this? A warrior with a maid's modesty?"

"Go below this blanket with that cloth, and I'll not bear responsibility for any consequence you find, lassie."

Brenna stiffened. Had the barrenwort failed? Is that what he wanted to hide?

"'Twas not my most favorite of chores anyway, Rory of the Road. I'll leave the washcloth and towels here for you to tend to yourself then, though I venture to say, there's naught for a maid such as myself to fear."

Rory's dark gaze sharpened. "How can you be so certain, Brenna of the hills?"

Glory be, what now? Brenna folded a towel to purchase time, but hot blood stampeded to her face. "If there be any mischief in ye, weak as ye are, Rory of the Road, methinks it's in your mind and naught else."

Taking his lack of response as the answer to her question, Brenna started to rise. "But I'll leave you to whatever modesty you require—oh!"

Rory gripped her arm with iron fingers.

His strength and suddenness so startled Brenna that she lost her balance and fell across him with a gasp. "What *are* you doing? You'll break open—"

"I think there is something on your mind, milady." His voice rumbled low and threatening from his chest, not unlike Faol's warnings. "Something you may wish to share with me."

Ho, *that* she was not about to do.

But before Brenna could collect herself, the blanket hanging over the entrance to the chamber gave way, and Faol bolted straight for them. His growl and bared teeth left little doubt of his intention.

"Faol, no!"

Brenna covered Rory's head and shoulder with her body before the wolf could reach his neck. With arm raised, she tried to ward off the attack. The move threw the wolf off balance. Faol's teeth caught on her sleeve, raking the skin beneath, but the momentum of his leap slammed into her.

"Back," she ordered, as the startled wolf threw itself away and landed, still snarling, head low. "To your rug. *Now!*"

The white wolf backed off a bit more, but not to the hearth. Brenna had never seen him so riled. But then no one had ever appeared to Faol to threaten her. He must have heard her gasp and the raised voices....

"Remain absolutely still," Brenna said softly to Rory. Then, ever so slowly, she crawled away from him, keeping between him and the wolf. Her knees shook as she gained her feet. "Rory meant no harm, pup," she cooed. "See? I'm not hurt."

Through the torn sleeve, her arm was red, but he'd not drawn blood. Faol would never hurt her intentionally. Brenna began to sing. *"You're my own little love ...."*

It was a lullaby, one Ealga had sung to Brenna and Brenna to the wolf since it was a pup. And she petted him until his predatory stance relaxed. When he at last took his gaze off Rory and raised his head for more attention, Brenna grasped the loose skin behind his neck and herded him over to the hearth. There she knelt, making him sit on the rug as well.

"Rory was in pain," she explained, as if the wolf could understand.

"You must be out of your mind to trust that beast," Rory sang to the tune of the familiar lullaby. He actually had a decent voice.

"I trust him with my life. You must understand, Rory. He

thought you were hurting me. If Faol so much as thinks I'm in danger, he … he becomes mad."

"I will definitely keep that in mind."

"He likes you, but not when you become so … so hostile."

It was a good while before Faol was at last satisfied that the aggression had passed. The wolf dropped on all four haunches, his gaze returning to Rory. But when Brenna ventured to rise, her pet started up with her. She pressed him down with her hand, petting him gently.

"Stay, *anmchara*."

"You call a wild *wolf* your soulmate?"

"Aye, I do, Rory. You may have a fine life beyond the walls of this cavern, but Faol and this cave are all I have." Leaving Faol at least semicontent, Brenna stirred the stew. "I'm sorry if I offended you, Rory. I only tried to lighten your sour mood and made you the worse for it."

Brenna waited for a reply, but when she looked, Rory was glaring at the ceiling of the cave, his face a mirror of frustration.

Shame on her. Here was a man used to fending for himself, and no doubt his pride was offended by his dependence on her. Brenna longed to put him at ease and yet was vexed as to just what to say to him.

Instead, she said, "Come along, Faol. Let's go for a walk and give Rory some time to himself."

With the white wolf eagerly at her heel, Brenna moved aside the curtain to the outer chamber of the cave and left the silent man inside to his surly dejection.

CHAPTER NINE

The Leafbud Equinox was nearly at hand, when day and night were equal. The forested hills were glazed with hints of new green. Heather had begun to sprinkle the hillside leading down from the rocky crags of Brenna's home with its purple hue, but it was the gorse that reigned over the landscape in bright robes of yellow. This year was surely its most glorious. But then, after the dark and dreary days of winter, Brenna thought that every year.

She carefully picked her way down a slope littered with scree, headed for the banks of the silvery spring that wound its way through the hermit's glen. One misstep could send her sprawling on her backside and all the splendor of early spring would not take the sting away.

"Almost there," she said to the equally cautious wolf accompanying her.

Upon reaching the spring bed, she spied smoke curling upward from Brother Martin's hut. The priest was home. She spied him working in his garden near to the stone-roofed abode. Although she knew she should respect his ritual isolation during the Lenten season, the tension growing between her and Rory had become untenable. Faith,

she spent more time out of doors than in—hunting, gathering ...
whatever might spare her Rory's prickly humor or the multiplying of
impulsive thoughts that invaded her mind.

Then had come last night's dream. A dream like none she'd
had before. One that left no doubt as to her future. Worse, she'd
awakened in Rory's arms, just as she'd seen in the dream. Except this
morning, it had been in the innocence of sleep. Not so in her dream.

Leaving Faol sniffing the air warily in the cover of the forest,
Brenna struck out into the sun-soaked clearing.

As though sensing her approach, the priest stopped his heavy
labor with the stick plow and turned, straightening stiffly. "Brenna!"

She smiled. Though she was clad in tunic and breeches, her hair
wound up beneath a cap, Martin knew her disguise well.

The voice of her mentor hastened Brenna's step. Indeed, the
priest had watched her grow into the woman she now was. Like a
father, he'd taken her dressed as a lad to spring fairs for trading and
taught her on academic and religious matters as diligently as Ealga
had healing. According to Ealga, the priest from a noble family had
been young when he'd first come to the isolated river glen. Now the
reddish-gold hair that spilled down to his shoulders from a druidic
tonsure was thick with threads of white and his still-broad shoulders
were slightly rounded. Nonetheless, his stride was long and powerful
as he closed the distance between them, his arms outstretched.

Brenna went into them willingly. "I have missed you over the
Long Dark."

"And I you, my child. But you look hale and hearty." His wide
smile wavered as he studied her expression. "At least on the surface,"
he amended. "What is wrong? Has something happened to Faol?"

"Nay"—Brenna chuckled, nervous—"he lurks in the wood, watching us even now." How was she to tell Martin of Rory? Worse, tell of these feelings her patient evoked in her? Or of her truly ungodly thoughts? Which was why she'd come up with a plan.

"But there is something," Brother Martin observed. "I know my girl."

He put his arm about her shoulder and shepherded her over to a crude bench beneath a shaded grove of oak. It was from there the priest spoke the Word to any of the villagers or hill folk who came on the seventh day of the week. Even though Rome had ruled the Sabbath be moved to Sunday two centuries earlier, the Celtic Church stuck to the traditions of its first-century founders, celebrating Easter along with the Passover that Jesus once celebrated.

Sitting next to the bench was a bucket of water. The priest dipped a cup and offered it to her. "Fresh drawn from the spring early this morning."

"Thank you, no." She patted a goatskin of water slung over her shoulder. "You didn't come up for your winter soak. Was the pass closed with snow longer than the first month?"

"No, I've been secluded, seeking God's will regarding a request to build a monastery and school here." Martin sounded as if he'd been asked to sin against God.

"But you are a wonderful teacher. Ealga said often that your gift was wasted on just one student."

"I was called to educate you, Brenna, just as I was called to this isolation, that I might become closer with God." He swung his arm wide, gesturing to his surroundings. "Look at this beauty. It was in the open-air forum of Solomon's temple that the Hebrews heard the

Word of God, you know. Jesus taught in the open air." He shook his head. "What a shame to defile God's handiwork with walls and clusters of huts."

Brother Martin's home was a special place. A sacred place once used by druids. Like so many Christian holy sites, it had been adopted from the older religion after countless druids of all degrees had heard the Word. Accepting Christ as their Druid, or teacher, they gave up their royal trappings for sackcloth and the humble service of teaching the Word to the common man per His example. Martin's own grandfather had been a Christian druidic teacher of mathematics and astronomy at the university in Bangor.

Yet while Brenna shared the priest's affinity for nature and loved Faol dearly, she would give anything to share her life in the wild with someone human.

"Do you mean it's a shame to defile it or to *share* it?"

Brother Martin snorted in humor. "You were always my challenge, Brenna. Quick-witted as a fox. But you did not come down from the hills to discuss my quandary, which is already settled in the Bishop of Llandalf's mind. He is sending twelve brothers to start the monastery after the Pascal celebration in Arthur's court at Strighlagh."

"Then why are you fretting if the church has solved your quandary for you?" she asked.

A sheepish look claimed the priest's reddening face. "Always on the mark," he lamented. "Now I must confess to my student that I am second-guessing God's decision."

Brenna seized at the unexpected opportunity to broach the topic that had brought her here. "That is exactly what I've been doing."

"I do not recommend it. In fact, I am praying God will help me to accept His will." Gone was Martin's gentle self-deprecation and in its place came steely conviction.

"But what if circumstances change?" She'd accepted the isolation imposed on her by her mother's prophecy, yet now it would appear that God had sent her someone.

"You've met a man." Martin's statement of fact was cloaked in dread.

"Aye, a good man." What would she do if her mentor refused her?

The priest reached over and folded her hand between his callused ones. "Tell me, child, all that is on your heart and mind."

So Brenna did, just as she'd rehearsed again and again on the way down the mountainside. Throughout the whole story of Rory's uncommon rescue by Faol and his healing over the weeks that followed, the priest's face remained inscrutable. But he managed a terse question now and then.

"Did you notice anything about the assailant that might identify him?"

"No … although I managed to put an arrow through his hand. It should leave a scar, were he ever found."

"You say the stranger rode a speckled horse?"

"Aye, a good three hands taller than our native stock."

"Did the injured man tell you his name?"

"Rory." The name rolled off Brenna's tongue, wrapped in the feeling she could no longer ignore. A feeling she feared and longed for in the same breath. *Is this what love is like?*

"And you are certain he is not an O'Byrne."

Brenna could still hear Rory's fevered ramblings. Could see the bloodshed though the glass of his soul as she'd held him. All those things too horrid for Ealga to tell her. Things Brenna would keep to herself for now.

"Aye. He was a soldier of fortune on his way to join Arthur when he accepted the O'Byrnes' hospitality and was attacked. I thought I'd lose him more than one night of fever, but by God's mercy he is recovering well now."

Besides, Rory had more than once apologized for his father's part in her family's massacre. It was only after she'd convinced him that she held no malice toward him, or even old Tarlach, that he'd truly begun to get better.

"You have your mother's gift then," Martin said. "And God's ear, of course."

But dare she go on? Martin's expression was as telling as the pile of stones at the far end of his garden.

"Soldiers of fortune are most often lacking in character, my child. Did you stop to think of your safety in taking this stranger in?"

"Of course," she replied, as though that were a given. "I have used a concoction daily of barrenwort to tame his beastly nature, just as Ealga taught."

The priest's gaze narrowed. "Still, you should have come to me rather than rely on herbal manipulation."

"The pass was closed," she reminded him. "And it's not manipulation. Manipulation is witchcraft. I *protected* myself."

"Then how do you know if Rory is a man of integrity or merely incapacitated by your *means* of protection?"

Her mentor had a way of getting to the core of things as well. Had she done Rory an injustice ... now that she knew him to be a man of honor?

"Rory has become as uncomfortable as I regarding my ministrations, now that he's grown stronger," she explained. "In truth, he keeps more and more to himself. Surely that's a good sign of character."

"Hmm."

Brenna scowled at the indistinct reply. "Regardless, I know he's noble enough to make a good—"

"Good *what?*" Alarm sharpened the priest's question, breaking the implacable facade of confessor.

"Husband." There. She'd said it. "And father to my son, if he's of a mind. I have a plan."

The priest's brow shot up. "You can't be serious."

"Oh, but I am."

Her reasoning poured forth like a mountain spring. There was no stopping it. Ealga had told her that Faol would bring her someone, and who was to say it wasn't the stranger? God knew that Brenna was lonely and that Faol could not live forever. Rory was a good man, although given to a life of wandering like his father before him.

Yes, she knew she'd have to let him go as she had all the living things she'd rescued. But if she could convince him to marry her and get her with child, then she'd be guaranteed the companionship she so desperately wanted. Nay, *needed*. Rory could stay or leave as he wished. Her demands were small, and she was certainly capable of caring for a child, even if she had to move to the lowlands in the west. As a healer, she could well support her son.

"The child will be a boy, Brother. I saw him. A beautiful baby boy with the same mark on his left hip as his father, shaped like a pledging hand. And that is why I came to you," she finished, nearly breathless.

Lost at her mention of *husband*, her mentor had yet to recover his priestly indifference. As she'd rambled on, Brenna had watched incredulity and alarm vie for dominance on the face of a man she knew to love her like a daughter. But now he met her with silence and closed eyes.

What if he refused her?

"How did you see the child?" the priest asked after what seemed an unendurable passage of time.

"In a dream. Eagla said my mother had prophetic dreams."

"She *was* gifted," Martin admitted with reluctance. "But how do you know it is not your emotions that put such ideas into your head rather than God?"

"Because I feel no waver of my spirit," she answered. "I know in my heart that this is right and good."

"Feelings and heart are temporal, my child, and often fickle. How does it measure with the eternal Word?"

The Word. "I believe this is the answer to my prayers for an end to my loneliness. But I will think on it more," she answered slowly.

"And pray."

"And pray," she agreed. There was no Scripture in her possession save the Beatitudes, artfully painted on a piece of slate … a gift prepared by Brother Martin himself for her sixteenth birthday. What Scripture she had to call upon was from memory, but the Gospels had been well seated there since early childhood, along with several Old Testament works. Ealga and Martin had seen to that.

"Are you equally yoked before God?"

Brenna hesitated. "I … I don't know for certain."

Her friend squeezed her hand. "Promise me you will pray on all we've spoken of and act on nothing until I've had the chance to speak with this man for myself."

Martin rose from the bench, Brenna with him.

"I was hoping you might come meet him today or tomorrow," she said. "I do value your opinion, and he seems most depressed—as though sinking into a hole of despair. Nothing I can say seems to improve his humor."

A hint of humor tugged at one side of Brother Martin's mouth. "Brenna, there is no guile in you. Your thoughts are written on your face."

Brenna resisted crossing herself, for she hoped her dearest friend could not read all that had crossed her mind in dream and thought.

"But I will not marry the two of you until I have spoken with him and prayed long over it."

"Then you'll come today?" That would be beyond her hope, though she'd have the wedding later, when the time for conception was best.

To her astonishment, the priest shook his head. "Sadly, I cannot. Not until after the Equinox feast at Glenarden. My presence at the keep there is requested. I cannot even keep my seclusion this little bit longer."

"Has Tarlach found the Lord then?" Hope sprang into Brenna's heart. If the old chief had come to terms with the feud of the past and present, then there might be hope for a life beyond the limits she had accepted for herself and her future son. Perhaps with her own kin.

"Nay, child, I fear not. His health and mind fail by the day."

Her hope spiraled down like a wounded bird.

"I am summoned there weekly at the request of Merlin Emrys to educate a young hostage assigned to Glenarden by Arthur's court," Martin explained. "A Gowrys prince."

"What?" Brenna gasped in disbelief. The two clans had raided each other in season since her family's slaughter, but this was indeed something new.

"And the Glenarden's youngest son is hostage with the Gowrys. It is Merlin's and Arthur's way of keeping each side in check after—" Brother Martin stopped, as though his words had struck a dam.

Or was there something he didn't want to say? Before Brenna could determine the nature of the pause, the priest continued. "Arthur has lost too many warriors fighting amongst themselves when such men are needed for the summer's campaign."

"Then that is indeed a hopeful thing. If only the Dux or his father before him had intervened sooner." Although, given all she'd heard of Tarlach's madness, he'd still have hunted her because of her mother's prophecy. "But I'll deem the news as a good sign. Perhaps peace will come to our hills after all." And it would not depend upon her.

"In God's time." Martin made the sign of the cross over his chest. "Until then, He has given me much to do and very little time in which to accomplish it."

"But you will come soon, won't you?" Brenna asked as she walked with him back to the half-furrowed patch of winter-hardened ground.

"Two weeks," he promised. "In the interim, let us both pray for God's will to be revealed to us ... and wait upon the Lord."

Brenna prayed the entire journey up into the hills that concealed her cave. But each time she waited in silence for an answer, nothing came beyond the dream. The dream of her lying clad in naught but nature's splendor in her husband's arms. The joy of holding their newborn son. Which meant that Rory might not take his leave of her after all. That they might have a real family.

God, could it be possible?

Familiar words came to her. *With God, all things are possible.*

Spurred on by the revelation, Brenna stopped waiting for the ever-curious Faol to check out this sound or that scent. Keeping in the cover of the pine that dotted the higher hills as she climbed slowed her enough. There was much she had to discuss with Rory, though in her heart she already knew their destinies were bound.

The first blue of dusk colored the hillside by the time Brenna reached her cave. Left to his own devices, Faol had wandered off to the west, so she entered the outer chamber alone.

"Rory, I'm back." She paused in case he needed a moment's more privacy. Upon hearing no answer, Brenna entered, expecting to see her patient sleeping on the pallet. But the bed was empty. A glance at the table showed the bannocks she'd made for his breakfast and nun-day meal were gone as well.

Had Rory left her? Brenna fought her alarm. Nay. He was not strong enough. Or had she underestimated him?

CHAPTER TEN

Perspiration beaded Ronan's face and caused his shirt to cling to his body. The steep descent, not to mention this eerie pit with its visible hot breath, was hardly the wonder Brenna had described. He felt as though he'd staggered into a dragon's mouth and down its long throat. The muscles of his legs had cramped as though clenched between unseen teeth. He'd suffered such cramps before, sometimes awaking him from sound sleep, but these were the worst. And now that he'd reached the dragon's belly, his limbs trembled like a newborn foal's.

By all the gods of this heathen place, for the animals and figures etched on the stone passage walls by ancient hands marked it as such, he'd never make it back up to Brenna's chamber on his own. How this place could be described as invigorating was beyond him. It sapped his strength. Each breath he took smothered him, leaving him lightheaded.

He had no idea how much time he'd passed focusing on the dome-like chamber that gradually took shape in the dim light of his lamp. Had he stumbled at the bottom instead of sinking against the wall, he might well have plunged into the murky water just a few lengths of an arm from where he sank to rest.

As his eyesight adjusted more, Ronan made out a ledge hacked out by human hands. There sat several candles, burned down to differing heights. Inscribed over them on the wall was a cross, declaring the site no longer pagan, but blessed for the purposes of God. He struggled up on his knees and, using the flame of the oil lamp he'd · brought with him, lit the lot of them before blowing out the lamp to conserve oil for the journey back. Exhausted, he closed his eyes and sank down near the ledge of the pool.

Would that his assailant had killed him and spared him this slow death. His sword arm was heavier than his weapon. Walking *downhill* sapped him of strength. But the loss that tormented him the most was that of his manhood.

This morning he'd awakened to find Brenna asleep in his arms. The sight of such innocence and beauty in sweet repose, the warmth of her curves pressed against him should have lit signal fires across the highlands. Yet nothing beyond the fire in his mind stirred. Nothing. He'd feigned sleep when she stirred and hastily wriggled out of his embrace as though burned by it.

But how could she know she had so little to fear?

Jaws clenched, Ronan slid forward, determined to be restored in this marvelous spring or drown trying. He tested the depth and found it shallow enough to sit in, at least as far as his extended foot could detect. The water was pleasantly warm. Though it appeared still, he could feel the slow-moving current flow from the yawning back of the cavern and out through what had to be a fissure in the opposite wall. Ronan's shirt billowed as he eased in the rest of the way. He should have taken it off, but his thoughts weren't the clearest.

This would save Brenna from having to wash it. How he wearied of this helplessness and her having to wait on him—

As if he'd conjured her in his mind, Ronan heard her voice in the distance. Her panic.

"Here," he shouted back. The reverberation in the small domed chamber nearly deafened him. But as it subsided, he thought he made out the sound of her making her way down the passage.

"I told you"—her disembodied voice traveled ahead of her—"not to come down here. What ... if you ... had fallen?"

Ronan smiled, picturing the indignation flashing in her gaze that he dared to disobey her. Not because she wanted to control him, but because she really cared. Of that, he had no doubt. Brenna had nothing to gain by saving his life and nursing him back to health. She said she did so because she was a healer, but it was more than that. Brenna of Gowrys embodied love. A love Ronan hadn't believed existed.

"I cannot believe you were so foolish as to come down here alone!" Her face flushed from the rush down the passage, Brenna halted at the sight of him sitting peacefully in the pool.

"As you can see, I am just fine. Stronger than you thought," he replied, with only a pang of guilt for not admitting she was right. Taking in her boyish attire piqued his curiosity. "You were gone a long time today. Where would you go that you need to present yourself as a laddie?"

"It was a fine day for a long walk and ... and I needed some time to myself. Time to think ... and pray."

Ronan lifted one brow. "And what do you pray for, Brenna of the Hallowed Hills?"

"Your healing." She tugged off her woolen cap, sending perspiration-damp black hair tumbling in disarray about her shoulders. "'Tis hotter than a baker's oven in here." Without a hint of self-consciousness, she pulled her woolen tunic over her head and dropped it beside the cap.

No silk-bedecked female had ever been so fetching as the one standing before him in plain linen shirt and breeches with deerskin boots laced to the knee. Ronan helped himself to a palm's dip of water.

"I've been doing a lot of thinking," she announced, dropping to the ledge, cross-legged.

Intense blue eyes delved into his, touching a part of him he kept hidden deep within, yet he resisted the urge to look away. "About?"

"*You*, who else?" she said with a snap of annoyance. "I can see you healing by the day—"

"You gave me no choice, milady. The sweetness of your voice drew me back from the Other Side as surely as I sit here." And it kept him in This World. She'd given him something worth staying for. Although after this morning, he had his doubts.

Her expression grew puzzled. "But life is a gift, Rory. Too precious to wish away. How could a man like yourself not want to live?"

"My life has been no gift, Brenna. No man should see the things I've seen, or done … some of the things I've had to do. It's the lot of … a soldier of fortune."

"I saw some of those things, Rory," she reminded him. "You must let them go, or you will never be whole, never live the life God has planned for you."

"It's not that simple." What would she know of the complexities of life? She'd grown up protected from them.

"But it *is* that simple … at least on God's part. It's us that makes it complicated."

And everyone and everything around us.

"How long have you been down here?" she asked, changing the subject.

"I only just made it into the water."

"Hmm." She hefted up one leg and began unlacing her boots.

"What are you doing?"

"I'm going to strip mother naked and jump in with you." She met his gaze head-on and took in his reaction straight-faced … for as long as she could. Dissolving into laughter, she focused on the laces of her boots again. "Fear not, I only mean to soak my feet. It was a long hike down to the glen and back."

Her feet. Heaven help him, the vision that leapt to his mind was not of her feet. If she was half as goddess-like as he imagined, his racing blood would set the pool to bubbling. If he were but half the man he'd once been …

"Then milady had best not be making promises she has no intention of keeping."

"Perhaps milord should avoid pursuing thoughts he has no—" Self-conscious, she glanced away. "My apologies, Rory. I only meant sport."

She knew. She knew of his impotence. Brenna of Gowrys might be a practiced healer, but guile eluded her. It was part of her charm and his curse.

She hauled off first one boot, then the other. Off came the stockings, revealing slender white calves and ankles in keeping with his imagination. She stopped to toy with her toes, separating and wiping imaginary sand from them.

By his worthless bones, this unwitting seduction was far more powerful than that of an accomplished temptress.

Even so, not powerful enough. "Are you going to soak your feet or not?"

Brenna started at the sharpness in Ronan's voice. "Clearly the calmative effects of the pool still have much work to do."

She rolled her breeches above her knees and with a wriggle that Ronan's stomach imitated, inched to the edge of the pool next to him. With a calculated look, she slapped her feet into the water, splashing him in the process.

"Is milord of discontent happy *now?*"

Ronan didn't answer. Instead, he eased his head back against the floor of the cave and closed his eyes. This misery was far worse than the pain and fever.

Brenna watched Rory as he slept, or feigned sleep to ignore her. He was getting restless, like any animal used to wandering free, and frustrated that he couldn't do as he pleased just yet. When she saw his cloak and breeches where she'd put them, her initial panic at Rory's disappearance had turned to confusion, for surely he'd not have left them behind. It was then she realized where he'd gone: to satisfy his curiosity about the warm spring she'd talked about....

"The water does seem to do my legs well, even if it hasn't

improved my temperament," he had said after they'd sat in the warm pool for a long while.

An apology. Likely as much as he could muster. Brenna chuckled. "Mayhaps I should hold your head under then."

"No, I mean what I say." He sounded surprised. "On the way down, my legs rebelled fiercely against me. The muscles nearly bound me over."

He should have waited for her. "And now?"

"They no longer plague me. They feel"—he searched for a word—"*restored* ..." He shook his head, as if that wasn't it. "Stronger."

"The fevers burn away at the body's muscles, like the sun does to dried meat. But there is something in this water that restores what the fever took away." Brenna rose to her feet. "Come now. Your fingers and toes will start to wrinkle."

"What kind of place was this? A pagan temple?"

"Before the water men came, most likely it was dedicated to Sulis, goddess of healing waters. But it has been a holy place since God created it, whether credit was given to Him or nay."

Brenna stood ready to help if Rory needed it. It pleased her that he did not.

"Water men?"

"Aye, our first Christian fathers. This was used for healing and for baptism, just as Saint John the Baptist used water. To wash away sins, that man might start afresh, learning and loving God. Merlin said there were many such places all over the isle."

Rory's brow shot up. "Which merlin is that?"

"I'm thinking his name was Emrys. I was just a little girl, but he visited once or twice with us and told the most wondrous stories. A strapping man he was, with black hair and expressive blue eyes. He was your Arthur's teacher, just as Ealga was mine. Can you imagine being tutored by the wonderful Merlin? Though he did say I was most bright for my age."

Rory stared at her in wonder. "You have friends in very high places, Brenna of the Hallowed Hills."

"It's Brother Martin who has the friends. Although Emrys is the only one he ever brought here."

"Martin." Rory mulled over the name, wringing the long tail of his shirt dry.

"Aye, I went to see him today. He's most anxious to meet you."

At this, wariness invaded Rory's demeanor. "Is he the priest in the glen near the river?"

"The same. He's known me ever since I can remember. In fact, he gave me my religious training." She glanced about. "I don't suppose you remembered to bring down towels?"

Clearly, from Rory's scowl, he hadn't. "What did the good Brother have to say about me?"

"Only that he looks forward to meeting you. 'Twas I that did most of the talking. I told him about the attack and how Faol came to your rescue. And how the fever nearly took you."

"Did he say anyone was looking for me?"

Brenna caught her breath at the alarm on Rory's face. Of course the murderer would be searching for him … if the coward had nerve enough to return after being attacked by a wolf and a ghostly bowman.

She caught Rory's face in her hands. "Don't worry your head over his telling anyone about you. He's kept my whereabouts secret for years. He'll do nothing to endanger either of us. He's a good man."

The corner of Rory's mouth twitched. "You see good in everyone, Brenna. Even the likes of me."

"Especially in you, Rory of the Road." The words spilled out before she could stop them, baring a heart about to burst. "I thank God for sending you to me."

Brenna knew she should look away from that warm russet appraisal. The line she'd drawn between her feelings and Rory dissolved with each breath she took.

"I do not deserve such honor." Rory put his hands upon her shoulders.

Heaven help her, Brenna savored their touch instead of pulling away as she should.

"What do you *see* now, Brenna?"

"I see you kissing me." Brenna stopped. She dared not look further, for what she saw would come to be and it mustn't. Not this soon.

"Are you enjoying it?" He pulled her closer, without so much as a wince of pain.

She went willingly, allowing his shirt to soak her clothing. "Most heartily, sir."

A half sigh, half laugh escaped the lips only inches from hers. "There is no woman like you on this side of Heaven."

She was going to swoon. It was the heat. His closeness. The fact that she'd stopped breathing.

"And who am I, then, Brenna?"

"The man I love." There. The truth was out, and she was about to drown in it most willingly.

"And who is he, my sweet?" His lips brushed hers, hesitantly. As if he was almost afraid of what she might say.

"The man I will marry when the time comes, if you'll have me and the son I'll bear you."

Rory stepped away so suddenly Brenna swayed and stumbled. She caught herself on the candle shelf, overturning one. Hot wax spilled over her hand. "Oh!"

"Brenna!" Rory seized at her hand and began to blow on it. "Forgive me, *a stór.*"

But the damage was done. Rory's reaction to her heart's desire slapped her as cold and harsh as winter's breath.

"It was a foolish notion." She jerked her hand away, but she couldn't help the tears glazing her eyes. The Devil take them. "But you asked me what I saw, and I told it as I saw it. It isn't set in stone." She sniffed hard and wiped eyes on her sleeve. *Or is it?*

"But you have a gift. You said you saw what I saw as a child when you held me ... and now this." Rory tried to close the distance between them, but she dodged him and reached for the pile of clothing she'd discarded.

"I also dreamed I could fly, but I'm not about to jump off a crag. Not *all* dreams come true." Only those she saw through the eyes of her soul.

"What if we want them to come true?"

Brenna froze in disbelief.

Father God, my heart cannot bear such leaps and lows. Her things clutched to her chest, she straightened and turned on bare feet. *"We?"*

Rory held up his hands in a show of surrender. "You have bewitched me, Brenna of the Hallowed Hills. You drew my soul from the depths of hell and breathed life into me with your song. You nourished my body with your herbs and loving care. It was for you that I came back from death's door. And it is only for you that I will remain on This Side, for I cannot imagine a future without you as a part of it." Rory glanced at the floor. "If you would have me, half the man that I am."

The torture in his voice pulled Brenna to him. She caressed his cheek. "You recover by the day, Rory. I promise you that you will be all you were before. You must believe me. Have I failed you yet?"

"Brenna, it is I who will fail you. I will give you no son."

"Of course you will. I've seen it."

"By my father's breath, must I say it, woman? My wounds have stripped me of my manhood!"

Brenna's thoughts reeled, condemned by the agony fueling his anger and frustration. Father God, forgive her. Brother Martin was right. She had harmed Rory most cruelly.

"I have *seen* our child. Not with the eyes of a dream, but with the eyes of my soul," she assured him. "As you recover, so will your manhood."

"How can you know?"

Don't make me tell you. Brenna looked away, but Rory cupped her chin, turning her traitorous face back to his.

"What"—he hurled each word with accusation—"have … you … *done* to me?"

"Nothing that cannot be undone this day," she managed. Now that she believed him to be honorable.

He seized her shoulders with a strength that astonished her. "*What*, Brenna?"

"I put herbs in your food and drink to protect myself."

With a growl, he thrust her away and paced along the edge of the pool, not unlike Faol.

"I took you in as a stranger. I saved your life. But until I came to know and trust you, I did what I had to do. What I will do no more."

"Indeed you will not," he snorted, shoving his fingers through his hair. "I'll prepare my own food from now on."

"No, Rory, you'll think about the logic behind my actions and then you'll see that what I did was right, given the circumstances. And you will believe me when I say that from this day forward, I'll hold no more secrets from you."

Still, when he turned to face her, suspicion clouded his face. Hurtful as it was, Brenna motioned toward the passage. "Now, you go up ahead of me. Should you become lightheaded, I'll be behind to catch you as I can."

Since Brenna had revealed her meddling with his food and natural desires, dreams Ronan prayed would not come true plagued his sleep. There were visions of Brenna in his arms, warm with desire, radiant … of their coming together and her laughing, no longer Brenna but some wild-haired witchwoman mocking his manhood. Yet when he shook off the nightmare, there she lay a short distance away, sleeping innocent as a lamb in the bed she'd maintained by the fire since revealing her secret. He missed the simple pleasure of awakening to her warmth. Of her touching his forehead and cheek to check for fever.

Now his fever was of the kind that made her decision to make up her bed by the fire a wise one. He rose up on one elbow to watch her. Next to Brenna, Faol opened one eye but made no threatening move or sound. Her lips curled ever so slightly upward. Whatever she dreamed was pleasant. Perhaps she saw him kissing her.

Ronan scowled. Her visions were unnerving at best ... if there was anything to them. Perhaps Tarlach had once felt similar anxiety before he went over the edge of reason and fell into murderous insanity.

Faol heaved a sigh deep enough to carry the burdens of the world with it and rose to his feet. After paddling across the distance between them, he nudged Ronan for a pet.

"I'll do all in my power to protect her," he promised the wolf. Oddly, the two of them had become friends as Ronan's recovery progressed. At least as long as Ronan kept his voice and manner amiable in Brenna's presence.

Once Tarlach met Brenna, the old man couldn't help but love her, Ronan thought. Especially since she had no desire to lead her own clan against the O'Byrnes. Such a match was indeed the answer to the prophecy of peace ... without bloodshed.

Although, given her fears about his male nature and the hostility of his clan toward her, better he marry her as Rory first. If he told her who he was, he might lose her forever. After a few days, he'd tell her the truth. By then, he'd have proven his love for her was real. And if her vision was real, she'd be with child. An heir that would unite the two clans. Then he could leave her in the safety of the cave while he went to prepare his family for her arrival.

Ronan scratched Faol's head absently, glad the wolf could not read his mind. Bad enough his conscience attacked him. But it wasn't as if she hadn't deceived him, he told himself. And his reason for lying was as valid as hers. More so. This time, his heart was at stake.

CHAPTER ELEVEN

A full year of marital bliss and Rhianon had yet to conceive the son who would become the O'Byrne, the chief of Glenarden. But this year she would have the blessing of her goddess *and* that of the church for Lady's Day. She'd invited Brother Martin to give a Mass here to celebrate the Annunciation, when the Virgin Mary received the blessed news that she would bear a son. Even now the cooks were busy preparing the feast and painting boiled eggs to adorn the Lord's Table.

"Careful not to anger the goddess, child," Keena whispered in warning. Not that her nurse had to speak lowly, for Tarlach's snoring could be heard through the thin wall separating his bedchamber from the one that had been hers and Caden's before Ronan's death. Rhianon had turned it into a chapel to please the Christian God.

Very much aware of her old nurse's scrutiny, Rhianon carefully, reverently, took the figurine of the fertility goddess Ostara out of the velvet pouch she kept hidden beneath the mattress of the bed.

Keena came closer to see it. "The Christian God is not the *only* jealous god. Ceridwen will not like this."

But Ostara was the goddess of fertility whose legendary pet rabbit gave her colored eggs. Rhianon carefully hid the disk-like Ostara

in an arrangement of fresh-cut flowers next to Ceridwen, triple goddess of the Celts. "She has had her chance, Keena. Perhaps Ceridwen
needs help."

Standing back, Rhianon made sure the visiting priest would only
see the flowers on the small altar shelf beneath the tapestry of the cross
Rhianon had made. He'd approve the banding together of the deities
no more than Keena.

"Faith is in the heart, not in some object or image," he'd chided
her when she expressed astonishment that there was no image of
God Himself.

Well, she'd prayed to get with child to His invisible God ever
since Martin had been tutoring the Gowrys hostage, and all to no
avail. Symbols worked better.

"If only I had a picture of the Blessed Virgin like Arthur has on
his shield." Rhianon sighed. "That would show God the fervency of
my desire."

"What would a Father God know of women's travails?" Keena
disdained. "Common sense tells me not a thing."

"The priest said He gave a woman more than *thrice* my age a son,
Keena. Enough now! I will have a son to inherit this kingdom, no
matter which god grants my desire."

Keena drew up to as full a height as her hunched frame would
allow, her dark eyes glittering. "I love you too much to lead you
astray, Rhianon. 'Tis the source of my words and has been since the
day you were born and handed into my care. Your desires are mine."

"And I love you for it." Rhianon rushed to embrace her nurse.
"But I am desperate. You know I am." She smoothed Keena's wild,
uncombed hair away from her withered face. "I need this babe."

"And, by the goddess, you shall have it, as your mother delivered you. I will see to it. And don't forget Heming."

Rhianon sobered at the mention of the hunter and soldier of fortune. She had not seen him since the Witch's End.

"I saw him this morning before you awoke. He asked for you."

Of course he would. One indiscretion when she was but sixteen and the oaf acted as if he had some claim on her. Rhianon had thought him still off with Arthur. The man was a worrisome shadow that could not be detached.

"Then I shall see him when … I see him," Rhianon finished. The hairy Welshman knew things about her that Caden had only begun to discover. And some that her husband would never know. "Surely—" Rhianon broke off at the creak of the door. "At the feast tonight," she finished, walking toward it.

Not certain what—or whom—to expect, Rhianon yanked it open.

No one. Not at the door. But close by, the Gowrys princeling wrestled a bone from one of Tarlach's hounds.

"You there, Daniel," she called to him. "Did you see anyone standing here at this door?" She preferred to keep her plans for Glenarden between her and her own.

Perpetually hungry, Daniel of Gowrys was like Tarlach's hounds—always hanging about the spit in the main hall or in the kitchen, hoping for a handout.

"Nay, milady." The lad hurled the bone, shaking his head. "Nary a soul." Both wolfhounds bounded over empty benches after the treat, knocking some over in the process.

Rhianon scowled. How she hated those dogs. And she didn't trust Daniel, either, and had told Caden as much. Wild and unkempt, Daniel skulked about the hall, always watching, always listening. He was old enough to slit their throats while they slept. For that reason, he was locked in a storage room at night. Fit enough lodging for him, even if Merlin Emrys insisted the lad receive an education from Brother Martin.

"Get out of here, you whelp!" Keena raised her cane and shook it at the boy. "And take those mange-ridden mutts with you until you learn to behave in a civilized hall."

At the awkward and gangly stage where boyish muscle raced to fill an increasingly manly frame, Daniel climbed to his feet and walked away from them. On reaching the door, he turned back, a murderous look simmering beneath the mop of unwashed hair that spilled over his brow.

"Look at me like that again, laddie," Keena warned, "and you'll never live to see that rat hole of a place you call home again."

The boy's mouth quirked, begging to curl into a snarl. He shifted his gaze from Keena to Rhianon, then back to the crone. Rhianon shuddered at its ferocity. But the enemy Daniel made was far more dangerous. It wouldn't be a matter of *if* Keena made good her warning, but *when*.

For now the timing wasn't right. It would lead to the youngest O'Byrnes' death. Then Caden would annihilate the Gowrys, with or without Arthur's blessing. And Rhianon would be queen of both the Gowrys hills and the lowlands of Glenarden.

Or would she be queen of ashes left by Arthur's warband? Nay, if war were to start, it must be clearly done by the hand of the Gowrys … perhaps even their princeling.

The Vernal Equinox. Light and darkness met on equal ground. From this day forth, seeds would sprout and grow into bounty. Nature would multiply. It was a time, according to the message of the robe-clad priest holding court in the open field, for rebirth.

Or love and lust, Caden thought, glancing at his wife. Clad in the green of the season with a wreath of first flowers crowning her golden hair, Rhianon took his breath away. Never had a woman had such a hold on him. The sun *and* moon would be hers, could he pluck them from the heavens.

Indulging in this celebration was the least he could do. Thankfully there would be feasting and song afterward. That is, if the priest ever ceased drolling on and on about gifts and God.

"Your Cymri forefathers worshipped creation. They saw a living god in the sea, the trees, thunder … *all* of nature," the priest said. His clear, strong voice carried over the crowd. "Today we know that it is the One Creator God, present in all living things, not many lesser dieties. That is why Scripture says that nature and the heavens declare the glory of the One Creator God. The One God who breathed life into it. So until the Word came to them, your forefathers could not have known that it was the One God's breath that grew the tree and moved the sea about us and the stars above us. Our God is so grand and far-reaching that our human minds cannot embrace all there is to know of Him." He chuckled. "And, for all my study of Him, I speak of the shortcomings of *my* mind as well."

Then stop talking and let's eat, Caden shouted at the priest in silence.

"Yet," Martin continued, "our druids knew this. The wisemen knew." The priest glanced at Ailill. The druidic bard nodded in affirmation. "But the old thought was that you, the common man, could not come to know a God whom you could not detect with your ears or eyes ... or by the touch of your hand. That wisemen, priests or druids, had to intercede on your behalf ... much like the Pharisees separated the Hebrews from a relationship with their Heavenly Father."

"This is *not* what I called him here for," Rhianon fumed next to Caden. "I am going to withhold some of our tribute."

"Besides, these men thought, how could one get to know a spirit God who created all life and breathed His power and life into them as you know your father or brother or friend?" Brother Martin raised both hands to the sky. *"Jesus Christ,"* he shouted, causing Rhianon and half the assembly to gasp.

"Jesus came to show us all, even the most learned of us, that we can ... we *must* ... and it is through Jesus that we can do this. God loves everyone from kings to paupers, from the learned to the feeble-minded. God longs for you and me—priest, chief, warrior, woman, and servant—to walk and to talk and to commune with Him. The God who made all wants to be our *anmchara.* Our soulmate. He wants to be our Father who loves each of us, even when we have not been lovable ... or good ... or just. He is a Father who loved us so much, that He allowed His Son to be sacrificed for all our sins."

"Good for us, but not for the Son," Daniel of Gowrys spoke up. Seated on the grass between Tarlach's gray wolfhounds, the young man stared at the priest as if daring him to reply.

An uncomfortable snicker fluttered through the gathered crowd.

Caden bristled with indignation at the affront to the priest. "No one cares what the likes of you thinks, Gowrys." Besides, the priest needed no reason to extend his talk even longer.

"*Christ* cares," Martin admonished Caden gently. "You see, Daniel, Christ chose to be the sacrifice—the last and only sacrifice that man would ever need to make—because He loved us and He knew that we could never follow the laws of God perfectly enough to have eternal life. He could have called legions of warrior angels to defend himself against His enemies—"

"But this is *Lady's Day*, Brother!" The nip in Rhianon's voice signaled her patience had reached its end. "Save your stories of Christ for your sessions with that unlearned oaf. Tell us of His mother, whose fertility was such that she could bear a child without knowing man."

"I prefer *our* way," Caden whispered into her ear.

"Shush," she replied, smiling at the priest as though she'd not heard Caden. But the telling color rising to her cheeks told him his wife had heard him well and agreed.

"As God created all of nature by the power of his Word, so His Spirit created the child in the Virgin's womb. As the farmer plants seed into the earth, so God's Spirit planted a son in Mary. And even today, as man and woman come together in love, it is His Spirit that gifts the union with fertility, for it is no secret that not all such unions produce children."

Now that *was* something every man present was surely thankful for. The squeeze of Rhianon's hand shot Caden through with shame at the drift of his mind. He knew she wanted a child. So did he. A son and heir to whom he'd pass Glenarden with pride and joy, not the grudging reluctance of Tarlach.

"Today, Heavenly Father," the priest began with what Caden hoped was a closing prayer, "we honor the willing heart of Mary to accept God's will. May our hearts be as willing to accept Your will for us. We honor the mothers, the mothers-to-be, and all of nature, asking God's blessing on them to bring forth new life after the Long Dark. Bless us with bounty in our crops and livestock and bounty in our cradles in this season of rebirth."

How holy men loved the sound of their poetry and praise.

In the corner of his eye, Caden spied the Gowrys prince ambling away from the gathering, the dogs and a guard assigned to watch him following. He and Tarlach were the only black clouds in Caden's brightening future, yet they ate away at his insides like lye.

When the priest motioned one of the servants forward with the bread and wine, Caden let out a long sigh of relief. It was almost over. Once he and Rhianon had partaken of the Eucharist, they would be free to return to the keep, where the steward and villagers had set up the feast.

"This bread and wine is the power of salvation through the sacrificed flesh and blood of the crucified Christ. It is the power enabling us to remember the Christ as He asked us to do each time we partake of it. And it carries us across the ages on the wings of His love to His table. Such is the threefold magic of the Eucharist given by our Lord to His apostles and posterity."

Rhianon's lips moved in fervent prayer as she accepted the bread and wine. Caden wanted to gather her up in his arms and tell her that a child would come when she stopped fretting over it. And it would be a beautiful son, crowned in golden hair with his mother's rosy cheeks.

"Rise and go forth in the name of the Father, the Son, and the Holy Spirit," Brother Martin said, making the sign of the cross over their heads.

Caden didn't realize his retreat from the Mass was so hasty until Rhianon grasped his arm. "Slow down, my love. My stride is not as long as yours."

"Will that sackcloth of wind leave after the feast, or must we submit to more of his preaching?"

"He will ask the Lord's blessing over our food and afterward light and bless the bonfires."

Caden groaned. "There'll be no child conceived this night if he catches a second wind."

"We will walk hand in hand around the fire to make us clean enough to receive the gift of a child. The priest will then anoint us with holy oil and bless us."

That his wife had conspired so with the priest was surprising, and, from the facial expression of that shriveled shadow of a nurse nearby, Caden was not the only one who disapproved. The old hag mumbled in indignant silence, no doubt hurling the spells of her sort at the priest.

"The rest, milord," Rhianon continued, snaking her arm about his to return to the hall, "is up to you and me."

chapter twelve

Brenna combed her hair in front of the fire, over which simmered a rabbit stew. Beyond her, Faol paced about the inner chamber of her home as if he knew that something was amiss, something that would change life as he knew it. He approached Brenna and nuzzled her, sniffing at the rose-scented oil she'd used on her skin.

"We're having a wedding, *cariad*. The man you brought to me is going to take me as his wife today, and I will take him as husband," she explained to him. "We'll be a family."

Restless, the wolf left her to sniff the freshly stuffed pallet in the bedbox.

Things had changed between them since she'd stopped putting herbs to curb his desire in Rory's food and tea. He'd eventually gotten over his anger at her for her precaution, or so he claimed, but his humor had been no less irritable, especially when she made up a bed on the rug next to Faol by the fire and left him on the pallet alone. Granted, it was hard and cold, but Brenna refused to let him take her place. The last thing he needed in his recovery was to take a chill.

With a half sigh, half growl, Faol abandoned her, proceeding through the blanket-covered passage to the outer chamber where

Rory awaited Brother Martin's arrival. Rory, her handsome husband-to-be. The father of the son she'd bear.

When her hair was mostly dry, Brenna rose to put on her mother's pale blue wedding dress. How she wished for Ealga as she pulled on the embroidered shift and then the gown.

Had her mother felt as sure of her future with Llas when she stitched its gold knotwork trim as Brenna was of hers with Rory? Had Joanna seen their dark end and married Llas anyway?

"Father God, let no darkness befall this union, but bathe it in Your light."

She fumbled with the laces at the back of the dress until her attitude of prayer became one of exasperation.

"May I come in?"

"I …" Brenna hadn't wanted Rory to see her until she was ready, but the dress was designed for a lady with a servant. "Yes, I need you."

Rory pushed the curtain aside and came in, Faol on his heel. The two had grown more accustomed to each other now that Rory was up and about and spent more time with the wolf.

"I need you as—" Rory stared at her as if seeing her for the first time.

His gaze warmed Brenna from bone to skin till she forgot why she'd invited him in. *The dress.* Yes, that was it.

"I … I have no servant to help me." Slowly she turned her back to him, exposing the loose lacings. "I'm tangled."

Instead of answering, Rory went straight to work, straightening the laces and pulling them until the gown conformed to her figure. When he'd secured them, he turned her to face him, spreading her unbound hair with worshipful fingers.

"You are too beautiful for words," he said hoarsely.

"Really?" Brenna's heart soared. Surely this man had seen the most handsome women in all Albion in his travels.

Chuckling, he drew her to him in a bear hug. "*Really*, Brenna of the Hallowed Hills."

In the magic of the moment, doubt melted away. This was what she'd been waiting for all her life, even when she wasn't aware of it.

Suddenly Faol barked, breaking the dizzying spell, and bolted out of the cave. A few seconds later, Brother Martin's loud "Hello, anyone there besides this hulk of a beast?" followed.

Brenna reluctantly gave up the haven of Rory's arms. "Coming, Brother." She grabbed a crown of spring flowers she'd made and placed it on her head so that the ribbons fell down her back.

"Perfect," Rory replied to her inquisitive glance.

Faith, she loved this man. Taking him by the hand, Brenna led him out to meet the priest.

Clad in a simple robe of gray sackcloth belted with knotted rope, Brother Martin waited near the cave entrance at his favorite spot—a boulder just the right height for sitting. Except that he stood in front of it with open arms and a radiant smile as Brenna emerged first, bringing Rory in tow.

Martin's admiration was not nearly so disconcerting. "My child, you have become a woman in what seems a matter of weeks."

Brenna returned his embrace. "Not so, Brother. I've been a woman for some time. There's just been no one to notice."

Rory cleared his throat behind her.

"Brother Martin, this is Rory of"—she hesitated—"of the Road. He is a soldier of fortune who wishes to stop his wandering to marry me and give me a son."

Brenna had always spoken her mind since Brother Martin, as her teacher and mentor, had encouraged it. But now he saw that he'd neglected to teach her when delicacy was required. Yet he'd never seen her more happy or unconcerned, and that did his heart good.

But not enough to offset the concern he harbored regarding her plan to unwittingly marry Ronan of Glenarden. "In good time, Brenna," Martin replied, "but I'd speak with your Rory of the Road in private as I am called to do prior to such matters as this."

"Of course. I've got to take the last of the barley cakes off and finish getting ready."

Brenna hiked her skirts and bolted into the cave that had been her home … and prison. In so many ways she was wise beyond her years and in so many ways innocent.

Heavenly Father, show me some way to spare her.

Martin was not comfortable with this marriage. But his instruction had come from the bishop himself through Merlin Emrys. The bloodlines must be joined. The prophecy must come to pass. The Celtic Church must be entrenched in the noble Scots and Britons to unite them against the invasion not only of the pagan Saxons' dominion but of Rome's doctrine.

"You have issue with my marrying Brenna." Arms folded over a broad chest, Ronan of Glenarden did not ask. He bristled. Tarlach had had no use for the hermit priest, and Ronan appeared much of the same mind.

"I do, *Rory*, if that is your name." Martin waited for Ronan to offer the truth. The priest had only seen Ronan of Glenarden at a distance during fair time. Yet this had to be the lost Glenarden.

"It is, Brother."

His unwavering gaze was almost convincing, yet Brenna could have rescued none other during the Witch's End. Certainly no mention had been made of this Rory, soldier of fortune. Martin had asked around at every nearby village and farm. Besides, that gash across this man's cheek did not lie. Many attested to the scar earned by the six-year-old Ronan in that unholy massacre. What mischief did Ronan of Glenarden play at?

What unseen scars of this man's soul might ruin Brenna's life forever?

"Brenna is like a daughter to me, *Rory of the Road*, so answer me true, or may God strike you down if you lie about this. Do you love her?"

At this, the hardness of the man's face melted like ice before the radiance of the sun. "More than my life. She is the only reason I live … or want to live."

It wasn't the words that swayed Martin, but the man's gaze. Beyond it, his soul swelled with unmitigated earnest.

"Are you prepared to risk everything you have for her sake? To forsake your family if need be to protect her?"

"Brenna is a part of me. If they cannot accept her, then they reject me and I them."

Just what Emrys predicted. The Glenarden heir would never forsake Brenna. And that would divide his father's house, exactly as

Joanna of Gowrys predicted. But the means to the foretold peace had long eluded Martin's grasp of this age-old conflict.

Man sees but one step at a time, Merlin had reminded him. *God sees it all, beyond the darkness.*

"You must tell Brenna the truth, Ronan of Glenarden," Martin said.

Upon seeing Martin's resolve, Ronan at last relented. "I will. You have my word, Brother … *after* I've prepared my family to receive her."

"Then wait to marry her. Do not taint your vows with deception."

"She has more protection as my wife and the mother of Glenarden's heir," Ronan pointed out.

That was true, but such security was brief. Many a woman's life ended with the delivery of an heir, and the death was not always a natural consequence.

"Besides, if you hadn't noticed, my bride is most set on this ceremony," Ronan said. "To the point that she would marry me even if I were to get her with child and abandon her." Again wonder claimed the man, taking away lines that a life of bitterness had etched on his young brow. "I do not deserve her."

"Aye," Martin agreed. He still didn't like Brenna marrying a man who would lie to her, despite his obvious love. "Things have changed at Glenarden. Caden rules in your stead—"

Ronan erupted in a short humorless laugh. "That does not surprise me."

"And your brother Alyn is now hostage with the Gowrys."

The man blanched. "What?"

"As the Gowrys prince is hostage at Glenarden," Martin hastily added. "In retaliation for your disappearance, Caden led a devastating raid against the Gowrys, killing the eldest prince. They pled for justice from Arthur, and Merlin Emrys conducted the exchange to keep peace."

Ronan stared up at the pine overhead, evergreen against the spring blue sky. "I hadn't thought about the consequences for the Gowrys regarding my disappearance. I thought Caden would have my bed in the master chamber before it grew cold, but—"

"So there is peace," Martin informed him, "tentative as it is. As such, the marriage could wait—"

"Nay, Martin. Marry us now." Ronan's fierceness softened. "Give us this night unmarred by my father's black deed. And I give you my word that I will go to Glenarden and right all its consequent wrongs."

"You'll take Brenna?"

"Nay." The man assumed a stance that told Martin he had no intention of being moved. "I'll not risk her life. She'll be safe here till I've prepared Father. Then I'll come for her."

"What of your lie to her? Will you marry her falsely?"

Ronan hesitated.

Martin allowed the man time to wrestle with his guilt. He was a good man ... but stubborn.

"Only till I'm certain she'll be safe."

"Son," Martin pleaded, "'tis no way to start a marriage. You've enough against your happiness as it is."

"I only led her to believe I was someone else because I feared for my life at first. Surely you can understand that."

"She loves you now, laddie. What will she say when she finds out she's not married to the man she fell in love with?"

"I am the same man."

"In your eyes, yes. But will *she* see you as the same man? She has opened herself up to you with complete honesty, complete innocence and trust."

"Then marry us again later," Ronan snapped. "Marry us daily if you must."

Martin held his peace, what little God afforded him in this. *Christ does not dictate. He gives free choice.*

"So tell me now, Brother. Will you marry us or nay?"

Martin shuddered. He had his orders. Yet he could not condone this. "I leave that decision to you, Ronan of Glenarden. How is it you would have your life with Brenna begin? In honesty and trust, or in the darkness that has plagued you and yours since your first breath?"

For a moment, Martin thought the Glenarden had been exposed to the wolf too long, for his lip curled into a snarl, silent, but no less hostile. With a muffled curse Ronan pivoted and stomped off into the forest that had once concealed Brenna's whereabouts … until she brought him there.

CHAPTER THIRTEEN

Something was wrong. Brenna knew it the moment she set sight on Brother Martin's face. Yet he insisted that Rory had gone off to pray after his confession.

"He'll be back soon, and we'll proceed as planned."

Confession, Brenna thought as she made tea to pass the time. What had Rory confessed? A child's part in the murderous raid on the Gowrys? Surely God had not held that against him.

The questions plagued her as she carried the tea out to Martin … until she spied Rory and Faol making their way up the almost hidden path to the cave.

"I'd begun to think you'd turned coward and run," she called out to him, smiling.

But Rory did not smile back. Nor could she see beyond the hard wall of his expression. Dread ran Brenna through. "What is it, Rory?"

Rory motioned toward the cave entrance. "I need to speak with you."

Brenna glanced at her mentor, hoping for some semblance of reassurance, but like Rory's, Martin's expression was masked.

"Go on. I'll enjoy my tea in this long-awaited sunshine." Martin shifted his gaze to Rory. "You are doing the right thing, son."

"Spare me, Priest." Rory's words dripped with bitterness.

Brenna felt the blood drain from her face and limbs with each step she took. Rory was married. That had to be it. She could think of no other reason why there was a problem.

Father God, please spare me that.

Yet she knew in her heart this marriage was God's will. There were fanciful dreams soon forgotten, if remembered at all. Then there were the visions, indelibly etched not just in her mind, but in her soul.

She went straight to the hearth, hoping busywork would help stay the trembling of her hands. "I made some tea—"

"None, thank you."

Brenna clutched the skirt of her dress, gathering courage as she spun to face him. "Then tell me what you must, for my heart can bear no more of this."

Ronan cursed the day he was born. He cursed his father. He was tempted to curse God for allowing this to happen, yet he could not. Not as he had before meeting Brenna. Not if Brenna was right: that God had brought them together.

Though He had left them in a black muddle with little light that Ronan could see. Except for this.

"Know first that I love you with all my heart and soul, Brenna of Gowrys."

But was it enough? Could Ronan accept it if she rejected him once she found out the truth?

Her shoulders squared. She lifted her chin to receive the anticipated blow.

"But I cannot marry you under false pretenses."

It struck full on.

"Oh." Brenna sank onto the bench next to the table.

That morning they'd shared breakfast there, swathed in love's giddy light. Ronan never dreamed he'd ever feel so young and reckless. But he'd been deceiving himself. He couldn't escape his past, nor bind her to it without her knowledge.

"Are you already wed?" she asked in a small voice.

"By my father's wretched bones, no!" His plight could be worse, Ronan thought. "No," he said, more softly. "You are the only woman I have ever loved. My heart and soul belong to you."

Relief released the breath she'd been holding. She struggled to smile. "I would have your heart, Rory, but your soul is God's."

She was as naive as the priest who taught her. Yet Ronan would give anything to experience such faith. To believe God really cared.

He clenched his fists. Just be out with it, and let God have His way. Then he'd see if God was working on their behalf. If God really cared about a man cursed from birth by his father's sins. Or if God existed at all.

"I am not Rory, nor am I a soldier of fortune. I lied to you."

"Because …"

Already he could see the hurt trying to contort her face, and he hated himself for it.

"Because you believe I am your worst enemy, even though I could never be. No one who knows you could *ever* wish you harm." Ronan reached for her, but she recoiled from his outstretched hand.

"You're … you're an *O'Byrne?*" Her voice clung to disbelief even as the bitter truth registered on her face and cast accusations at him.

But I trusted you.

I saved you, and you repaid me by lying.

You let me fall in love with you.

And he was guilty of them all.

"I am Ronan O'Byrne, eldest son of Tarlach. I was there when my father murdered yours. I saw your mother fall on her own blade rather than submit to my father's mad ravaging. I received this scar"—Ronan pointed to his face—"defending myself from the blade of one of the Gowrys men. And I killed him."

Brenna covered her ears with her hands. "Noooo …"

"I have led raids on your people to keep them confined to the highlands, subservient to mine," Ronan shouted. He stepped into her path as she rose to run. And when she tried to duck around him, he grabbed her arm. "I was the monster you feared, spawn of the Devil himself—"

"Let me go … please …"

Ronan couldn't deny her. Couldn't blame her. He dropped his hand and watched, helpless, as she raced out of the chamber. She passed Faol on his way in. Instead of attacking him, the wolf stopped, seemingly bewildered by Brenna's hasty exit. After an assessing glance at Ronan, he turned and followed his mistress.

Ronan wished the beast had torn out this throat. Such a fate was far more merciful than this.

The sun moved past midday before Brenna returned to the cave, her eyes red and swollen with the toll of Ronan's betrayal. She'd argued with him over and over in her mind. Try as she might to win, to make him a monster, she couldn't. Had she been in his place, she would have done the same thing.

Faol agreed.

Sometimes the best counsel is a quiet one, and Faol indeed was that. One who listened and showed her nothing but unadulterated love and support, enduring her hugs and soaking in her tears, while she foundered in a maelstrom of confusion and emotion.

And hadn't she kept a secret from Rory—*Ronan,* she amended—to protect herself? Had he done any differently? If she were the wolf-woman-witch hunted by his clan each year, he'd have good reason to fear her.

That is what reason told her.

God told her to forgive him as she'd expected him to forgive her.

And there was the vision. Was it from God—or a hopeful, lonely heart? For the first time, Brenna began to doubt, for it had not shown the whole truth.

One step that thou might see.

Brenna groaned. That small, still voice was ever at odds with her impatience.

Ahead, Brother Martin waited on the stone near the mouth of the cave, head bowed in quiet contemplation. Earlier, she'd blindly brushed past her old friend and mentor, too upset by Ronan's confession to make sense of anything, much less speak. Desperate just to get away from the pain, to run until she could run no farther, until she could hear no voice except that of God.

"When did you know?" she asked, looking about for Ronan.

"He's inside," Martin replied to her unspoken question.

"Good." It was Martin she sought, now that she'd had time to think. Now that her emotions had been wrung dry. "When?" she prompted softly.

Guilt grazed the priest's face. "I suspected, even feared it, when you came to me a few weeks ago. After seeking all the information I could, I concluded your stranger could be no other."

"Yet you came to marry us?"

Martin glanced away from her accusation. "My superiors are in agreement that this is a good marriage."

His superiors. The same lot who arranged for her mother to marry the man who eventually murdered the one she loved and drove Joanna to suicide.

"How can you trust such men?" she asked. Had Martin betrayed her, too?

"I sought their counsel, child, but I was not convinced that this was a good match until Ronan did right by you and told you the truth of his identity."

Brenna hiked her brow. "And you are convinced now, that this is right in God's eyes?"

"He loved you enough to tell you the truth, even though that truth could drive you away from him," Martin assured her. "He loved you enough to risk losing you as Christ loved us enough to lose His life."

Brenna's heart staggered within her chest.

Did she love Ronan *that* much? Enough to let him go?

Yes. She'd already said as much when she thought him a soldier of fortune.

Did she trust him with her life?

Yes. He could have done her harm, had he wished. Yet, foul humors aside, he'd treated her with utmost tenderness and care. Even after she'd stopped giving him the barrenwort.

A blessed assurance settled over her. "Then marry us, Brother, for I have seen it and trust God and my heart on this."

"God be thanked."

Brenna turned to see Ronan standing in the mouth of the cave. His jaw was seized as tight as his fists. As if he held back a fierce tide, one that might break free if he so much as twitched. But his bright gaze bridged the distance between them, reaching for her, beckoning her with the signal fires of his soul.

Brenna glanced down, suddenly conscious of the clinging wolf's hair and the brambles caught in the fine weave of her mother's dress from her headlong plunge into the woods. Reaching up, she felt for the flowered wreath she'd painstakingly made, only to find it gone. What a sight she must—

"Like a wild rose," Ronan assured her.

Brenna's eyes widened in surprise, not that he'd just read her thoughts, but that he could still find her pleasing in such disarray.

"Indeed she is," Brother Martin agreed. "But I'm accustomed to the bride and groom being close enough to bind in matrimony with my belt … that is, if there is to be a wedding this day."

Yet Ronan didn't move. Not until Brenna tilted her head in silent invitation. And suddenly his embrace was real, his kiss taking her breath away, lifting her off her feet. Like a leaf falling from a treetop, spinning helpless, yet reveling in the flight.

Until, from somewhere outside the sweet gale of emotion, someone cleared his throat. Ever so reluctantly she drifted back to the earth. But Ronan's warmth was still there. And his eyes still refused to let her go.

"That is usually reserved until *after* the ceremony," Martin reminded them wryly.

"*That*, good Brother," Ronan said, "was gratitude for the grace I do not deserve."

"None of us do, son," the priest replied. "None of us do. And so," he announced, assuming a posture of authority, "the two of you come together under God's sky this day to enter into the holy alliance of marriage. No longer alone, but together, you will take on life's joys and life's heartaches, clinging to one another and offering each other comfort in prosperity and woe."

Brenna had only seen a wedding from afar, heard bits and snatches of what was said. Had she been closer at that time, tears would have pooled in her gaze at the beauty of the soul-melding words ringing beneath the canopy of the trees, accompanied by birdsong.

Faith, now she couldn't even see Ronan's face as he pledged that gone hence were his ancient ways, replaced by his devotion to her and only her ... with all himself, his being, his heart and worldly store—his *life* till death take him was hers ... because it was she that gave it back to him.

"May this kiss press my words into thy heart, for you art flesh of mine own flesh from this moment hence."

She couldn't even see her hand through the veil of tears as he took it and pressed it to his lips. But she felt her swelling heart branded by the innocent contact. Suddenly, she was aware of another presence wedging between them. Faol.

Instinctively, she started to shove the wolf aside. "Nay, darling, not—"

"Let him be, *a stór*," Ronan interrupted. He patted the wolf's head. "I owe my life to him as well as for bringing us together. His presence seems only fitting."

Brenna hardly thought her heart could grow even fonder of this man, yet it did.

Later that afternoon, Ronan could not take his eyes off Brenna as she busied herself with dishing up the stew she'd prepared for their wedding feast. There were no secrets between Ronan and Brenna now. No lies to threaten their love.

A shudder ran through Ronan at just how close he'd come to entering into this marriage on a lie. Martin had been a godsend, rather than the threat Ronan had first thought. Doing the right thing, even though it might cost him Brenna, made the union between them real, not the sham Ronan had been willing to accept.

Thank You, Heavenly Father, for saving me from myself.

"What's that you're sprinkling on?" he asked as Brenna stirred in some dried seasoning.

She glanced up, beaming with a saucy smile. "Nothing you should worry about, *Husband*."

Husband. Desire coiled within him. Her trickery had run its course.

"Just a touch of tarragon to enhance the taste."

Food was the last thing on his mind. Thank Heaven theirs was a simple, private ceremony with no formalities to endure. Just the two of them, doing what they wished in their own time. Even Faol had followed Martin down the hillside. And this time Ronan hoped the wolf would stay away for a while.

"I wish you didn't have to return to Glenarden."

The comment took Ronan by surprise. From the moment he'd heard about Alyn's being taken as hostage, he'd been planning that, but he'd not mentioned it to Brenna.

"I have to let them know I'm alive. I'm the reason the feud reignited and my brother was sent to the Gowrys."

Brenna put a wooden plate on the table. Steam rose from the contents. "And what will *I* do?"

"You'll go with me." At the hike of her brow, Ronan added, "After I've had the chance to prepare my family for your arrival, of course." He'd never think of taking Brenna into that den of wolves without making sure she'd be accepted. "I gave my word to Martin that I'd take care of this, let them know I'm alive."

Brenna eased next to him at the table. "So, when will you go?" Resignation tainted her question.

"Three days from now."

With a look that tore at his heart, Brenna reached for his hand and bowed her head. "Father God, we thank You for this bounty and for the grace You have extended to us in Your love. May we be nourished by both to serve You and each other, whatever betide. Amen."

Instead of letting her hand go, Ronan raised it and pressed it to his lips. "Amen."

Brenna couldn't imagine leaving her home. What would Faol do? He was half wild. Even if she could adapt to living with the same people who'd hunted her for so many years in order to kill her, could he? Leaving was not in her plan. Living with the O'Byrnes was certainly not. Was this part of her mother's prophecy?

Next to her, Ronan wolfed down his stew and oatcake, while she mostly moved hers around the dish, her stomach knotted. Not even the honey mead Brother Martin had brought them could relax the tension building within.

"You've hardly eaten a bird's share."

Brenna lowered her head at Ronan's gentle observation. "I cannot. I—"

"Don't tell me you are just now becoming the nervous bride. Most maids would be surrounded by others, being pampered from head to toe, whilst you, Brenna of the Hallowed Hills, trapped and skinned a rabbit this morning, prepared the bridal feast and bed, and forgave this undeserving groom for his treachery. If anyone should be nervous, it should be me."

Ronan shoved the plates aside. Taking her hands in his, he drew her from the crude bench and into his lap. "Do you fear me so much, Brenna?"

"Nay." Brenna curled against his chest, welcoming his embrace. "I love you, Ronan, with all that I am. It is the future I fear. Would that we could stay here forever, where only love lives. I am not accustomed to others, nor is Faol. What will become of us?"

"I will protect you with my life," Ronan whispered against the top of her head. He nuzzled her hair, his embrace tightening about her as if to make her part of him. "And your wolf."

"*Our* wolf," she corrected.

She felt her hair part at her neck and the warmth of the kiss Ronan planted against her skin. Frissons of awareness shot through her, scorching the fingers of anxiety winding about her thoughts. Resistance never crossed her mind as Ronan turned her and those lips found hers.

"But why do you fret about tomorrow, *a stór*, when we have the night yet ahead to pass?"

Brenna didn't answer. She couldn't. Not when Ronan's kiss sealed her lips with promises that set her head to spinning. And through the blur, she could see and feel them fulfilled. They snatched her breath away and made her pulse leap and bound like a brook in spring flood.

"Do you trust me, Brenna?" Ronan whispered raggedly, drawing his lips along the taper of her jaw and down to the pulse point drumming in her neck.

"Y-yes."

He rose, scooping her up like a child in his arms. "Then love me now, Wife, and let us face the future when it comes."

ChAPTER FOURTEEN

The forested hills were decked in a haze of spring green as Caden and his party made their way into their leafy depths. Hounds yelped, eager for the hunt.

Give me the feel of a good horse beneath me, good companions about me, and the lay of my own land before me any day over the tedious administration of Glenarden, Caden thought. With winter's last breath expelled, farm, hall, and village came to life with work to be done— ground to be plowed and planted, calves and piglets to be delivered, and whey, buttermilk, butter, and cheese to be made to replace the winter stores. But the simple peasantry couldn't seem to work out their differences without the lord's interference. It was small wonder his brother Ronan had little sense of humor, given the petty complaints brought before him.

Then there were Rhianon's preparations for the Pascal celebration and her family's visit. With luck, fresh venison would accompany the lamb on the feasting tables. Or boar. Perhaps both. Meanwhile the steward, Vychan, had put out the word to local fisherman for salmon and trout to complement the meal. Aye, this freedom of the outdoors was the sort of pursuit Caden preferred.

A glimpse of something white flashed against the green of the forest. Something large as a deer, but white. The dogs saw it too. The nature of their yelp changed from playful and excited to on-the-hunt. A woman couldn't tell the difference, but a huntsman and houndsman knew. Caden licked his lips, anticipation surging through his veins, and nudged Ballach into a run. The day was off to a fine start.

Brenna sat on a gorse-dotted crannog overlooking the pass through which Ronan had disappeared a little after daybreak. Though bathed in the rays of the midday sun, she was cold, lost without his nearness. How quickly the three glorious days they'd spent together as husband and wife had flown. With Ronan, her fear of the future fled, but now that he'd left to prepare his family to receive his bride, it was back in manifold force.

How had she spent her days before Ronan came into her life? Sure, she couldn't remember. Yet she'd been diligent, always busy hunting or gathering, preparing for the Long Dark or for trading at the Leafbud and Sun Season fairs. The blue flowers of rosemary were in bloom, and white-blossomed wild garlic awaited in the shady damp of the forested streambeds. Perhaps she should go back for her basket and digging stick—

Brenna cocked her head, listening. In the distance, the faint sound of hounds in pursuit echoed from the forest below her perch. Her pulse quickened. A hunt, and here she was an hour's climb from her home in a dress that stood out like the sun in a clear sky. Her hand flew to her waist. And she was weaponless. Ronan had made her forget what she *was* as well. *Hunted.*

Brenna hastened up the steep mountainside, following deer paths easily overlooked, unless one knew where they were. Overhead, a breeze whispered through the canopy of oak and hazel, carrying the sound of the hunt. The dogs were closer now, spurring her into as much of a run as the uneven ground would allow. She heard the thundering of horses' hooves … and their riders' shouts.

"It went this way!"

This way seemed to be the same route Brenna pursued. For every change in direction she took, the hunters followed, though they were still a distance behind. Briars picked at her skirt and skin as she stumbled uphill, tripping on her hem. In braccae, she would have been able to move as easily as Faol in the forest.

Faol. Brenna had last seen the wolf following Ronan through the pass, keeping to the edge of the trees as he always did. A terrible foreboding seized her. Grabbing the trunk of a hazel, she paused, gasping for air.

"I think I hit it," a loud voice called.

It. A dizzying wave washed over Brenna. She had to get back to the cave. If Faol was in trouble, he'd head there. Brenna plunged ahead, but a hurried climb up uneven ground spotted with slippery moss and lichen-covered rock was impossible without risking a broken neck. She'd never make it to the safety of her cave. And neither would Faol, if he was the target of the hunt. A white wolf pelt would bring a handsome purse for any man.

Above her, pine thinned to a ledge notched by time into the side of the mountain. From it spilled a stream, forming a waterfall that pooled on a wooded plateau that dropped off sharply beyond. The pool was a favorite, shaded spot to spend time and find wild garlic.

If she could make it there, Brenna might call Faol to her. They could hide behind the icy water spray. It wasn't that far. Underbrush of heather and juniper and bramble shredded her stockings and skin as she made for the pool.

Dare she call for Faol? If he was safely watching the hunt …

Sodden winter leaves gave way beneath her foot, and down she went with a startled cry. *The baby.* Brenna crawled to her knees and forced herself up. She had to think about the baby she knew she carried. She'd known the moment the child was conceived. She'd seen the newborn squirming in her arms in the midst of passion's dizzying storm and knew.

The fall of water splashing upon a rock bed penetrated Brenna's dazed thoughts, turning memories of bliss into present horror. Faol bolted up the hill toward her, limping. She couldn't see the hounds on his trail, but she could hear them—and the excited shouts of the hunters.

She stepped out into the wolf's path. "Come on, laddie, let's go."

As if understanding her intent, Faol passed her, moving toward the fall. Brenna fell into a staggering run behind him. They could make it. There was still time. The dogs would lose their scent in the water. It would be freezing cold, but the fall was large enough to hide them until the party gave up. When it was safe, she and Faol could return to their home, where she'd see to the arrow lodged in Faol's hindquarter and heal it.

Father God, let it be so.

How could she have been so foolish? Faol limped ahead of her, and while she had nothing but scratches, her legs grew heavier with each step she took. Blood pounded in her ears so loud it seemed to shake the ground beneath her. But she could see the waterfall now. See Faol stop and turn.

The hair on the wolf's body stood straight up, making him look half again his size. And she could count every tooth in his head, bared as they were. He hunched, the way he always did when he was about to attack—

"Well, what have we here?"

Brenna spun so abruptly at the man's voice that she nearly lost her footing. Fingers of iron clasped her arm, preventing her fall. She looked at them, her gaze skimming up a well-muscled arm to broad shoulders swathed in the colors of an O'Byrne. A fair-haired giant of one.

"Spare my wolf. He's a gentle—"

A gray wolfhound shot through the periphery of her vision, followed by another.

"No!" she screamed.

The wolf and hounds clashed in a fury of snarls and snaps.

And Brenna's heart was at the center. "Stop them, sir. I beg you. I've raised him from a pup. *Please*."

Caden O'Byrne looked deep into the wide blue gaze turned up at him, tugging at him with a power that left him unsettled. There could be no doubt who this was. So why he felt compelled to help her was a mystery.

"Gillis, leash the hounds." Had she bewitched him already, to make him believe a wolf such as this could be tamed?

"There's no stopping them now, milord," the hounds master said, breathless, as he caught up with Caden. "That wolf'd chew a man up as soon as them. Them, too, in the middle of a fight."

"Then give me the leashes," the woman pleaded. "*I'll* put them on. He'll not harm me."

Caden didn't know whether to trust her or not. Comely and convincing as she was, who was to say she'd not shift into a she-wolf and take on the other dog? Yet he saw no conniving in her gaze. Only fear. Stark fear and pleading.

Curiosity to see what she might do got the better of him. "Give her the leashes."

In a flash, the woman seized them and raced straight into the fray. Quick as lightning, she slipped a leather noose about the dog circling the embattled two and tossed it in Gillis's direction. The hounds master grabbed it and, with the help of a second man, hauled the straining, startled wolfhound away.

She had courage, Caden would give her that. Or she was as mad as a swineherd.

But as she reached the wolf and second wolfhound, the sickening snapping of bone stopped her still. The gray and bloodied wolfhound went limp, its last breath escaping in a strangled whine through the clench of the white wolf's powerful jaws about its neck. The wolf held it a moment, looking beyond the woman, as if she were no threat, at the other dog being hauled away.

"Faol." She sank to her knees, weak with relief. "Father God be praised."

Behind Caden, servants led Ballach and the other mounts up the hillside. The forest had become too thick and the hillside too steep to risk a misstep with the horses, so they'd been left behind and the hunt taken up afoot.

"Come, Faol," the witchwoman said, opening her arms to the wounded, bloodied wolf.

The wolf hunkered down, growling at Caden and his companions, never moving.

"Husharoo, my love."

She sang to the savage creature as though to a babe. Mesmerized, Caden waited along with the others, some with ready spears, others with axes or knives, all poised for what might happen next. The scene and all in it grew still as a tomb.

Until sunlight beaming through the canopy of leaves caught and danced off the woman's extended hand, drawing Caden's attention to the gold ring adorning her thumb. His body tightened, cold with recognition. It was Ronan's. By his father's aching bones, now he knew what had become of his brother.

"Cursed Gowrys!" Caden started for the woman.

It was all the provocation the wolf needed. Instinctively, Caden drew his knife. He heard the woman's "No, Faol!" Saw relief turn to horror as she rose too late to stop the beast. Watched as the white fury seemingly took flight, coming straight at him. There was no time to think. Only to drive the dagger deep into the animal's throat. Its running leap took Caden down. As he fell, his sense of place and motion slowed, giving him plenty of time to jerk the knife, making certain the wolf's lifeline had been severed. But no chance to brace himself. He struck the ground with a bone-jarring thud. The beast's hot blood spurted over him, its last growl filling Caden's nostrils with feral breath.

But it was the anguished wail from the woman that seized his senses. Before Caden could throw the animal off him, she pulled it away.

Hysterical, sobbing and mumbling, she held the wolf's head, oblivious to the blood ruining her tattered blue gown.

"My fault," she groaned, rocking back and forth. "Oh, Faol ... m-my fault."

So much for the shape-shifting legend. She was just a madwoman who'd made a pet of a wolf. A madwoman who'd killed his brother. The woman his father had hunted all these years. Maybe, at last, she would be the key to Tarlach's approval.

"Seize her," Caden ordered, climbing to his feet. "And skin the wolf. 'Twill make a fine trophy."

His order penetrated the captive's fit of grief. "Nay," she sobbed, swatting at the men who reluctantly approached her.

More superstitious fools.

"L—" She forced steel into her voice. "Leave us be."

"She's naught but a weeping female with no more powers than that dead wolf," Caden admonished them. "Seize her."

The men moved in, but still no one dared touch her. No one but the huntsman from Gwynedd. Yet as he reached for her, she stiffened, lifting a face to him smeared with the blood of the beast she'd nuzzled in her agony. Caden didn't know if it was the sight of such beauty despoiled by savagery or the way she curled her lip at him, wolf-like, that made the man pause.

"Touch me, and I'll draw blood," she growled lowly. Gone was the broken demeanor, and in its place was something else entirely.

The sinewy way she moved her body, crouching, shifting back on her haunches, it was unworldly. "One bite or a scratch from me, and men will be hunting you for your pelt come nightfall."

Heming glanced at Caden, unnerved by the threat. "I say kill her, dead as the wolf." Stepping back, he slipped his bow off his shoulder.

What game did she play? For surely she could do no harm to them. Certainly she couldn't turn them into wolves as she suggested.

"She plays at your fear," Caden said. "And you're the fool for believing her."

"Her mother was a witch," someone in the company reminded him.

"Aye, and *she's* a witch who killed my brother. See, she wears the O'Byrne ring." Pure gold it was.

The woman leapt to her feet, hands poised claw-like as she turned, glaring at Caden. "Nay," she said. "One of you killed him, as sure as you killed Faol. And there's the horse to prove it." She jerked her finger at Ballach. "Speckled as the day I last saw it."

"God in Heaven," Gillis said, crossing himself. "She turned Ronan into a wolf."

The possibility staggered Caden for a moment.

"And I'll do the same to you, if you so much as touch me," she warned Heming.

The man took another step back, preparing his bow. "Give me the word, milord, and I'll put an arrow between her eyes."

This was nonsense. "You may be crazy, woman, but you've no more power than I," Caden retorted.

"Better to kill her and be sure," Heming told him. He nocked an arrow, eager.

Too eager, a small voice told Caden. "Hold, huntsman. I'd have her alive."

Caden made to grab her arm, but the wench was as fast as she was cunning. With a twist, she bolted toward the waterfall. Caden pursued her, determined to show his men there was nothing to fear, but slight as she was, she seemed to work her way through the trees like the wind, while he caught the slap of the brush and branches in her wake.

"Shall I loose the hound, milord?" Gillis called after him.

"Nay—" Caden broke off with a curse, spitting out a mouthful of leaves. Suddenly the left side of his head exploded in pain. Once his vision cleared, he saw her loose another stone. Instinctively he raised his hand and deflected it, though its sting shot from his wrist up his arm like a lighting bolt. His arm grew numb as the prickling burn ebbed.

Caden leaned into a tree, heaving a sigh of relief. His arm was heavy, painful to lift, but he still could feel the rough bark against his skin. Sure, he'd struck his elbow and felt the same sensations. No witchcraft like that which had left his father's axe arm useless for life.

Still, she *was* as canny and dangerous as her wolf.

He flexed his fingers, satisfied he was unharmed. "Surround the pool," he shouted to the others, who scrambled after him. "Don't let her escape, but I'll be the one to take her."

Although from the anxiety drawing their faces, he needn't worry about someone taking his prize. Gaze narrowing in determination, Caden brushed away the blood her first stone had drawn from his temple and strode at his leisure to close the distance between them.

There was nowhere else for her to go now, but into the pool at the base of the waterfall.

Which she did. And straight into the cascading white water pouring down the cliffside, where she vanished.

Oaths and cries of astonishment echoed among the men who saw the roaring water curtain swallow her.

"By my faith, she's vanished."

"Turned to water like a fairy."

"'Tis just as well. No good can come of this."

Caden was stunned as well, but more from surprise than fear. *Clever girl, this one.*

Drawing his sword, Caden plunged into the pool, disrupting the plant growth that still swayed and quivered in her wake. Had she been supernatural, her path wouldn't have been marked. The water was a sharp breath short of freezing, seeping into his boots, soaking them. She'd pay well for this … and the hound her wolf killed. After he presented her to Tarlach and showed the old man that his fears were for naught.

Standing before the fall, Caden poked his sword into the wet curtain. He couldn't see her, but he knew she was there. He'd held flesh and blood in his hand earlier, nothing more. But the blade touched nothing but the water pouring over it. He extended the sword even deeper, until the fall threatened to consume him as well. He felt space behind it. Space enough to hide a woman.

And space enough for him to enter. Using the sword as a probe, he forced his way through the downpour pounding on his broad shoulders, eyes shut until the water eased away to naught but a mist. Caden blinked away the water, his gaze settling on the woman pressed against the stone wall at her back.

"My father's been waiting years to meet you"—his lips curled with sarcasm—"Milady *Wolf.*"

Even with her soaked gown plastered against her body, she was a handsome woman. Slight compared to Rhianon, but handsome nonetheless. Had she thrown herself at his mercy, Caden may have felt more charitable toward her, but his soaked clothes and bleeding temple, not to mention one dead and costly hound, had done little to improve his humor.

Terror seized her face as he started toward her. Good, he wanted her to be afraid of him. She should be. Her white fingers splayed against the wall as if drawing strength from it. Or perhaps she was grappling for a weapon for her incredible aim. She began to waver, as if trying to decide whether to make another run for it, or stay and face her fate.

"You can't escape," he told her. "Your days of haunting the hills are done ... wolf-woman."

She shrank away from his approach, but something in her gaze triggered an alarm.

Too late. His boot slid out from under him on a slick patch of pond growth, sending him into a groin-tearing split. But for the buckling of his knee, which slammed onto the hard rock beneath, it might have been weeks before he could walk with a normal gait.

"By all the gods, I'll—" His minced oath broke off.

She was gone, out into the sunlight.

Swearing to diminish the torture of overextended muscle, Caden regained his footing and followed. The brilliant light and water temporarily blinded him, but he could hear the shouts of his men as they tried to stop her. To warn her. But from what?

It wasn't until his gaze adjusted to the light that he saw them gathered at the crag holding the pond nestled in its belly.

No.

Heart sinking to his stomach, Caden slogged through the water and peered over its hedge of rock. Below was another shelf of ragged rock. And splayed upon it was the raven-haired nymph, still as death.

Heming's voice penetrated the disbelief numbing Caden's brain. "I tried to stop her, sir, but she wrestled free of my grasp and sooner than be captured, jumped."

"Fetch her body then," Caden said woodenly. He'd wanted to frighten her as she'd done so many, but not kill her. From the moment she'd looked into his eyes, pleading for the life of her wolf, he'd seen something special.

He shrugged off the pall of guilt smothering him. Regardless, Tarlach would have to acknowledge him for accomplishing what neither the chieftain nor his idolized eldest son could. It was going to be a good night at Glenarden.

CHAPTER FIFTEEN

It was well past nun day when Ronan reached the plateau overlooking the river where Glenarden's keep rose in regal fashion, banners flying over its stockade. He'd passed through acres of freshly plowed farmland sowed with peas, beans, and corn. Seen carefully chosen lumber cut and stacked at the edge of Glenarden's thick forest—some for sale and some for further construction within the walls of the stockade. It appeared that Caden had slid into Ronan's role well—a surprise given his younger brother's usual indifference to such matters.

It was partly pleasing. Ronan wanted Caden to be a capable administrator. But someone had tried to kill Ronan. Was he a chance horse thief or the hireling of an usurper? Regardless, Ronan now wore the simple garb of a farmer, borrowed from a trusted servant who'd been out in one of the fields. If someone at Glenarden wanted him dead, better Ronan slip in unnoticed to observe the changes that had taken place … and to speak to his father.

Slipping through the hall was easier than he'd anticipated. It teemed with servants preparing for the Pascal celebration—tomorrow, if his sense of time was right. Brother Martin had said he was invited to officiate.

"You!" Lady Rhianon pointed an imperious finger at Ronan. Clad in apron and kerchief, she jerked it toward a heaping barrow of fresh hay. "Help spread the new threshing. I should hate to choke on dust still floating in the air during supper."

Wondering how the old steward Vychan had accepted her take-over, Ronan bowed his head in acknowledgment and walked to the barrow. 'Twould be quite a setback for the imperious Rhianon when Brenna became mistress, especially now that his wife was with child. Brenna had told Ronan the morning after their wedding night that she had conceived. And knowing his new wife as he did, he believed her.

With an armload of threshing, he worked his way toward the back of the hall, where Tarlach's bedchamber had been made of an anteroom. The door was closed. After spreading the hay along the wall, Ronan stepped into the chamber. It was dark ... and musty. The housekeeping outside had clearly been overlooked in here.

Ronan couldn't see a thing. If not for a small lamp on a table and his knowledge of where Tarlach's bed lay, he'd have been lost indeed. By the time he reached it, his eyes had adjusted more to the dim light. He could make out his father's sleeping form, curled on its side.

And it was after midday. Usually by this time, Tarlach would have ridden over the fields with him.

Alarmed, Ronan touched Tarlach's shoulder and shook it gently. "Father, the day is half wasted."

"Get away." Tarlach shook off Ronan's hand. "Leave me die in peace."

"Are you ill?" Ronan found his forehead beneath a tangled shock of hair. Save Tarlach's blinking eyes, his face was all but covered in it.

With a low growl, Tarlach rolled to his back, the gnarled fist of his good arm drawn. "By the Devil's own breath, I'll have you—"

"Father, it's Ronan." Ronan tugged off the hat so that the dim flame on the bedside table illuminated his face.

Tarlach's fierceness gave way to a sob. Half fear and half hope, it gurgled in his throat. He shrank into the coverlets.

"I'm no ghost." Ronan reached for his trembling hand and squeezed it. "See? Flesh and bone, same as you."

The old man tugged Ronan's hand to his mouth, kissing it over and over, his groans wrenched from his shuddering chest. He rocked like a child. A drooling, distraught child.

It shook Ronan to the core that the angry, wounded bear Ronan had left behind at Witch's End was reduced to this. The squalor and stench. The behavior. Had Tarlach gone totally mad?

Ronan had been prepared to face the bear. Not this.

He pulled Tarlach upright with the hand his father would not let go. At least his strength survived in that good arm. It felt awkward for Ronan to put his arm around the old man's sob-racked shoulders, but he did so anyway. Ronan hated Tarlach's obsession, but not the man who'd made him his pride and joy.

God, help me. I know not how to deal with this Tarlach.

Ronan heard no answer. Perhaps one had to know God longer than he for prompt replies. Helpless, he simply held Tarlach in his arms until the tears and sobs were exhausted.

Had Caden done this? As soon as Ronan thought it, he minded that the door had not been barred.

Vychan. He was the one who could explain.

Tenderly, Ronan eased away from Tarlach, though he had to pry away the old man's crooked fingers from his hand. "I'm not going anywhere," he promised his father. "I'm only going to send for Vychan. I am not going anywhere."

Once free, Ronan donned the hat again and, opening the door, caught the attention of a passing servant. He changed his voice as best he could.

"Milord calls for Vychan. See to it, woman. Tarlach's in a mood."

The maid gave Ronan a hard look before acknowledging with a disdainful sniff. Clearly the hall staff thought themselves superior to the ones who worked the fields to fill all their bellies.

Behind him, Tarlach pulled himself upright with a rope affixed to a beam for such purpose and swung his bare legs over the edge of the leather-strapped bed. The effort cost him his breath. He held onto the rope as though he might fall back if he let it go. "Where … have you … been?"

"It's a long story, Father. For now, just know that I am returned, hale and hearty."

Hale and hearty enough. The wounds still let him know they were there if he twisted the wrong way or strained overmuch. But his strength had come back. He handled the sword he'd left behind with the field hand well enough.

"Are you well enough to get up and dress?"

Tarlach smiled. At least Ronan thought he did behind that matted bush of a beard. "I am now."

After a short knock, Vychan let himself into the room. "Milord, you're up," he exclaimed, both surprised and pleased, by the sound of it.

"I want a celebration, Vychan. The biggest we've ever had."

"Milady Rhianon is working on that as we speak, milord. But she will be pleased to know you are up and attending."

Tarlach snorted. "Not the Pascal. *There's* the reason." He gestured to the shadows behind the door where Ronan stood.

From the look on Vychan's thin face, Ronan knew the loyal steward had nothing to do with the attack. Pure joy lit upon it. "My lord Ronan!" And then the man grew speechless, a rare occasion in any circumstance, for Vychan always had an opinion.

"Vychan, it is good to see you again, my friend." Ronan grasped his arm firmly. Thin, but wiry like the rest of him. "Now tell me, what has happened to my father, that he lies listless in bed after midday?"

"Your loss, milord. We thought you dead, murdered by the Gowrys."

Stunned, Ronan spun to face his father. "You did this to yourself, when Glenarden needed you more than ever?"

"Your brother was more than eager to take over Glenarden," Tarlach mumbled.

"Not to mention her ladyship," Vychan added, mouth twisted awry.

"As they should have … under Father's approval," Ronan told them.

"Don't lecture me, boy. My old heart has been broken," Tarlach huffed. "And it may take some time for me to gather the pieces. So help me get dressed. I've a celebration to plan."

"Father, I would rather no one know just yet."

"But why, milord?" Vychan asked.

"Because someone attacked me and left me for dead. Someone whom, I think, rode with us at the Witch's End."

For a moment, Ronan thought Tarlach would sink back on the bed. But as the words penetrated, his jaw took on a familiar set. "Would you recognize him?"

Ronan's shoulders dropped. "I was wounded by arrows before he openly attacked me. 'Twas his sword I watched, not his face. But for the interference of a cave hermit, he might have finished me. But the hermit's dog and keen skill with a bow scared off the villain."

Ronan purposely left out Brenna's identity for the time being— and Faol's. He still wasn't sure of Tarlach's state of mind.

"You can't hide in here forever, Son."

"Aye, he's right about that," Vychan chimed in.

True. Even if Ronan could stand the stench, he couldn't remain undetected for long.

"Then let us keep a sharp eye out for any who seem overly astonished or upset at my resurrection from the dead," he agreed at last. "Meanwhile, Vychan …"

"Milord?" the steward replied.

"Have this pigsty cleaned and aired. And a new mattress. And send a man to see Father bathed and shaven properly."

"I'll see to your father myself."

"Do the two of you think I'm deaf?" Tarlach demanded from his bedside. As if to prove himself, he used the rope to pull himself to his feet, but his knees nearly buckled in spite of its support.

The old man had not lost his fight after all.

"Nay, Father, just weaker of body from lazing about and," he added, waving his hand across his nose, "stronger of bouquet."

"I'll have my mustache."

"I'll personally see to it that you do, milord," Vychan assured him.

"And tell that woman we'll sup outside the hall tonight, for there'll be no room for all who will want to see my son again."

"I'll have the bonfires lit," Vychan said, "and help milady set up the guest table at the top of the steps for milord's family and guests." The steward seized Ronan's hand, shaking it again and again. "This is a joyous day, to be sure. I'll have your room restored to you as well."

"Perhaps after the Pascal guests have left. I'm not oaf enough to displace Lady Rhianon without warning."

By then, Ronan would have prepared his family and gone to fetch Brenna. Just the thought of his wife filled him to a completeness he'd never known. As she'd breathed new life into him, Ronan had no doubt that she would do the same to Glenarden.

Somewhere between This World and the Other World lies a place where the spirit may continue its journey forward or go back. Brenna did not want to go back to where danger and treachery awaited her and the tiny life within her womb. She could not see the child's spirit, but held it with her own. The joy was tenable, lifting her into a light so brilliant, she could not see. Yet she knew.

She knew Ealga was there, embracing her and the babe.

And there was her mother and father ... without form, but surrounding her with all that they were. Their love renewed her, vanquishing her pain and fear. Then gently, firmly, they pushed her back toward the bruised and broken body waiting in This World.

"You must return, child."

That voice. She knew it well. Not that of anyone she'd ever known on This Side, but the still, small voice that had been her companion for as long as she remembered. It was the voice of her Shepherd.

"Where have you been?" she shouted at Him. "Why did you let this happen to me and my baby?"

"I will never leave thee nor forsake thee."

"And Faol? He did nothing wrong but love me."

"A gift for a season lives forever in your mind. As for you and your child, you will be safe, for I have plans that you should prosper ... and make my people prosper."

"No."

Never had she spoken so to the Shepherd, but it was too much. More than she could bear.

But the grasp of This World would not relent, no matter how many times Brenna's consciousness recoiled from the sharp pain jabbing at her head. Nausea roiled from her belly to her throat. Every joint screamed. And then the agony let her go once more to drift, beyond physical sensation. But this time there was no loving embrace of light, only pain-free darkness. Her soul sank into it. She was back in This World to stay ... at least for a season. And it didn't feel as if her Shepherd had returned with her.

The gray-marble of smoke hovered over the village before thinning ever upward as Glenarden's horsemen approached the gatehouse. A banner with pale blue and black colors of Rhianon's visiting family flew opposite the red, black, and silver of the O'Byrne. The guests from Gwynedd had arrived. A glance at the horizon told Caden there would be time before purple twilight gathered over the western hills to wash away the blood and filth of the hunt for the feasting to follow.

His procession of triumph, though, would not wait. He had caught the long-sought witchwoman. The pall of the prophecy would lift forever when he presented her to Tarlach. Granted, Caden would have preferred presenting the living, breathing, helpless creature whom Tarlach had feared for so long. Even if his father didn't recognize Caden as rightful lord of Glenarden, the people would recognize the superstitious old man for the mad soul he was. This was the beginning of a new age for Glenarden.

But the fall had killed the madwoman. Her breathless, broken body was rolled in a blanket and secured across Ballach's flank. Behind them followed Caden's fellow hunters with the fine bucks they'd come upon not long after she'd thrown herself to her death … and a make-shift rack with the trophy wolf skin stretched for proper drying.

The guards in the gatehouse hailed the approaching hunters and opened the gates to receive them. Caden slowed Ballach. Where was the crowd? Had he not sent runners ahead to let the keep know the men returned, not only with meat for the tables, but a spectacular prize? He'd sworn them to secrecy as to the latter's nature, of course. Yet, aside from the usual watchmen manning the gate, there were no onlookers to cheer his return.

Uneasiness pricked at his senses. This was not right.

"Tell the men to have their weapons ready," he said to Heming.

"Aye, something is amiss to be sure," the Gwynedd man agreed.

"How goes the day?" Caden shouted to one of the guards. He recognized the man, as well as his companions. "Where is our welcome?"

"On the inner grounds of the keep, milord. 'Tis a most wondrous day for Glenarden."

Well, his father wasn't dead. *Wondrous* would hardly be used to describe a clan chief's death. Yet something clearly had happened.

"And why is this day so wondrous?" Caden asked, for clearly the oaf was going to shed no more light on the mystery.

"We are instructed by Milord Tarlach to tell you Glenarden is received of a most welcome and esteemed guest."

Tarlach was up and about? No amount of beseeching on Caden's part had roused the old man from that putrid den of grief. By the gods, what game was the madman about? And before Gwynedd's guests? Rhianon must be as fitful as a hen in a fox's teeth at this.

Unless Arthur had come to Glenarden. That had to be it. They had a royal visitor.

"Enter straight and proud, men," Caden called over his shoulder. "It seems we have an honored and unexpected guest to welcome."

The village beyond the stockade enclosure was all but abandoned. A few dogs frolicked unchecked, driving fowl up to the low-hanging thatch of the rooftops. Ballach strained at the rein, eager to return to the stable and a handsome helping of grain. Struck with an anticipation of a different sort, Caden allowed the steed to break into a slow canter.

Because of his maternal connections to nobility, he'd grown accustomed to Queen Gwenhyfar's visits, but Arthur had never been to Glenarden.

Ahead, the great hall rose in its stone and timber majesty above a skirt of tents, set up by Gwynedd's entourage. Rhianon had insisted on preparing the master bedchamber for her parents, while the rest of the visitors would sleep either in the hall or in their tents. But if Arthur were here, new arrangements would have to be made.

And given the massive spread of people, that was surely the case. The Pendragon himself, Dux Bellorum of Britain ... *Caden's* guest. Pride swelled in Caden's chest, leaving hardly room for breath.

The crowd parted to allow Caden and his men to ride straight toward the steps, where a banquet table had been set. Here and there amidst the carpet of people, the smoke of bonfires wafted up, indicating the festivities were expected to continue well into the spring evening.

Caden reined in Ballach. Where was Arthur's banner of the Red Dragon?

"Welcome home, Son." Definitely not at death's door, Tarlach shoved himself to his feet behind the board table. He was not without trembling and leaned heavily on the board before him. Still, his great mustache had been trimmed, hanging like an oxbow on an otherwise clean-shaven face, and his silver-gold hair had been combed and braided. Next to him, the seat of honor stood empty.

The bench Caden usually shared with Rhianon was empty as
well. But then, she might be busy. Perhaps even washing the guests'
feet, as was only fit hospitality.

Caden nodded to his father-in-law, Idwal, and his wife, Enda. "I
bid my Gwynedd family welcome."

Idwal and his lady nodded stiffly, both shifting uncomfortable
gazes from Tarlach to Caden. Perhaps his father had insulted them?

"We have a great s*h*uprise this day," Tarlach informed him.

No. Tarlach was not going to steal his moment.

"As have we, Father," Caden announced. Not even Arthur would
take this from him.

Caden slid to the ground from Ballach's back. Pain burned in
his overstretched groin muscles, but he hid it. Instead, he worked
loose the knots securing the body of the witchwoman. After heaving
her over his shoulder, he approached the steps of the keep, his limp
slight. At their bottom, he unrolled the blanket, depositing the lifeless body at the bottom of the steps before the head table.

"Behold, Father, the wolf-woman … the *witch* you've feared all
these years. *Brenna of Gowrys!*"

A collective gasp erupted from the crowd. The closest onlookers took a step back as one. The old chief blanched, pale as the
still figure on the ground. Clutching at his chest, Tarlach sank into
his chair, shaken to the core at the sight of the still and bloodied
corpse.

Suddenly everyone was talking, staring, pointing. Caden stood
proudly over his prize, taking his due recognition. Like Beowulf over
Grendel, like Jason with the Golden Fleece, like—

"What … have … you … *done?*"

The words that rose above and quelled the cacophony came at Caden like the roar of the beasts of old. No war cry Caden had ever heard compared to their rage … and lust for blood.

The urge to race toward Ballach and his sword stopped as though hitting a mountain wall at the sight of his eldest brother, dressed in the finest red, black, and gray brat and embroidered linen tunic—the one that Tarlach refused to give to Caden.

Ronan! Caden blinked in disbelief, unable to move. *But Ronan is dead.*

At least Ronan had the pallor of the dead. His eldest brother stood equally frozen, not by the sight of Caden, but by that of the body of the woman lying at his feet. Then with an unearthly howl of rage—or agony—Ronan came down the steps in two bounds. Caden stepped back, bracing himself, but instead of attacking him, Ronan gathered the wolf-woman up in his arms.

"Brenna!" His sob was loud enough to wake the dead in Erin a sea away. "Brenna!" He kissed her face. Her head. Her neck. Again and again. And shook her.

Caden couldn't believe what he saw. The ghost of his brother, come back in the flesh, hysterical over the death of a witch he'd hunted a lifetime.

"Come back to me, Brenna of the Hallowed Hills."

Brenna of the Hallowed Hills?

Ronan was as crazed as Tarlach.

"At least we know that Ronan was not the wolf," someone observed dryly from among the horsemen.

Bewitched, Caden thought. *That's the only explanation. Maybe something to do with the ring on her finger.*

Ronan gently laid her down and raised her hand to his lips, kissing it as though it were some religious relic.

"She killed herself," Caden heard himself saying. "Ran over a cliff, rather than be caught. She went crazy when I killed the wolf, but it attacked—"

Without warning, Ronan shot up from his crouched position and drove what remained of Caden's breath out of his body. He struck the ground, his elder brother atop him. Instinctively, he fought back, striking Ronan in the jaw, but the blow didn't faze him. Caden drew up his leg in an attempt to throw Ronan off and the pain that ripped through his groin nearly made him faint. Yet he dare not. Not with the feral look in Ronan's gaze. Not with the snarling flash of his teeth. His time with the wolf-woman showed in his every mannerism.

Why didn't someone try to pull them apart? Ronan was mad, and Caden's men knew he'd been hurt. Caden swung at Ronan again, blinded by pain. He missed his brother's face, hitting him squarely in the shoulder. With an agonized cry, Ronan gave way, stumbling backward, favoring it. Having found a weakness, Caden hit him again.

Where was everyone? What was the matter with them? Not even Tarlach allowed his sons to fight. Matters between him and Ronan were often settled far away from the keep and their father's eye.

Ronan rolled away with a grunt and to his feet, shaking his head as if to shake away his obvious pain.

"Caden!" Heming tossed Caden his sword.

Caden seized it and gingerly hauled himself upright. He could hardly straighten. Blood ran from his nose down the front of his hunting vest.

"Use that sword, Brother, because if you do not, I will kill you." Head lowered, holding his bad shoulder with his free hand, Ronan peered at him as though to run him through with gaze alone.

"Then come get your due, *Brother,*" Caden taunted. If Ronan were to die on his sword, best he run into it, because at that moment, Caden could not bear to step forward. Instead he braced as the steam of Ronan's fury built, heaving breath by heaving breath.

But Caden didn't want to kill him. He wanted to find out what had happened to him. He tightened his grip on the handle of the blade. Perhaps he could knock some sense into Ronan with the pommel.

"Someone stop him, before I have to draw his blood," Caden shouted to the onlookers. What was the matter with the lot? They were as frozen as a winter lake while Ronan seethed, rocking, ready to charge. Ready to—

His brother took one step forward and stumbled to a sharp halt, reined in by a woman's voice. "No, Ronan!"

Caden turned to see the source of the voice and understood why no one had moved to interfere with his battle. Indeed, he felt the white wash of fear drain blood from his face, his very limbs. The dead had come to life. There could be no other explanation, for surely she'd had no beat in her throat when Caden checked. Yet the wolf-woman struggled to her feet, her long black hair tangled with bits of heather and brush, her gown tattered and stained with blood. The sight rendered Caden as motionless as the rest.

But not Tarlach. The chieftain trembled visibly, but he took action. "Unleash the hounds," he ordered. "Kill her. A fine prize to the man who—"

"Death to the man who listens," Ronan countered, bellowing even louder.

But Gillis had already unleashed the wolfhound. It bounded toward the unsteady female, spurred on by his attack command. Before Caden knew what his brother was about, Ronan snatched away Caden's sword to race to her aid. Yet Caden knew Ronan would not reach the woman in time.

But someone else did. Out the multitudes stepped Daniel of Gowrys.

"Cú, to me!" the youth commanded.

Instead of attacking the woman, the dog that had been the boy's constant companion since his arrival stopped, scattering dirt at the woman's feet, and bolted toward Daniel. Never without pilfered food, the hostage rewarded Cú with some dried meat.

"Blessed be," the wolf-woman whispered. Swaying unsteadily, she started toward the boy and the dog. "You have a gif—"

"Brenna!"

The world resumed its right motion. Ronan threw aside the blade and caught this Brenna as her knees gave way. With a grimace, he hauled her into his arms. "Blessed be, God has given you back to me, Wife."

"Wife!" Tarlach gasped.

"Wife?" Caden echoed. Surely this was a dream. A nightmare. Nothing so far-fetched was possible.

"Tell me this is not so, Son," their father demanded weakly. Only the astounded silence of the multitude enabled him to be heard. "It cannot be. You know the prophecy. You heard it firsthand. And already you and your brother try to kill each other."

Ronan cradled her to his bosom, stubborn as a bear protecting
its young. "*With a peace beyond your ken,*" he reminded Tarlach. "You
always leave that part of the prophecy out, Father. And loving her has
brought me that, Father. That peace beyond your ken."

He lifted her higher, as though to show her to all. "Mark it
well," he shouted. "Brenna of Gowrys is my wife and mother of your
grandson. Heir to Glenarden *and to Gowrys.*"

"Not as long as I live!" Tarlach struck the table with his fist, but
his effort was more than he had strength to carry out. Those who
did not see it never heard it. He reached for Ronan as though his life
depended on it.

"Bewitched." With that garbled sob, Tarlach's panic-stricken
eyes closed.

Chapter Sixteen

Rumors abounded. The wolf-woman had been caught. A dead witch had come to life. Ronan had been bewitched. Now the chief of Glenarden lay on his deathbed.

Ronan paid the rumors no heed. His father had made his choice—the same superstitious mistake he'd made years earlier. If he was against Brenna, then Tarlach was against Ronan.

All Ronan cared about at this point was that Brenna was alive.

If he so much as reflected upon the vision of her lying in the dirt, tattered and white as death itself, his stomach turned so fiercely that he feared fainting. Or a reason-blinded rage stalled his brain. Neither extreme was familiar to Ronan, but then neither was this love he felt for his wife.

But she breathed, blessed be, though her semiconscious state was fraught with moans each time she moved, or was moved. And she was sick. Wretchedly so. Therein was another change Ronan saw in himself. Before, such things had made him as queasy as the person who was ill. But for Brenna, he would do anything.

The village midwife had come to his aid as he carried Brenna into the keep. Old Dara had witnessed the scene, saw the dead come to life, yet showed no fear as she gently washed away the dried blood on Brenna's flesh. There'd been so much. Thankfully, most of it was Faol's. He'd given his life to save her.

Caden swore he'd had no choice but to kill the wolf or be killed. He said he'd not harmed Brenna. That the dogs had followed Faol to her. He'd expressed incredulity that she'd tried to save the beast, racing into the savage animal fight without fear and emerging without so much as a scratch when not even Gillis would attempt to interfere. But in her panic to escape Caden and his men, she'd gone over a rocky ledge and plunged three spears' lengths to yet another ragged protrusion. Far enough to break bones, yet her worst wound was the gash on her head.

"I thought her dead," Caden declared to Ronan in defense of the unceremonious transport he'd given her to Glenarden. "Life did not beat in her throat, nor did she draw breath."

The men vouched for his brother's story. All of it.

"When I saw the ring, I thought she'd been responsible for your death … er … disappearance," Caden amended.

That his brother had been truly threatened by Faol, Ronan was forced to accept. He'd seen firsthand how protective the beast was of Brenna. But it was Caden's zeal to capture the wolf-witch that Ronan thought responsible for his wife's near death.

"Milord," Dara said, straightening up from the sweet-scented bed that Caden and Rhianon had prepared for her parents in the upstairs master chamber, "if you would send in a servant to help me, I'll see what injuries lie beneath this rag of a dress and put a clean shift on …" Dara paused before deciding her next words. "Your *lady*."

She chose well. But Ronan was loath to leave Brenna's side, for even a moment.

"I'll help you, Dara. Brenna *is* my wife," he insisted. "Wed before God four days ago."

Dara gave him a stern look. "This is woman's work, milord. On my life, I will look after Lady Brenna. 'Twas her own sainted mother who taught me many things about the childbed."

Ronan blinked in surprise. "*You* were schooled at Glaston?" Dara was but a peasant, uneducated beyond her common knowledge of nature's secrets.

"Nay, milord. I was midwife during your birth," she reminded him, "long before my hair turned the color of dull iron. But for Lady Joanna's instruction, both you and your mother might have been lost."

"I'm sorry, Dara. I'd forgotten."

"Worry not, milord. I've special cures for the womenfolk. Now do as I say, that your wife might rest clean and comfortable as my herbs will make her, given her condition."

Ronan scowled. "But you said you saw no sign of broken bones or internal injuries."

The lines furrowing Dara's shriveled face lifted with her laugh. "Aye, milord, but that doesna change the fact that she's carryin' your child. Both mother and bairn have wills of iron, it seems."

"You can tell so early?"

Dara's humor wavered. "I take the word of milord … for now. Now let me to my work, so that I can see if it's wishful thinkin' you're havin' or if God has seen fit to fulfill the prophecy. This old head can think of nothin' short of a blood heir to both clans to settle the madness at last."

God. Dare Ronan believe the Creator God was truly with him? It was something he longed for with desperation. He'd need help of the supernatural to offset the superstition and treachery plaguing Glenarden.

Had he not faltered in his determination to confront Tarlach upon his arrival, Ronan's announcement might not have been so disastrous. Instead, Ronan had left Tarlach to gather himself properly and gone to bathe and dress in his finery. And in doing so, come face-to-face with Lady Rhianon in the adjoining chamber, now turned chapel from the bower she and Caden shared.

Such a shriek he'd never heard. Down she went in a dead faint. Had he not been quick on his feet, Rhianon might have crumpled hard upon the floor. Instead he caught her and broke her fall. From that point, the word that Ronan had returned from the dead spread like a wildfire from one end of Glenarden to the other. Its people began to gather in the inner yard to see for themselves. With a hasty change of clothing and a still hysterical Rhianon in her servant Keena's care, Ronan went straight to assisting Vychan in taking charge, for the party from Gwynedd had arrived.

The guests.

Ronan was certain his brother Caden entertained their guests, but he would check on his way to his father's chamber. Besides, he needed to speak to his people. They deserved an explanation. Or as much of one as Ronan could give them.

God, You have given me Brenna and spared her for a purpose. I believed her when she said as much. Give me words, for my brain is fraught with worry.

Ronan descended the steps to the main level of the hall and

sent one of the housemaids to Dara. The great room was astir with servants coming and going from the kitchen, but the main of the celebration was still in the courtyard of the keep. Taking advantage of the opportunity to see Tarlach unnoticed, Ronan started for the door to the antechamber, guarded by a servant. On the way he spied the young man who'd stopped Tarlach's wolf-hound from attacking Brenna. The lad was wrestling playfully with the dog.

"Daniel of Gowrys. The hostage," Dara had told him.

Upon seeing Ronan, Daniel's boyish grin and play with Cú ceased.

Ronan approached the lad, extending his hand. "I owe you a great deal of thanks, Daniel of Gowrys."

Instead of accepting it, Gowrys stared at it as if it oozed with the pox. "Is it true she is Brenna of Gowrys?"

"Aye. She and her wolf saved my life."

"Then she didn't know who you were."

"No, she didn't. But it was a strange rescue, one that could only have been arranged by God, for nature went against itself."

Daniel's gaze sharpened with interest.

One person at a time. If that's what it took, Ronan would repeat the strange story to every man, woman, and child in Glenarden *and* of the Gowrys. So he did, riveting the young man's attention with how Faol had risked his life to save Ronan and keep him warm in the snow until it was safe for Brenna to help him.

"And for it, his skin hangs like a trophy." Daniel jerked his head to where it hung on its drying frame next to the elegant hunting tapestry adorning the wall. Another wave of rage broke over

Ronan at the sight. With a smothered oath, he strode over to the wolfskin and took it down. He'd not have Brenna see it day after day. Not like this.

"Will you do her another kindness, Daniel?" When the youth didn't answer, Ronan explained. "I would not have my wife reminded so cruelly of her loss ... *our* loss."

It surprised Ronan to hear himself admit the wolf had worked its way into his heart as well. But for Faol—

"Will you take it to the tanner's shed and ask the man to keep it for me?"

"He won't listen to the likes of—" The lad broke off as Ronan withdrew his money pouch and retrieved two coins, ancient and Roman, but of value nonetheless.

"One for each of you," he said, handing them over.

"And what do you think you're doing with that?" a belligerent voice boomed from the hall entrance. Caden staggered inside, then recovered himself. "I made the kill. It belongs to me."

"That wolf belonged to us—my wife and I. The sight of it would pain her." Ronan would not waver on this. "Given the damage you've done, giving up the hide is the least you can do."

"You are only lord by a thread, Brother, so tread lightly."

"And until our father or kinsmen elect you, that thread still holds. 'Tis you who'd best tread lightly."

"My wife wishes our bedchamber returned to her parents and then to us." Caden's hand rested on the dagger sheathed at his waist. Drinking increased his aggressive and impulsive nature.

"Better we remain closer to Tarlach, so you shall have it," Ronan conceded. Sleeping in the master chamber didn't matter a whit to him. What Ronan wanted to do was finish the fight Brenna had interrupted. *"After* my wife is well enough to move."

"Can you not carry her to the antechamber?"

"Can your wife's relatives not sleep there?"

The questions spurred the men closer, step by step.

"They are our guests."

"Your reckless chase put my bride in that room."

"You married our sworn enemy."

"She saved my life." Ronan could smell the wine on Caden's breath. It wouldn't do to push him further. But questions burned amidst his anger and frustration. "After I was abandoned by you and left for dead, Brother."

Ronan anticipated Caden's flashpoint and seized his wrist as he went for the dagger, staying it.

"I thought you'd returned to the keep," Caden grated out through clenched teeth.

Faces nearly touching, pure muscle to muscle, each held his own. The dagger rocked between them.

"You took my place readily." Ronan stepped forward, forcing Caden to brace himself with a backward step. A wince grazed his younger brother's face. Sweat began to film on his brow as it did on Ronan's.

"Avenged … your death," Caden pointed out through the strain.

How many times they had played at this, two bulls with locked horns, neither giving. They'd beat each other bloody, return to the keep, and swear to Tarlach they'd fallen.

"Your drink has impaired your brain, Brother." Faith, his wounds were beginning to halt his breath. "I … will … not … yield … on the wolfskin … or my wife's … welfare."

Ronan threw his entire weight into Caden. Caden's stance broke. He stumbled and caught himself against the wall, cursing all that didn't curse back. The confrontation, combined with a wolfhound's excited bark, stopped the servants scurrying about in their tracks.

Ronan kept his eyes on Caden but shouted over his shoulder, "Carry on. We have guests to attend to. My brother and I are agreed that Glenarden's hospitality comes first, are we not?" he asked Caden.

"It is *all* we are agreed upon, Brother." Caden held up his fingers, as though rolling wool between them. "By a thread, Brother. By a thread."

This was far from over.

Ronan relaxed only slightly as Caden tore away and staggered out through the kitchen.

"I'd be watching my back, if I were you, sir," Daniel said, his blue eyes dark with warning. "Least when I'm locked up at night, mine's covered."

CHAPTER SEVENTEEN

Brenna drifted in and out of pain, as if her brain were trying to break free of her skull, rendering her helpless as a babe. She had no choice but to trust the tea her wizened caregiver offered her. But it *felt* right. None of Brenna's innate alarms sounded when something passed her lips that could cause harm. There was no check in her spirit. No tingling in her jaw muscles. No palpable draining of strength. If only her mind were as keen as her other senses. And her guilt.

If she'd not been so preoccupied with Ronan's departure, she'd not have exposed herself so. Faol might have escaped. She wouldn't have plunged over the ledge. Had her feet not tangled in her wet skirts, she could have made the leap, jolted, but sound. Though where she'd go from there, she'd had no idea. All she wanted to do was run. Run from the hunters, the dogs, the sight of Faol's lifeless body, his beautiful white fur stained bright with blood.

Faol.

A sob tore from Brenna's throat. Then another, and another. "Faol."

"Hush, *a stór.*" Arms cradled her. Strong and familiar arms. "I know, I know." The voice of love. Of her husband. "Would God that I could take your pain."

Ronan squeezed her as though he might force it out. It hurt, but not as much as his intention soothed her wounded spirit. Brenna wanted to look into his eyes but feared the head misery would come back. In this semidream world, it remained at bay.

"But you are safe and alive. I owe God my life for that."

God. The irony of Ronan's statement was not lost on her. When he'd been angry at God, even doubted His existence, Brenna had insisted God had brought them together.

"Faol was ours for a season, but God spared you and the bairn."

The baby. Brenna remembered its bright spirit, part of her and yet not. And Ealga ... and her parents. And the gentle voice of her Shepherd saying the same thing. He had a plan for her, for Ronan, for their child.

Like before, Brenna hesitated, not really wanting to abandon the space between This World and the Other Side.

"Come back to me, Brenna. I need you as I need breath," Ronan pleaded.

Love. Pure love. It poured from those words into her ears, filling her, forcing out her dread. Even her pain, she realized as she pried open her eyes. At least it was bearable, not waiting with swords and hammers to beat her back into unconsciousness.

"Ronan." She breathed his name.

His face took shape above hers, strong, handsome, fraught with a mix of concern and ...

"Praise be to God, you are back with us!"

Joy.

"Shall I call Dara?" The mattress beneath them crackled as he leaned over and kissed her on the forehead. "Do you need anything?"

Brenna shook her head, slowly. "Where are we?" She smelled lavender ... and heather.

"In my bedchamber, Wife. Where you belong."

Fragments of memory flashed before her. People. A multitude. Ronan fierce as she'd ever seen him, about to charge a warrior's sword. An old man shouting, clearly disturbed.

"How?"

Brenna listened as Ronan explained how his brother had come across Faol during a hunt.

So the blond giant who'd killed Faol was Ronan's brother.

"Caden thought you dead. So did"—Ronan's voice broke—"I."

Brenna raised her hand to his cheek. "I was," she whispered softly. "The Shepherd sent me back to you."

He nestled her hand to his lips. "I'm so sorry for leaving you. I should have taken you with me. It's my—"

"Shush. My own pain is enough to bear without yours. God has a plan for us ... for our love and our child."

Skepticism lifted his brow. "Are you sure?"

Fear circled like carrion over Brenna's spirit. Still, she nodded and sought his embrace. There it felt as though nothing could harm her.

We are troubled on every side....

Even in her weakened state, Brenna knew that her husband had at least one nemesis among the many surrounding her. One who wanted him dead ... nearly killed him. She prayed on.

... yet not in despair. Thou art with us. If You are for us ...

A knock sounded on the door before she could add, *... we have nothing to fear.*

"Milord, it's Dara. I have the lady's breakfast."

Dara. The name of the healer who'd tended her.

"A moment, Dara." Ronan rolled out of the bed, slinging aside the covers. Naked to the waist of his laced braccae, he hustled across the plank flooring and opened the door. "She's with us again, Dara."

The pure joy of his words put a smile on Brenna's face. But secretly she wondered if she'd have been able to finish her prayer with a whole heart after all that had happened. Her soul cried out in panic.

Father God, help my unbelief.

Ronan couldn't believe his eyes. Within an hour of taking breakfast, Brenna entered the hall, lovely in a green hand-me-down from Rhianon, who was suddenly glad to have a sister. Ronan resisted asking what had changed her since yesterday when she could be heard screaming that he was supposed to be dead and that witch had no business in Rhianon's bedchamber. But then, Rhianon was fickle and high-strung.

Brenna, on the other hand, was ... *full of grace*, he thought, watching as she hugged Dara and thanked her for her help.

"With just a few stitches, she made it fit," Brenna told Ronan, turning carefully so that he might see. And then to Dara, "You must have tea with me after the Pascal service, milady, so that you can tell me more of my mother." The moment Brenna had heard Brother Martin was giving the Pascal service, she had insisted she was well enough to attend.

"Ach, I'm no lady, milady," Dara protested. "I'm just a lowly servant … a midwife. Not born of the blood like yourself."

"You are my friend," Brenna insisted, turning to Ronan. "Tell her, Ronan."

Ronan's lips twitched. "You heard my lady, Dara."

Dara puffed up, affording him a sharp look. "I know my place, milord, and 'tis best for her ladyship if she learns hers."

Dara was right. If Brenna was to be the queen of Glenarden, she had to learn to act like one, lest the people disrespect her. Though Ronan loved her as she was, uninhibited and filled with life and love.

"In time, Dara." He couldn't resist touching the ugly purple swelling running from under Brenna's hairline to cover her left temple. Such bruises were matched in many places hidden by the garment. Each one, he knew. He'd helped Dara rub ointment on them. Or, rather, Dara had humored him by letting him help.

Funny how a woman who was almost a nonentity in his past figured so prominently in his present. How many other good people had Ronan overlooked in his prideful role of princeling?

"Oh my!" Brenna's gasp banished his introspection as she took in the huge expanse of the hall, the weaponry hung on the walls and beams, the tapestries. "Arthur's own Camelot can be no grander than this!"

Ronan was glad that he had the chance to show his wife his keep in relative privacy. "There are grander," he assured her.

She shook herself from the enchantment. "Where is Brother Martin?"

"Aye, he's with the others out in the orchard." Weather permitting, the Resurrection service was always on the fourteenth day of Nissan, or Passover, held out of doors where both high and low of station might worship together with the Creator's sky as the ceiling of their temple.

"Then we must hurry. I've so wanted to hear the church service from within the throng instead of from without."

"It's a good walk," he warned her. "I could arrange a private service for you after—"

The stubborn jut of an otherwise perfectly shaped chin cut him off.

"You waste your breath, milord," Dara tutted. "She says the more she moves about, the quicker she'll recover. I only hope her head agrees."

"There's hardly a dull ache now," Brenna assured her. "The fresh air will do it good."

"All the same, this *friend*," Dara reminded her, "is not leavin' your side." To prove it, the old midwife stationed herself on Brenna's other side as they stepped out into the sunlight.

The inner grounds where his jaded homecoming celebration took place the day before drew the same awe from Brenna as the hall. "You must introduce me to every cow, calf, sheep, and lamb. And the chickens," she said as a mother hen strutted from one of the sheds with a small band of chicks in her wake. "Have you named them?"

Keenly aware of Dara's observation, Ronan hesitated. "No," he said finally, "but you may, if you wish."

A hint of a smile touched the old woman's thin lips.

"Brenna has a love of animals," he explained.

"And fire pits. Sure, you'll be feeding an army today," she marveled. "And look at the beautiful banners on the tents. It's like a grand fair."

"Lady Rhianon has a talent for hospitality." At least Glenarden sported more flair than it had before the lady came to it. Even Vychan had reluctantly given her that.

"Well, I have never seen such a fine keep and grounds. And look—" Brenna pointed to the gate of the inner stockade. "A village beyond. I'm sure it's filled with good people, if you and Dara are any example."

Good but superstitious people. Some of whom still might believe Brenna a witch of dubious powers. Ronan's chest tightened. Should he have insisted she remain inside?

"Come on." Brenna tugged at his arm when he slowed his step. "We'll miss the Eucharist."

Not all the villagers were in the orchard. Some clung to the old gods. Some to the old deities *and* the One God. The few who remained behind peered at Brenna from behind the hide coverings of their windows. The less discreet stared openly at the legendary wolf-woman. Ronan sensed curiosity, but there was fear as well— fear mingled with its companion, animosity. It was especially evident in the women who gathered children into their huts as though looking upon the lady in the pale green dress might some-how bewitch them.

Yet the cool reception didn't seem to bother Brenna. Gone was that *little girl lost* who'd sought the reassurance of Ronan's embrace that morning.

She now waved at total strangers, calling out, "Blessed be" and "Glorious day" to any within earshot. All the while, Dara would whisper the name of the person who ducked behind a curtain and doorway … or who ventured to wave back.

The morning sun beat warmly down on meadow grass beyond
the village gates. Wildflowers of yellow, red, blue, and white adorned
the spread of green waving in the gentle breeze that carried the priest's
booming voice to them.

"I invite thee to the Lord's Table to partake of the bread and
wine in remembrance of Him and His great sacrifice for us, while we
were still sinners."

As was their place, the guests proceeded toward the priest, who
today was accompanied by twelve assistants garbed in mean gray
robes. With Tarlach and Caden conspicuously absent, Rhianon led
the way. Ronan pulled Brenna forward that they might take their
rightful place in the fore, but she held back.

"I will wait my turn with my people … and the young man with
the dog, whom, I believe, saved my life."

Daniel of Gowrys and Cú stood at the edge of the crowd, watching Brenna's approach. By the time they reached the lad, Dara had
shared her opinion of the hostage. A decent enough lad, but strange.
And who could blame him for keeping to himself, situated as he was
amidst sworn enemies?

But as they approached, Cú lowered his ears and growled. Daniel
jerked his leather collar, and the dog sat, but it was still guarded.

Unlike Brenna, who approached the beast with open arms.
"Listen to you, now, growling on such a day as this," she admonished
the dog in a whisper. "I hold no grudge for you. Have you a name?"

"Cú," Daniel replied, holding it even tighter. "Careful, milady,
he's a fierce one till you get to know him."

"Cú," she said to the dog in a voice that would have made Ronan
roll over and do anything she asked of him.

"Brenna—" Ronan reached for the hand she extended to the dog's nose, but she resisted.

"Smells are important. We are getting acquainted … aren't we, Cú?" Though she continued to whisper, attention was turning their way down the line. "You've a horrid case of mange on your flank. I've just the thing to make it stop itching and heal. If you're willing, that is." The same singsong voice she used on Faol lifted the wolfhound's ears.

"Caw, I never," Daniel said in wonder when Cú tentatively licked Brenna's hand.

Or was it the way she held the dog's gaze with heartfelt concern that transcended words?

To Ronan's dismay, Brenna knelt so that the hound could have killed her with a simple snap of its powerful jaws. Instead it hunkered down and allowed her to stroke its wire-bristled fur. "How long has his fur been thinned so?" she asked Daniel.

"Was that way when I came here, milady."

Brenna glanced up at Ronan. "We must get my things from home."

"We will, *cariad.*"

"I've a dog suffering the same malady," a man standing nearby spoke up. "Bites hisself bloody, he does. Hurts me to see it."

"Hush," the woman next to him hissed. "'Tis witch's magic."

"'Tis God's gift of nature's bounty, milady," Brenna said gently. "Given for the good of His children."

"The same as the drawing salve you get from me for your boils, Ina."

Ronan turned to see Brother Martin standing next to them, flanked by Rhianon and her guests. Upon seeing Brenna's approach, the priest left his companions in charge of the Eucharist to come to her aid.

"Or the medicinal teas for your plaguing coughs or distressed bowels. This lady has prepared them for you for years, and I have seen that they reached those in need."

A murmur of surprise wafted through the crowd.

"The church believes Lady Brenna is a gifted healer like her mother before."

"Her mother was a witch," Ina said.

"Only in my father's fevered mind," Ronan replied. "Ask *your* father, Ina, or any of the men who were present at the Witch's End, if they sleep well at night after the wrong committed upon Tarlach's orders."

"I have heard their confessions," Martin said. "But for God's grace, they would carry the burden of their guilt to their graves." He canvassed the crowd with a piercing gray gaze. "You men know who you are."

The edge of hysteria surrounding them began to dull. Yet Ronan knew it could sharpen with a turn of phrase.

"I can't believe I'm hearing this!" Rhianon stared at Ronan and Brother Martin as if they'd grown horns and tails. "Are you accusing your father of senseless murder before his own people? Oh, would that my husband was here to defend him, instead of abed with the same terrible head pain as his father!"

The lady didn't finish her accusation, but her nurse did. "Aye, the same curse as her mother put on Tarlach."

Whispers and gasps rippled through the gathering throng who had abandoned the young priests and the communal wine and bread.

"Nonsense," Ronan countered. "Caden suffers from too much of the heath fruit last night. As for Tarlach—"

"Superstitious nonsense." Like a great oak seizing Heaven's replenishment, Martin raised his clenched fists. "With God on our side we have nothing to fear. Sin and sin alone caused Tarlach's disability, and bitterness has fed his madness. God strike me down now if I am wrong!"

Whether the crowd believed him or whether they awaited God's verdict, the murmurs quieted.

"Martin is right," Ronan said. "I was there. Father's rage came from a spurned heart, not a just cause. But I believe that God has given Glenarden a second chance to redeem itself … through my wife."

"What about the prophecy?" someone called out.

"Father only quoted part of it—the part where Glenarden will be divided," Ronan told the onlookers. "But the most important part that you need to know is this: *And bring a peace beyond the ken of your wicked soul.*"

"May I speak?" Brenna rose, a bit unsteady, and brushed off her gown. She was pale, drained from the exertion of coming out to the orchard. Yet again Ronan was struck by her determination and courage.

"By all means, my love."

"The same prophecy that has kept you at war with my kinsmen has kept me imprisoned for twenty years, hidden away from the people God intended me to heal. I prayed for an answer to my dilemma, and He sent me Ronan, whom I love with all my heart." Brenna linked her arm in his. "By God's union of marriage, his people are now my people. If you be divided," she charged, "then you are divided between continued war and the chance for peace and prosperity for all."

"That is easy for you to say, now that you have married into authority," Rhianon challenged. "But do you have your people on your heart—or ours?"

"I have the welfare of the O'Byrnes *and* the Gowrys on my heart, milady," Brenna replied. "As proof, it is my hope that *you*, Lady Rhianon, will do me the honor to continue to run the household as you have done so well. For I am a healer and unschooled in such affairs. I wish only to serve God's people in that capacity."

The thin line of Rhianon's lips slackened with shock. Beside her, her mother, Enda, squeezed her hand. As for Idwal, Ronan couldn't be sure. Had Brenna won Rhianon's father over or not?

But behind her, Keena mumbled, "The proof will be in the pie."

Brenna stepped up to the crone and hugged her as Brenna embraced all of life—with boundless love.

"Then let us make—" She stepped back, a flicker of discomfiture grazing her impressive show of confidence and grace. Her glance darted to Brother Martin, then back to Keena's impassive face. "Then let us make delicious pie, dear friend. Together as sisters of God."

Brother Martin raised his voice with ecumenical authority. "God be praised that on this day, we celebrate not only the Resurrection of the Christ, but the rebirth of peace and friendship between Glenarden and Gowrys. Allies for Arthur and Albion, brothers and sisters in Christ. Amen."

Amens scattered through the throng, but Ronan would have wished for more.

CHAPTER EIGHTEEN

Brenna rolled over, half asleep, and stared in the dim light at the thick-beamed ceiling of the anteroom bedchamber next to that of Tarlach O'Byrne. Upon hearing how Rhianon and Caden had been ousted from the master bedroom on the second floor, Brenna pleaded with Ronan to move to the makeshift chapel at the rear of the hall.

"Christ the King dwelt *among* his disciples, not above them," she reminded him when he expressed second thoughts regarding his right as lord of the keep. "Besides, I am ill at ease in such luxury, and it means much to Lady Rhianon. The smaller room will do us just fine."

Though it had no hearth like her cave to glow warmly in the night, it was not in the updraft of the main floor's fires like its elegant but smokier counterpart. Its beams hung with Brenna's fragrant herbs while her scant belongings—Ealga's old cabinet from the cave and the bed box—served as ample furnishing. Bless them, Brother Martin and his companions had moved them for her the week before the Pascal celebration.

With a yawn, Brenna reached for Ronan but found his side of the bed empty. Her eyes opened wider. What time was it? A thin line of light reached in from under the door, enough for Brenna to

find her old shift and tunic and slip them on. Just as she was about
to braid her hair, a miserable wail came through the wattle and daub
wall separating the two anterooms.

It wasn't the first such complaint Brenna had heard from
Tarlach's room. His cries awakened her several times during the night.
According to Rhianon, the chieftain reached fast for the gateway to
the Other Side. Yet, healer that she was, Brenna had been forbidden
to see him for fear of speeding him on his way all the more quickly.
She knew that she could ease the man's passage, but Ronan would
not budge on his decision.

"I'll not have anyone saying you are responsible for my father's
death. Let Keena and Dara do their work."

Keena. Brenna shuddered as she made hurried work of her
braid. It went against her nature to dislike someone, but there was
something about Rhianon's maidservant that drove dread through
Brenna's chest like a spear. Though she'd only been taught about pure
evil, surely Keena's presence was what it felt like.

Brenna found Vychan, Glenarden's steward, seated at the plank
table in the hall. He was the picture of desolation. At the end, Caden
slept on folded arms, snoring softly.

"Your lord is worse?" she asked.

"Aye, milady. I fear the end is near. He is spent from this stomach misery that has beset him. The women despair of keeping clean
linens on the bed. The stench is unbearable."

"Who is with him?"

"Your husband … and the women."

Brenna, frustrated, studied the closed door. "It isn't right that I,
a trained healer of Avalon, cannot go to his aid."

The door opened, and Dara emerged, looking weary.

"Dara, have you given him elderberry?" Its juice was soothing to the stomach.

"Aye, like I told you last night … thrice, it was."

"And the slippery elm?" It stopped loose stools.

Dara shot her an annoyed look and held up three fingers.

"Watch yourself, woman," Vychan reprimanded. "You forget your place."

Brenna put her hand on Vychan's. "She's been up most of the night doing what you could not and what I was not allowed to do."

Dara's scowl disintegrated. "I am sorry, milady. It's just that I canna understand why nothin' helps. His lordship is a strong man and suddenly—"

"*She* appears?" Caden lifted his head suddenly and leveled a red-eyed accusation at Brenna.

Her husband's brother was hard for Brenna to read. There was no consistency to his personality. Emotion clouded his vision when she assured Caden that she understood why he'd killed Faol. That she forgave him. Yet, at other times, he seemed totally without tenderness. Either wooden … or afire with anger.

"Milady, I dinna know you were up and about," a maidservant exclaimed upon entering the hall and seeing Brenna. "I'll fetch your tea and fresh-baked scones."

The girl was gone before Brenna could stop her. Brenna loved going out to the kitchen, a separate building next to the tower with far more cooking capability than the fire pit that had served the original builders of the keep. She and the cooks had talked for hours about herbs and seasonings.

"Milady, forgive me." Vychan stiffly rose to his feet. "It seems Dara is not the only one who has forgotten her station. I should have seen to your—"

"You should rest, Vychan. You, too, Dara," Brenna added as her new friend sought to sit by the fire pit in the center of the hall to ward off the early morning chill.

Around her and the few still, sleeping figures of children, servants set up benches that had been stored against the wall during the night to make room for the keep's inhabitants to bed down. Soon the little ones would be awakened, and the hall would be filled as morning chores were completed.

"When it's done, milady," Dara replied. "When it's done."

At that moment, Lady Rhianon emerged from the stone stairwell looking fresh as a wild rose. Keena followed like a frostbitten counterpart.

"Good day, Rhianon," Brenna called out. "And to you, Keena."

Rhianon gave Brenna a semblance of a smile. "I hear the old man still hangs on to life," she replied, plopping down on the bench next to her husband and rubbing his back. "Would that God would put him out of his misery."

Keena never answered Brenna at all but headed out of the keep.

"Perhaps God is not through with Tarlach," Brenna suggested. From what little she'd seen and heard, Tarlach's was a tortured soul. Tortured souls fought death and the demons that were said to wait for the unsaved dying's last breath.

Rhianon gave her a sharp look. "Then you have a most cruel god, Lady Brenna. Vychan," she said to the steward, "I'll have my tea and breads now."

The steward bowed stiffly. "I'll see to it."

"My God loves us even when we are not so lovable, Rhianon," Brenna replied sweetly.

She'd heard that Rhianon sought the approval of many gods, including the One God. At some point, perhaps Brenna might help her to see that her gods were no more than the One God's creations. That His was the life breathed into them. In time.

For now, Tarlach was Brenna's mixed bag of concern. Part of her feared the old man, while the healer longed to ease his misery.

"I believe God wants Tarlach to have His peace, that he might not fear death." Just as He wanted her to have the peace to help him, if they would but allow it.

Caden snorted, coming to life again. "Why should Father have peace when he's afforded none to anyone else in all his years?"

Brenna could almost taste the man's bitterness ... and the deep wounds that spawned it. 'Twas enough to make her ill. Never had she been exposed to such hostility and anguish in one place, not even at the hospital on the Sacred Isle. "Yet God loves him, even with his faults."

Caden and Rhianon exchanged rolled gazes of skepticism.

Just as I am trying to do with you, Brenna finished in silence. *Father God, help me. I am only one healer. I cannot do this alone. Show me what to say, what to—*

The door to Tarlach's room opened abruptly, and Ronan stepped out. He was pale. He sought Brenna with eyes circled with weariness and dull with resignation.

"Is he gone?" Caden asked, his bear of a voice no more than a whisper.

Ronan shook his head, without taking his eyes away from Brenna. "He wants to see your mother. He's begging"—Ronan's voice caught—"like a whimpering child to see her."

"He must think you are Joanna," Rhianon suggested. "It would make sense, his seeing you after all these years."

"She is her mother's image," Ronan agreed.

Nodding, Brenna rose from the table. This was her path—who she was meant to be. God's reassurance spread through her, warm as the cup of tea that the girl brought in from the kitchen along with a plate of scones.

"Give those to Lady Rhianon, please ..." Brenna gave the girl a plaintive look, for she'd forgotten the servant's name. There were so many to learn.

"Mab, milady," the girl replied.

"Thank you, Mab."

Ronan stopped Brenna short of the door. "Are you sure you want to go in there?"

Would that the same reassurance flowed through her husband.

"'Tis what I've asked to do for the last few days, Beloved. What God has called me to do. Your father needs me ... or at least my mother." And Brenna could see for herself the poor man's state.

"Then let me go in first and be sure he's fit to be seen," Dara announced from the hearth and charged for the bedchamber.

"Aye," Ronan said, "and the rest of you come as well. I'll not have you claiming she did a thing to him but try to comfort a dying man."

Rhianon wrinkled her nose. "I'd rather not. I've no stomach for—"

"You can stand at the door, milady … for your husband's sake," Ronan added, "if for none other."

It was a sickroom and smelled as such. Brenna forced herself to breathe through her mouth as Ealga had taught her and approached the bed to help Dara. Tarlach lay on his side, curled away from the door on a scant mattress of straw. Eyes clenched so that his thick brows nearly touched his cheeks, he grasped his abdomen as though impaled there.

This whimpering, shriveled soul was the fierce savage who'd slaughtered her father and driven Joanna of Gowrys to take her own life?

"Husharoo," she sang, gently reaching out to stroke the hair away from his face. "Is the pain in your head or your belly, precious one?"

Tarlach lurched, trying to throw himself on his back. "Where are you, lassie?"

"Here. Let me help you turn." Brenna worked her arm beneath Tarlach's afflicted shoulder and lifted him. Beside her Ronan moved in to help, but Brenna shook her head. She'd moved Ronan more than once like this. It took a moment for Tarlach's bent form to straighten. "You mustn't lie in the same position for so long."

"That's what you always say," Tarlach grunted.

Brenna's heart smiled. So her mother had given him the same advice.

Tarlach jerked his hand at Ronan. "Fetch a light, laddie. Can't see a cursed thing in here."

The light drove home just how sick Tarlach was. His complexion was cold and wet, with death's pallor and sweat. Drool dripped from the slack side of his mouth and down his oxbow mustache.

"I ... it *is* you." His breath heaved out the words, sour with sickness ... and something else that set Brenna's senses on alert. "I have prayed for this day and here"—he seized another lungful of air—"you are." His eyelids fluttered and head trembled as he tried to lift it from the pillows. "Jo ... anna."

Garlic. Ever so faint, but unmistakably garlic.

"How long has he been sick to his stomach and loose at the bowels?" Brenna picked a cup up from the bedside table and sniffed it. It smelled of cold tea laced with herbs to heal the misery of the abdomen.

"Only since you arrived, milady," Dara informed her. "Just a bit at first, but it's gotten worse, little by little."

The contents had been nothing she wouldn't have prepared herself, garlic included. Yet, when she touched a damp remnant lying in the bottom and put it to her tongue, her jaws tingled with warning.

"I must speak with you, Joanna. I must," Tarlach moaned, his face plowed deep with anguish. He motioned her closer.

Brenna put the cup down, leaning in. Garlic in food often hid more sinister tastes ... like sandarach. But surely that was absurd. Use of the arsenic stone required sophisticated knowledge. "I'm here, milord."

Tarlach tried to touch her face, but his good arm trembled with weakness and fell to the bed. Brenna lifted it to her cheek.

"Joanna." The name was breathed in worship. "Soft as a ripe peach. I canna believe my eyes, but you feel real to me."

"I am real, milord." She folded his gnarled hand in her own, taking note of his discolored nails. How could this be?

"I am dying, Joanna, but I must beg your forgiveness. I canna leave this world without it." Tarlach tried to squeeze her hand. A faint attempt.

"The old man's as good as gone," Caden grumbled somewhere behind her. "At least his mind has."

"Then permit what's left of it to gather what peace he can," Ronan warned. "God knows he's suffered with his guilt too long. We all have."

"*Say* you forgive me." A sob strangled in Tarlach's throat. "Llas was my friend. You were my heart." Tarlach's wide shoulders heaved with the emotion bursting free, emotion that had been locked inside for twenty years.

Brenna held his head between her palms to ease the pressure pounding there. Tarlach wasn't fevered, but oh the torment he felt, present and past. The reassuring light within that she carried into the room staggered at the sinister onslaught of rage. The swing of a blade. Blood. Horror.

"Father God!" she gasped, reeling at the vision of a man's head cleaved from his shoulders, his own blade still in midslash, as though his body carried on its last command. And steps, narrow and ascending … she climbed them, the head held in front of her gaze. Tarlach's gaze. A feeling of raw vengeance assailed her, poisoning whatever it touched. But just as her heart would burst from the beating, a pair of hands clamped on her shoulders, drawing her out of the living nightmare and once more into the light.

"Brenna," Ronan whispered.

And the hatred disappeared, destroyed by a surge of something stronger yet. *Love.* The press of her husband's body against her back reminded her of all that was warm and wonderful in the present. And of all that would be. It was for that she reached with her flagging soul.

Forgiveness. It was the only balm that would work. Even as the answer came to her, Brenna sensed that the dark spirits, clinging with menacing claws to this broken man-child, were digging in even deeper.

Tarlach gasped, arching against the bed, as though the demons had seized his last breath.

"No!" Brenna grabbed him by the shoulders, drawing him to her, shouting into his ear. "In the name of Jesus, you are forgiven, Tarlach. Nothing can separate you from God's love or mine. Call His name," she pleaded. "Call Jesus!"

"In the name of the Father ..." Dara prayed close by.

Tarlach's face screwed up with a terror worse than Brenna had seen while holding him. He saw them. The demons. She clung to him tightly.

"Pray!" she commanded to any who had the ears to hear. "I won't let you go. *Christ before me, Christ behind me, Christ beside me, Christ within me.*"

"Christ before me," Ronan chimed in as she repeated the prayer.

"Call on Jesus, Tarlach," Brenna said, clutching his fevered body tightly to her. "Call Him!" She was losing the battle. Tarlach wasn't responding. "Jesus, help us."

Suddenly Tarlach stopped trying to pull away and lurched against Brenna, reaching past her at the air. "Jesus." It was no more than a garbled sob, but the Name above all names loosed the fierce lines drawing Tarlach's brow ... and the hold of permanent darkness.

He fell slack in her arms, suddenly too heavy to hold, now that he was fully back in This World. This time when Ronan helped her ease him back on the bed, Brenna allowed it.

"You will not die today," she heard herself say. Shock constricted Brenna's chest. *Why, Lord? I cannot make such declarations.*

"What?" The exclamation bounced from one to another behind her. *You've never fought darkness like this before.*

Her Shepherd strengthened her so that all heard her pronouncement. Or was it His? "You are poisoned, sir. But it is not too late."

Ronan pulled Brenna about to face him. "Are you certain?"

She was. Her jaws did not lie. Nor did her Shepherd. "I do not know with what exactly, but I have my suspicions. Right now I need to fetch my medicine bag."

"I'll get it," Vychan offered.

"It's hanging over our bed." An embarrassed flush warmed Brenna's face. It was still strange to use the word *our*, as in forever bound as one. Behind her, Ronan gave her a hug, driving to heart all the more this bond they shared.

"That is outrageous," Rhianon protested from the door. "Who would want to poison Tarlach?"

"Half of Glenarden on any given day," Caden remarked cryptically. "You know what a beast he can be."

Beast. Had they prayed the beast out of the old man? Perhaps the spiritual one, but the poison remained.

"What have you done, you old crone?" Rhianon accused Dara.

"As God is my witness, I've given him naught but the best of care. Your own nurse saw to him as well, milady," the midwife answered.

"Perhaps it's accidental," Brenna suggested. Not that she believed it. What she wouldn't give to go through the bag Keena kept slung about her bony hips. Although Keena's motive—

Brenna reined in her galloping thoughts. There wasn't much time. If she could induce him to drink a concoction of charcoal and black cohosh …

"No one here would dare poison me," Tarlach objected from the bed, his voice weak but thankfully coherent. Strangling on a bit of drool, he went into a fit of coughing. "Besides, what has an old man left to live for?"

Her heart cringed for him. Brenna leaned over, speaking into his ear. "A grandson, Tarlach. Our grandson. Your heir."

Tarlach grew still. "Here?"

"Nay, but he is coming nine months hence."

The old man lowered his voice. "You've seen him, haven't you?"

"Aye, I've seen him."

"I can't listen to this nonsense," Rhianon exclaimed. "How can she be so blessed certain and they've only been married—" She stopped to calculate. "Well, not long enough."

Brenna heard her stomp away from the door. Ignoring the distraction, she continued. "His hair is the color of roasted chestnut, and his eyes are as blue as a starlit sky."

"And?" Tarlach prompted. Excitement built in his weary gray eyes.

"What else could there be to say, Father?" Ronan asked.

Her husband thought she was humoring Tarlach, but even as Brenna started to talk of the child, he appeared to her, lying in her lap, naked as he came into the world. "A beautiful baby boy …"

Amazement tripped her. Before, she'd seen as through a fog, but this was so clear. "With ... with a birthmark on his hip, shaped like a pledging hand."

"An O'Byrne of the Red Hand," Tarlach cried out.

Judah's twin. The Red Hand of Zarah, father of the Celts, whose offspring married his royal brother Pharez's descendants and thus preserved the Davidic kings. A new sense of awe washed over Brenna as the bigger picture formed ... bigger than a child to bring peace to warring clans. Her son's father of the Red Hand. Her own of the Arimathean lineage. These were the same holy bloodlines as flowed through the Christ. King, peacemaker, healer, counselor ... what was her baby's destiny? Brenna trembled to think of it.

Forgetting his disability for the moment, Tarlach threw aside the light coverlet as though to get up. "God be thanked!"

"Nay, sir!" With Ronan's help, Brenna kept Tarlach from flinging himself off the bed.

As Brenna tucked him back in, she asked, "So, milord, will you do as I say and get well so that you may bounce that baby boy on your knee?"

"I would fetch the moon for you, lassie. Ye ken that."

"Here's the bag," Vychan announced upon entering the room.

Beyond the steward, she could hear Rhianon ask Caden from the other room, "Are you certain you want *her* tending to your father?"

Brenna would have to deal with their superstition later. For now, a greater task lay ahead of her. "I'll need water and honey, Dara. And tell the cook to boil eggs, put on beans to mash, and onions, lots of onions. Such foods will offset the effects of the poison."

"Aye, milady, right away."

"And garlic. I'll need garlic. And salt." He'd lost so much body salt through perspiration and water from his digestive tract. If only they were closer to the cave, she'd soak him. "Ronan?"

"Aye, Love. I'll not leave your side."

"But you must. I'll need as much water from the hot spring as can possibly be brought down from the mountain. Take as many men and horses as you can."

With those words, the door of Brenna's past life closed behind her. Her refuge would be well known now. No longer could she go back. It was time to go forward. Time to share her gifts ... and God's. With God beside her, what had she to fear?

Besides ambush and poison, that is.

Father God, You have brought me safe thus far. I count on Your promise never to leave or forsake me ... or mine. In the name of our Savior and Druid Teacher, Jesus Christ, amen.

Chapter Nineteen

While Vychan and the family sought to find the source of the poison, Brenna never left Tarlach's side for the rest of the day and into the next. It was essential to get the poison out of his system by emetics, which she laced with oil, charcoal, and black cohosh. The poor soul retched until he could retch no more. Then they would start again. But his determination to be rid of the venom became a matter of mind over physic.

"If any sends me earthways," he gasped weakly, "'twill be the Lord." Another breath, fiercer this time. "Not a cowardly assassin."

This glimpse of Tarlach's vengeful side couldn't help but give Brenna second thought. For now, he thought she was his angel, Joanna. But what would happen when he fully came to his senses?

It didn't matter. Just as she'd risked her life to save Ronan, she'd do so for Tarlach. Hadn't she prayed for the chance to heal others as she'd been trained to do? God had answered.

When all that could be done to expel the poison had been done, Brenna coaxed spoons of beans, mashed with more herbs, into his mouth to absorb or counter what remained in his system. Knowing it was critical that his bodily humors, or fluids, be restored, she instructed Dara to keep the patient covered with towels soaked in saltwater until Ronan could return with the healing waters from her cave. It would also offset the fever.

Meanwhile, Brenna urged Tarlach continuously to sip watered-down wine. "No more," Tarlach mumbled, turning his head away from one of the new garnet glass goblets that Rhianon's visiting parents had given to her. She'd offered it for its alleged property of changing color, should it contain poison.

Brenna trusted her instincts more. "Would you see your grandson, or nay, sir?"

"He has the birthmark?" Tarlach rallied.

"Aye."

"I had it. My own father and Ronan didn't. See?"

"Aye, I've seen," she replied, staying him from the exertion of exposing his hip. And she had seen. More times than they'd repeated this conversation. "Now take some nourishment."

Like a young robin, the chieftain opened his mouth with a trust not shared by the rest of his family. Brenna could well imagine the effort it took, her own stomach recoiling in empathy. Yet patient and healer both did what needed to be done. By all her knowledge, for the poison had had more than its necessary time to take Tarlach to the Other Side, the man shouldn't be alive, much less have the fortitude to fight so for his life. Truly it was God's hand and not Brenna's that was at work here.

Having sent Dara to rest, Brenna cast a wondering glance to where Vychan and Keena drifted in and out of sleep at their posts by the door. Caden and Rhianon insisted the old woman be present at all times to keep an eye on Brenna. Every morsel or drink that came into the room was checked by Keena's cherished unicorn's horn, which she insisted was endowed with the power to keep the chieftain from further harm. Looking more like a narwhal tusk Brenna once saw at a fair, it was said to sweat when it detected something deadly in the nourishment given to Tarlach.

The precautions were not one-sided. The tangle of who was watching whom would have been amusing, were the situation not so dire. Ronan put Vychan there to protect Brenna, and Brenna made certain Tarlach was not left alone with Rhianon's old nurse.

God forgive her if she judged Keena unfairly and spoke idle words of caution to Dara, but Brenna's intuition was rarely wrong. She exchanged the last of the towels for a freshly dipped one, closing her eyes.

If I am wrong, Lord, I will plead for her pardon once Tarlach is restored to health.

"How is he?"

Brenna started at the sound of Ronan's voice in the doorway. "You're home!"

Feet that had been leaden moments ago suddenly grew light with joy. Wiping wet hands on her shift, she bound toward him before the steward could shake himself from sleep and rise to his feet.

"You must have traveled the night, milord," Vychan mumbled.

The steward was right. Getting to and from the cave was less than a day's journey, but carrying barrels of water with horse and cart—

Brenna looked beyond him to where the light of dawn flooded through the open doors of the hall.

"Don't ask me to leave you again, milady," he said, drawing her into the hall and into his arms. "Not even for Father's sake."

Brenna captured his face in her hands. "He is better. In all my days at Avalon, I have never seen such strong will."

"It will grow more stubborn as he recovers," Ronan warned her.

"Well, this healing water will do wonders to restore his humors."

"Then let us hope it only restores his good humor," he replied dryly, "and that the rest is tossed with the dirty bathwater."

Brenna shook her husband's face in admonishment. "It seems your father isn't the only one in need of better humor."

"There I am, asleep in my new abode," Brother Martin complained as he rolled a sealed barrel to the door, "and an army of men with empty casks assails me." With a grunt, he straightened, clutching a stiff back. "All is well?" he asked of Brenna.

She nodded ... after a moment's hesitation. There was much more than she could say within earshot of Keena, who surely listened. "He is weak, but most determined to survive. Though he may still think I'm my mother."

"So I heard. The miracle in Tarlach's sickroom speeds through the kingdom like a highland wind. Wrestled Tarlach from the brink of death with your own hands, did you?"

Heavenly Father! Brenna cast her dismayed gaze to the floor. "You know that is not true. 'Twas God who spared him. But I would speak to you of it, Brother, for it was most terrifying."

"Later," Ronan intervened. "I don't know which of us is the more weary, but I am taking my wife to bed. After a good rest, the two of you can speak all you wish."

Brenna lowered her voice. "I cannot leave Tarlach alone." She jerked her head toward where Keena feigned sleep.

Martin shooed her off with a wave of his hand. "Don't look at me as if I'm still a bairn on the breast," he said, voice raised for Keena's benefit. "I think your husband's idea is a fine one. I will see to Tarlach."

"But you've been up all night as well," Brenna said.

"I, my dear, am not with child."

Martin was right, of course.

"Well enough," she conceded. "I've laid hands on him to balance his complexions and—" She ended with a startled squeak as Ronan swept her off her feet.

"The priest has tended the sick before, Wife."

"Aye, medicine is part of our training," Martin reminded her.

Of course her mentor knew what to do. He must think her addled. But then, in her husband's embrace, she was. "If you grow weary, send for Dara."

"Aye, between Dara, my colleague Brother Michael—" Martin motioned to a young red-haired priest struggling through the door with yet another barrel of water and added with a conspiratorial wink, "and *Keena*, I'm sure Tarlach will be well attended."

The reassurance melted the last wall of resistance to the fatigue Brenna had battled from dawn last to dawn present. As it triumphed through her limbs and laid claim to her brain, she managed one all-encompassing *Thank You, Lord,* grateful that He had given her the strength and endurance she'd needed for as long as she'd needed it.

Provision. Grateful that He had spared Tarlach's life.

Grace. Grateful for Ronan's safe return as he carried her through the door of their bedchamber and deposited her in the bed box that had cradled her since she could remember.

Protection. Grateful to feel his body join hers, as he took her into his arms until they were cozily entwined.

Peace. Grateful for the bond that held them to each other and to Him.

Love.

The day after Ronan's return from the cave, the hall was filled to the beams with revelry and Glenarden's bounty. Conspicuously absent was the party from Gwynedd. Once assured that Tarlach would recover, Idwal and Enda took their leave, lest they become burdensome. Or poisoned.

Regardless of their motivation, Ronan was glad to see them go. Ronan didn't care to have Glenarden's dark drama played out before another clan. Bad enough they'd seen his bride brought in like a carcass of meat and the clash between him and his brother, resulting in his father's brain fit. But the poisoning was a disgrace. Common enough in kingdoms throughout Albion, but an affront to the honor of the clan.

Who would dare? Ronan scanned the room like a hawk for a mouse, looking for the slightest flicker of guilt in a glance. A difference in behavior. Was the would-be assassin the same who had tried to murder him? If so, Brenna's suspicions of Keena were unfounded.

His family stood the most to gain by his and his father's deaths. He cut a sidewise glance at them. Her work as grand hostess done, Rhianon sat next to Caden at the family board as if her family's departure had taken away her vigor. As for his brother, there was nothing secretive in his behavior. Caden cared not who saw him drink himself into oblivion. Nor did Caden seem to care if Ronan saw the raw hatred of the gaze that met his. Poison was too cowardly for his middle brother. Face-to-face combat was Caden's style.

There simply were no clues leading to the culprit. Or culprits, if Ronan's attack and Tarlach's poisoning were not perpetrated by one and the same. If only Ronan or Brenna could recall something distinctive about his would-be murderer. Questions regarding the poisoning revealed that the food had been prepared and served by the usual people in the usual way. Every store had been checked for molds, and mushrooms were examined meticulously. Nothing. It was assumed an accident, though in private Brenna vowed on her gift it was not. She suspected wine tainted with the poison stone.

"The residue in his cup made my jaws tingle."

Ronan reached out and covered his wife's hand, drawing her smile. He didn't understand her gift, but he trusted it. "Have I told you how lovely you look tonight?"

"Twice."

If it kindled what Ronan saw in her gaze, he'd tell her a dozen more times before the night was out. But it was true. Even in her plain brown dress and shift, she glowed.

"I still cannot believe all this." Brenna motioned toward a group of people seated in a cluster near the hall door. A farmer with a chronic cough. A woman with female ailments. And these were just from among those who'd heard of Tarlach's miracle.

Proud as a mother hen with a chick, Martin had done his part in fanning the wind speeding the news along. The secret he'd kept for so many years was out at last. He told to all who'd listen of Brenna's extensive training at Avalon. How she'd been chosen for it by Merlin Emrys himself when she was of toddling age and assigned to Martin as his ecclesiastical student. But who could wonder at her gift, given her priestly lineage, traceable back to the union of Bran, the Blessed, the first Christian British king, with Anna, daughter of Joseph of Arimathea.

"Sure as Joseph was a tin man," Ronan heard Martin say, for it was known throughout Albion that Arimathea was not only a member of Jesus' family, but that his wealth came from the tin trade between the isles and the East.

As for Brenna *saving* Tarlach, Ronan was at the least disconcerted by what he'd witnessed that day. Spiritual warfare, Martin insisted. In the absence of a priest, she had fought for Tarlach's soul with prayer. Only after it had been spared in Jesus' name had she been able to nurse him back to health.

"I think once the brethren finish their huts in the glen," Martin said to Ronan, "we'd best be thinking of adding a hospital." Which meant Glenarden should provide the materials and what labor or skill the brethren could not.

"*We?*" Brenna teased. "It sounds to me as if you are warming to the idea of a bishopric, *hermit.*"

Martin shook his head vehemently. "Not for me. I like my solitude. Perhaps Brother Michael here."

Michael grew the shade of a beet, a horrid contrast to his carrot red hair. "You honor me more than I deserve. But such a future"— his hawkish face contorted—"would overwhelm me."

It was the most Ronan had heard the painfully gaunt young man say since his arrival.

The elder priest laughed. "I'm sure God will provide. He always does." He shifted his attention to Brenna. "In the meanwhile, child, do not overtax yourself. Your most important calling for now is that of motherhood. You must avoid contagion at all costs."

"Dara has already warned me," Brenna informed him. "And Ronan."

"But this is the child the church has ordained for the peace of your peoples. A generation late," Martin said, referring to the ill-fated match between Tarlach and Joanna, "but the key, nonetheless. They must become one in blood and faith."

The weight of the priest's words bore down upon Brenna. Covering her flat belly with her hands, she leaned into Ronan as though to draw strength. Ronan felt it too. For if this child were divinely appointed for the task of peace, a great responsibility lay on the babe as well as the parents. A passage of Scripture flashed to Ronan's mind. That of Simeon as he praised God for being allowed to see the salvation of mankind in the holy babe … and as he was warned of the heartache it would bring his mother.

Ronan had no illusion that their child was equal to the baby Jesus, but the task ahead of him would be a treacherous one. Albion was as plagued by the worst of mankind as Jerusalem had been.

"Maybe I should cede Glenarden to Caden and take Brenna and the bairn to Brittany, someplace safe," he thought aloud. Numerous noble families had abandoned their ancient lands to the invaders and settled there.

Brenna looked up at him, shocked. "If this is God's will, I've no mind to run from it and wind up in a whale's belly."

Martin covered his mouth, but the wine he'd just sipped squirted out his nose instead. Even Brother Michael laughed audibly.

How could Ronan not join them? He drank in the flash of Brenna's gaze. *Prickly. Mischievous. Fearless.* She was all of them and more.

"We are born to this, Beloved. Our blessings multiply by the day," she told him.

Would that Ronan had her faith. But while she'd been reared in grace and protection, he'd led a far more worldly life. "Mind the dangers do as well."

"Nothing God cannot face with—"

A commotion at the other end of the hall interrupted them. Ronan stood as the doors burst open, allowing a guard from the gatehouse in.

Flushed, the man stopped to catch his breath, then shouted, "The O'Toole is returned from the Orkneys campaign! Cennalath, that Saxon-loving Pict, is dead. Long live Arthur!"

ChAPTER TWENTY

The incense in Keena's hut made Rhianon's head swim. Or was it the bittersweet concoction of wine and herbs she'd taken to enhance communication with the Other World? Rhianon wasn't certain, but after the miserable attempt to kill Tarlach and tie his demise to Brenna's appearance, and the departure of her parents fraught with concern rather than filled with praise over her accomplishments, it felt glorious.

It almost made Rhianon forget her trepidation over reaching out to spirits for help. She was comfortable with her goddesses, but they had failed her. *Still* Rhianon had not conceived. She'd even tossed her grandmother's solid gold armband into Ceridwen's sacred pool to make amends for her infidelity with the other gods. Yet the poison stone they'd put in Tarlach's wine was as useless as a common fieldstone, not possessed of magic properties as Keena had said.

There was no choice but to appeal to the stronger spirits at Keena's hand.

Rhianon opened her heavy-lidded eyes, making out Keena's rocking, chanting figure. The crone prayed, first in her Cymri mother's ancient tongue, then in her Saxon father's. Each prayer summoned powers that Rhianon had not yet learned to command. But she'd felt them, thought she'd seen them … with her Spirit Eye. At the moment, all Rhianon saw was an old woman dipping her fingers into one of her magic powders, sprinkling it first on the fire, where it manifested a shade of blue that defied the best efforts of the dye women. Then on Caden's naked body.

If Caden knew, he would kill the nurse. He'd warned her and Rhianon against using their magic on him. But plied with wine and just enough henbane to induce a drunken sleep, he would never know dream from reality. It had been no challenge for Rhianon to coax him into a walk to distract him from the woes of Ronan's return with a promise of a night of pure ecstasy, much less to get him to down the alleged aphrodisiac.

By the goddess, it was hot. Her dress lay in a heap near the wall, and her linen shift clung to her like a second skin. Perspiration gleamed on Caden's splendid form as well. Rhianon blinked as smoke thickened over her husband's abdomen. From the power or powder?

"Friend of the Dark, give him courage to fight for what he desires." The eyes painted on Keena's lids folded up beneath her wizened brow, revealing her real ones, black as polished coal in the firelight.

"Yes!" Keena raised her arms, naught but leathered flesh over knotted joints of bone, toward the ceiling of the hut. "You are the desire of our desire, milord. Fill this mortal that he may be worthy of you … and of your priestess."

Caden began to jerk as though pierced by the fingers of black smoke surrounding him. Rhianon's heart beat faster as her husband inhaled a gulp of air, swelling the muscled ridges of his chest even more.

With a satisfied cackle, Keena struggled to her feet and motioned Rhianon to hers. "Milord awakens and awaits his priestess most eagerly." She loosed the bodice of Rhianon's shift and let it drop to the earthen floor. "Please him mightily, and he will do the same for you, child."

Brenna checked Tarlach for fever the following morning. He was cool. The chieftain slept like a babe, curled on his good side. Weak as one as well, but improving. Would that she could return to bed, for sleep had been scant with the needs of Tarlach taking precedence. Yet some of the villagers already waited to seek her advice for various maladies.

"He should not have lived," Brother Martin said, entering the room. He was dressed for travel—his plain gray cloak slung over his shoulder like a sack.

It broke Brenna's heart to see him leaving so soon. If ever she needed his mentoring, it was now. "God has a strange sense of justice that the daughter of the people Tarlach slew should be the one to save his life from his own kin."

"*When you expect God to do one thing, He may surprise you by doing something else ... usually something better than what you wished for to begin with.*" Ealga's words were sound, but nothing her nurse could have told her prepared Brenna for the speed at which her life had been turned about. Rescuing her enemy. Falling in love with him. Losing Faol. Captured as a fugitive and now hailed as a miracle-working healer. No time to grieve or celebrate, much less make sense of it all.

How could her priestly mentor leave her now? The brethren in the glen could not possibly need him more than she.

"A healer *and* a prophet." Martin's words pulled Brenna back to the bedside. "Ealga would be so proud of you."

"Prophet." Brenna scowled. "You keep saying that, Brother. I wish you would not."

These people did not understand who or what she was. Already the maidservant Mab had asked Brenna to ask God if a young warrior would ask her hand in marriage. The very idea appalled Brenna. The future belonged to God, not her.

"You say you trained me in the Word, that I might prophesy, but are you and Merlin certain this gift is *God's* calling?" Brenna challenged him. She had visions or dreams like her mother, but *her,* a prophet? Surely she'd not walk in the sandals of Isaiah and godly men of his ilk. Her visions pertained to her life and hers only. Perhaps it was intuition. Or worse, what if it came from darkness rather than light?

"Have your visions ever been wrong?"

Not that Brenna could recall. "But I can't tell when they will happen or ask and receive them on demand." She'd also explained that to the maidservant. "My visions come as they please and as vague as they please."

"God does not give His chosen these visions or words on their demand, but in His time and manner. That is what separates the prophets of God from those who use their gifts for personal gain. A soothsayer always has an answer and, ofttimes, it's wrong."

Martin chuckled, then grew grim as death itself. "That is why now especially, you must trust God's voice and stay close with Him. There is an evil in this place that will draw you away from Him, if you let it."

Brenna's flesh pimpled, swept cold by the memory of holding Tarlach, of pulling him away from unseen forces. Martin and Ealga had both counseled her on treating the spirit as well as the body, but never had she imagined the likes of that moment.

"I thought I saw demons trying to take him away," she confided, still in disbelief. "Or rather, felt them. I … I can't explain it any more than I can my visions."

And she'd actually seen the babe in her womb. Faith, she'd been so busy with Tarlach, she hadn't had the chance to think about either till now. It made her knees weak and her stomach tightened with dread. Nay, panic.

"You've taken your visions for granted till now, haven't you, child?" Martin placed a comforting hand on her shoulder.

"You and Ealga led me to think they were to be expected."

"For the daughter of Joanna of Gowrys."

"And I didn't believe in them until recently." Ronan strode into the room, looking the O'Byrne chief in the black, red, and silver of his clan.

Yet it was his nearness, not his finery, that renewed her. *Love.* Hadn't St. Paul declared it the greatest of all good things?

Her husband sat on a bench near the bed and drew Brenna into his lap with no heed that a priest watched them. "Tell me, Priest, just who is this enigmatic creature I've married?"

"Ronan," she chided, squirming with embarrassment.

He held her fast. "Still, *mo chroi*. Brother Martin knows we are properly wed."

My heart.

How could Brenna resist such an invitation? In the beam of Martin's smile, she curled against her husband's chest. After the late evening of celebrating the return of Glenarden's warriors from the Orkneys, it felt good. But her mind could not rest.

"So tell me, *please*," she implored, "of these demonic visions I saw over Tarlach." What she'd seen, or thought she'd seen, had haunted her since.

"Even my lay observation could see something otherworldly was amiss," Ronan agreed. "Something so sinister that I could not move to help her."

Brenna's pulse tripped. What exactly did Ronan think of her now? A healer was one thing. This was something else—and altogether frightening, even for her.

"Brenna is a healer, both of the physical and spiritual body. She is trained after the ministry of Jesus and His disciples in Scripture and medicine ... although she does not have as much learning as Merlin Emrys wanted due to having to hide her for so many years." Martin recovered from the resignation in his voice with the brightness of his faith. "But God gives us all we need, even if it's not all we would have."

The comment piqued Brenna's curiosity. "What else did Merlin want me to learn?"

"Astrology," the priest replied.

Ronan stiffened. "Astrology? I thought the church frowned on that."

"The Scripture admonishes against *worship*," Martin emphasized, "of the stars and heavens. Such worship was punishable by death.

"But David wrote in Psalm 19, that"—the priest quoted—"*The heavens declare the glory of God; and the firmament sheweth his handywork. Day unto day uttereth speech, and night unto night sheweth knowledge. There is no speech nor language, where their voice is not heard.*"

"God speaks to us through the heavens and stars, Ronan." A sweet memory came to Brenna's mind of Ealga and her staring at a starlit night in utter wonder. "He gives us signs of weather to come—"

"And of the Messiah's birth and death," Martin added. "Every astrological scholar of Jesus' time could read the heavens like a missive from their king. These magi knew what the Star of Bethlehem meant. And they knew as well that Heaven itself mourned Christ's death with darkness and earthquakes at midday, not just in Jerusalem, but in every country under the sky and on His earth. These things were recorded by historians of many nations as well as in the Scripture."

"That is why the Druids knew who Jesus was, of His birth and death," she stipulated, "*before* His disciples brought the news of His sacrifice and resurrection to Albion's shores." Brenna thought a moment, how best to illustrate. "The heavens were like God's scroll to all the world ordaining Jesus as King of Kings, Messiah, Son of God. It was surer than Merlin Emrys' recital of Arthur's genealogy at his coronation."

Skepticism still ruled her husband's face.

"Think, Ronan," Brother Martin urged. "Man in his fallibility might have misrepresented who Jesus was, but only the Creator God Himself could declare His Son's birthright, by writing with the stars upon the parchment of Heaven's own sky. What greater witness can there be?"

"Still, it smacks of heresy, Brother," Ronan replied. "So close that I fear my wife would be accused of it. Just like her mother."

"Yet Scripture says that these are divinely given gifts," Martin reminded him. "How the gift is used and to whom the glory is given for it determines its source. If of God, it is used for the good of others according to the Word, not for personal gain, and it glorifies the Father in the name of the Son and Holy Spirit."

"Like fire, Ronan, it can serve us or destroy us. Hence it is treated with the utmost respect and caution."

Yet, even as Brenna spoke, a coldness seized her, much like the one she'd felt while praying over Tarlach. And the one that had awakened her last night. Instinctively, she'd snuggled close to Ronan for his warmth, unable to explain it, given the moderate climate. And unable to go back to sleep, she'd lain awake for what seemed hours, troubled by that which she could not see or fathom.

"But what if we don't want the gift?" she asked Brother Martin.

"That is up to God, my child. The church's duty is to recognize and nurture it with the Word toward good fruit. Or to battle and condemn it and its source, if used for evil. Just remember: It is never the gift itself that is good or evil, for nothing from God is evil. It is the fruit of that gift that determines it one way or the other. Matthew says, *Ye shall know them by their fruits.*"

Brenna wriggled out of Ronan's embrace and stood, facing her mentor. "Then, if you believe as I do, that something evil lurks here at Glenarden, how can you in good conscience leave me to face it alone?"

"I agree with Brenna," Ronan said. "Clearly she hasn't your experience in dealing with such things."

"I am a healer. I thought my visions were only for me. How can you leave me now, when I first find there is more to them than my own interest and that of my child?" Brenna pleaded.

"Aye, there's the bairn to protect, Martin," Ronan reminded the priest. "Part of a greater plan, you say, yet you are abandoning the child and the mother."

"I am."

The serenity in her mentor's demeanor bewildered Brenna. How could he have such peace in the midst of something like this, much less answer her with that benevolent smile?

"God has a plan for each of us," Martin reminded them. "Yours, Brenna, is for here and now. Yours, Ronan, is to believe in her and protect her the best way you know how. But mine," he continued, "is elsewhere."

"Even when I've been summoned to Strighlagh?" Ronan shot back.

Last night Egan O'Toole had given Ronan a message from Arthur, demanding he go to the fair at Strighlagh a fortnight hence, to meet with the Gowrys and straighten out the mess of hostages that Caden had created with his impulsive and unjust raid.

"Mind you *both* have been summoned," Martin said. "But neither of you will need me. God is with each of us. He is sufficient."

Brenna crossed her arms and turned away. The priest was right. The Word said it. She believed it. But she sure didn't feel it.

"You can trust God always, lassie, but you canna always trust your feelings."

Easily said, Ealga, Brenna silently argued with the nurse in her mind.

Father God, I believe ... but help my unbelief.

A loud creak on the bed drew everyone's attention to where Tarlach had rolled on his back. His eyes were open, staring at Brenna as if for the first time.

His chest rose, pulling in breath and strength, then collapsed with a heavy sigh. "You are not," he accused, "Joanna."

The despair in Tarlach's words tugged Brenna to his side without thought to herself. She perched on the edge of the bed and took his hands into hers. "Nay, milord, I am not. I am Joanna's daughter. And on my soul, I give you my word, you have nothing to fear from me. What is past is past and forgiven." She leaned forward and planted a kiss on his cheek. "We must look to the future now. To your recovery and to the grandson you shall have ... with the mark of the Red Hand on his hip."

A flicker of recognition registered in Tarlach's dull gaze.

"We must stand together as O'Byrnes, Father, for Brenna is my wife, one with me, and mother to your grandson," Ronan said, closing in on the other side of the bed. "There is an enemy within us so vile that both you and I were nearly sent earthways, but for Brenna's intervention. She has saved us both."

"I have seen this myself, sire," Martin spoke up, earning a flicker of a glance.

Brenna tried to read Tarlach, but he was unfathomable. Whatever emotion or thoughts existed behind his gray gaze remained his and his alone.

He lifted his hand with a tired wave. "Tell me."

CHAPTER TWENTY-ONE

Ronan reined in Ballach to keep the horse from leading Brenna's smaller one into a trot. He'd chosen the gentlest of the stable for his wife to ride over Glenarden and introduce her to its heart—the people who tended the fields and livestock now out to pasture after the calving. Although given his choice, he'd have insisted on a cart, or that she ride with him on his stallion.

"I am with child. I am not an invalid," she'd insisted. "And I've longed to ride a pony since leaving the Sacred Isle."

How could he deny her? She had taken Glenarden as she'd taken his heart—with her bubbling love and genuine humility. Vychan and Dara hovered over her like mother hens, determined to teach her her proper place and duties as lady of the keep, but Brenna's innate humility was impervious to such things. The household authority she deftly deferred to Rhianon.

"My sister has been trained to oversee such a grand keep. An eagle doesn't swim, nor a fish fly."

Then there was Daniel and Cú. Even though Dara accompanied Brenna into the village to visit the sick and distribute alms at the gate, the awkward youth and dog guarded her flank. They also served as witness to the effectiveness of her balms, for Cú's mange improved by the day, now that he'd stopped biting it. And only yesterday Daniel and Brenna had carefully bound the broken leg of a rabbit that had run afoul of a trap.

"Daniel has a special heart for God," Brenna told Ronan when he'd teased her about being jealous of her time spent with the lad. "And a way with wild creatures. I shall call his attention to Merlin Emrys when next I see him."

For the first time since returning to Glenarden, the tightness in Ronan's neck and shoulder muscles relaxed beneath the fingers of the early morning sun.

"So many times I've looked at these fields and pastures from the cover of the hills. Never did I see myself riding through them on my own pony. And her name is perfect, isn't it, Airgid?"

One might have thought he'd offered her the horse's weight in silver, rather than one of the older stable steeds, broken by experience and time. "'Tis a high name for such a lowly beast," he teased. "But I'll find a more worthy mount for you at the fair."

"Hush, now." She leaned forward to cover the pony's ears. "She can hear you. He didn't mean it, Airgid. I vow you shall be mine for as long as God allows it." She ran her hands along the mare's gray neck.

Something told Ronan the wounded rabbit was not the last of the animals that would find a home in Glenarden's sheds. He thought about Faol, amazed that he missed the beast. He'd never been much for pets, even as a child. His heart and soul had been bound in the past ... until Brenna. Now seeing ordinary people, even animals, through his wife's eyes was seeing beyond the physical to an extraordinary, most individual spirit. She had made his old world new.

"I've been thinking," he said aloud. "Perhaps we'll find a good pup at the fair." Especially since a new horse didn't seem to be in order.

The same cloud that tamped his spirit grazed her sunny expression. "Maybe."

Would that he'd kept his mouth shut. He grappled to recover the sun. "Well, definitely fabric. I'll have my bride bedecked with dresses in every color of the rainbow."

She thought a moment. "Perhaps a blue, like the one that was ruined. That would be lovely." She glanced down at her boyish attire. "Though I can't see wearing a dress for riding." Second thought creased her brow. "Unless you think me unfit to be seen with."

Ronan groaned. What a muck he made word by word. "Milady, I'd find you most fetching in anything you choose to wear ... or not wear," he added with a rakish grin. Ronan shifted uncomfortably in the saddle, stirred by the look she gave him. With the sunlight dancing off her raven hair and her blue eyes brighter than Heaven's own sky, no man with a heartbeat could resist the urge to spirit her away to a private place and—

"Lady Brenna!"

Across the meadow to the east, making his way through the heather and spring's bouquet of wildflowers, came Daniel of Gowrys, Cú bounding ahead of him. At a distance, one of the guards assigned to keep him from running off watched.

Ronan couldn't say if the Gowrys lad was intrigued by Brenna and the aura of mystery that surrounded her, or simply smitten. Either way, confound his timing.

"There's a woman waiting with a crippled boy to see you beside the gate. She's come down from the uplands."

"A Gowrys?" Ronan exclaimed, astonished.

The young man shrugged. "I've ne'er seen her, but she's nigh worn out from the journey, dragging the boy on her cloak when his leg gave out."

The same way Brenna had dragged him to her cave, Ronan recalled.

Brenna must have had the same thought. "Oh, Ronan, we must hurry. Come along, Airgid." She nudged the mare's sides with her heels. "Quickly now." The gray mare took off at a teeth-jarring trot, Brenna holding onto its mane for dear life.

"Brenna, wait!" he shouted. At the click of his tongue, Ballach bolted forward and caught up with the smaller steed in six great strides. Ronan reached down from the stallion's back and caught up the reins his wife had dropped. "Ho, Airgid. Ho."

The mare eased back into a walk. Brenna, beet-faced, straightened in the saddle and gave him a sheepish grin. "You must teach me to ride again, it seems."

Had Ronan ever been so frightened? He wanted to strangle her. Had Brenna ever been more precious? He wanted to love her as if there were no tomorrow.

"If you will run ahead," she said to Daniel, above the heart pounding in Ronan's ears, "tell the lady I will be there as soon as my mare will carry me to her."

"Aye, right away." The lad gave her a courtly bow and bounded off, dog at his side.

Ronan tamped down the feelings stampeding through him.

"Come along—*cautiously*—milady." He handed her Airgid's reins. "Your people await you."

Let God be his witness. He loved her so much it hurt.

Brenna glanced over her shoulder to check on her new charge, wondering if Bron was as excited to be attending the fair as she. A week ago, the peasant boy now riding in the cart with Tarlach, Rhianon, and their companions had been a penniless cripple with a clubfoot. There were some things even the gifted could not heal, but Brenna did discover a rare artistic talent in the lad. Another way he might help provide for his widowed mother. The wolf he'd drawn on his mother's cloak with charcoal while they awaited Brenna's arrival was Faol's very image. So real Brenna could almost smell his fur, rife with the scent of the sun and forest. And she knew God had provided another way.

Ronan paid the mother a handsome price for it and it now hung, nicely framed, in their bedchamber. As for Bron, his mother agreed after some persuasion to trust her son to Brenna's care, at least until after the fair. Upon seeing the lad's rare talent, the women of Glenarden had scrounged every scrap of cloth to be found for more sketches, that he might sell them at the fair. Some had already set about embroidering those lifelike images he'd given to them for their kindness.

At first, Rhianon protested the peasant's company in the cart … until Bron offered to sketch her likeness along the way on one of the precious sheets of vellum that Brenna had secured from the brethren.

As for Tarlach, the old chieftain was indifferent to the boy. He catnapped along the two-day journey ensconced in his leather chair, which was secured to the cart, while Cú and Daniel walked behind. Tarlach's stubborn will amazed her. He insisted on attending the fair to show anyone—peer or would-be assassin—that he was still alive and in control of his kingdom.

Now, ahead of them, stood a fortress of stone and timber belonging to Angus, known in Arthur's brotherhood of the Round Table as the Lance of Lothian. Perched on the ancient black rock standing sentry over the Firth of Forth, it flew banners of blue and gold on white. Above those, a Red Dragon fluttered unfurled, indicating Arthur was in residence there. Hence, it was Camelot for as long as the Pendragon remained.

"See how it shines in the sunlight!" Brenna took in Strighlagh's whitewashed timber and stone fortress high upon its rock pedestal. "It's the most beautiful place I've ever seen."

"Raised in the darkness of a cave, I would think so." Caden sneered from the brown horse beside her.

Insecurity bullied its way into Brenna's delight. Self-conscious, she glanced from the red tunic and braccae that Dara and the women had made for her to Rhianon's elegant peony gown.

"No beauty compares to you, milady." The look Ronan gave her riddled her to the core. But what a marvelous warmth it was.

"Aye, but beauty must know its place," Caden pressed with a pointed look at the bow and quiver of arrows slung across Brenna's back. "My wife has no fear that her husband can't protect her."

"With a tongue as sharp as well-aimed spit, Rhianon needn't—"

"Ronan," Brenna softly stayed his reply.

Given any chance, her husband's middle brother would ruin Ronan's peace with his barbed remarks. They escaped like steam from a pot about to boil over, Ronan had observed.

"Caden has every reason to be as proud of Rhianon as you are of me," Brenna pointed out, pragmatic beneath her husband's skeptical look. "And each of you for reasons that are as different as Rhianon and I are."

She turned to Caden, encountering the glacial sting of his gaze, yet unable to see beyond or through its gray fog.

Devoid of humanity.

"I have no fear that Ronan is unable to protect me, Caden." Brenna forced herself to ignore the chill. "As you said, I was raised in a cave, and this weapon is like a second skin to me when I am in unfamiliar territory. But I will put it away, if it offends you."

"Pay him no heed, Brenna," Ronan spoke up. "I am proud to have you just as you are as wife. That is what makes you extraordinary in an ordinary world."

As though bored, Caden kicked the sides of his steed. "I'm riding ahead to secure our place for the tents," he called over his shoulder.

Brenna reached across the distance between their mounts and squeezed Ronan's hand. "I'm grateful I've married the stronger man—one who has the courage to turn the other cheek."

"Until he presses too far with this jealousy and ambition of his."

Ronan's undertone pierced Brenna with alarm. The prophecy that she would divide the O'Byrne household was happening, and Brenna could see no way around it. *Father God, what must I do?*

The answer came clearly: *"Let love pull hatred's teeth."*

Except that kindness only seems to madden Caden and Rhianon all the more, she argued.

"Doing right is never wrong."

"But for now," Ronan announced, breaking into her battling thoughts, "I look forward to enjoying the fair with my most extraordinary wife."

Once they reached the edge of the nobles' encampment, Tarlach insisted he be helped upon his horse. Riding straight as his ague-plagued limbs would allow, he passed upward through the menagerie of tents and clan banners to his rightful place of encampment as kin to Strighlagh's Gwenhyfar and battle lord under Arthur. The reception was warm enough. Several chieftains hailed him as friend, although some seemed more surprised than others to see him up and about, affirming that the rumors of his death had made their mark.

But even more attention focused on Brenna. She was grateful to have her father-in-law on one side and husband on the other. Even so, she could feel the eyes upon her—some curious, some anxious, but all interested in the prophesied return of the daughter of Joanna and Llas of Gowrys.

"Where are the Gowrys camped?" Brenna asked Ronan.

"You'll see them in Arthur's court soon enough," Tarlach grumbled. "Nor will you seek them out, if you're wise. I forbid it."

Aside from asking about her unborn son, this was the most her father-in-law had said to her since he'd regained strength.

"The Gowrys will be camped farther downhill toward the river … where the ground rent costs less." Ronan pointed to a sea of banners and tents situated alongside the sun-bright curl of water. "Beyond the bridge."

"You've nothing to fear from me, milord," Brenna assured Tarlach.

"'Tisn't you I'm worried aboot, woman. 'Tis the bairn."

Brenna instinctively covered her abdomen. Surely her own clan wouldn't do anything to threaten her or her child.

"There's Caden now!" A jubilant Rhianon waved her handkerchief at her husband.

Another man joined him on the shoulder of the hill. Brenna studied him—his fine green tunic and brown breeches. Suddenly recognition clicked into place. He'd been with the hunters who had captured her.

"That's that ghost of a huntsman from Gwynedd, no?" Tarlach asked. His forest of a brow knit as he squinted in the midday sun.

"Aye," Ronan replied. "Heming, I think."

"Ghost?" Brenna questioned.

"He lurks about as though always stalking. Here a moment, then gone. Not the most sociable sort."

As if to demonstrate, the hunter faded into the hubbub of activity in the campsites surrounding Glenarden's.

"Heming spends more time in the wood than at court," Rhianon complained. "Good riddance."

Brenna would have thought the Lady Rhianon would have been glad to see someone from her homeland. Certainly she and Keena, who was also from her homeland, were as close as peas in a pod, always whispering in Brenna's presence as if she weren't there.

"When can we go down to the fair?" Brenna asked, watching Caden help his wife down from the cart. For all his strength, he handled her as though she might break. Perhaps Rhianon would be the key to unleashing the goodness suppressed by his jealousy and anger.

"Now … if you're not too weary from the morning's ride." The mischievous twist of Ronan's lips said he knew better. "The servants will set up our encampment while we take in the sights."

Beaming with excitement, Brenna dismounted from Airgid. "I must pinch myself to believe I am here. And to meet Arthur and"— she edited out *Gowrys* quickly—"and others I've only heard about. Soon as I've rubbed down Airgid and watered her, I'll fetch my skins and medicines.…"

"Milady, allow the servants to do their jobs," Ronan chided. "As for your *trading*, Vychan is most adept at business."

"But I need the money from my goods to purchase vellum and supplies for Bron." Reminded of the boy, she turned to see him standing at her heel, crutch beneath his arm. "And Bron," she said, ruffling his mop of brown hair, "has trading to do as well."

"There will be time to take care of all this business," Ronan assured them. "Today we shall see what is here and perhaps buy something to eat from the vendors. As soon as the rest of your entourage catches up with us."

Brenna followed his pointed look to where Dara, Daniel, and Cú made their way toward them. Her husband was right … about the looking. She'd do well to familiarize herself with the goods and prices as she'd seen Brother Martin do at the small fair near Glenarden. If he were here, her life would be complete joy.

"Take two men with you," Tarlach insisted. With Vychan's help, he eased into his chair, which had been placed under the shade of an oak. His face was flushed from the effort of dismounting, but he seemed otherwise invigorated.

"I'll ask O'Toole," Ronan agreed. A cocky grin claimed his handsome features.

How Brenna loved it when he smiled, though it was rarely outside the privacy of their bedchamber. It ate at him that his and his father's would-be assassins were still at large, despite his exhaustive efforts to find them. Hence, they might still be in their midst, though none had a scar from the arrow Brenna had shot through his hand.

Sharing his son's rare humor, the old chief's mouth pulled up on the one good side. "Aye, I'd wager he's enough, weapons or nay."

To keep the peace, no weapons beyond a dining dagger were allowed on the fairgrounds except for trade or competition, but what Egan lacked in weaponry, he made up for in sheer mass.

After a downhill walk through too many other campsites to count, Brenna's entourage entered the main street to the makeshift village of merchants from all over Albion and beyond. There were Saxons, Frisians, Franks, Spaniards, Italians, Jews, and Middle Eastern vendors, all plying their goods from buildings, tents, and stalls rented from the landowners. Never had Brenna heard so many languages and accents or seen so many luxuries.

"Can you imagine the world beyond Albion?" she exclaimed, fingering an Italian silk in awe.

There was glassware, displayed like the colors of the rainbow, the beautifully crafted ceramics, dye-stuffs for Glenarden's clothmakers, cotton fibers for armor padding and quilts, leather goods…. Brenna wanted to see and touch them all. Even the armor. Her astonished squeals were only surpassed by Bron, who rode astride Egan's broad shoulders.

"Methinks we have two youngsters," Egan said with a laugh as Brenna tugged him and Bron toward a puppet show on a flat of land cleared for entertainment. "Mayhaps now we might roost long enough to eat. I'm hungry as three horses."

Food. "I forgot." Brenna glanced at the sun, surprised to see it had moved several more degrees westward than it had been when they arrived.

"I'm still not hungry," Bron protested, and Egan slid him down to his feet.

"Speak for yourself," Daniel of Gowrys teased, handing the boy his crutch. Both strangers in Glenarden, the two had become best of friends since Bron's arrival. Daniel had given his word to Ronan that he'd not try to escape and, having saved Brenna by calling down Tarlach's wolfhound and with the champion Egan as watchdog, that was enough. "Cú, stay with Bron."

"And you, Bron, stay here with the ladies," Egan said. "Ronan and I'll be along with food directly."

As the menfolk set off in the direction of a row of food vendors, Dara hauled a light blanket out of the sack she'd carried slung over her back and spread it on the ground. "To tell the truth, I forgot food meself," she admitted. "I canna mind when I last came to the big fair ... and so much to see."

"I have to say, now that we've settled," Brenna confided, "the scents excite my stomach as yon puppets do a certain lad I know."

"May I move closer so's I can hear?" Bron asked. At Brenna's nod, the boy eased his way closer to the stage, a curtained cart with a window where the puppets performed. Obedient, Cú inched forward behind him.

"I canna believe the change in that beast since young Daniel came. Same as its master ..." Dara paused. "Well, the whole lot of us," she continued, warming Brenna in her approval. "'Tis the prophecy to be sure."

"Nay, 'tis God's love. Words and efforts are vain without it."

Brenna turned to watch the show, but her mind wasn't on it. *Father God, they place too much credit with me. Expect me to work miracles. Help me turn their thoughts from me to You.*

"Brenna of Gowrys?"

Father God, more for miracles?

"Aye?" Brenna looked up to see three men gathered round her. The one who spoke was a bear of a man, draped with a brat of faded red and green.

"Father, save us," Dara gasped as two of them hauled Brenna to her feet. "'Tis the *Gowrys!*"

CHAPTER TWENTY-TWO

Dara didn't wait for God's intervention. The midwife launched herself at the leg of one of the men and bit for all she was worth with the few teeth she had.

With a startled curse, the Gowrys clansman shook the older woman free, kicking at her when she tried to bite him again.

"Stop it, *all* of you," Brenna protested, tugging as her captors lifted her free of the ground.

"Bring her along," the leader ordered.

They'd taken leave of their senses to abduct her here in the midst of a field of witnesses ... although none of the shocked onlookers seemed inclined to intervene.

"If you are my kinsmen, I demand you put me down."

They did, although Brenna wasn't sure if it was her authority that stopped them in their tracks or the gray wolfhound that leapt into their path, snarling lowly.

"Gentlemen, I assure you, one of you will not shake Cú off so easily, if you persist in this indignation."

"Caw, he even looks like Tarlach—gray and evil," one of the men remarked, hand easing for his dining dagger.

"Lord Ronan!" Dara screamed. Brenna turned in time to see Ronan parting the thick crowd between the food vendors' stalls like a raging bull.

"Act as gentlemen, or it will go badly for you," she warned them, for Egan O'Toole was on her husband's heels and him just as beetled-red mad.

At their leader's nod, the men lowered their arms to their sides.

"Bow and kiss my hand, Donal of Gowrys," Brenna ordered one of the men.

With his coal black hair and blue eyes, the older version of Daniel cocked his brow in astonishment.

"And nothing will be said, right, Dara?" Brenna asked.

"His bleedin' leg will tell enough." Dara gave the man a defiant sniff.

Fear stabbed at Brenna, despite her bravado, as a seething Donal of Gowrys bent over, head low, and kissed Brenna's hand. "So it's true you're with them of your own accord?"

They were but a breath, a word from bloodshed.

"Aye, and now I'm with you *both*," she emphasized. Brenna turned away and held up her hands in feigned exasperation.

"Then get me my boy back," she heard Donal growl.

She had seconds. Just seconds.

"Ronan, where is the food?" Brenna called out in a bright voice. "We've *guests*."

Father God, this is calling black white if there ever was such a case.

But Brenna wanted them to be guests. That counted, didn't it?

"I dinna like this," Dara grumbled.

Ronan slowed only slightly, yet he was hardly winded when he reached them. Nor did he believe Brenna's claim. "Get away from my wife, Gowrys. What mischief are you about?"

"She's my cousin, as well, is she not? Daughter of my father's brother?"

"She's an O'Byrne now." Ronan inserted himself between Donal and Brenna, ignoring the Gowrys' hand upon his dagger. "Honorably wedded, bedded, and carrying Tarlach's heir in her belly." Her husband's hand was also on his blade.

"And our *murdered* chieftain's heir as well." Nose to nose with Ronan, Donal refused to back away. "Like your brother murdered my eldest son."

Around them, some of the crowd had risen and gathered, more interested in the prospect of a good fight than a puppet show. Brenna wanted to pull Ronan away, but Donal might take advantage of the distraction. Already the other two clansmen hefted dining daggers to match O'Toole's. One misspoken word and someone would be maimed.

"That was wrong, no doubt," Ronan admitted. "But stealing my wife is no way to settle this."

"Nor is taking my only son left hostage for a wrong we did not commit," Donal responded.

"Father!" Daniel of Gowrys approached, his arms loaded with mangled pies heaped upon loaves of bread and a large chunk of cheese dangling from a string about his wrist.

Gowrys backed down from Ronan's hard glare, dagger hand dropping to his side. "Son." Emotion cracked the grizzled Donal's voice.

"The laddie's put on weight," the red-haired Gowrys observed.

"Nay wonder. Lookit what he carries," his kinsman quipped.

"This isn't over," Donal growled beneath his breath to Ronan.

"Oh yes it is." Brenna motioned to the food. "Will you and your men join us for a repast? Dara, help Daniel, please."

"I'm not hungry." Donal may not have been, but the expressions on the other men's faces told Brenna otherwise. All three bore the look of a hard winter, wiry and broad of frame but gaunt beneath their bearded faces. And their clothing naught but rags holding rags together, a stark contrast to Glenarden's well-dressed party.

It took a moment to unload Daniel so that he could greet Donal properly. Just their hug softened Donal's belligerent humor a bit more. "You look well, Daniel."

"I am well treated." Daniel glanced at Brenna. "Especially since Lord Ronan arrived with our kinswoman as his bride. For the first time in all my days, Father, I've a hope for peace."

The Gowrys exchanged dubious looks.

"What of my brother Alyn?" Ronan interrupted. "We'd like to see if he is as well treated as our hostage."

"He's treated as well as any of us can afford to treat him," Donal said, "given both our homes and cattle have been unjustly ravaged."

Daniel had told both Ronan and Brenna of how difficult it was to scratch a living in the highlands. Without the good ground that was once theirs beneath the lake rath, their winter stores barely kept man and beast alive. Cattle they needed for breeding died of starvation and served as food. Hides would be as good as they could bring for trade at the fair.

"My brother was wrong, though he did what was reasonable,

given I'd disappeared from where he left me, leaving only blood and arrows fletched with your red and green."

Donal snorted. "It was not us."

"I believe you," Ronan told him. "And I do not need the Pendragon's order to give you back your son—"

Brenna's heart skipped in anticipation.

"—when you return my youngest brother."

The surprise on Donal's face turned to distrust. "And why should I trust *your* word?"

"*I* will guarantee it." Brother Martin's voice boomed behind them.

Brenna had been so engrossed in the exchange that she'd not seen the priest approach them.

"Meet Daniel, O'Toole, and me at the tavern this night. 'Tis a neutral place well patrolled by the Angus' guards, so both clans need not worry about violence." Ronan extended his hand. "This blood feud has lasted long enough."

"I agree, Father," Daniel said.

Donal ignored him. "This will not change what the O'Byrnes owe us for their wrongful attack."

"Let the Pendragon decide that," Martin said. "It is as I've told you, Donal. With Joanna and Llas's daughter at Glenarden, the promised peace is close at hand."

So *that* was the pressing matter the priest had sped away to after he'd left her.

"We have a *mutual* enemy who would keep that peace out of reach," Ronan said to Donal. "The one who left me dying with the Gowrys colors run through me. He is more responsible than Caden for the outrage against your clan."

After an eternal pause, Donal replied, "Tonight, then." But suspicion weighed heavily on his demeanor. With a jerk of his head, he said the word "Go," and his men fell in behind him as he walked away.

"Wait!" Brenna stopped them. "You might as well take these pies." Before they could refuse, she gave one to each man. "They're as much as crushed from too much pie and not enough Daniel to carry them."

The carrot-topped man grinned at her desperate stab for humor. "Thank ye, milady. If your husband dinna—"

"By all means." Ronan's clipped reply displayed none of the relief washing over Brenna.

With his men smoothly eased from his control by Brenna's generosity, the Gowrys chieftain shot a defiant look over her head at Ronan. "'Twill take more than a pie or two to settle this." With that, he led his men away.

How long the lot of them watched the colorful sea of fair attendees, even after it swallowed the Gowrys, Brenna had no idea. But Ronan's grasp on her shoulders would surely leave bruises.

It was Bron's hail that finally cracked the shell of anxiety enveloping them.

"Lady Brenna, look!" The lad hobbled over on his crutch, fairly bubbling with excitement. "Do you see it?" He pointed to the stage, oblivious to the drama that had transpired. In front of the covered cart, a man led about a shaggy black and white pony for people to examine, while two others hung a sign from the wagon.

"He says it's the prize for the archery contest tomorrow morning."

The boy's longing was so palpable, Brenna hugged him. Or perhaps it was for breaking the tension. But she saw Bron riding the pony from village to village, leather sacks with his drawings and supplies hung over its flanks, his crutch slung from the saddle. *She* wanted it for Bron as much as he did. As much as she longed for peace among their clans.

"Sir, may women take part in the contest?" she called out to the man with the pony.

The man afforded her a curious head-to-toe look, but only after he spied Ronan and Egan flanking her did he reply. "Only if she can pay the fee and shoot a straight arrow. Can ye do them things, lassie?"

"Caden is going to leap for joy at this," Ronan griped behind her.

She spun about. "Is it well with you, milord? For *you* are all I care about."

Ronan grinned. "Who cares for Caden? I can refuse you nothing, *mo chroi.*"

Joy shot Brenna through. Or was it love's own arrow?

"Aye, sir," she shouted back at the skeptical pony man. "I can do both."

Caden laughed out loud at Brenna's announcement that she was competing in the morrow's archery tournament. It covered the cold fury gripping him when Tarlach accepted Ronan's proposition to exchange the hostages without protest. As always, Caden was in the wrong. It was *his* fault that Glenarden would be seen as owing compensation to their sworn enemies.

"I did *nothing* wrong," he fumed.

"Brother, I am not saying that you did, given what you knew," Ronan said. "You did the wrong thing for the right reason."

Tarlach held up his good hand to Caden. "Let your brother finish."

The knife at Caden's waist burned there, just as the desire to use it upon both his father and brother burned in his mind. He could hear nothing else but the thought fueling the flames. *They deserve to die.*

"Caden." Rhianon put a cool hand on his bare arm. "Let us leave this matter. I need to walk, lest I go mad with boredom."

Madness. By his father's lips, that's what it felt like. Caden had never liked Tarlach, but he loved him. Tarlach was his father in every way but heart. Caden swallowed, but his parched tongue stuck to the roof of his mouth. What was wrong with him? If he did not rid himself of the dagger this moment, it would blister him.

"For our child," Rhianon enticed with a whisper, "I need escape the smoke of the fire."

Our child. The one his wife pleaded be kept secret, for fear the witch would do it harm to protect her own. Caden would have shouted the news, but he dared not. He'd seen half of Glenarden bewitched by Brenna, his father and brother to the point of insane judgment.

Caden stood up from the plank table assembled by the fire, nearly flipping the board nearest him. His fingers fumbling as though listening to two masters, he managed to remove his dagger from its sheath. But instead of sending it flying at Tarlach or his brother, he buried it in the thick oak, bringing an abrupt end to the conversation.

"You know my feelings. Give them nothing they don't deserve."

Relief washed through him, for the burning stopped. He stared at the silver-handled dagger Rhianon had given him as a wedding gift as if it belonged to someone else.

But the voice of his wife, Caden knew, and he would follow it anywhere. "Come, Love. 'Tis a lovely night."

CHAPTER TWENTY-THREE

"I've never been inside a tavern, have you, Daniel?" Brenna asked, walking behind Ronan, her arm linked with that of the Gowrys lad.

Alert to any nuance of danger, Ronan looked past the patches of torch and firelight to the night beyond as he escorted his wife and Daniel through the camps and stalls of the fair. His keen gaze glided from one group of revelers to another for any possible hiding places for brigands.

Ronan was still put off by the events of the afternoon. The sight of Brenna being carried off by the Gowrys that afternoon, feet flailing, had knifed Ronan through with a two-edged blade—one of panic and one of naked fury. Tonight, apprehension riddled him, though the other blade was not far from him. Against all logic, he'd agreed to let Brenna accompany him to the exchange of hostages. He, and more amazingly, Tarlach, yielded, albeit grudgingly, to her argument that a greater power accompanied her than their muscle and steel.

How Ronan's fury had vanished at the touch of her hands still made him wonder. He'd been primed for a fight—no man, friend or foe, would lay hands on his wife—not for the reconciliation that spilled from his lips. Nor had she needed his or Egan's help. Her protection had been a dog, a crippled child, a widow woman, and her Shepherd, she insisted, before he and his champion could offer it.

Could her Shepherd—God—be as tangible as she believed? For, while Ronan walked like a man on edge, her childlike enthusiasm for life and all it brought was undaunted. Even now she approached such a simple occasion as exploring the nightlife of the fair as a grand adventure full of wonder.

Maybe there was something to Caden's accusation that Ronan was bewitched. Or as addled by Brenna's lack of guile as Caden was by Rhianon's manipulation. Ronan at least still carried his dining dagger and kept both hands free for the dirk in each boot in case of an ambush.

Father God ... Humor tugged at his lips as he reached out to Him who was higher than his understanding. He even called God as she did, now that he ventured to call at all.

The sight of Brother Martin waiting with Donal and three other men under the painted *Red Lion* tavern sign cut his prayer short. The benches set in front of the two-story building to accommodate the overflow of customers were all taken. Dust kicked up by the reveling clientele floated in the light of lanterns strung overhead from tree to tree. Music and laughter wafted out through the open doors and windows, revealing a crowd thick as hornets on a hive inside. Two of Strighlagh's guardsmen chatted near a corner post.

Ronan continued to scan the area, looking for any sign of additional Gowrys, but given that their chief was the only one who wore the colors, it was hard to tell, even in daylight.

"Ronan!"

It took Ronan a moment to recognize his youngest brother. Alyn broke from the group, rushing to embrace him. Ronan could feel the young man's ribs through the linen of his tunic. Yet his face was flushed and, from what Ronan could tell, his eyes were bright … overly so. Alyn had not yet learned to hide his feelings well.

"I thought you were dead. We all did."

"I was left for dead but was rescued." Ronan turned to introduce Brenna as the rest of the Gowrys party caught up to them.

"I know," Alyn said. "Brother Martin told us the whole wondrous story. Can you believe how God has worked in our lives?"

God. Dare Ronan fully accept what his younger, less-jaded brother did? What Brenna did? That God was working through the circumstances and events of their lives? Yet here he was, married to the enemy he'd hunted until just months ago and now ready to negotiate with her kin to help stop a twenty-year war. What other explanation could there be?

Even more, he was offering prayers to her God under his breath, as if it were second nature to him.

"*This,*" he said, "is Lady Brenna of Glenarden, the lady who changed my heart forever."

Alyn bowed with all the grace his tall, gangly body would allow. "Milady, at last I meet you. And you look nothing like a wolf."

Ronan allowed himself a chuckle to Brenna's melodious laughter.

"And I at last meet you, Alyn of Glenarden," she replied. "You put me to mind of your eldest brother."

"We take after our mother. Caden is the golden Glenarden."

"Let's make the exchange and be done with it," Donal of Gowrys said. Like Ronan, his gaze darted about to shadows with equal distrust. Or was he looking for a sign from an accomplice?

"Daniel, you are free to join your kinsmen," Ronan said. "But we hope that you will not be a stranger to Glenarden. Cú will sorely—"

Something set off an inner alarm, that sense of being watched … closely. As Ronan turned, a hooded, cloaked figure shot up from the nearest bench and plowed into him, sending him sprawling off balance. The hiss and thud of an arrow registered in an alder just beyond them.

Had the man just attacked him or saved him?

Charging through Ronan's confusion came one main thought. "O'Toole! Get Brenna to cover."

"Cover them all," the unknown man ordered, his deep voice ringing with authority. "In the name of the Pendragon."

The men previously seated with the stranger rushed to form a circle about O'Byrne and Gowrys alike. Beyond, the two guards had broken away from their conversations and raced off in the direction Ronan's mystery figure pointed, as if they'd been waiting for this to happen. As O'Toole steadied Ronan on his feet, the stranger removed his hood, revealing a mane of white hair and piercing gaze beneath the snowdrift on his shaved high brow.

"By the Father's grace, Merlin Emrys," Brother Martin exclaimed.

The priest started toward his friend, arm extended, but Merlin held up his hand. "Later, friend, once we reach a safe place. All of you—come with us to the Eccles."

The walk to the small church that served the valley of the Forth near Strighlagh seemed to take an eternity, given with each step, Brenna expected another arrow to fly at them. At Ronan. The thought of losing her husband nearly made her sick to her stomach. She clung to his arm like moss to a tree, as though she might somehow protect him and at the same time draw upon his strength.

The red and green fletching on the arrow stymied everyone, including Donal of Gowrys. This time, it wasn't the word of Glenarden against Gowrys about a mutual enemy; it was proof. Merlin Emrys, on hearing of the mutually agreed-upon exchange from Brother Martin, anticipated such trouble. So he'd had men watch both clans carefully to be certain no one from either side was at the source. Unfortunately the guards who pursued the would-be assassin—or searched the direction from which the arrow came—found no one.

The old church reminded Brenna of a great overturned boat made of dry masonry. At Merlin's instruction, only Ronan, Brenna, and Brother Martin entered the structure through the single door from its west end. The rest remained with the royal advisor's men outside. Inside, the wall rose, half again a man's height, before it curved inward and upward, narrowing to a point, or upended keel, overhead. A small stone altar stood opposite the door, hollowed out to hold water. Lamp stands to either side illuminated the gable wall.

"For as many wonders of God's creation that meet the eye, there are even more that do not," Brenna whispered to Ronan.

"What?"

"If the recollection of my studies serves me, this church is strategically located where two underground streams cross. This alters the nature of the water placed in the cup, making it more beneficial to health ... like the healing waters of our—"

A rustling of fabric in the silence of the great chamber drew Brenna's attention from the candlelit altar to the sides of the room, where a group of robed figures filed out of the shadows. Merlin Emrys bade her party stand just inside the door, while the figures formed a half circle to either side of the altar. Half were clad in red, the other half, when Merlin shed his cloak and joined them, in white. At the center a tall, fair-haired hulk of a man in both red and white robes trimmed in gold took the seat that one of the others placed in the center of the half round.

"Arthur of Dalraida," Brother Martin whispered to her. "Born of the Lions of Judah in red *and* the Josephs of Albion in white."

Brenna nodded. A king of kings after the example of Christ, with twelve warrior and priest-like disciples.

The saintliest of Briton's bloodlines assembled here with the kings and queens of Judah, the Davidic descendants from the breach marked by a scarlet cord, the stolen birthright in Genesis—a breach repaired as prophesied by Isaiah centuries before by the marriage of Pharez's princess and Zarah's Red Hand prince.

Martin identified them. Merlin Emrys, Arthur's great-uncle, stood with his protégés Arthur and Percival. Vivianne, Arthur's aunt and Lady of the Lake, with her protégés Gwenhyfar and the Angus or Lance of Lothian. There was Gawain, Arthur's right arm....

Arthur was so much older than Brenna had thought. At least compared to Lance of Lothian, the Pendragon's left arm.

Merlin Emrys tapped his staff on the hard earthen floor. At that moment two men in robes wordlessly lit the lamps hung on the walls. Immediately the scented oil began to offset the inherent must and mold of the stone enclosure. "I call this Council of the Grail to order," Arthur said after the men in robes left. His voice filled the room—before them, above them, and behind them. "In the name of the Father, the Son, and the Holy Spirit. Amen."

"Amen," Brenna echoed with them. She'd heard of such meetings, but they were usually reserved for the Holy Isle.

"Why are we summoned, Merlin?" Arthur asked quietly, the chamber amplifying every sound.

"Brothers and sisters, warriors and warrior queens, priests and priestesses of the Celtic Church of Christ, the matter of the O'Byrne and Gowrys may not wait until the political court to be held at the week's end lest there be more bloodshed," Merlin explained. "This night an assassin tried to take Ronan O'Byrne's life for the second time, even as the leaders of both clans sought a righteous and peaceful end to this bloodfeud. Thankfully, Brother Martin made me aware of their honorable and peaceful intentions beforehand."

Merlin Emrys handed Arthur the arrow he'd fetched from the tree before leaving. "Do not touch its tip," he warned. "Had the Brother and I not foreseen trouble, this poison-tipped arrow might have found its mark."

Brenna grew weak at the knees. Had it so much as nicked Ronan—

"It is poorly disguised," Merlin went on, "just like the previous ones that nearly took this young man's life." He leaned his staff toward Ronan, casting darts of light about the lusterless stone walls. "But the nature of this poison alarms me far more than its disguise."

"A knowledge of nature magic abused by a black soul," Gwenhyfar remarked upon taking the arrow from Arthur. The queen tossed the arrow to the ground. "Faith, I can feel the darkness." She crossed herself and held out her hands, palms up. "Take this from me, Father." She grabbed Arthur's hands. "And from our king."

"Amen," the gathering chorused together.

"What of Merlin?" Brenna asked Martin, as Merlin picked it up and wrapped it in the folds of his discarded cloak. "He touched it too."

"It is his path to the perpetrator of this deed," the priest answered. "This is more than a clan war, Brenna. If we cannot find and stop those who abuse such sacred knowledge of creation for their own gain and glory, the church itself is at risk. We all, Christian and pagan alike, shall be washed in the same black water regardless of our fruit."

"That," Merlin addressed them, "is a battle for another day. Tonight we judge Glenarden for its trespasses against their neighbors."

Ronan's muscles tensed even more beneath Brenna's hand. Had she heard right? They sought to judge Ronan for *Tarlach's* misdeeds?

"Come forward for your father's sake, sir," Arthur commanded.

"'Tis unfair," Brenna protested beneath her breath to Brother Martin. She started forward with her husband, but Arthur palmed his hand at her. "Alone," he stipulated, adding more gently for her sake, "for now." He stood. "Ronan of Glenarden, for a moment I will make you king. Go on, take my chair."

Ronan cast down his gaze. "Milord, I cannot—"

"Take my chair."

Brenna gripped Martin's arm. What could Arthur possibly mean to—

"Your Majesty," the Pendragon said, addressing Ronan as he settled on an upholstered cushion with rich, tooled Spanish leather at his back. "I have in my kingdom a chieftain blessed with abundance. His dominance is over all the land he can see, high and low to the western hills, including that of smaller, weaker peoples—a gift from his Pendragon, my father, conquered in the name of Christ for the glory of the God that granted us victory."

"Milord, a demon jealousy has consumed my father all these years," Ronan replied. "I do not excuse his slaughter of my wife's kin."

"No," Gwenhyfar said to Ronan's right. "No son raised in the faith by a strong Christian mother would."

"And so," Arthur carried on, "this chieftain continued to oppress the lesser clan, denying them their former landholdings, the only ones arable enough to provide sufficient food for winter stores. Each winter many of them died from starvation, punished for *his* misdeed, while he and his kin feasted and their servants cast excess to the swine."

"It was wrong." Ronan's hands clenched white on the claw arms of his chair.

"And yet that is exactly what *you* did—" Arthur's shout was deafening—"Ronan of Glenarden."

"Nay, milord, not Ronan," Brenna blurted out.

Only Martin's grip on her held her from rushing to Ronan's defense. "Quiet," he ordered, voice hushed with a fierceness she'd never heard from her mentor's lips before.

Ronan rocked as though he'd been struck silent by a physical blow.

They accused *him?*

No. He'd honored his father. *Who was a madman.*

Tarlach cared for his people. *But not the enemy Christ charged him to love.*

And Ronan had gone along with him, because—

That was the way it was.

Even as he summoned his excuse, it fell apart. He'd been wrapped up in what he *didn't* have, instead of using what he *did* have for everyone's good … including his own. He could have stood up to Tarlach—he was the only one who could do so and live—but he hadn't. While Ronan hadn't known of the Gowrys desperation, he'd not bothered to find out the reason they continued to fight. Instead, if they raided for cattle, he'd come back at them with stronger forces and taken his cattle back … and more.

Nay, he'd been too occupied wallowing in Tarlach's bitterness and guilt. It had so consumed Ronan that there was no room for God beyond meaningless ritual, when obligated.

"Father God, I *am* that man," he said numbly, dropping to his knees from the chair. A sob tore from deep within his chest. He'd done as much wrong as Tarlach … by doing nothing. His sense of nobility and justice were founded on the same.

Nothing. That was what he'd been. What he was now.

Ronan looked up at Brenna. "How could you marry me? Better you had let me die as I deserve." He was unfit to touch the hem of the distraught woman who pulled away from Brother Martin and rushed past Arthur to Ronan's side.

Collapsing in a heap of skirts, she gathered Ronan into her arms, shouting for all to hear, "Because God sent you to me broken and showed me how to heal you. Because my life was meaningless and empty, and you gave me purpose and made me whole. The decision was neither yours nor mine, but God's."

She faced the council. "My lieges, I have forgiven this man *and* even his father for what they did because I believe God has ordained our union, in spite of our flaws, to bring peace and glory to His name. And both Ronan and Tarlach are changed by God's grace."

"This is true, milord," Brother Martin spoke up. "This woman fought demons with prayer for Tarlach's soul. He should have died of poison, but he did not."

Gwenhyfar stepped forward, smiling down at Brenna. "You are truly your mother's daughter. Many of our council knew it."

"And I am my father's son," Ronan managed hoarsely. "*Cursed!*"

"Nay, Beloved," Brenna said, lifting his face to hers. "You are forgiven."

But his beautiful wife was too tenderhearted not to forgive. God, on the other hand—

"Forgiven," the gathering repeated. "In the name of the Lamb, by the Father, through the Holy Spirit."

The essence of the words spiraled and vibrated around and through Ronan.

Forgiven.

Name of the Lamb.

By the Father.

Through the Spirit.

Knots of guilt Ronan did not know existed unraveled, releasing light long constrained. His body grew weightless with its buoyancy, and his skin tingled, as though it glowed for the eyes of the Father alone. The others no longer existed. Not even Brenna. Just Ronan ...

and the Father. Or rather, the Light that engulfed them. There were no words to express what Ronan felt, only tears wrung from places they could no longer hide.

At last Arthur burst the ethereal globe surrounding Ronan. "You have been given uncommon grace, Ronan of Glenarden."

Once again Ronan became aware of where he was and the presence of the others. Had they seen what he had—that Light like no other on this earth?

"The question remains," the king said. "What will you do with that grace?"

Ronan knew the answer. It was what Brenna had been leading him toward all along. But before, he'd gone along with her wishes because he loved and believed in her enough to take a risk. Because he'd begun to search for her God. But now, he knew, his motivation could no longer be to please his wife. It had to be to please her God. *Their* God. The One who had given him a much undeserved second chance.

CHAPTER TWENTY-FOUR

Ronan was spent by the time he, Brenna, and Alyn, accompanied by Merlin Emrys and his company, returned to Glenarden's campsite below the great rock. At least Donal of Gowrys and his son returned to their camp with good news—better than the cattle they'd intended to ask for. Ronan had pledged to return their land and provide some of the timber to rebuild the fort on the lake. All this under the protection of the O'Byrne.

Gowrys never questioned Ronan's intent, for only a fool would falsely pledge such things before the Pendragon and his esteemed council. Donal had been brought in after Ronan's trial, and though the Gowrys chief didn't know all of those present, he knew enough to heave a great sigh of relief once outside the building again.

"I dinna ken all that aboot our quarrel and the survival of the church," he confessed, shaking Ronan's hand before departing. "But the Devil's had his way long enough."

Ahead, the Glenarden scarlet, black, and silver banners marked the clan tents. Ronan didn't delude himself into thinking a celebration awaited him. He had to convince Caden and Tarlach this was for the best. Yet before Ronan could form the prayer to ask for the strength and wisdom to do this, his beleaguered mind cleared. His body became invigorated … as if God knew his needs before he asked.

Blessed be!

Caden sat by the fire, drinking straight from a flagon of Flemish wine. Tarlach had waited up as well and slept in his chair, bent over the plank table with his head cradled on his good arm.

Just as Ronan opened his mouth to hail them, Alyn launched himself past Ronan and at their middle brother with a roar. Caden jerked up his head, eyes bulging in alarm as Alyn bowled over bench, wine, and his brother. His reflexes dulled by drink, Caden swung the flagon and thankfully missed Alyn's head. Slipping from Caden's grip, the cup flew onto the fire, crashing, contents sizzling.

Before Caden could recover from the impact of his body weight being hurled onto his back, the younger lad sat astride him, knees pinning his shoulders, and boxed his older brother's ears.

"Miss me, Brother?" Alyn chortled in delight. The youngest O'Byrne might have lost weight, but he'd not lost his penchant for mischief.

Ronan rushed between Alyn's back and the fire as Caden hunched his powerful shoulders, lifting the lighter man in the process. With a swing of his leg, he hooked the off-balance Alyn by the neck and threw him aside. Ronan was there to block the lad from rolling into the bonfire.

"For the love of your departed mother, are you trying to kill your brother?" Tarlach bellowed, awakened by the turmoil. As he pushed himself up from the table, Vychan rushed to his aid.

"Which one of us?" Alyn asked, propping himself up on his elbow. His grin was a delight for Ronan to behold after all those months.

"Aye," Caden said, climbing to his feet. He brushed the dirt off his tunic. "Which one? *As if I didn't know*," he added beneath his breath.

But for Alyn, Caden smiled, walking over and hauling the lad to his feet. "Seems the ache in my bones is exchanged for a pain in my—"

Alyn lifted a cautioning finger. "Ladies present," he reminded his brother. "Speaking of ladies, where is Rhianon?"

"Off walking with her nurse. Sure, newborns need less coddling." This was the old Caden, Ronan observed. Belligerent, cross.

"Well, you young whelp, have you nothing to say to your father?" Tarlach held out his good arm, inviting his youngest into such embrace as the old man had.

"You were sleeping so soundly, I thought I'd first give you a chance to knock the fog from your brain." Alyn hugged Tarlach. When the young lad locked his long arms behind the old man and tried to lift him, Ronan was tempted to believe that all was back to normal.

"Nay, you knocked *mine* out instead," Caden teased. The light in his gaze died upon seeing Tarlach make an effort with his invalid hand to gather Ronan's.

Instead of taking it, Ronan stepped behind his father and clapped him on the back. "Now you've all *three* sons again." He extended an arm to Caden. "Join our reunion, Brother. And then we must talk," he announced. "For I've had an audience with Arthur."

It wasn't until they'd moved the table, end to the fire, and settled on benches around it, that Tarlach saw Merlin standing in the shadows. His companions had vanished.

"Emrys, how long have you been here?" Tarlach demanded of his old friend.

"Long enough to see joy on your ugly face one more time," Merlin replied. He moved to the space Ronan made between himself and Tarlach, while Alyn took that yielded to him on their father's other side by Caden.

"Faith, I'm hungry enough to eat a full-grown boar by myself," Alyn declared.

His eyes rounded with delight when Vychan appeared with two maids bearing platters of cold meat, cheese, and bread. The steward placed a tray with a new flagon of wine and cups for all on the table.

"Vychan, what can I do?" Brenna asked. She shot an apologetic glance at Merlin. "I've been taught many things but am still learning a wife's duties at the board."

"Your duty is at your husband's side and with the infirm, my dear," Merlin told her. "We all must act according to our gifts. As I recall, Caden's lovely bride is most adept at running the household."

"Rhianon is no servant of Ronan's wife," Caden challenged.

"She is not," Emrys answered. "Yet we are all called to be *God's* servants, to do whatever our task as if for Him, and in that she excels with her hospitality, milord."

If Caden sought to stare Merlin Emrys down, he had second thoughts after a prolonged silence. He took up the cup Vychan served him and downed it straight away. "So, Brother," he said to

Ronan. "What is to be our penance for defending ourselves against our enemy?"

Merlin answered first. "To make right the wrong committed by Tarlach in the past and by you and your family ever since."

"Until I lived with them, I had no idea the Gowrys were in such dire need," Alyn told them. "Since I have been there, two babes and a childbearing mother have died, too weak from lack of nourishment to survive." Emotion clouded his voice. "More than one night I went to bed cold and hungry after being given the best they had to offer. It—" he paused and swallowed— "it made me ashamed to be their neighbor."

"So what do they ask for?" Sarcasm dripped from Caden's voice. "For us to give them food and blankets every winter?"

"Nay," Ronan said. "They ask for the return of their lowlands to grow the food and healthy livestock for themselves."

Caden slammed his empty cup on the table. "And give them an open door to our prime pastures to pick and choose our cattle at whim?"

"Llas and I shared pastureland." A distant look softened the haggard lines of Tarlach's face. "We alternated with the seasons so that none were overstripped."

"It may come to that again, God willing," Ronan told him. "I hope it does." And God in Heaven knew Ronan spoke from his heart.

Tarlach turned to the merlin. "It's time, isn't it, old friend?"

Ronan squeezed Brenna's hand under the table. Tarlach was at last ready for peace.

"Aye," Emrys replied. "That is why I came, to bear witness. He's ready, acknowledged by the elders."

Confusion reined in Ronan's relief. "What ... *who* is ready? For what?"

Tarlach called Vychan from where he served Egan O'Toole wine. The champion had taken up a guard position by the laird's tent on their return. "You and Egan fetch as many of the clan as are in the camp. Tonight I step down as the O'Byrne and hand the lairdship to my firstborn son."

Caden thrust up from the table, knocking the bench out from under Alyn. For a moment Ronan thought his middle brother would draw his dining dagger as before, but this time thrust it into Ronan's heart. Instead, Caden's fingers wrestled with the silvered hilt, drawing, then shoving it deeper into its sheath. But oh, the daggers of his gaze were well aimed.

"Call all you will, old man," Caden hissed through his teeth. "But *these* eyes will not bear witness. For as sure as I breathe, you bring about the fall of your own house, Tarlach. And no witch's peace will save it."

Images from the night before still played through Ronan's mind the next morning as he watched Brenna wait in line to pay her fee to enter the archery contest with money she'd received for her herbs and furs earlier. Sleep had been scarce for them both. The clan warriors had assembled in front of the laird's tent beneath a high moon. When Tarlach presented his case and named Ronan as the Glenarden, not one accepted the old chieftain's invitation to object. If anything, there was relief. But then, Caden was conspicuously absent.

As for the news of the agreement with the Gowrys, it was better received by the O'Byrnes than Ronan had anticipated, though warily accepted. Merlin's presence lent it more authority. "These eye-for-an-eye disputes will soon blind us all, and the Saxon white dragon will then devour us as it has our brothers to the south and east. Will we unite as Britons—or perish?"

"I mind there's enough Picts and Saxons to keep us busy," someone shouted from the ranks.

"Aye, gi' the Gowrys a rest," said another.

So now, on his first day as the O'Byrne, Ronan suffered from too much *uniting* over the drink that flowed afterward. He hadn't noticed when Merlin slipped off undetected or when O'Toole and Vychan carried Tarlach to his bed. But the rest of the men—especially those who'd been rounded up from the tavern—were in the humor to celebrate with Ronan.

Thankfully Brenna had saved him at last from his own clan, pleading that his heir needed rest and that she would need all of their support at tomorrow's archery tournament. Only his enigmatic wife had the charm to send a band of rough and rugged revelers willingly to their bedrolls.

Today a good number of them lined the edge of the field, ready to cheer Lady Brenna of Glenarden, although the organizers of the contest didn't bother to suppress their shock and subsequent disdain at the tall, slender woman in tunic and trousers when she dropped her purse in front of them.

If it bothered Brenna, it didn't show. She was fixed on winning that pony for Bron.

"Watch Bron while I go over there," Egan whispered in Ronan's ear, pointing to where a group of men were taking bets on the outcome of the tournament. The champion had taken a liking to Brenna's latest stray and carried him effortlessly on his shoulders wherever they went. Perhaps he missed his daughter, Kella, who visited her late mother's kin in Erin every spring.

"I wouldn't bet against her," Ronan advised dryly as Bron scooted closer to him, his lame foot stirring up more dust to assault the throat and nostrils.

Tied about the boy's neck was his own purse, heavy with coin from the drawings he'd sold while accompanying Brenna to the dry-goods vendor stalls at sunup. Seeing the same potential for the lad's artwork as Brenna did, a thread merchant had bought all of the lad's goods right off. Despite Brenna's insistence that she'd only wanted blue fabric for herself, Ronan authorized Dara to purchase what she saw fit for his wife's wardrobe while Brenna was distracted by the tournament.

"Ye think I should place a bet, sir?" Bron asked, fingering the coins through the leather pouch.

"I'd think of your mother's joy when she sees what you've earned and not risk a copper of it," Ronan advised. "Unless you've money you don't need."

The boy frowned. "Who doesna need all his money?"

"Exactly," Ronan said. "With what you have there, you might buy a goat or chickens that will provide milk and eggs. And if you choose later, you could get your money back for them."

"Or sell the milk and eggs."

"But if you put your money on a tournament, you might win more. Or you might lose it all and have nothing to show for it."

"And I'll always have my goat."

"Right."

"Unless it dies."

"All the more reason to take good care of your animals."

And one's people, Ronan thought, spying the Gowrys gathering on the opposite side of the field. Only the nobility was allowed in the seats covered by bright red and white canopies where he and the lad were. The rest stood on the sidelines.

"There Ronan is," Alyn announced loudly from a distance away, "dressed fine as you please and sporting the O'Byrne brooch."

Ronan heard his youngest sibling before he spied him. Alyn made his way with Daniel of Gowrys to the O'Byrne seats. Evidence of blackberry tarts about their mouths incriminated both young men.

"Good day, Daniel," Ronan greeted the guest.

"And a fine brooch it is," Daniel concluded, admiring the ruby-jeweled pin that had belonged to Ronan's father and his father's father. "Alyn told us this morning how you were elected the O'Byrne last night. I've more hope for peace than ever in my life now."

"Alyn should not have left camp without escort this morning," Ronan chided, "as we still have a mutual enemy of our alliance about." The reckless abandon of youth was a luxury Ronan had never had. "But I will do my best to keep my promise to your ... my *wife's,*" Ronan amended, "people. You are family now. In fact, I'd like to invite your father to join me here ... as my kin. Would you two renegades deliver the invitation for me?"

"Has Lady Brenna had a turn yet?" Alyn asked.

"Nay, the elimination trials have just begun." Ronan searched the cluster of contestants and spied her scarlet tunic and the plumed hat he had purchased for her that morning. Black with a dyed-red peacock feather.

"We'll be back, then."

Restless as two penned pups, the youths climbed down from the stand and disappeared into the crowd. Ronan smiled to himself. *Indeed, an unlikely friendship following an unlikely marriage.* Ronan allowed himself a bit of Daniel's optimism.

CHAPTER TWENTY-FIVE

Donal of Gowrys sent his thanks but declined Ronan's invitation. Ronan supposed twenty years of enmity could not be forgotten with a handshake, even if it was in the Pendragon's presence. Still, the Gowrys made their support of Brenna known. They'd cheered loudly as she effortlessly survived the elimination trials. If anything, the cheering had become a contest between the O'Byrne and Gowrys contingent, one that would likely leave them all without voice.

"Well then …" Egan slid onto the bench with his leather mug filled to the brim with ale. "Me whistle's wet and me bet's made."

Though Ronan prided himself on not being a betting man, he realized as he watched Brenna emerge triumphant from yet another round that he'd wagered more than coin. He'd wagered his heart … and gladly.

When the trials had narrowed down the contestants to six, the Pendragon's court arrived, buglers heralding their approach, to occupy the canopied dais directly behind the archers. The contestants remained bowed until Arthur and Gwenhyfar, both resplendent in blue and white, took their seats along with Merlin Emrys.

And suddenly Brenna appeared nervous. Ronan watched her fingers fumble as she nocked her arrow. She found her anchor point and released the arrow. The shot veered astray of the target's center. It was the first time she'd missed the inner rings, and shock rippled through the onlookers. Thankfully her next two shots struck the black center dead on, leaving her one of the three archers left to contend for the pony.

As the targets were moved another spear length away, a herald announced the finalists to the onlookers. "Murray of Clockmanan, Heming of Gwynedd, and Brenna of Glenarden."

"Gowrys!" her kinsmen shouted above the clamor of the onlookers. There could be no doubt who had become the favorite.

"Formerly of Gowrys," the herald added, casting an apologetic glance at the O'Byrne side.

Ronan swelled with pride.

Brenna went first at the insistence of her gentlemen competitors. Her first arrow struck the outer ring of the target. Her next was dead center. Her last landed a hand's width from it, still within the black.

"I'd think thrice aboot makin' that one angry," Egan teased. "She's as good as our finest."

Ronan nodded, but his gaze was fixed on where Brenna and Heming exchanged words, while Murray of Clockmanan took his turn. Mostly likely about the contest, though Heming looked as though he could devour her like a meat pasty.

Murray's first shot barely hit the target's edge.

The second shot landed equidistant from Brenna's to the center.

The third arrow hit squarely in the outer ring, eliminating him from the contest.

When Heming took his turn, it was quickly over. One arrow to the outside. Two dead center to Brenna's one.

"I can't believe my eyes." Bron shrank against Egan O'Toole with a moan. "She lost."

"And cost me good silver," Egan admitted. "Though she gave us a fine show."

Ronan didn't answer. He was already pushing against the departing crowd toward the green. Brenna leaned on her bow at the edge of the winner's place, trying to smile as Heming was awarded the pony. But her over-bright eyes gave away her disappointment.

Upon seeing Ronan, she shrugged. "I tried."

"That you did," he said, gathering her to him in a consoling hug.

"And I prayed, but … is Bron too disappointed?"

"He won't be." Ronan had already made up his mind what he was going to do upon seeing her disappointment. For her *and* the lad. "Come along."

He ushered Brenna to where an admiring throng surrounded the champion.

"Heming," Ronan called out, "how much will you take for the pony?" But with so many talking at once, he had to get closer. "Heming!"

Intoxicated by victory, Heming of Gwynedd waited until Ronan of Glenarden waded through the crowd before acknowledging he'd heard the man. The gods were still with him. Neither Ronan nor his comely wife recognized him from the day of the Witch's End. But now Heming knew exactly who had shot an arrow through his hand. A woman. One who did not know her place and had nearly bested him ... *again*.

"What was it you said, milord?" Heming asked. "There is so much noise about."

"I would like to buy that pony," Ronan told him. "Name your price."

"For the crippled boy I told you about," Brenna explained.

Heming cared no more for the boy than he now did for Lady Rhianon. He had them all fooled. But Rhianon wasn't happy with that. She'd insulted his cunning, insisting he leave Glenarden, lest they might mind something of the attack. And last night she'd berated him soundly for his risky shot to Ronan's head with a stomp of her delicate slippered foot.

"I told you to gather your friends and stay out of sight until we leave," she'd warned him.

But he'd been in no danger of being caught. Heming could blend into a tree like its own limb. Had she come to him alone, Heming would have taken the wench then and there. But his crone of an aunt was with her. *In time.* The old woman hadn't said it, but she'd warned him to be patient with that chide many times.

How he looked forward to seeing Rhianon's face when he returned to the Glenarden encampment as champion of the day. Heming scratched his unshaven cheek, savoring his victory. Since the fates smiled on him, he might as well get an invitation.

He handed Brenna the pony's reins. "Take it, milady."

"What?"

One would have thought he'd offered her the world from the wonder on her face.

"What use have I for such a small pony?" he asked. "I came for the competition, and you gave me an ample dose."

"B-but—"

Heming folded the lead rope in her hand with his gloved ones. "Besides, there is no question. You were today's favorite. Am I not right, good people?" he asked in a louder voice.

A great round of "Huzzah" rose from the bystanders close enough to know what was going on. And as the word spread, the approval grew even louder. It was more heady than the drinks that were being offered him from every direction.

But while the wench was speechless, staring at him as if a halo had appeared over his head, her husband was not. "Thank you, but I'll pay you."

Ronan reached for a purse tied at his belt, but Heming caught his wrist. "It is done. Consider it compensation for the many nights of hospitality I have enjoyed at your keep. An offer of friendship between Gwynedd and Glenarden. To refuse would be an insult."

"That is the last thing on our minds, good sir," the lady said, finding her voice at last. "You must join us tonight for the evening meal, if you have no other obligation."

"You are too kind, milady." *And predictable.*

"Nay, sir," she demurred. *"Your* kindness and generosity shall not be forgotten all my days."

Such lovely eyes, filled with a goodness that would be her undoing. How he'd enjoy taking this one as Keena promised.

Heming brandished a courtly bow. "My pleasure is yours … *for all your days.*" Which were numbered. And he would have the pony back to boot.

For all your days.

Brenna might have attributed the strange wording as evidence of Rhianon's estimation that the huntsman lacked basic social graces. But at the touch of his hands, she'd sensed a cold darkness about him, even through the leather of his gloves … so contrary to the warmth he exuded on the surface. His eyes put her to mind of colored glass that hid the true nature of their content.

"Tell me more about this Heming," she said to Ronan as they led the new pony back to the family campsite with a very happy Bron astride it. Alyn and Daniel of Gowrys talked with the boy behind them, the latter promising to teach Bron how to get the pony to kneel, so that the boy might mount it easier. "Heming's a queer sort," Ronan told her. "Came from Gwynedd as a huntsman, though I suspect there is more than a wish to serve his lady's new family. He is devoted to Rhianon. Too much so, if you ask me. Were I Caden, I'd watch him closely."

"The attraction doesn't seem mutual. She esteems him an oaf."

"Why do you ask?"

"Was he present the day you were injured?"

Ronan hiked his brow. "You think Heming was my would-be assassin?"

Brenna couldn't make an accusation like that. "Nay. Perhaps it's the man's awkwardness … like Rhianon said." Although she'd know more if she saw his hands. Perhaps tonight when he joined them for the evening meal....

Ronan read her doubt. "What?"

She shrugged. "There's just something about him that puts me off. A contradiction of character that confounds—"

"Ronan!" Ahead, Caden pushed his way through the crowd toward them.

Speaking of contradictions. Brenna stiffened. Caden had made himself scarce since last night's events.

"What is it?" her husband asked when his brother caught up to them.

"It's Father." Caden glanced at Brenna. "He's had another brain fit. He can barely speak, but he managed your name."

Father God, not now. Not when all begins to go well with us.

"I'll see that the lad and his pony get to the camp," Daniel assured her quickly. "A trot might shake him off."

Brenna called, "Thank you, Daniel" over her shoulder as she and Ronan hurried after Caden and Alyn. She would have asked more questions, but it was all she could do to keep up with the brothers' long strides. By the time they reached the uphill encampment, Tarlach lay, eyes closed, propped up on his cot by all the bedding Vychan could muster.

"He insisted on sitting up," the steward told her. "Said that if we laid him down, he'd die."

Brenna felt Tarlach's forehead. It was cool, and his color a deathly cast of gray.

"Was he out of his mind?"

"Not as I could tell. He was sitting at the board, when suddenly he grabbed his head and began to shake." Vychan imitated Tarlach's shaking for Brenna. "Told me his head was about to burst like an overripe boil and to send for you. Caden went for you while I tried to get him to bed."

Seizure? Apoplexy? Both?

"Milord Tarlach," Brenna said, turning to her patient, "do you hear me?"

"My … y … " He dragged the word out and, with the last ounce of that breath, finished, "Head."

"I took the liberty of getting your bag," Vychan said, handing Brenna the sack in which she kept her herbal supplies when traveling.

"Wonderful." She took out a small sack, sewn in overlapping fashion, and handed it to him. "Put on hot water for tea—"

"Done, milady. It should already boil."

"Then our concoction of oak bark, cowslip, and nutmeg should relieve the pain and soothe his brain." Cold humor or touch required hot treatment.

"He shouldn't have made the journey, just recovered from the poisoning," Rhianon fretted. She nuzzled Caden's arm, clinging as though it alone kept her from swooning with concern.

Although he never opened his eyes, Tarlach lifted his good hand and grunted, drawing Brenna's attention.

"Yes, milord?" she said, taking his hand in hers. It, too, was cold.

"Ro … nan."

"Aye, Father, I'm here." Ronan moved to the other side of Tarlach's cot and grasped his withered hand.

"Take ... me ... home," he slurred. "Will not ... die ... here."

Should we move him? Brenna read the question in Ronan's lifted brow.

Tarlach had survived the poisoning by sheer will and God's grace. This episode might yet take him. She pulled Tarlach's hand to her face, pressing it to her cheek, and closed her eyes, waiting, hoping.

Father God, what shall I say?

Nothing came. No vision. Just the pouring of her heart through her hands and into Tarlach's cold one.

"No more talk of dying," Brenna said at last. "You promised me that you would see our son."

A tug of a smile lifted the unafflicted side of Tarlach's mouth.

"So we go?" Ronan asked.

Tarlach nodded. "We ... go."

CHAPTER TWENTY-SIX

Ronan set up camp that night by a narrow burn that ran down from the highlands and over a rock fall into the curling inland fingers of the Clyde. Although he'd given the warriors who'd fought recently with Egan O'Toole against the Orkney Picts leave to remain at the fair, he'd kept enough on hand for protection. Still, most volunteered to return to Glenarden with their new chieftain … and their dying one.

"Some of us have fought at Tarlach's side too often to abandon him in his final battle," Egan told Ronan as they sat around the fire that evening. "And we done our tradin' wi' our battle prizes the first day. Besides … " He sniffed the air. "I know trouble when I smell it."

"That was me, you old fool." Caden snorted. He stood and stretched. "'Twill be good to rest in my own bed tomorrow. The ground becomes less and less hospitable by the day." He looked over to where Rhianon piled bracken beneath a clump of birch to soften the rocky bottom beneath their blankets.

"Marriage has made you soft," Alyn teased. The youth stuffed the remains of a meat pie, purchased at the last moment before leaving the fair, into his mouth.

Alyn hadn't stopped eating since rejoining his clan. With such a constant reminder of his shortcomings, Ronan had sent Daniel with funds enough to purchase food and drink for the Gowrys as a token of goodwill, even though his father, Donal, had declined Ronan's invitation at the archery meet.

Had it only been hours ago? It felt like yesterday. With the celebration of Ronan's new lordship, they all needed sleep.

"Aye," Caden replied to Alyn's charge. "And Rhianon's restless as a snake on a hot stone. I think I'll break out a new cask of beer and lift a few mugs with the lads. Mayhaps that will soften the ground, eh?"

"I'll join you," the youngest O'Byrne suggested.

But Caden held up his hand. "I can handle my heath fruit. You've not enough bulk for serious drink."

"Then I shall drink accordingly," Alyn shot back.

Caden turned to Ronan. "Has your wife a thimble in that bag of hers that our upstart might use for a cup?"

Ronan chuckled. It was almost like old times, now that Alyn was with them again.

As his bickering siblings wandered over to where a second campfire had been kindled for the men, Ronan glanced to the wagon, where Brenna had made Tarlach as comfortable as possible.

Pray. That's what she told Ronan when he asked what could be done. There were some things that no amount of nature magic could heal. Herbs, stones, hands … they had their limits.

"It is up to God, if Tarlach is to live or die from this."

As Ronan got up to see how Tarlach was faring, Brenna lifted the old man's lame arm, bending it and stretching it gently. "It helps to get the blood flowing warm," she explained, reading the question on his face. "Given his cold humor, Dara is making warm tea and heating stones for compresses. We'll have you snug as a bairn in a blanket," she told her patient.

"Hate"—Tarlach dragged in more breath—"this."

Brenna gave him a stern look. "Then get better, milord, so you can soon hold your own grandson."

It was incentive for Tarlach to recover before. Perhaps it would work again.

"I'll make up a bed for us next to the wagon," Ronan offered. At least he hoped his wife would share it. Given Tarlach's condition, she might well sleep next to him. Ronan wouldn't begrudge her charity, but he would miss her closeness. Holding her in his arms completed his world.

As he worked next to the cart, he listened as Brenna conversed with his father, encouraging him to respond as best he could. How ironic that only a few months ago, Tarlach wanted her dead. Today, he would do anything to please her. Even drink the tea laced with cayenne from the East.

"How I wish you could tell me about the good times you shared with my father. I've heard more of my mother than of Llas," she said.

"Hah." Egan O'Toole meandered to the opposite side of the wagon from Ronan. "Now them were the days, weren't they, old friend?" he said to Tarlach. "I mind two upstarts joining the Pendragon—he was Prince Aedan in them days, Arthur's da," he added. "And the both of ye, hopin' for land of your own."

"You ... rr whelp," Tarlach slurred.

"Aye, I was a whelp, not yet dry behind the ears ... and Dalraida

Irish like yourself and the Pendragon." He glanced at Brenna. "Yer
da was Cymri from Caerleon. Hair black as night, like yours. Ye got
them loch blue eyes from him *and* your maither."

"I thought you'd be lifting a cup with Caden and the men,"
Ronan teased.

Egan grunted. "I lifted one cup too many last night, and it's left
me with no taste for more. Unlike the time me and your fathers," he
began, referring to Tarlach and Llas, "went to Aedan's coronation at
Dunadd. Mind ye that night, milord?"

Ronan recalled the tale. And how later the priest Columba predicted that Aedan's rebellious son Arthur would not follow his father
to Dalraida's throne at Dunadd. Ronan wondered if prophecy had
troubled the Pendragon as much as Ronan's had secretly nagged at
him. Not that he could complain about the way his had unfolded.
His had brought light into his dark world.

Amazingly, Tarlach rallied with Egan's tales of youthful escapades
and battle fury. Granted, his comments were more oft grunts or one
word, but his mind seemed sharp on those times. Just speaking of
them relaxed the deeply etched lines on his face.

"Afore yer maither," Tarlach said a good while later, exonerating
Llas from a dalliance with a Pictish princess that nearly got them
skewered with iron.

After Tarlach finally drifted off to a peaceful sleep, Brenna
climbed down from the wagon. "I think your father enjoyed Egan's
tales," she told Ronan. "I know I did." She covered a yawn with her
hand. "Have you seen Bron?"

"Over by the warriors, sketching designs on their shields. The
wolf is their favorite."

For a moment, their gazes locked. Ronan could almost see Faol's image in Brenna's mind. Had their time at the fair not been cut short, he might have found a pup—

"Mine, too," she said softly. She stepped against him, slipping her arms around his neck. "For it is by the wolf that God sent you to me. It was by Faol's devotion that I learned unconditional love."

Ronan snorted. "I don't think his love for me was unconditional."

"No." She made a cute noise, half chuckle, half sigh. "But he did save you."

Ronan kissed her ear. "You look weary, *a stór*, and I know I am. How about joining me for a long night's embrace?"

"Give me a moment, and I'll be delighted to. I need to bid Airgid good night and give her some of my fruit from dinner."

The horse. How she loved the horse.

But that was why he loved her. Brenna embodied love.

While Ronan waited for Brenna, he checked the guard, doubled to make certain the camp was secure. Already Egan and some of his men began to settle about the fire nearest the O'Byrne's cart. This bit of glen was the safest place to stop along the road to the higher ground of Glenarden, but forest thickened in the distance. It was a perfect cover for anyone bent on mischief … or murder.

The howl of a wolf penetrated Brenna's restless slumber. Men crept stealthily through the trees near a moon-glazed ribbon of water. Bloodthirsty renegades all, like their leader. Ah, there he was. Heming crouched like a wolf ready to pounce, his black hair greased slick for battle. Brenna saw him as clearly as she had at yesterday's tournament. Saw that sinister smile as he said, "My pleasure is yours for all *your* days."

With a gasp, Brenna bolted upright, staring with wide eyes at the figures sleeping peacefully around the campsite. She placed a hand over her pounding heart to keep it housed within her chest.

"What is it?" Ronan's hand tightened on the hilt of the sword next to him.

Was it only a dream?

No. The force of her conviction chased the remaining fog of sleep from her brain.

"He's here. Heming … and a score or more of men. In the woods."

"You're sure?"

Brenna nodded, though she hoped she was wrong.

Ronan seized her arm. "I want you to crawl under the wagon and into it on the other side."

"Aye, my bow is there."

"Nay, I'd have you keep down, protect Father."

"As you say." But she'd not hide when her new family was in danger.

"Do it!"

As Brenna rolled under the wagon, Ronan crawled toward Egan, who snored loud enough for the men in the woods to hear. But before he could reach the champion, Caden's voice carried across the campsite.

"Going somewhere, Brother?"

The eerie nature of her brother-in-law's voice raised the hairs on Brenna's head as she emerged on the yon side of Tarlach's cart. The sound was amplified, as if through a hollow reed. And now Caden was standing over Ronan, who was still belly to the ground.

"We're under attack." Ronan started to get up, but Caden pressed the sword to his throat.

What was wrong with the man?

"That witch of yours is good ... but not as good as mine." Caden inclined his head toward the woods, where the men Brenna had seen in her dream emerged from cover, along with Rhianon and Keena.

Brenna reached blindly into the cart where she recalled having stashed her bow. She could easily hit Caden from this distance.

But Caden's pride at the way his devious plan was coming together gave Ronan the chance he needed. He knocked Caden's sword away, plowing into his brother and shoving Caden over the sleeping Egan O'Toole.

"Glenarden to arms!" Ronan roared. "To arms!"

Egan was on his feet before Brenna could climb into the cart, but the champion groped at an empty scabbard in bewilderment. Caden's work, no doubt.

For the span of a lightning flash, there was deafening silence filled with a thousand thoughts and questions. Then, pandemonium. The attackers rushed the campsite, screaming like banshees. Ronan and Caden locked in hand-to-hand combat on the ground. Egan raced from man to man on the ground, trying to wake them, but to no avail. A few staggered to their feet as though drunk, but most of Glenarden's warriors would not stir.

Could not stir.

It wasn't Caden's handiwork this time, Brenna knew, but that of the crone dancing amongst the attacking hoard, her gnarled cane raised over her head in triumph.

Without second thought, Brenna strung her bow and nocked an arrow.

One of the charging Saxons dropped, felled by Brenna's first shot. Beside her, Tarlach struggled to get up. "Mm … *axesh.*"

She loosed another arrow, striking a second man in the knee before she rummaged for the old chieftain's axe.

Ronan and Caden separated, each with swords recovered and ready.

"Hold!" Caden's shout halted the charge, but his gaze never left that of his brother. "Circle them. Spare any who sleep."

The villains closed in on where no more than a handful of Glenarden's warriors crawled in confusion. And in their midst stood Egan and Ronan back to back, Egan brandishing a sword recovered from the overzealous, hence careless, assailant lying still nearby.

"Drop your bow, Brenna, or I'll set my wolves upon the sleeping men and all will die. As for you, old man"—Caden glared at Tarlach—"your threat to us has long passed."

With a growl of outrage, Tarlach tried to raise his axe, but it tumbled from his weak grip to his feet. The sob that gurgled in the old man's throat as he sank to his knees tore at Brenna. Reluctant, she tossed her bow to the ground.

"You and Egan as well, Brother," Caden ordered. "Put down your weapons."

"You betray your own clan? Your own blood?" Incredulity vied with contempt in Ronan's charge. As much as Caden had rebelled hEALER 327

against him, he still didn't want to believe his brother capable of such betrayal.

"Actually, Ronan, we've *spared* our men," Rhianon said with a feline drawl. "If they don't wake up, we won't have to kill them." She batted her eyes at Ronan in such a way as to make Brenna's blood boil. "Unless you resist. Then we'll kill them one by one until your swords are handed over."

Reaching down, Rhianon slashed the neck of one of the men, a warrior trying to fly in his madness. His lifeblood spraying her skirts, he collapsed in death's throe.

To think Brenna had been glad to have this woman as a sister. "If there is a witch among us, it is not I," she declared. "*You* abuse God's gifts, nature's properties, for dark and devious ends, Rhianon. But this will return to you. As you sow, so shall you reap."

"Is that a *vision*, milady?" Rhianon jeered.

Brenna shook her head. "Nay, nor my promise, but God's Word."

"*Nay, nor my promise, but God's Word,*" Keena mimicked. She peered over Rhianon's shoulder at Brenna. "What a shame you'll take credit for my handiwork"—she spat out the word—"*healer. Miracle* worker."

"What madness do you speak of, woman?" Ronan demanded. He'd yet to drop his sword.

"Our warriors will believe me when I tell them that *your* witch-woman put a spell on them so that her clan could slay you and our father," Caden replied.

Brenna shivered involuntarily from the icy indifference in his voice.

"Though I'm not far from the truth," he added. "Brenna *has* bewitched you and Father."

"Caden," Brenna pleaded, "this is not your doing. *You* are the one bewitched."

Why hadn't she seen it before?

She had. His gaze had been as soulless as a glass cup for some time. Brenna had learned of such things, but never seen the like. But, like Ronan, she hadn't wanted to believe the worst in Caden.

"We're *both* bewitched, aren't we, darling?" Rhianon snaked her arm about Caden's waist, cooing, "By love."

Caden groaned, submissive as a dog to a belly rub, as she tripped playful fingers up his muscled arm, reveling in her control.

"Only *my* brave, strong husband is going to save me. *Yours* will die." A perfect rose of a pout formed on Rhianon's lips. "Sadly, so will you."

Suddenly her crone spun about and pointed to Heming. "Go on, laddie, what are ye waiting for? Claim your prize."

Heming gave Ronan a gloating look. "No one to save you now, *Glenarden,*" he said in contempt. "Not wolf, nor merlin ... " He cut his gaze to Brenna. "Nor witch."

"It was you," Brenna declared. Why hadn't she listened to her instincts?

And why, Father God, had they come so late? Brenna couldn't help but feel God had betrayed her. What was the point of her gifts, if she was to lose the only man she'd ever loved? *Where are You, Father?*

"See if your prize still works miracles," Keena told Heming. But her hateful gaze wasn't on the hunter. It was on Brenna.

That same smile Heming had given Brenna yesterday and again a short while ago in her vision accompanied familiar words. "My pleasure is yours for all *your* days." The implication curdled her blood. And her without so much as the dining dagger in her sack to defend herself.

"No!" Without thought to himself or his men, Ronan tore from his defensive position at Egan's back. He slashed his way at the warriors who blocked his path to Heming, while more closed in at his back in a circle of certain death.

Helpless, Brenna reached from her very soul's depths for the God who seemed to have abandoned her.

"Father God!"

"For Glenarden!" a chorus of men shouted at the same time from somewhere behind her.

Angels? She glanced over her shoulder in disbelief.

Men. A score or so. Stampeding across the shallow burn, beating their weapons against wooden shields, shouting. "For Gowrys!"

Time slowed itself, and trapped all in it. Brenna clutched the side of the cart, gaze riveted on Ronan. The warriors surrounding him stood frozen in disbelief before the charging phantoms that had appeared from nowhere. Bleeding from a gash on his arm, Ronan skewered one diverted Saxon and kicked another away. As her husband turned to deal with the second man, a hand clamped vice-like about Brenna's ankle.

Heming! For the blink of an eye, she saw beyond his leering face. On horseback, Donal of Gowrys directed his ragtag force. They swarmed like hornets about Caden's renegades, their sting death-dealing. Beside Donal was the shocking image of Brother Martin, crosier raised in one hand and the Gowrys colors in the other, bellowing prayers for his king like an ancient bard.

Heming snatched at Brenna's foot with such force that the amazing sights vanished. Down she went, hard, on the wagon bed.

"You're coming with me," he shouted above the din of clashing wood and metal.

Brenna grabbed at the rail, at Tarlach's leg, anything to hang onto, but Heming's strength was compounded by the panic in his gaze. As the wagon bed raked at her back, Brenna seized one of the arrows from her quiver. The moment she was close enough, she thrust it, dagger-like, at her assailant's eye.

He turned too quickly. The tip slashed across his jaw and snagged his ear.

"Witch!" He backhanded the side of her face, knocking her to the ground.

How her head spun! The men fought about her, moving like ribbons on a Maypole.

Brenna shook off her dizziness. She had to keep Heming from taking her. She crawled under the wagon, reaching for the sack next to her bedding. Digging frantically, she found her dagger, shoved it between her teeth, and latched onto the wheel with her arms. She drew up her ankles, ready to kick.

But there was nothing. Nothing except a heavy thud at her feet. Beyond them was the bulging stare of Heming's lifeless eyes, now separated by Tarlach's battle-axe.

CHAPTER TWENTY-SEVEN

"'Tis a fitting death." Tarlach's last words were as clear as his speech had been in his prime.

Ronan tried to grab his father's flailing hand, but he wouldn't take it. Instead, the dying man reached with his good arm toward something just beyond his grasp, something he wanted with all his being; something not of This World. Then it dropped, leaden, across his chest as breath left him for the last time.

"He … he died saving me," Brenna cried softly. She closed the old chieftain's eyes with her fingertips. Her gown was bloodied from tending the knife wound in his chest. Heming's last murderous deed. She'd left the blade there and packed Tarlach's brat about it to stifle the bleeding until death stilled it.

A blade of rage edged with grief wedged in Ronan's throat. "'Twas a fitting death for a warrior, more so than choking abed on his own spittle." As though putting a child to bed, Ronan covered his father with the stained black, red, and gray plaid of his clan. "God was with him … as He was with us all."

Through the dust and smoke from the fire, scattered in the midst of the fray, Ronan surveyed the bodies strewn about—some dead to all that had happened with sleep. Others dead to This World, or soon to cross over to the Other Side. He said what he believed about God, but still his blood roiled from battle.

Ronan helped Brenna down from the wagon and held onto her as though she alone kept him from such a crossing. He would kill Caden for trying to take this from him. Gone was the fraternal bond that had kept Ronan's suspicion at bay.

But in his desperation to protect Brenna, Ronan had lost track of his brother during the melee. Now the Gowrys beat the predawn forest for those who'd fled their charge: Caden and the women among them.

Caden. The very thought turned Ronan's blood hotter and hotter. He would hunt his brother down and avenge his murderous plot. Draw his innards from his belly and feed them to the dogs while he watched. Even then, that would not be enough.

"I should help Brother Martin tend the dying." Brenna pulled away from Ronan's embrace with reluctance.

Bitterness tinged Ronan's words. "Tend only *our* wounded."

Not that there were many. A few cuts and bruises for sleeping in the midst of a full-fledged battle.

She slanted a reproving gaze at him. *"All* must receive the comfort and knowledge of Christ."

"Their souls be cursed to eternity."

Brenna caught Ronan's arm as he turned away. *"You* may damn them, but I cannot deny them the same mercy you have received."

Ronan bit his lip. He could not argue with truth.

But he had been a boy, led by a madman—not a full-grown coward attacking incapacitated innocents in the night.

He looked at the bloodstained sword he'd planted in the earth. It was still there, by the cart, when he had abandoned it to be with Tarlach once the enemy had fled for the woods. Ronan felt no sorrow for the fiends he'd slain this night. Taking up the weapon, he wiped it across his thigh, staring into the wood.

His heart hardened even more. "And the killing is not yet done," he growled to himself. For a moment the image of Faol, baring his teeth to protect Brenna, flashed into his mind. Aye, the beast lived. In Ronan himself. This time, in the form of a man.

The sun broke over the horizon, bathing the green skirts of the cloud-cloaked mountains rising to the north and the woods thickening about the burn. With the dawn, the effects of the taint in the men's beer began to wane. Caden and the women were still missing when most of the Gowrys returned to the camp with the prisoners they had been able to capture.

"Isn't there anything you can do to speed the return of the men's senses?" Ronan demanded of Brenna. He wanted to find Caden before he had the chance to leave the area, for his brother would not dare show his face at Glenarden again.

"I've given them something for their aching heads and thick tongues, but no. Keena's henbane, or perhaps mandrake, must run its course," she snapped. "Be thankful they are alive and well, not among the dead. Those are dangerous herbs in evil hands."

Even Brenna's ever-loving nature had been tested by the carnage. She glanced to where the Gowrys dug a deep trench for the bodies stacked beside it. Catching her lip between her teeth, she shuddered and blinked away the weariness and grief clouding her eyes. "I must get away from this."

"Wait." Pricked by guilt, Ronan caught the sleeve of her dress. "I'm sorry. I'm not the saint you are."

Brenna didn't reply. She merely stared at his hand until he released her. As he watched her head for the sparkling stream away from the main body of the camp, he knew he'd hurt her. But she could not understand this anger....

"You need to get away as well, son."

Brother Martin approached, hearty as he'd been in leading the Gowrys hours earlier. Druids and priests were exempt from harm, even on the battlefield. At least by law.

"How is Alyn?" Ronan asked.

Evidently the youngest O'Byrne had not practiced the moderation he preached and had slept like a babe through the bloody conflict.

"Slight as he is, he's taking longer to come around, but the women are nursing him with sips of tea like a babe. Likewise the boy, Bron. But *you* need to take time to count your blessings," the priest advised. "I'll tend to Alyn."

Not what Ronan wanted to hear. "Caden betrayed us," Ronan ground out through his teeth. "He will pay."

The priest crossed his arms, thinking aloud. "Actually he did as much to bring peace between you and the Gowrys as any edict from Arthur."

As absurd as Martin's finding merit to Caden's betrayal was, Ronan knew he should thank the priest again and again for urging Donal and his clan to cover Ronan's back ... for reminding the Gowrys that they'd not seen the last of their common enemy. But if he did as the priest said, Ronan would lose the edge of his rage, and that was something he could not afford to do until he'd sent Caden earthways.

"I nearly lost her." The hungry way Heming had looked at Brenna, the sight of her reeling from his backhand—thinking of those images kept Ronan's rage sharp and ready.

"But you *didn't*." Martin clapped Ronan on the shoulder. "Go to her, laddie. You need each other ... and time with God."

Lips thinned, Ronan looked to where Brenna knelt beside the burn. She had edged downstream, toward the falls, and beneath an umbrella of alder and hazel. Leaning over, she splashed the running water on her face and arms, washing away the blood and dirt. And, judging by the way she scrubbed and scrubbed, she was attempting to erase the horrors of what she'd seen.

"When the Hebrew warriors returned from battle," Martin said, "they cleansed themselves physically and emotionally by spending a week away from their loved ones until the battle rage was replaced by God's peace."

Peace. Would Ronan ever have it?

"*You* do not have that luxury with your wife. Seek your peace together."

At this moment, in this time, Ronan didn't even want such peace. At least not for himself. But he did for Brenna. And that desire clashed with his blood's clamor for more carnage. Yet, with it, he might at least take some of the nightmare away from her.

Brenna was crying when he reached her. Sobs wracked her shoulders as she tried to rub the dried blood from her skirts. Were it in his power, she'd never face such a day as this again. Ronan gently pulled her to her feet and into his arms.

"I told the truth back there," he said, ignoring the cold dripping fabric now soaking his clothes. "I'm *not* the saint you are." He kissed the top of her head. "I'm just a man who faced losing the most important thing in his life, and it still haunts me. I want to protect you, *a stór*."

"Such things are beyond our power." Brenna jerked her arm toward the camp. "I c-couldn't save any of them." She fought for a steady breath. "The Gowrys are d-deadly foes." The next breath was no less shaky. "You want to protect everyone, and I want to save them, but … but sometimes, we j-just *can't*."

"I know." Ronan's reply was as inadequate as he. He wanted to take away her tears. Take away her fears, her pain. But all he could do was feel. Worse, what he felt could not be put into words. But he tried. "I love you, Brenna, with all my heart and soul."

Ronan lifted her chin, his gaze meeting her own. Instead of seeing his declaration sink in, perhaps hearing it returned, he saw terror. Sheer, speechless terror.

Looking over his shoulder, he saw Caden coming at his back, knife drawn.

There was no time to speak, only to act. Ronan twisted sideways. His hand caught Caden's wrist, halting the downward swing of the blade. With his other, Ronan pushed Brenna away. Heard her splash as she fell into the burn.

"One of us will die," Caden rumbled from deep in his chest, "this day."

Perspiration pushed its way through the skin on Ronan's forehead. He struggled to hold the knife at bay, all the while reaching for the dagger in his belt with his free hand. But his brother's uncommon strength, the prick of his knife against his skin, forced Ronan to use both hands to stop it. Blood thundered in his ear so loud it was hard to think about what Caden might do with his other hand.

But Ronan had to do something. Caden would not stop with taking his life. He would kill Brenna as well.

"Praise God the Father Almighty and Jesus Christ, Lord of all!"

Caden's strength faltered at Brenna's shout. Enough that Ronan regained some of the footing he'd lost.

"Let go of me, woman!" Caden roared.

In the periphery of Ronan's vision, Caden shook Brenna from her hold on his free hand. Something clattered from it. A knife?

Ronan couldn't look. Now he dealt with the force of *both* of Caden's hands on the knife poised at his throat. And his feet would not hold in the moist earth beneath him.

"This is not you, Caden." Brenna was back, embracing Caden about the waist. "In the name of Jesus, the Christ, begone demon of lust and greed, for this soul belongs to Him, not the likes of you. I cast thee out in Jesus' name."

Caden shuddered, weakening enough for Ronan to push the blade away at his arm's length. They locked at his elbows. Although how much longer Ronan could sustain this muscle to muscle—

"I praise the name of Jesus," Brenna cried out, "who seizes you by your neck and casts you out!"

An angry "Nooo!" erupted from Caden, along with a force that knocked Ronan nearly senseless to the ground.

Breath? Muscle? Maybe both. Something had bowled Ronan over like a toddling child. Caden stood above him, chest heaving, nostrils flaring, his knife still clutched in his hand. But instead of finishing off Ronan, the man seemed to struggle with himself.

And still Brenna clung to him. "I cast you out in the name of Jesus!"

"Let me go, woman!"

Caden would kill her. No doubt in Ronan's mind. Renewed by desperation, Ronan rolled away and struggled to his feet, drawing his sword.

Caden drew his as well, but Brenna would not let him go.

Even when Ronan begged her, "Brenna, run!"

"I claim this man in the name of Jesus—"

Caden shoved her face away with the palm of his free hand.

"—and I banish you," she stubbornly resisted, "demon greed and ambition. I banish you, demon lust and envy. All of you in the name of Jesus."

Spittle sprayed from Caden's snarl as he tried to twist from her grip. He lifted his sword as though to strike her with its pommel. Ronan lunged at him with his own weapon. The blade glanced off his mail shirt but diverted Caden's attention from Brenna. As Caden's blade clashed with Ronan's, Caden sent Brenna flailing to the ground with his boot.

Clutching her abdomen, she rolled to her knees and screamed, "Martin!"

Alarm shot through Ronan like ice falling into a blazing fire, steaming his desire for blood. Had Caden hurt her or the babe, Ronan would kill him twice! Dagger in one hand, sword in the other,

he flew at his fair-haired brother, slashing, blocking, thrusting, parry-
ing. Again and again he met steel. And with each clash Caden gained
ground, fed by Ronan's fury.

Ronan winced as Caden's sword found the meat of his thigh—
and leapt away when Caden, distracted by Brother Martin's loud and
angry Latin verse, failed to follow through.

"Spiritus, ego te ligo in nomine Jesu, potestate ...."

Brenna repeated the prayer in her native tongue, this time keeping her distance as she circled Caden. "Spirit, I bind you in the name
of Jesus, by the power of the cross and His blood ...."

Ronan watched for another chance, the right slip. With their
distraction he might overcome Caden's incredibly sharpened battle
prowess.

At long last men from the camp had heard the sound of combat
and rallied at full run.

But Brother Martin stayed them with an authoritative, "Back!"
between his rants, for such a prayer as this Ronan had never heard.
"Et per intercessione omnium sanctorum, te impero recedere, Caden ..."
the priest continued.

"And by the intercession of all the saints ..." Brenna joined in.

"Brenna, get away from him," Ronan ordered.

Instead she boldly seized Caden, who seemed stunned, even ill,
from behind again. Brother Martin laid his hands upon him as well.

"I command you to leave Caden of Glenarden and return to thy
lowly source."

Ronan wanted to pull her away to safety, but Caden faded by the
breath, by the groan, by the unseen power that ran him through the
gut and dropped him to his knees.

"Spirit, I bind you in the name of Jesus," healer and priest began—one in Briton, the other in Latin.

Caden's eyes rolled back in his head, but it was his rippling abdomen that riveted the attention of all who'd gathered. The hair stood up on Ronan's neck. It was all he could do not to back away as some of the others did.

"Return unto thy lowly source...."

Arching backward so abruptly that Brenna just escaped, Caden fell to the ground, writhing and groaning in agony.

Both Brenna and the priest followed him, keeping their hands on his body.

"In the name of the Father, the Son, and the Holy Spirit," they finished together.

Caden coughed. It was the only sound in the eerie silence.

Then an unearthly scream erupted from a cluster of rocks near the falls. Some of the men turned to run, while others stood motionless, hands on the hilts of their weapons.

Keena raced out from cover, tearing at her hair with her hands and racing up and down the bank.

Following the nurse was Rhianon. The lady was blanched of color and as oblivious to their audience as the crone. "Cease, Keena. You must gather your wits!"

But Keena whipped a blade out from her sash and turned on her young charge. "Back," she hissed through her scant remaining teeth. "Back, or I'll kill you."

Rhianon stilled, shocked. "Keena, nay. You must—"

Keena raised her blade at her audience. "Curse you all, your God and your saints," she shrieked. Except it wasn't the voice of an old woman, but of something dark and otherworldly. The same something that had haunted Caden's voice. Its timbre stroked Ronan's spine, lifting the very hairs along it.

"I'll kill you, all of you," the crone warned. Whatever it was that forced her backward, she slashed at it with all her fury. "Take that … and that."

Even as she went over the edge of the fall, she cursed at it … or them.

"Keena!" Rhianon's scream echoed to the highlands and back. She rushed to the precipice and peered over at the river below in horror and disbelief.

For a moment no one moved, save Brother Martin and Brenna, who continued to pray over Caden in a mingle of Latin and British.

Ronan grappled for his senses. "Seize her!"

But everyone else was held suspended by what they'd just witnessed.

Rhianon stiffened at the sound of Ronan's command. Her gaze shifted from panic to calculation as she took in the men's reaction. Or lack of it.

"I'll do it." Just as Donal of Gowrys moved forward, Rhianon pointed an imperious finger at him. The chieftain stopped in midstride, halting anyone else of a mind to follow.

"The first man to touch me will suffer the same fate as my husband," she warned, her voice bordering hysteria. She ventured a hasty glance over the edge where Keena had disappeared. "And now that my nurse is gone," she declared, growing bolder, "I'm even stronger."

"This is no ordinary foe, Glenarden," Donal said to Ronan, almost apologetic.

Using Caden's discarded sword as a crutch, Brother Martin rose on stiff knees. *"I'll* face her."

"Do you think I fear *you*, Priest?" Rhianon scoffed.

Benevolent to her contempt, Martin walked toward her, smiling. "You have nothing to fear from me, child. It is my Lord who makes you tremble so. Let us praise Him together."

He cast the weapon aside, arms widening in invitation. As did Rhianon's eyes. Furtive glances from priest to precipice showed her clearly torn between the appeal of the two options.

"Praise God Almighty," Martin sang in a fine baritone. "Ruler of Heaven and earth."

Rhianon put her hands over her ears.

"Praise Jesus, Son and Demon Conqueror, Victor over death and sin—"

"Curse you, Martin." Rhianon accented her defiance with a stomp. And with a sweep of her bloodied skirts, Rhianon spun and leapt over the fall.

The scene grew still as a tapestry. There was no trip of the burn over the rock ledge. No bird song. No movement of man or beast. No scrap of weapons against leather or mail.

Until Caden groaned and tried to rise.

"Be still," Brenna cooed in a voice that gentled wolves.

But not the wolf in Ronan.

Ronan sprang at his brother's prone figure and pressed his weapon at Caden's throat.

It was only Brenna's sudden and tight clutch of the sword blade alone that kept Ronan from ramming it into that place where his brother's life still beat without right.

"Let it go, Brenna," Ronan said.

"Aye," Caden said in gravelly agreement. "I deserve no less."

"I'll not let you do this, Ronan," she said.

"Do it, Brother," Caden implored. "Let this be done between us."

Brother Martin joined them. "Remove your hand from the blade, Brenna," the priest told her. "This is Ronan's test, not yours."

"Test?" Ronan echoed.

"It is your choice to make. Will you submit to God's will, or insist on your own?" Martin asked. "Will you remember your blessings or your rage? Will you feed the beast within you as you fed Caden's, or starve it with gratitude for the miracles that have taken place in these last hours?"

Miracles. They tumbled across Ronan's mind.

The Gowrys and that crazy priest spewing from the tall grass on the other side of the burn. Ronan thought he'd hallucinated at first.

The image of Tarlach rising like an ancient phoenix from the wagon bed with battle-axe brandished and letting it fly straight at Heming's head.

His men lying asleep and unharmed thanks to the herbs that had been meant to render them helpless. Had they not slept through the fighting, it would have been hard to discern the Gowrys from his captors.

Heartened by Ronan's hesitation, Brenna stroked Caden's wild, flaxen hair off his face. "In the name of Jesus, thy spirit be healed, Caden of Glenarden, freed by Him who has fought the battle for you and won."

"Thy spirit be healed."

The strange voice in Ronan's head conjured the image of Faol—one moment bearing his teeth at Ronan and the next, laying his snout on Ronan's hand. Healed of his distrust. Forgiving.

Then there was Brenna's pardon … and Arthur's.

Father God, I cannot be so merciful. I do not have it in me.

"I *am in you.*"

God? In me? Even as he wondered, Ronan could feel, could see in his mind's eye, the beast lie down. Thus enabled, he withdrew his sword from Caden's throat. The beast was still wary, but willing.

"*A willing heart is all I need.*"

Ronan became aware of the men gathered 'round them, watching him. Waiting for him to lead them. To be worthy of their loyalty. He sought out Egan O'Toole and Donal of Gowrys.

And suddenly birdsong burst from the trees beyond them, celebrating the new day. The frolic of the burn resumed.

"Bind him soundly," Ronan ordered, taking the caution of kicking the discarded daggers away from his brother's reach. "Arthur be your judge on This Side," he told Caden gravely, "and God on the Other."

epilogue

Brenna tried to reduce the swelling in her tear-swollen eyes with cold water before rejoining the people of Glenarden and their guests at Tarlach's funeral feast. She'd forgiven Tarlach but never dreamed she'd grieve him so. It had been two weeks since they'd returned to Glenarden. Two weeks since the Christian burial the family and Brother Martin had given the old chieftain in the glen that Tarlach had ceded to the church years before at the behest of his wife, Aeda.

Ronan's mother would be pleased to see that her hope of an outdoor chapel was soon to become a small church—the beginning, perhaps, of a monastery. Brother Martin's new helpers were most industrious.

The door to the small bedchamber that she and Ronan still occupied opened, admitting her husband. Concern darkened his gaze as he took in her sadness.

"The feast is near its end," he told her. "Are you ill?"

"I wish I'd known your mother," she lamented. Faith, would this waterfall ever cease?

An empathetic smile creased his lips. "She would have loved you." He closed the distance between them and placed his hand on her abdomen. "Perhaps you and the little one should rest. There is no need for you to endure Caden's judgment."

With the feasting complete, it was time for the business Merlin Emrys and the queen were to officiate. How sad that they should mourn the father and condemn his son on the same day.

Brenna shook her head. "I ... *we,*" she insisted, "are fine. It's my eyes that won't stop watering. Poor Vychan has had all the preparations fall on his shoulders—"

"Vychan is glad to have his household return to order," Ronan assured her.

With the fair at last ended, it was only natural for the Glenarden's friends and family to pay their respects and for Arthur to deal with Caden's murderous treachery. The prodigal himself had remained in Glenarden's prison, shunned by all save Brenna and Brother Martin, who'd prayed for him daily.

Brenna would be there to speak on the broken man's behalf, whether Caden wanted it or not. "I shall blame Ailill for my distress," she announced halfheartedly, turning to rummage through her medicine bag.

Ronan's fervent "Aye" echoed her sentiment.

During the course of the feast, the bard's dramatic rendition of the peace and battle betrayal had sent shivers up and down Brenna's spine and wrenched her heart. In perfect rhyme and meter so as never to be misrepresented, Tarlach, the redeemed murderer, emerged as the hero. It was, as he'd said himself, a fitting end.

"There," she said, pulling out a small jar. She opened it and dabbed a little of the drawing cream under her eyes. "If they look like red puffing toads after this, then so be it."

"Those eyes could never resemble anything but the blue of a highland lake." Ronan took time to kiss each one before they entered the hall proper.

Brenna chuckled. "Now who's the poet?"

The hall was filled with delicious scents of food, drink, and fresh threshing. As Ronan escorted her to her seat next to his in Tarlach's tooled leather chair, Merlin Emrys, Martin, Egan, and Alyn rose. Such attention caused Brenna's cheeks to warm. It still seemed unreal, this new life of hers. Yet there was Queen Gwenhyfar at her side taking in every aspect of Brenna's appearance with her slanted green gaze.

"Worry not, Lady Brenna. All expectant mothers develop an odd connection between the bladder and the eyes," she confided behind her ringed hand. "I remember well my term with Lohot."

Arthur's heir, now a warrior in his father's warband.

"That would explain it then, Your Highness," Brenna replied.

"To Joanna's daughter, I am Anora."

"Anora." The queen's given name? Then Gwenhyfar *was* a title, wife to the Arthur, even if Arthur happened to be this one's given name as well.

"I am honored ... Anora."

The appearance of the guards in the main hall entrance with Caden, arms bound behind him, cut their conversation short. Cut all conversation in the hall off completely, so that their footfalls on the plank flooring echoed their approach to where the Glenarden and his guests sat. Ronan stiffened next to Brenna. Since he'd walked away from Caden the day of his capture, he'd not allowed her to speak of his brother in his presence. Caden was dead to him, even if he still breathed.

Merlin Emrys gathered his staff and rose on stiff knees to leave the table and face the accused alone. Shed of his cape, the older man was not nearly as imposing. Still tall, his shoulders were bent from the weight of time and the service he'd dedicated to the Creator God. But when he spoke, he swelled with authority.

"Caden of Glenarden, you stand accused of the lowest treachery and grievous ambition. This is your chance to defend yourself. Do you understand?"

"Aye," the prisoner responded.

Caden looked horrible. He'd lost weight. His normally clean-shaven good looks were shaggy and filthy with neglect from refusing the bathwater and soap provided him by Brenna. But it was his eyes that told it all. They were empty, truly empty this time. No hate, no jealousy … no hope.

"Did you not conspire to murder your father and brother … and any who sought to stop you from becoming chieftain of Glenarden?"

"I did." Caden's answer was as hollow as his gaze.

"Had you any cause beyond greed and ambition?"

"I did not."

Brother Martin cleared his throat. "If I may, Merlin." At Merlin's nod the priest spoke on. "Many, including myself, were witness to a most unusual circumstance. From my knowledge of Scripture, this man had been possessed with a demon summoned by necromancy."

A wave of uneasiness rippled through the onlookers.

"He wasn't himself," Brenna chimed in, half-rising from her bench. At Merlin's reproving look, she sat back down. Better Brother Martin testify. He was the knowledgeable one.

Brenna herself could hardly recall what had happened that morning. Just this driving desperation to help her husband, to stop Caden. But the moment she'd laid hands on the man, she saw, not Caden, but something so hideous it still turned her blood cold. It frightened her, for in her soul, she knew no sword or stone threatened it. Only the praise of God, the declaration of Jesus' name. In desperation she had grasped at God's Word, repeating what came to her mind, praying from the bottom of her faith.

"The only demon at fault was me," Caden said.

"I saw it," Brenna blurted out. She caught her lip belatedly.

"*We,*" Martin said, sending a glance of approval her way, "fought it with praise and prayer."

"*Unto you it is given to know the mysteries of the kingdom of God: but to others in parables; that seeing they might not see, and hearing they might not understand,*" the merlin quoted from Luke.

"If, and I mean *if,*" Ronan emphasized, "there was such a demon in my brother, then it had food to feast upon."

"He speaks truth," Caden agreed, adding with sarcasm, "as always, the *good* brother, aren't you, Ronan?" The man would not help himself. "You said yourself, Brother Martin, that no demon could possess a man filled with the Holy Spirit."

"I also said that you were by God's grace given a second chance to invite it in."

"I wouldn't dirty His linen," Caden replied.

"So you are unrepentant?" Merlin Emrys asked the prisoner.

"If you mean, do I regret what I did, then, aye, I do. So much so that if you champion any real justice … or mercy," Caden added for Martin's sake, "you will give me death."

Now the room buzzed with anticipation. Merlin Emrys' face gave no hint of what was going on behind the steel of his gaze.

"That is what you have requested," he said after a lengthy pause. "But that request is denied."

Ronan shot to his feet. "What?"

Brenna closed her eyes. *Father God, help me crack the shell he's put about his heart.*

"In time."

"You are hereby exiled from Glenarden," Merlin announced. "Return by penalty of death."

Several protests rose from the men who had been drugged by Caden, who believed him responsible for the Glenarden's death and nearly their own. Others more loyal to Caden contested the objection, declaring Rhianon and her nurse the real villains.

Ronan sat stone-like, his only movement the twitch of muscle at his temples.

Brenna placed a hand on his arm. "I pray that if our son is ever in serious trouble, that God will extend the same mercy to him … for I could not bear it, otherwise."

The twitch stopped. The veins hedging it faded with the unclenching of her husband's jaw.

"You are a hard woman to argue with," he said without looking in her direction. Instead Ronan watched his brother being led out. Alyn, who until now had remained silent, left the table to rush after his exiled brother.

"God has plans for you, Caden," Brother Martin called after them. The promise from Jeremiah rang loud and clear above the din of dissension. "Plans to prosper, not harm you. Plans to give you hope, Caden. If you will but call to the Father, He will harken."

"God may harken," Ronan drawled laconically, "but it will be a long time before I can find forgiveness in my heart for what Caden's done."

Brenna folded his hand over hers and kissed it. "Then I shall spend a long time tending that heart until it's fully healed."

For her Shepherd's plan was for *all* of His children.

... a little more ...

When a delightful concert comes to an end,

the orchestra might offer an encore.

When a fine meal comes to an end,

it's always nice to savor a bit of dessert.

When a great story comes to an end,

we think you may want to linger.

And so we offer ...

AfterWords—just a little something more after you

have finished a David C. Cook novel.

We invite you to stay awhile in the story.

Thanks for reading!

Turn the page for ...

GLOSSARY

Alba—Scotland

Albion—the Isle of Britain

Alcut/Alclyd—Dumbarton on Firth of Clyde

anmchara—soulmate

arthur—title passed down from Stone Age Britain meaning "the bear," or "protector," connected with the constellation of the Big Dipper; equivalent of Dux Bellorum and Pendragon; the given name of Arthur, prince of Dalraida

a stór—darling

Ballach—Ronan's horse, meaning "speckled"

behoved—beholdened

Ben Ledi—Mountain of Light, the first of the highland mountains beyond Stirling's pass

braccae—Latin for woolen drawstring trousers or pants, either knee- or ankle-length

cariad—dearest

Carmelide—Carlisle

Cennalath—*ken'-nah-lot*, Pictish king of the Orkneys

Dux Bellorum—Latin for duke of war, commander general; see *arthur*

earthways—to death/burial

fell—rocky hill

fodere—deceiver

foolrede—foolishness

Gwenhyfar—*Guinevere;* considered by some scholars to have been a title like *arthur* and *merlin,* as well as a given name. Some scholars believe the Pictish Gwenhyfar was called Anora.

Joseph, the—the high priest of the Grail Palace on the Sacred Isle

Long Dark—the winter

mathair—mother

merlin—title for the advisor to the king, often a prophet or seer; sometimes druidic Christian as in Merlin Emrys, or not, as Merlin Sylvester

Merlin Emrys (Ambrosius)—the prophet/seer/Celtic Christian priest descended from the Pendragon Ambrosius Aurelius, thought to be Arthur's Merlin, suggested to be buried on Bardsley Island

Merlin Sylvester—the prophet/seer to Gwendoleu of Gwynedd's pagan court; the bard said to have gone mad after the Battle of Arthuret

mind—remember or recall

mo chroi—my heart

Mountain of Light—see Ben Ledi

nun day—noon-day meal

Pendragon—Cymri for "head dragon," dragon being a symbol of knowledge/power; see *arthur*

rath—walled keep and/or village

sandarach—arsenic mentioned by Socrates in fourth-century BC

souterrain—underground chamber for storage, defense, and escape

Strighlagh—*strī'-lăk;* Stirling

Sun Season—summer

tuath—*tŭth;* kingdom, clan land

widdershins—counterclockwise

❧ARThURiAN ChARACTERS

Most scholars agree that Arthur, Guinevere, and Merlin were titles shared by various personas throughout the late fifth and sixth centuries. These are the late sixth-century characters. Because of inconsistent dating, multiple persons sharing the same titles and/or names, and place names as well as texts recorded in at least six languages, I again quote Nenius: "I've made a heap of all I could find."

* historically documented individuals

*Arthur—Prince of Dalraida, Dux Bellorum (Duke of War) or Pendragon/High King of Britain, although he held no land of his own. He is a king of landed kings, their battle leader. A Pendragon at this time can have no kingdom of his own to avoid conflict of interest. Hence, Gwenhyfar is rightful queen of her lands, Prince Arthur's through marriage. Arthur is the historic son of Aedan of Dalraida/Scotland, descended from royal Irish of the Davidic bloodline preserved by the marriage of Zedekiah's daughter Tamar to the Milesian king of Ireland Eoghan in 587 BC. Ironically the Milesians are descended from the bloodline of Zarah, the "Red Hand" twin of Pharez (David and Jesus' ancestor) in the book of Genesis. Thus the breach of Judah prophesied in Isaiah was mended by this marriage of very distant cousins.

*Aedan of Dalraida—Arthur's father, Aedan, was Pendragon of Britain for a short time and prince of Manau Gododdin by his mother's Pictish blood (like Arthur was prince of Dalraida because of his marriage to Gwenhyfar). When Aedan's father, the king of

Dalraida, died, Aedan became king of the more powerful kingdom, and he abandoned Manau Gododdin. For that abandonment, he is oft referred to as Uther Pendragon, *uther* meaning "the terrible." He sent his son Arthur to take his place as Pendragon and Manau's protector.

Angus—the Lance of Lothian. Although this Dalraida Arthur had no Lancelot as his predecessor did, Angus is the appointed king of Stirlingshire and protector of his Pictish Queen Gwenhyfar and her land of Strighlagh. Like his ancestral namesake Lancelot, his land of Berwick in Lothian now belongs to Cennalot, who is defeated by Arthur. (See *Cennalot* and *Brude*.) Angus is Arthur's head of artillery. It is thought he was raised at the Grail Castle and was about ten or so years younger than his lady Gwenhyfar.

Scholar/researcher Norma Lorre Goodrich suggests he may have been a fraternal twin to Modred or Metcault. In that case it would explain Lance not knowing who he really was until he came of age, as women who bore twins were usually executed. The second child was thought to be spawn of the Devil. Naturally Morgause would have hidden the twins' birth by casting one out, only to have him rescued by her sister, the Lady of the Lake, or Vivianne Del Acqs. This scenario happened as well in many of the saints' lives, such as St. Kentigern. Their mothers were condemned to death for consorting with the Devil and begetting a second child. Yet miraculously these women lived and the cast-off child became a saint.

*Brude/Bridei—see *Cennalot/Cennalath/Lot of Lothian*.

*Cennalot/Cennalath/Lot of Lothian—Arthur's uncle by marriage to Morgause. This king of eastern Pictland and the Orkneys was all that stood between his Pictish cousin Brude reigning over all of Pictland. Was it coincidence that Arthur, whose younger brother, Gairtnat, married Brude's daughter and became king of the Picts at Brude's death, decided to take out this Cennalot while Brude looked the other way? Add that to the fact that Cennalot was rubbing elbows with the Saxons and looking greedily at Manau Gododdin, and it was just a matter of time before either Brude or Arthur got rid of him.

*Dupric, Bishop of Llandalf—wants to start a monastery on land where Brother Martin lives (a historical bishop who *may* also be Merlin Emrys per Norma Goodrich).

Gawain—son of Cennalot/Cennalath and Morgause, brother to Modred/Metcault, and cousin to Arthur; Arthur's right-hand man on the battlefield and much older than Angus/Lancelot.

*Gwendoleu—kingdom between Strathclyde and Rheged invaded by Riderch of Alclyd/Strathclyde.

Gwenhyfar/Guinevere—High Queen of Britain. This particular Gwen's Pictish name is Anora. She is of apostolic line and a high priestess in the Celtic Church. She is buried in Fife. Her marriage brought under Arthur the lands of Stirlingshire, or Strighlagh. Her offspring are its heirs, as the Pictish rule is inherited from the mother's side. There were two abductions of the Gwenhyfars. In one she was rescued. In the other she *slept*, meaning she died (allegedly from snakebite), precipitating the fairy tale of *Sleeping Beauty*. Both in Gwenhyfar's abduction and in that of Sleeping Beauty, thorns surrounded the castle, thorns being as common a defense in those days as moats were. Also note the similarities of names, even if the definitions are different—Anora (grace), Aurora (dawn).

*Merlin Emrys of Powys—a Christian druidic-educated bishop of the Celtic Church, protoscientist, advisor to the king, prophet after the Old Testament prophets, and possibly a Grail King or Joseph. Emrys is of the Irish Davidic/Romano-British bloodline as son of Ambrosius Aurelius and uncle to Aedan, Arthur's father. Merlin Emrys retired as advisor during Arthur's later reign, perhaps to pursue his beloved science or perhaps as the Grail King. In either case he would not have condoned Arthur's leaning toward the Roman Church's agenda. Later the Roman Church and Irish Celtic Church priests would convert the Saxons to Christianity, but the British Celtic Church suffered too much at pagan hands to offer the good news to their pagan invaders. (See *Dupric, Myrddyn,* and *Ninian.*)

*Myrddyn (also known as Merlin Sylvester or Merlin Wilt, meaning "wild")—a pagan druidic bard of Gwendoleu, often confused with Arthur's Merlin. (See *Merlin Emrys of Powys.*)

*Riderch Haol of Alcut or Alclyd in Strathclyde—historic Coeling king. His relationship with Arthur, Urien, and the other kings of the North was tenuous. Arthur punished him for invading Gwendoleu to avenge his ambitious brother's death. Yet he rode later on with Arthur, his father, Aedan of Dalraida, Urien, Gwendoleu, the deposed Morcant Bulc of Bryneich (now Saxon Bernicia), and others against the Picts and Saxons in the Battle of Camlan.

*Vivianne Del Acqs—sister to Ygerna and Morgause of Lothian, she is Arthur's aunt and Lady of the Lake. Vivianne is a high priestess and tutor at the Grail Castle. It's thought that she raised both Gwenhyfar and Angus/Lance of Lothian, all direct descendants of the Arimathean priestly lines.

*Ygerna—Arthur's mother and a direct descendant of Joseph of Arimathea, was matched as a widow of a British duke and High Queen of the Celtic Church to Aedan of Dalraida by Merlin Emrys to produce an heir with both royal and priestly bloodlines. It is thought her castle was at Caerlaverock.

The Grail Palace

Norma Lorre Goodrich suggests that the Grail Palace was on the Isle of St. Patrick, and recent archaeology has exposed sixth-century ruins of a church/palace there. But what was it, or the Grail itself, exactly? Goodrich uses the vast works of other scholars, adding her expertise in the linguistics field, to extract information from Arthurian texts in several languages. Weeding out as much fancy as possible, it was the palace or church/place where the holy treasures of Christianity were kept (not to be confused with the treasures of Solomon's Temple, which are alleged to have been taken to Ireland in 587 BC by Jeremiah and Zedekiah's daughter Tamar or found by the Templars during the Crusades). The Grail treasures consist of items relating to Jesus: a gold chalice and a silver platter (or silver knives) from the Last Supper, the spear that pierced Christ's side, the sword (or broken sword) that beheaded John the Baptist, gold candelabra with at least ten candles each, and a secret book, or gospel attributed directly to either Jesus, John the Beloved, Solomon, John the Baptist, or John of the Apocalypse.

Or was this book the genealogies of the bloodlines, whose copies were supposedly destroyed by the Roman Church?

If the house of the Last Supper was that of the wealthy Joseph of Arimathea, is it possible that Jesus used these rich items and that Joseph brought them to Britain in the first century as tradition holds? The high priest of the Grail Castle tradition was called the Joseph. Of all the knights who vied for the Grail or the high priest position as teacher and protector of the bloodlines and treasures, only Percival and Galahad succeeded. Did they take the place of Merlin Emrys, when he passed on?

The purpose of the Grail Palace beyond holding the treasures was one of protecting and perpetuating the apostolic and royal bloodlines … hence the first-century Christianity brought to Britain by Christ's family and followers. It was believed that an heir of both lines stood a chance of becoming another messiah-like figure. Such breeding of bloodlines was intended to keep the British church free of Roman corruption and close to its Hebrew origins. Nenius, who was pro-Roman to the core, accuses the Celtic Church of *clinging to the shadows of the Jews*—the first-century Jews of Jesus' family and friends.

But by the time the last Arthur fell, the hope of keeping the line of priests and Davidic kings, as had been done in Israel prior to Zedekiah's fall, was lost. With the triumph of the Roman Church authority, political appointment from Rome trumped the inheritance of the priestly and kingly rights divinely appointed in the Old Testament. Celibacy became the order of the day to keep the power and money in Rome.

Based on Goodrich's insights, it's suggested that there were three Grail brotherhoods: Christ and the Twelve Disciples, Joseph of Arimathea and his twelve companions, and Arthur and the Twelve Knights of the Round Table. After Arthur's death, the order of the Grail with its decidedly Jewish roots gave way to Columba at Iona and the Roman Church. The Grail treasures—which had been brought from the Holy Land by Joseph of Arimathea, first to Glastonbury and later, after Saxons came too close for comfort, to the Isle of Patrick off of Man—had to be moved again. Percival and

Galahad returned it to the Holy Land. And it is there, centuries later, that the Knights Templar allegedly entered into the mystery, perhaps with privileged information kept and passed down among the sacred few remnants of the bloodlines that shaped early Christian Scotland, England, and Ireland.

Etienne Gilson said the Grail veneration started in Jerusalem with Arimathea and Jesus' family and friends and that it stood for grace. God's grace. Christ's grace by sacrifice.

Or is it that only those truly baptized by Pentecostal fire are fit to care for the Grail treasures, just as only the high priest of Aaron was allowed into the Holy of Holies in ancient Israel? And is finding the Grail a metaphor for the Holy Spirit embodied in the apostles, or entering into the presence of God? Lancelot only dreamed of it, while Percival and Galahad actually achieved it as evidenced by the fires on their tunics.

The truth has been veiled by time, muddied or intentionally destroyed by later anti-Semitic factions in the church, and turned into a fantasy by later medieval writers who vilified most of the women, romanticized the men, and changed the now-lost original accounts to suit the tastes of their benefactors. Yet still this quest haunts the imagination and the soul—to be like, and hence in the presence of, Christ.

bibliogRaphy

For Readers Who Want More:

There are *over* seventy-five books from which I've garnered information and inspiration for this novel. However, I am listing those of the most influence for the reader who wants to delve into the history and tradition behind this work of fiction.

David F. Carroll makes a case for the historically documented Prince Arthur of Dalraida as *the* Arthur. This documentation is why I chose his story as the background for this series, while incorporating many of Norma Lorre Goodrich's observations as well. Her scholarly analysis of Arthuriana suggests that there is more than one Arthur, Guinevere, and Merlin. This, and the fact that there was no standard for dating, explains Arthur and company having to have lived for nearly a hundred years and the many dating discrepancies in historical manuscripts. She, among others listed, uses geographical description and her knowledge of linguistics to place Arthur mostly in the lowlands of today's Scotland. Shortly after she suggested the location of Arthur's Grail Palace on an island near Man, the ruins of a Dark Age Christian church was discovered there.

Isabel Elder's *Celt, Druid and Culdee* provides a wonderful insight into the origins of the early church in Britain and how the similarities of these three groups made them ready to make Christ their Druid or teacher/master. A must-read to understand the New Age philosophy of today. Andrew Gray's *The Origin and Early History of Christianity in Britain—From Its Dawn to the Death of Augustine* is fascinating and impacts *Healer* as it lends some credence to some of Goodrich's observations on Arthur and the church.

The oral traditions about Joseph of Arimathea and Avalon/ Glastonbury are underscored by ancient place names and Roman, British, Irish, and church histories in books by Gray, Joyce, McNaught, and Taylor. They also provide a compelling case for the British church's establishment in the first century by Jesus' family and apostles. Books regarding the Davidic bloodlines preserved through Irish nobility that married into the major royal houses of western Europe, Britain in particular, include those of Allen, Capt, and Collins.

To separate magic from science from miracle throughout history, I found Charles Singer's book one of the best I've read for clarification. Kieckhefer's is also an excellent historical resource for medieval customs, superstitions, and medicine and their darker side as well.

I do not advocate the practices featured in Buckland's book on witchcraft, although reading it has helped me develop a clearer understanding of where much New Age thought comes from, that I might more effectively witness to the similarities and differences in the future in my case for Christ. After reading the above and more on my magic-miracle-science research, I found the scriptural perspective in Rory Roybal's *Miracles or Magic? Discerning the Works of God in Today's World* reassuring and spiritually grounding. And, of course, enough can't be said of the King James Version of the Bible quoted throughout *Healer.*

Arthurian Works

Barber, Richard. *The Figure of Arthur.* New York: Dorset Press, 1972.

Blake, Steve, and Scott Lloyd. *Pendragon: The Definitive Account of the Origins of Arthur.* Guilford, CT: The Lyons Press, 2002.

Carroll, David F. *Arturius: A Quest for Camelot.* D.F. Carroll, 1996.

De Boron, Robert. *Merlin and the Grail: Joseph of Arimathea, Merlin, Perceval.* Translated by Nigel Bryant. Rochester, NY: D.S. Brewer, 2005.

Goodrich, Norma Lorre. *Guinevere.* New York: HarperCollins, 1991.

_____. *The Holy Grail.* New York: HarperCollins, 1993.

_____. *King Arthur.* New York: Harper and Row, 1986.

_____. *Merlin.* New York: Harper and Row, 1988.

Holmes, Michael. *King Arthur: A Military History.* New York: Blandford Press, 1998.

Reno, Frank. *Historic Figures of the Arthurian Era.* Jefferson, NC: McFarland & Company, 2000.

Skene, W. F. Edited by Derek Bryce. *Arthur and the Britons.* Dyfed, UK: Llanerch Enterprises, 1988.

Church History

Allen, J. H. *Judah's Sceptre and Joseph's Birthright.* Merrimac, MA: Destiny Publishers, 1902.

Capt, E. Raymond. *The Traditions of Glastonbury.* Thousand Oaks, CA: Artisan Sales, 1983.

Missing Links Discovered in Assyrian Tablets: Study of the Assyrian Tables of Israel. Muskogee, OK: Artisan Publishers, 2004.

Collins, Stephen M. *The "Lost" Ten Tribes of Israel ... Found!* Boring, OR: CPA Books, 1995.

Elder, Isabel Hill. *Celt, Druid and Culdee.* London: Covenant Publishing Company, 1973.

Gardner, Laurence. *Bloodline of the Holy Grail: The Hidden Lineage of Jesus.* New York: Thorsons/Element, 1996. (Used for tracing Jesus' family and apostles, not His alleged direct bloodline.)

Gray, Andrew. *The Origin and Early History of Christianity in Britain—From Its Dawn to the Death of Augustine.* New York: James Pott & Co., 1897.

Joyce, Timothy. *Celtic Christianity: A Sacred Tradition of Hope.* New York: Orbis Books, 1998.

Larson, Frank. *The Bethlehem Star,* http://www.BethlehemStar.com (accessed January 1, 2008).

MacNaught, J. C. *The Celtic Church and the See of Peter.* Oxford: Basil Blackwell, 1927.

Taylor, Gladys. *Our Neglected Heritage: The Early Church.* London: Covenant Publishing Company, 1969.

General History

Adomnan of Iona. *Life of St. Columba.* Translated by Richard Sharpe. New York: Penguin Books, 1995.

Alcock, Leslie. *Arthur's Britain.* New York: Penguin Books, 1971.

Kings & Warriors, Craftsmen & Priests in Northern Britain AD 550-850. Edinburgh: Society of Antiquaries of Scotland, 2003.

Armit, Ian. *Celtic Scotland.* London: B. T. Batsford, Ltd., 2005.

Ashe, Geoffrey. *A Guidebook to Arthurian Britain.* London: First Aquarian Press, 1983.

Ellis, Peter Berresford. *Celt and Saxon: The Struggle for Britain, AD 410-937.* London: Constable, 1993.

Evans, Stephen. *The Lords of Battle.* Rochester, NY: Boydell Press, 1997. (Excellent resource for the life of a warlord and his men.)

Fraser, James. *From Caledonia to Pictland: Scotland to 795.* Edinburgh: Edinburgh University Press, 2009.

Hartley, Dorothy. *Lost Country Life.* New York: Random House, 1979. (A wonderful look at country life in Britain by the season.)

Hughes, David. *The British Chronicles, Book One.* Westminster, MD: Heritage Books, 2007.

Johnson, Stephen. *Later Roman Britain: Britain before the Conquest.* New York: Charles Scribner & Sons, 1980.

Laing, Lloyd and Jenny. *The Picts and the Scots.* UK: Alan Sutton Publishing, 1993.

Marsh, Henry. *Dark Age Britain: Sources of History.* New York: Dorset Press, 1987.

Snyder, Christopher A. *The Britons.* Malden, MA: Blackwell Publishing, 2003.

Magic, Miracle, and Science of the Dark Ages

Buckland, Raymond. *Scottish Witchcraft, The History and Magick of the Picts.* St. Paul, MD: Llewellyn Publications, 1999.

Kieckhefer, Richard. *Magic in the Middle Ages.* Cambridge, UK: Cambridge University Press, 1989.

Roybal, Rory. *Miracles or Magic? Discerning the Works of God in Today's World.* Longwood, FL: Xulon Press, 2005.

Singer, Charles. *From Magic to Science: Essays on the Scientific Twilight.* Mineola, NY: Dover Publications, 1958.

SCRIPTURE REFERENCES

Prologue
Greater love hath no man than this, that a man lay down his life for his friends.—John 15:13

The secret things belong unto the LORD our God: but those things which are revealed belong unto us and to our children for ever, that we may do all the words of this law.—Deuteronomy 29:29

Chapter Two
Inasmuch as ye have done it unto one of the least of these … ye have done it unto me.—Matthew 25:40

Chapter Five
For I know the thoughts that I think toward you, saith the LORD, thoughts of peace, and not of evil, to give you an expected end.—Jeremiah 29:11

Chapter Nine
With God all things are possible.—Matthew 19:26

Chapter Fifteen
I will never leave thee, nor forsake thee.—Hebrews 13:5

I have plans that you should prosper … and make my people prosper.—
see Jeremiah 29:11

Chapter Seventeen

We are troubled on every side, yet … not in despair.—2 Corinthians 4:8

Chapter Eighteen

Nothing can separate you from God's love.—see Romans 8:39

Chapter Twenty

The heavens declare the glory of God; and the firmament sheweth
his handywork. Day unto day uttereth speech, and night unto night
sheweth knowledge. There is no speech nor language, where their
voice is not heard.—Psalm 19:1–3

Ye shall know them by their fruits.—Matthew 7:16

Chapter Twenty-three

The saintliest of Briton's bloodlines assembled here with the kings
and queens of Judah, the Davidic descendants from the breach
caused by a scarlet cord and stolen birthright in Genesis—a breach
repaired as prophesied by Isaiah centuries before (see Isaiah 58:12)
by the marriage of Pharez's princess and Zarah's Red Hand prince
(see Genesis 38:29–30).

Chapter Twenty-six

As you sow, so shall you reap.—see Job 4:8

Epilogue

Unto you it is given to know the mysteries of the kingdom of God: but to others in parables; that seeing they might not see, and hearing they might not understand.—Luke 8:10

Plans to prosper, not harm you. Plans to give you hope.—see Jeremiah 29:11

ABOUT THE AUTHOR

With an estimated million books in print, **Linda Windsor** is an award-winning author of sixteen secular historical and contemporary romances and thirteen romantic comedies and historical fiction for the inspirational market. Her switch to inspirational fiction in 1999 was more like Jonah going to Ninevah than a flash of enlightenment. Linda claims God pushed her, kicking and screaming all the way. In retrospect the author can see how God prepared her for His writing in her early publishing years and then claimed not just her music but also her writing when she was ready. At that point He brushed away all her reservations regarding inspirational fiction, and she took the leap of faith. Windsor has never looked back.

While all of Linda's inspirational novels have been recognized with awards and rave reviews in both the ABA and CBA markets, she is most blessed by the 2002 Christy finalist award for *Riona* and the numerous National Readers Choice Awards for Best Inspirational that her historicals and contemporaries have won. *Riona* actually astonished everyone when it won against the worldly competition in the RWA Laurel Wreath's Best Foreign Historical Category.

To Linda's delight, *Maire,* Book One of the Fires of Gleannmara Irish Celtic series, was rereleased by Waterbrook Multnomah Publishers with a gorgeous new warrior queen cover in 2009.

Christy finalist *Riona* will be rereleased with its heroine on an all-new cover in summer 2010.

Another of her novels, *For Pete's Sake,* Book Two in the Piper Cove Chronicles, is winner of the 2009 National Reader's Choice Award—Best Inspirational, the Golden Quill Award—Best Inspirational, the Best Book of 2008 Award—Inspirational (Long & Short Reviews), and Best Book of the Year—Inspirational (*Romance Reviews Today*). *For Pete's Sake* also finaled in the Colorado RWA 2009 Award of Excellence and the Southern Magic RWA Gayle Wilson Award of Excellence.

Linda's research for the early Celtic Gleannmara series resulted in a personal mission dear to her heart: to provide Christians with an effective witness to reach their New Age and unbelieving family and friends. Her goal continues with *Healer* of The Brides of Alba series, which reveals early church history, much of which has been lost or neglected due to intentional and/or inadvertent error by its chroniclers. This knowledge of early church history enabled Linda to reach her daughter, who became involved in Wicca after being stalked and assaulted in college and blaming the God of her childhood faith—a witness that continues to others at medieval fair signings or wherever these books take Windsor.

Windsor is convinced that, had her daughter known the struggle and witness of the early Christians beyond the apostles' time and before Christianity earned a black name in the Crusades and Inquisition, she could not have been swayed from her early faith. Nor would Linda herself have been lured away from her faith in Christ in college by a liberal agenda.

Linda's testimony that Christ is her Druid (Master/Teacher)

opens wary hearts wounded by harsh Christian condemnation. Through her witness, admitted Wiccans and pagans have become intrigued by the tidbits of history and tradition pointing to the how and why druids accepted Him. She not only sells these non-believers copies of her books, but she also outsells the occult titles surrounding her inspirational ones.

When Linda isn't writing in the restored eighteenth-century home that she and her late husband restored, she's busy speaking and/or playing music for writing workshops, faith seminars, libraries, and civic and church groups. She and her husband were professional musicians and singers in their country and old rock-and-roll band, Homespun. She also plays organ for her little country church in the wildwood. Presently she's trying to work in some painting, wallpapering, and other house projects that are begging to be done. That is, when she's not Red-Hatting or, better yet, playing mom-mom to her grandchildren—her favorite role in life.

Visit Linda Windsor at her Web site:
www.LindaWindsor.com

Don't Miss the Stunning Sequel

Thief

Book Two
The Brides of Alba
Linda Windsor

*"Love of our neighbor is the only door
out of the dungeon of self."*

When Caden O'Byrne fails to find the death he seeks as an end to his miserable exile from family, country, and faith, an old Scottish proverb challenges him to move on. But doing so means traveling deep into Saxon territory to bring home a young woman abducted as a child by Saxon raiders. Little does Caden know that a familiar enemy awaits him—one more dangerous than a Saxon blade.

Sorcha's troubles are finally behind her with her betrothal to a good, if elderly, thane whose wealth will enable her to continue rescuing British children from the Roman slave market. Then a stranger arrives and tells her she has an inheritance from parents, who never tried to find her when she was a young, frightened captive. Sorcha's heart is torn between her passionate calling and an intense longing for what might have been back at her childhood home.

When treachery strikes, Caden and Sorcha are forced on a dangerous journey that neither could have imagined.

PROLOGUE

Lothian
Leaf Fall, late sixth century AD

It was a good day to die. But then this warrior had lost count of such days, hoping that each one would put an end to his miserable existence … to this exile of body and soul. Beneath him, his horse strained at the reins, eager to join the fray between the Pendragon's forces and the Saxon invaders seeking to win yet one more chunk of the ever-shrinking Bryneich. Once it had swept to the North Sea, but the Sassenach had hacked away its coastal settlements with their axes. Now they wanted more.

Caden O'Byrne held his stallion back, waiting with the other mercenaries for the signal to sweep down the hill and relieve the first line of warriors already engaged. None of them knew him by any other name but Caden. Like everything else that mattered, he'd left clan name behind. Only shame followed, haunting him night and day.

The clang of blades, the cries of rage and anguish rose in a dissonant chorus from the edge of the autumn-tinged forest of oak and alder that had hid the enemy—or so they thought—until the last moment. Anxiety weighed upon the faces of Caden's battle-hardened comrades—at least those with something or someone to go home to. But there were a few, like him, who grinned, teeth bared in anticipation of, if not death and escape from their personal demons, at least a chance to take out their pent-up need for vengeance on an enemy they could see and lay hands on … an enemy they could kill.

Down the line, Modred, Arthur's nephew and now regent of Lothian, sat upon his horse, clad in somber priestly robes, his arm raised. Priests and druids were untouchable in battle, at least among the tribes of Britain. That made Modred a bit of a paradox in leading the Lothian warband, though *coward* came to Caden's mind. He wondered if Modred following his mother Morgause's calling into the high Celtic church made the man fit for the Lothian kingship he'd assumed from his late father, Cennalath. Or loyal enough to his uncle, Arthur, now engaged in the battle below. After all, it was Arthur—known as Pendragon to the Welsh, Dux Bellorum to the British, and High King to the Scottish Dalraida—who was responsible for the Saxon-loving traitor Cennalath's death.

But who was Caden to judge when he was naught but a mercenary bound to the highest bidder? In this case, the priest-king Modred.

Besides, in these times of rivaling British kingdoms, today's enemy was often tomorrow's bedfellow, especially when the Saxons entered the scene. It was the Christian High King's mission—and nightmare—to unite the squabbling Christian and pagan Britons as one against the wolfish enemy who would devour—

Modred lowered his arm, commanding the signaler to blast his horn. Caden forgot about the questionable loyalty and merit of his employer and gave Forstan a nudge with his knees. The steed, aware of the meaning of the horn's blast, shot forward, shuddering not at the sound of clanging swords and death as some of the other horses did. Like its rider, the costly stallion—worth two years of war prizes—seemed to crave it. Unflinching bravery had earned Forstan his name. Caden's courage stemmed from the will to die.

Joining the roar of the charge, Caden rode straight for the well-executed chaos. That was Arthur's genius, the reason he led Britain's kings, though he had no proper kingdom of his own. It was what the church had trained him to do: lead kings. The Britons had the best ground, the best warriors hewn from experience, and word that the Saxons were on the march along the Lader Water. Some said this good fortune was all due to the image of the Virgin the Arthur wore on his shield, but Caden leaned toward experience and skill over the painted face of a woman.

Like the one on Caden's own shield, though his had been nearly beaten into oblivion. Hretha, the name lettered around the image of the Saxon pagan goddess, certainly hadn't brought glory or victory to its previous owner. Nay, it was skill and passion that won the day. And Caden sported Hretha now, not for the goddess's protection, but for the well-made wicker and leather laminate backing her image.

Caden's blood began to race at battle speed, its cadence matching that of Forstan's muscled flesh hurling downhill toward the fray. Above it flew the banner of Arthur's Red Dragon, the rallying point.

The Saxons also had reinforcements. Caden spied them in the periphery of vision. Perhaps, just perhaps, the enemy would put up a fight worthy of a warrior's end. The drums thundering in his head drove Caden into the dust cloud enveloping the battlefield. He inhaled it and exhaled fury. A wild-haired Saxon with a deep red scar across his cheek rushed to meet him before he could dismount, hurling a lance with all his might. It glanced off the stallion's breastplate.

"Your gods take you if you wound my horse!" Caden slid off Forstan's back and broke into a dead run toward the unfortunate warrior now brandishing an axe. "I was going to dismount to meet you fairly." Horses were used like chariots before them, to deliver men fresh to the thick of battle and carry the weary off, though Caden had done his fair share of fighting from horseback. But he had no use for cowards who targeted a man's horse.

While Forstan cantered off, trained to await him a distance away, Caden unsheathed Delg, a prize from another battle and more deadly in his skilled hands than the thorn after which he'd named it. The Saxon charged, his axe forming a deadly sphere of continuous motion— down, around, up, around again, ever forward. Caden cut its frenzy short with a hard blow. Hretha's oak and leather took the brunt of the impact and sent the weapon flying. Good for the old goddess, who was credited for March's victory over winter's end … and for Caden's strong arm behind her.

The Saxon made the mistake of looking after his weapon in disbelief. He still wore that expression when Caden separated the man's head from his body with Delg. Easy. Too easy. Thanks to Egan O'Toole, the O'Byrne champion from another lifetime, Caden had been trained to incorporate skill and instinct into one. Plunging deeper into the thick of dust and battle, Caden faced enemy after enemy after enemy. And with each kill, the drums in his head grew louder. His breath became bursts of rage until he no longer faced men but the demons that deprived him of peace with their ceaseless torture.

Just then, one of the Saxon curs approached the back of the Pendragon, whose blue and white tunic had long since been stained with dirt and blood from those who'd fallen victim to Excalibur. Arthur had led his men into the first clash and fought not only his own demons but, it seemed, those of his nephew, Modred, who watched safely from the heather-dashed knot above them. Caden judged the pace of the running yellow-haired warrior, whose axe was aimed at the Pendragon's back.

So much for the protection from the Virgin on Arthur's shield. Caden hefted Delg like a spear and gave the sword a mighty thrust, closing a distance he could not make in time afoot. True it went, straight into the heathen's abdomen. It stopped the assailant long enough for Caden to set upon him and end his writhing misery.

Arthur spun at the unholy death scream, but instead of a flash of approval or gratitude on his beleaguered face, there was warning. Before Caden could comprehend the look, a shaft of blinding agony entered his back. He swung about, pulling Delg out of Arthur's attacker in the process and slashing at his cowardly assailant. The tip of his blade laid open the man's neck.

But Caden kept spinning. Blood-splatter, autumn colors, blue sky, and dust—always dust—swirled about him. Arthur, his men, the Saxons ... all were consumed by it. Thick and gray it was, choking out everything except the pain. Only when it turned to blessed blackness did the pain go away. One thought drifted up through the abyss, pulling the corners of Caden's mouth into a smile. *It's a good death.*